Airing Out

Dirty Laundry

Latisha Patterson

Library of Congress Control Number: 2011927368

ISBN: 978-0983-1669-4-8

Cover design: Donna Osborn Clark at creationsbydonna@gmail.com

Editing and Publishing Assistance: 21st Street Urban Editing & Publishing www.21StreetUrbanEditing.com

Interior design: Glenda Wallace at interiorbookdesigns@gmail.com

Cover Model: Tiffany Brooks

This book is dedicated to Darian, one of my best friends. Thank you for standing by my side through the rough patches of my life. You inspired me to write this book, and I will forever be grateful for your friendship. You will always have a special place in my heart.

Acknowledgments

First I would like to thank God for giving me a creative mind and the drive to do something constructive with my time. Writing this book helped me through a trying time in my life. I want to thank my mom for her great book titles and quotes on life. Thanks for believing in my work and standing by me when times were hard. I want to give a special thank you to my cousins, Tiffany and Ashley Brooks, for reading my entire manuscript. I appreciate your feedback and support. Tiffany, I will forever be grateful for you taking on the role as my cover model. You better work it, Diva!

To my favorite sister, Latoya Patterson, thanks for believing in me and donating your hard-earned money to help make my dream come true. You are the best little sister a girl could have.

My two daughters, Mikiya Patterson and Tayanna Bradley, I love both of you dearly and I am so proud of both of you. You all are the reason I decided to follow my dreams and I hope I inspire both of you to do the same.

Phoenix Jackson we have been friends since the fourth grade and I have so many fond memories of us growing up. We were so close people thought we were related and even though it is not by blood, we are sisters. Thank you for your friendship, it helped me create the bond between the characters in this book. Your input and suggestions were much appreciated.

Casilia "Big Mike" Williams, we go way back and have had some fun times. I appreciate your ability to turn my bad mood into a good one. When I have had a rough day and I'd call you about it, you would have the ability to make me find the humor in it. By the time I get off the phone with you I am in tears from laughing so hard.

Dianna Auston, you have become one of my best friends. It is ironic how we met but despite all of the drama, we have managed to become family. Thank you for typing up my manuscript and listening to all my ranting and raving.

Ryan Gardner, you are a true friend. I love the way you are blatantly honest with me, there is no sugar coating with you. You are the sensible one that tries to keep me on the right track. We do not always agree but that has never affected our friendship. Thank you for pushing me to move forward with publishing this book.

Ashley D. Redwood, thank you for being my personal assistant. I appreciate the pre-editing of my manuscript, revising my synopsis, and putting together my media kit. Your help is deeply appreciated.

Janelle Ellis, I have to thank you for keeping me sane. I am not the easiest person to get along with but we made it work. Living with you for about five months was indeed an experience. I remember all the late night talks we use to have and those short stories you had me write.

Ananda Sykes, you are the big sister that I never knew I needed. Boy do we have some stories about the things we went through. Thanks for helping me stay out of trouble and motivating me to finish writing this book. Talking to you helped me get through those rough days. Now that I have my book in print, I need you to get moving and get your book published.

Angel Williams, when I need an honest opinion on something I know exactly who to ask. Thank you for the book title and all of your feedback on the book cover and synopsis. All of your suggestions were appreciated.

I cannot leave out my family. It is too many of you to name so I will just say without **ALL** of you; my book would not be possible. Through all the ups and downs, I still love all of you. From the bottom of my heart, I want to thank you for all of your support. I am proud to call all of you my family.

To my former co-workers at AIC, I appreciate all the support you all have given me. Without all of your candy bar purchases, I would have overdosed on chocolate, and this book would not have made it to print.

A special thank you goes out to Donna Osborn Clark who designed my book cover and flyers. Donna did a great job on all of my promotional materials and became a friend in the process. She is a pleasure to work with and I look forward to her designing the cover for my next book.

The finished product would not be possible without Niccole at 21st Street Urban Editing. Niccole, thank you for being patient with me and answering all of my questions during the publishing process your knowledge is appreciated. I could not have asked for a better person to work with.

There is no way I can end my acknowledgements without giving a huge shout out to my "Dirty Laundry Street Team" you are the best group of people I could ask for to help me promote my book. Without your help I would not have made it this far. I thank all of you from the bottom of my heart.

Last and certainly not least, I would like to say a big thank you to everyone who purchased this book. I appreciate your support and I hope you enjoy this book as much as I enjoyed writing it. I fell in love with the characters and I hope you do too...

Chapter One

Skye

Today, it's all about me. I'm in desperate need of some alone time. I decide to spend a couple of hours at Sylvia's Day Spa - you know, get a massage, facial, manicure, and pedicure, just pamper myself. Lord knows I need it.

As I'm lying on the massage table, getting one of the best massages ever, my cell phone rings. At first, I ignore it, but someone keeps calling back. I pick up my Blackberry Curve and notice the number on the caller ID. It's Omar, my boyfriend.

"Hello!!" I yell into the receiver, completely agitated.

"Hey, baby. Why are you yelling? Is something wrong?" Omar asks, sounding shocked by my tone.

"I thought we talked about this. Today is for me. M–E…just me, Omar. I want to relax and be alone for a couple hours. I thought you understood that," I reply, my anger growing.

"Well, I do … but, umm, I just wanted to talk to you. I miss you. We just wanted to make sure you were a'ight. Skye, you know sometimes out of frustration people say things they don't necessarily mean."

I could hear in his voice his feelings were hurt, but at this point I really don't care. "In this case, I meant what I said. I don't have time for this Omar; my patience is wearing thin. If everything is okay with Omari, then there is nothing more to say. I'll see you when I get home." Click! I hang up the phone before he can utter another word. Damn! There goes my day of relaxation right out the window.

Trying to calm myself, I resume my position on the massage table, and begin reflecting on how things had gotten to this point. My life is so hectic right now. Who would've thought Skye Ariel Jordan would be at her wits end! I've always considered myself to be an intelligent black woman, with too much style and grace for all this drama.

At twenty-five, I have a pretty decent job at Richmond Premier Staffing. The agency I work for is well-known, and I'm paid a yearly salary plus commission. I'm an account executive, responsible for filling temporary job positions for local companies. My job is the one thing in my life I truly enjoy.

Omar and I have a beautiful two-year-old daughter, Omari. She's so precious, and the only good thing that came out of this dysfunctional relationship. Omari has a golden-brown complexion and green eyes like mine, but she looks exactly like Omar. There is no mistake, she's his daughter. She even has black curly hair and a small round nose like her father. The only difference is the chubby cheeks that carry her deep dimples.

We've been together for about four years. Omar is the hotel manager at the Marriott Courtyard located in the West End of Richmond. He makes way more money than I do, so I guess you could say we are financially stable. We live in a two-story brick house in a middle class neighborhood called Glenden Hills.

Don't ask me why we have a five-bedroom, two-and-a-half bath house when it's just the three of us. Omar wanted to go all out when it came to purchasing a home, so we ended up with this big house. The subdivision was new, and we got our house built from the ground up. I picked out everything.

Omar's an excellent provider and a great father. Omari adores him. He spends a lot of time with her. He reads her bedtime stories, gives her baths, and tucks her in at night. I don't even take her to daycare or pick her up, because he does that too.

Omar has proposed to me millions of times. Of course, I always turn him down. I'm not ready for marriage. I can barely deal with having him as a boyfriend.

On the outside looking in, one might say I have a good life and a good man. Yeah right, on the surface, maybe. No one really knows or cares to understand how I feel. Omar is too clingy and emotionally needy. It's like he has to be with me 24/7. He's smothering me with way too much love and affection. I don't know how much more I can take. Lying here thinking back, I'm trying to remember if I missed something, like a sign - a bright neon sign that said, "Run, this nigga is crazy!" Who knows? Everybody always says, "Love is blind." Well, now it seems I have 20/20 vision. This brother seriously has some deep-rooted issues, and I don't know if I'm equipped to handle them. My mother and father both think he's God's gift to the world. All of my friends, except one, are envious of my relationship with him. I guess my girl Coco is the only one with some damn common sense. Everyone else always takes his side.

What about me? What about my feelings? I always find myself asking. My married best friend, Jamyya, says in disgust, "Skye, you're too spoiled; everything is not always going to go your way. You have to compromise sometimes. That's what relationships are all about. Omar loves you and just wants some attention. He's a good man. I don't understand your problem."

I quickly reply, "Compromise; yeah, that's what I want him to do. He's always underneath me. I need some space, Jamyya. Why can't anyone understand that?"

I find myself having this same conversation with her day in and day out. Frankly, I'm tired of all this shit. I hate to admit it, but maybe I am spoiled. I guess being the only child does that to you. My dad and I are also really close. You got it - I'm daddy's little girl. So, yeah, I'm used to having things my way. So what?

***

It all started four years ago when I met Omar at a VCU vs. ODU basketball game hosted at the Siegel Center downtown. I should've known I was going to pull a bunch of niggas, 'cause my gear was hot like fire. My girl, Coco, is a stylist, so my hair was definitely laid. Those honey-blonde highlights she added to my hair drew more attention to my green eyes. I'm about 5'6, have a golden-brown complexion, and long wavy hair. And yes, my hair and eyes are real. There's nothing fake about me at all. My hips and butt are kind of big for my size-4 frame but that's what the guys like, so I use that to my advantage.

When I walked in, all eyes were on me because I was "fresh to death" in my dark denim Seven jeans, red fitted T-shirt, and red Jimmy Choo pumps. Hmm ... you couldn't tell me nothing. My dad had bought me a pair of two-karat diamond earrings and a diamond necklace with my name on it, so you know my neck and ears were blinging. Actually, my whole crew was turning heads. I can't be hanging out with no "bamas."

I roll with a crew of five. Yeah, the Fabulous Five, that's us. It's Jamyya, Kori, Damisha, Jasmine, and me. Jamyya and I go all the way back to middle school. Kori who everybody calls Coco is what I call "ghetto fabulous". She grew up around Creighton Court projects, but she stayed fly. Coco always had the latest gear.

Can you believe that one time, Coco got the new Dooney & Burke bag before I did? I know what you're thinking, but it was authentic. Me and my crew didn't mess with the bootleg, counterfeit, Chinese store shit.

Damisha, better known as Mimi, is my girl from way back too. We went to the same high school. Everybody was hatin' on me and Mimi 'cause she's half Filipino and half Black. Well me, I just look good, plain and simple. You know how girls are when you got long hair and light eyes. They instantly become jealous. So me and Mimi became friends because I wasn't intimidated by her beauty.

Jasmine, whose nickname is Jazz, is the youngest of the bunch. She moved in down the street from me and didn't know anyone, because she had just moved there from Philly. So me, being the nice person that I am, invited her to join my crew, which is nothing short of a privilege.

During half-time I decided to go get something to eat from one of the concession stands. "Anybody want to go with me to get something to eat?" I asked the girls.

"I'll roll wit' you, Skye," Jazz replied, getting out of her seat. People were everywhere. I turned as we approached the concession stand and accidentally bumped into a tall fine chocolate brotha.

"Excuse me. I didn't mean to bump into you. My bad." I was embarrassed.

"Shawty, that's a'ight just be more careful next time," he replied, laughing in a low tone. "I'm just joking. My name's Omar. What's yours?"

"Skye."

"Really, Ma, what's your name?"

"My real name is Skye. That's what my parents named me. Do you have a problem wit' dat?" I asked with an attitude, holding up my chain.

"Naw, actually it's kind of fly. It's just different, that's all," Omar said smiling.

Damn, he sure does have some pretty dimples, I thought to myself.

"So, do you have a man, Miss Skye?"

"Not at the present time, but then again, I wasn't looking." I stood there with a smirk on my face and my hands on my hips.

"That's a shame. You might pass up something good."

"Like you?" I questioned with my eyebrows raised.

"Yeah, like me. Why don't you give me your number so we can hook up sometime?"

"You're not crazy, are you?" I asked in a joking manner.

"Only a crazy person would dignify that with an answer."

I looked at him with inquisitive eyes, but gave him my number anyway. What could it hurt? A brotha as fine as he is couldn't be all that bad. I stood still for a moment, taking in everything about his physical appearance until Jazz screamed my name, which broke me out of my trance.

"Skye, come on here," Jazz said very curtly.

Damn. I had almost forgotten what I had come out there for. I made a U-turn and headed toward the concession stand to get a hot dog.

"Let me find out a man got Skye all hot and bothered, don't know which way to go," Jazz teased.

"Girl, shut up. He was cute, but it ain't all like that," I said as I handed my money to the short lady behind the counter.

"Jazz, did you want a soda or something?"

"Yeah, I'll get a Pepsi and some onion rings."

"Make sure you got some gum for that onion breath," I joked, and we both laughed and headed back to our seats.

"Girl, what took y'all so long? I was about to call the search team to come find y'all," Jamyya said, laughing at her own sarcasm.

"You know Miss Fly had to stop and have a conversation with every man that looked her way," Jazz said jealously.

"Actually, I bumped into this tall, fine, chocolate brotha, and he asked me for my name and number," I said, matter-of-factly.

"Really?" Jamyya said in a questioning manner.

"Yep, he is the cutest one I've seen so far tonight."

"So, what's the deal with him? Did you give him the digits?"

"Hell yeah, I gave him the number! I told you he was fine. Anyway his name is Omar, and he's about 5'10". He's got dark brown eyes, pearly white, straight teeth, the deepest dimples I've ever seen, and his smooth milk chocolate skin made my body shiver. That's about all I know".

"She ain't lying, neither. Mr. Omar had my girl gone as soon as he flashed that Colgate smile," Jazz said laughing.

"Seems like you noticed a lot. No wonder it took you so long to come back," Jamyya said, cutting off Jazz.

"Oh, yeah, I almost forgot. He's got long pretty cornrows, and he was G'd up in his LRG outfit."

"Mmm, guess I missed out. Maybe next time I'll roll wit y'all. These lazy heifers don't ever want to mingle. We walked around for about five minutes then 'grandma' said her legs were tired. So we came back to our seats," Jamyya said, looking at Coco and Mimi smiling.

"Who's 'grandma'? I asked, looking at Jamyya

"Coco; this heifer just had to ruin the fun."

"Who in the hell are you calling a heifer? Everybody ain't a hoe who's on the prowl for every man she sees," Coco retorted, loudly cutting off Jamyya.

"I was just joking. Chill out. What got your ass all on your back?" Jamyya asked, trying not to get upset.

"Girl, she's just mad 'cause she saw André with some chicken-head hanging all over him," Mimi said, trying to whisper to the rest of us.

"Thanks for telling all my business, Mimi," Coco said, rolling her neck.

"You're welcome. You know they were going to find out anyway. Everybody knows I can't keep a secret," Mimi said laughing, hoping to lighten up the situation.

***

A week went by before Omar finally called me - not that I was sitting around waiting. I believe it was a Sunday evening, around seven o'clock. I was just chilling in my room watching the Lifetime Movie Network. Suddenly, my cell phone started to ring. I looked at the caller ID, but didn't recognize the number.

"Hello?"

"Did I catch you at a bad time?"

He had such a deep voice.

"No, not really. Who's this?" I asked, acting as though I didn't know who he was.

"My bad, ma, this is Omar, you know, the nigga you met at the VCU vs. ODU game last week."

"Yeah, I remember. What's really good wit' u?"

"Nothing much, just been working. I had some free time today so I thought I'd give you a call and see when we could hook up. You know, go get a bite to eat, catch a movie or something."

His voice was so sexy.

"Umm, well I don't have much going on this week. When would you like to hook up?"

"Friday, around eight o'clock is good for me."

I nonchalantly answered, "Yeah, that will work."

We continued to have small talk, the usual basic get-to-know you conversation. Omar appeared to have it all together at twenty-three years old. He was three years older than me, but I liked that. I needed a mature man. He'd graduated from VCU two years ago with a Bachelor's degree in Hotel and Restaurant Management. He was currently working at the Marriott Courtyard as a shift supervisor, but he aspired to be the manager. You've got to start somewhere. At least Omar had goals he wanted to obtain.

Omar was a perfect gentleman on our date. He picked me up from my house at exactly eight o'clock. He didn't come empty handed. He arrived with a bouquet of pink chrysanthemums. He opened and closed the car door for me, and even pulled out my chair at the restaurant. Not once did he try to make a move on me. After dinner and the movie, he drove me straight home. He kissed me gently on the cheek and walked me to the door. This guy was different from anybody I had ever dated before. I called up all my friends and said, "I think I've got a winner. Omar is definitely a keeper."

Soon, I would find out how wrong I was.

***

After six months of dating, I decided to introduce Omar to my parents. This was going to be good. Mr. Omar Keith Rhodes was about to meet Vivian and Paul Jordan. At this time, I was still living with my parents in their tri-level home located in Springdale Estates. My mom said to me, "Skye, darling, your father and I would love to meet this young man you're so fond of. Why don't you invite him to Sunday dinner?"

Reluctantly I replied, "Sure, that sounds great, Mom. What time should I tell him?"

She pulled up a chair to sit beside me. "Is something wrong, dear? Are you embarrassed of us?" I could hear a hint of hurt in her voice.

"Oh, nothing like that. I just don't know how he would feel about it. Meeting parents is like taking the relationship to another level. I'm not sure if he's ready for that type of commitment," I said, wondering if she would change her mind.

"Well, honey, just ask him and see what he says. No pressure. Just ask if he would like to come to dinner Sunday at six o'clock."

"Alright, Mom, I'll let you know what he says."

Embarrassed? Ha! I think to myself, how could I possibly be ashamed of my parents? My mom's forty-two years old, but she looks young. Everyone always mistakes her for my older sister. We do look a lot alike. My mom is about 5'8" and has a smooth pecan brown complexion. Her eyes are green just like mine. She started getting gray hair, so she dyed it spicy cinnamon. The color looks great on her short, spiked haircut. Even after having me, my mom still has a great figure. She's a size ten. Her job is the bomb. She's the regional manager for Victoria Secret stores. So, you know my lingerie drawer is off the hook.

I couldn't be any more pleased with my father either. My father is forty-six years old and wears a pair of small round frame Hugo Boss glasses. He's kind of tall, about 5'11", and his complexion is a shade darker than my mom's. He has a full beard with a low haircut, and unlike mom, he doesn't dye his gray hair. My father has a nice build, too. His waist is a 36 and he has wide, broad shoulders. I always feel so safe in his arms. To him, I'm still a little girl. My daddy buys me everything 'cause he has plenty of money. He works at Merrill Lynch as a financial advisor. With parents like these, what would a girl have to be embarrassed about?

I called up Omar and asked him to dinner on Sunday.

"Oh, now you want me to meet your parents," he said excitedly. He had been asking to meet them for a while, but I declined. I didn't know if I really wanted to take this relationship to the next level. To me, Omar was just too nice and considerate. Something had to be up with him. This good boy act was killing me.

"Yeah, I feel it's time," I responded after several seconds of silence.

"What time should I come?"

"Be here at six. My mom's a good cook, so come hungry," I said, trying to sound cheerful about the whole thing.

Sunday came quicker than usual. This was a special day, so mom pulled out all the stops. She cooked roast beef with potatoes and carrots, macaroni and cheese, collard greens, corn pudding, homemade biscuits, and for dessert, strawberry cheesecake. My parents don't drink soda so she made Lipton ice tea.

Omar arrived on time, as usual, which gave him extra points with my dad. My father is very big on punctuality. I was still upstairs getting ready, so my mother opened the door.

"Come in, honey, and have a seat. Skye will be done in a couple of minutes," Mom said with a warm smile.

"Thank you very much for inviting me, Mrs. Jordan. These are for you," Omar said, handing my mother a bouquet of white Calla lilies.

"Oh, honey, thank you. You are such a nice young man. Please, call me Vivian. Omar, this is my husband Paul."

"How are you doing, Mr. Jordan?" Omar asked timidly.

"I'm fine son, please have a seat. No need to be shy. I'm not going to interrogate you. We just wanted to meet the young man that was taking up so much of our baby's time," my dad stated, trying to ease Omar's nervousness. Dad and Omar chatted, getting to know one another while mom finished last minute preparations in the kitchen.

I came down the stairs.

"Hello, Omar. I hope my dad's not harassing you," I said half-jokingly.

"No. Not at all. Actually, your father's pretty cool."

"Everything is fine, honey. Why don't you go help your mother in the kitchen?" my father said waving me off.

"Good idea, 'cause I'm starving," I said, rubbing my stomach as I approached the kitchen.

I helped my mom put the food on the table. "So mom, what do you think?" I asked anxiously. I couldn't wait to know what my parents thought about Omar.

"Well, honey, your father seems to like him a lot. I haven't had a chance to talk to him, but he seems like a nice young man. Look at those Calla lilies he brought me. That was a very sweet gesture." My mom was smiling.

"Yeah, Mom he's always like that. That's what worries me. He seems too good to be true."

"Well, honey, some people are just genuinely nice. Maybe he was brought up in a good Christian family. Have you met his parents?"

"No, I've been making excuses to get out of it, but since he has met y'all, I'm supposed to meet them this coming Sunday." My voice was full of skepticism.

"Honey, I'll talk with him at dinner and let you know what I think. It wouldn't hurt to meet his family. Maybe it'll give you some insight about him," my mother said reassuringly.

My mother and I were interrupted by my father. "Is the food ready?" he asked. "This young man and I want to eat."

"Yes dear, come on in and have a seat."

My father sat at the head of the table and my mother sat at the other end. We ate, and my mother got her chance to converse with Omar. I must admit the evening turned out pretty well. Omar stayed for nearly three hours before leaving. I walked him to the door, and he kissed me lightly on the lips.

"Your parents are wonderful, Skye, you are lucky to have them."

"Yeah, they are very special people," I said, feeling sleepy.

"Goodnight Mr. and Mrs. Jordan. Dinner was absolutely delicious," Omar said, heading out the door.

"Goodnight," my parents yelled simultaneously from the other room.

It was a hit. Both my parents liked Omar very much. Picture that. I wish I was into him as much as they were.

Over the next couple of months, my father and Omar grew closer. He eventually was spending more time with my dad than he did with his own family.

***

It had been three months since Omar had met my family, and the time had come for me to meet his. I could not put it off any longer. Every time I was supposed to meet Omar's family, I came up with a good excuse. After three months of dodging the meeting, now was the time to go through with it. He never knew his father because his mom had him at fourteen, and his father hadn't bothered to stick around. I would just be meeting his mom, two sisters, and three brothers. The two youngest lived with his mom in a three-bedroom house on the Northside of Richmond.

Omar had his own apartment and had been living on his own since he had graduated from college.

It was around 5:30 P.M. Sunday evening when Omar came to pick me up in his black Honda Civic. It was a very nice car. He always kept it clean, plus it was only two years old. He told me that his grandparents on his father's side bought it as a graduation gift for him.

"I guess they feel bad that my father had nothing to do with me. They told me they were proud of me and thought I could use a car," he told me nonchalantly.

On the way to his mom's house, Omar tried to give me the scoop on everybody. "My mom's name is Shakita, and she works at 7-Eleven as a cashier. She can't cook like your mom, but don't worry, I'm sure she ordered some good take out. Then there are my sisters, Kenya and Tamara. Kenya is twenty-two and has two kids—Kayla, who's four years old, and O'Ryan, who's three years old. Tamara is eighteen years old, and this is her last year of high school. She also has a little boy, Kemonni, who's two years old. I also have three brothers, and none of them have kids. Damon is twenty and is visiting this weekend 'cause he usually stays on campus. This is his sophomore year at Norfolk State. Tyquan is sixteen and Devin is fourteen. They both go to John Marshall High School. My family is a bit different than yours, but everybody is really nice. Please just look over their flaws and give them a chance," he said, pleading his case.

"A'ight, baby, I'm sure your family is not as bad as you make it seem," I said, trying to remain positive.

We pulled up to the one level brick house on Crafton Lane, and I saw four boys playing football in the yard. "What's up, lil bro?" Omar yelled out the car window at the boys playing ball.

"Hey, Omar. We just playing a little ball," Devin replied.

Omar opened the car door for me, and we approached the front door. Since this was his mother's house and the door was already open, we just went on in. "Hey, Mom, it's me. Where are you?" he yelled.

"I'm in the kitchen, boy, trying to get dinner straight," she said with attitude.

"Mom? I know you didn't cook," he asked, sounding scared.

"Hell no, you know I can't cook! What you want me to do, scare the damn girl off? Y'all just have a seat in the living room. I'll be out in a few. Have you seen your brothers?" Her voice was extremely loud.

"Yeah, they out front playing ball wit' some friends. Where is everybody else?"

"Kenya on her way over here, and I sent Tamara to the store to get some ice and sodas. Act like you got some manners, boy, and see if the chile want something to drink."

"Would you like something to drink, Skye?" Omar asked, trying not to be embarrassed.

"Well, I can wait until your sister comes back from the store." I was unsure of what to say.

"Mom, she said she'll just wait for Tamara to get back."

"Alright, baby."

Omar's mother finally came into the living room to introduce herself. She was a short lady, about 5'3", with a milk chocolate complexion - the same as Omar's. She also had two deep dimples. Her hair was braided in small micro-braids with burgundy hair. Her petite shape held wide hips and a big ghetto booty. She was very pretty and looked younger than thirty-eight years old. She also had two gold teeth. Shockingly, her outfit was banging. She had on a pair of tight Baby Phat jeans with a brown and gold Baby Phat shirt to match. Even her gold Baby Phat boots were cute.

"Hey, baby, nice to meet you. My name is Shakita but you can call me Kita," she said, extending her hand to shake mine.

"Nice to finally meet you. Your outfit is very cute." I was trying to make conversation.

"Thank you, baby. I got it from Citi Trends about a week ago. You ever go there?"

"Yes ma'am, I go there all the time. I also go to Marshall's and A. J. Wright too," I said excitedly.

"Oh, girl, I like you already. Maybe we can go shopping together sometime. I can tell by your outfit you got style," she said, smiling.

A few minutes later, a tall, skinny girl with a mocha-colored complexion walked in. She had long black hair in a layered wrap and was carrying two brown paper bags as she tried to hold a little boy's hand.

"Hey Omar, I sure could use some help!" She definitely had an attitude.

"Why didn't you get Tyquan or Devin to help you? They were out front playing ball in the yard," he asked, trying to be smart.

"Well, they ain't out there now, jackass. Don't you think I would've asked them first? Use your college brain sometimes." She was frustrated and out of breath.

"Skye, this is my rude-ass sister, Tamara. Tamara this is my girlfriend, Skye. Baby, I'll be right back," Omar said looking at me.

"Okay." I was wondering what was going to happen next.

"Honey, excuse my daughter, she just don't know how to act sometimes." Shakita rolled her eyes at Tamara.

"Oh, I'm sorry, Skye. I've just had a bad day. It's nice to meet you." She was trying to be pleasant.

"Don't worry about it. I have my moments too." I tried to laugh it off.

Omar came back in with two grocery bags and a large bag of ice. As he walked in, a tall, fine chocolate brotha was with him. Instantly I knew this had to be one of his brothers. They looked just alike. I guess they all look like their mom, because Omar said they have different fathers.

"This is my brother, Damon. Damon, this is my girl Skye," Omar said, smiling.

"Nice to meet you, Skye. You are prettier than Omar said," Damon said, flirting. He proceeded to kiss my hand.

"You better get off my girl before I beat your ass." Omar was angry. I had never seen or heard Omar act like this before.

"Calm down, O, I was just being friendly. I got my own fan club at school anyway," Damon said, laughing.

Damon went on to tell me that he was a wide receiver for Norfolk State. According to him, he was a star player and all the girls wanted him. Tamara came in the living room after putting away the groceries and joined the conversation. Finally, the food was ready and Shakita called everyone to the table. As soon as we sat down to eat, Kenya and her two kids came strolling in.

"Hey, y'all, sorry I'm late. Do you have enough for us? Who's this?" She pointed at me.

"This is my girlfriend, Skye. Skye, this is my sister Kenya and her kids, Kayla and O'Ryan." Omar tried to remain cool.

"Hey, girl, that's a cute outfit you got on. I see my brother finally got a girl wit' some style." She laughed.

"Thank you. You look cute yourself." I was complimenting her on her Chanel dress. She was rocking the hell out of that dress with a pair of high black Chanel boots and Chanel glasses to match. She was truly getting it, I had to admit.

Omar was right. His mom did order take out, if that's what you want to call KFC. She had three big buckets of chicken, extra crispy, with the sides and biscuits. She had two-liters of Pepsi, Dr. Pepper, and Sunkist Orange sodas to drink. Everyone was hungry, so no one really talked much while eating. For dessert, we had banana splits that Shakita and Tamara made.

Although their Sunday dinner was different than my family's, I had a good time. After we ate the banana splits, Omar's two younger brothers came in, and we all watched "American Gangster" on DVD. I really had a good time.

It was time to go, and Omar drove me home. "So, what did you think?" he asked hesitantly.

"They were really nice, a bit ghetto, but I liked them a lot," I said, smiling.

"I'm glad, because I could tell they liked you too." He sounded happy.

My thoughts of how Omar and I met were interrupted by Martha softly nudging me. "Skye, your massage is finished. Kim is over at the pedicure station waiting to do your facial and pedicure."

"Girl, have a seat and put them feet in this water. While your feet are soaking, I'm going to start your facial. Would you like the cucumber or mud mask?" Kim asked while she set things up.

"I'll take the cucumber!!" I say excitedly, as I lie back in the chair and continued reminiscing.

***

A year had passed since I'd met Omar's family, and we were still together. Lately, I hadn't been feeling well. I had been vomiting and sleeping more than usual. I called up my girl Jamyya.

"Jay, I think I'm pregnant. I've been throwing up for days, and it seems I can't get enough sleep. My period is late! What am I going to do?" I screamed into the phone frantically.

"Calm down. Have you taken a pregnancy test yet?" she asked in a calm voice.

"No. I didn't really think about it. We have been using condoms, plus I'm on the Pill. What am I going to do? This can't be happening! I just started my college classes. Damn. My life is over!!" I said, still not calming down as Jamyya had suggested.

"First, you need to find out if you're pregnant. Go to Walgreens and get two different pregnancy tests. Come to my house and take them. We'll see what they say and go from there. Please Skye, pull yourself together," Jamyya said, trying to comfort me.

We were the same age, but Jamyya was much more mature. It's probably because she had to raise her younger brothers and sister. Her mother was a dope fiend almost all her life, so she had to grow up quick. She also got pregnant at sixteen and decided to keep her baby. When she turned eighteen, Jamyya and Keenan got married and moved into a three-bedroom apartment. Her mother was in and out of jail, so she took her two brothers and sister with her.

Keenan is such a good man. He never ran from his responsibility. He was only two years older than us, but he became a father to their child and her siblings. They now have four children together; twin boys and two girls. Their daughter Ke'Asia is the oldest.

Anyway, I headed to the store as Jamyya suggested. I picked up a "Fact Plus" that had two tests inside and a "First Response". I quickly drove to Jamyya's apartment. She lived about fifteen minutes away from my house in an apartment complex called Fair Oaks Apartments. I made sure I parked my silver Lexus in the visitor's parking space. This was no time for me to get my car towed. Now, I know what you're thinking. How did a twenty-one–year-old girl with no job get a Lexus? Well, that's simple - I'm spoiled. My mom and dad bought it as a high school graduation gift.

I ran to the door and knocked three times very hard.

"Damn Skye, you didn't have to knock like you was Five-O," she yelled as she opened the door. "The kids are taking a nap so try to be quiet. I have a million things to do," she said in a much nicer tone.

Ke'Asia was five years old and in kindergarten, so she was at school. Tamia was three and the twin boys were nine months. Their names are Keontaé and Deontaé. Jamyya's sister Jamesha, who was the youngest, was now fourteen and in her freshman year at Highland Springs High School. She was the only one of her siblings still living with her. Her two brothers James and Jamal were now eighteen and nineteen. They both got scholarships for college. James played football. He went to Virginia State University. Jamal got an academic scholarship and decided to go to Hampton University.

"I'm sorry girl, I forgot all about the kids. I guess I was just too wrapped up into my own problems," I said apologetically.

"That's okay girl, let me see what you got in that bag."

I pulled out the pregnancy tests and showed them to her. She said they were good ones, and I trusted her judgment. Besides, she had four kids.

I went to the bathroom and took both tests. We had to wait about five minutes for the results.

"So, what are you going to do if you are pregnant?" she asked, trying to break the silence.

"Girl, I don't know. I haven't even told Omar I missed my period. I have no idea how he'll react. Everything has been so good between us. I knew something bad was bound to happen," I stated, feeling really depressed.

"Well, it's time to check the results. I'm sure Omar will support you, just like Keenan did me. Omar is such a sweet person. I couldn't imagine him turning so cold," Jamyya said, trying to smile.

"I hope you're right, because it looks like I'm pregnant," I said sadly.

"It's not the end of the world, Skye. Sometimes things happen, and it seems it's not the right time, but everything will turn out fine. Just remember you'll always have me. I'm your best friend, and I'll support you till the end," Jamyya said, hugging me tight.

"Well, I better make an appointment with my gynecologist. Thanks for being my rock. You are always holding me up. What would I do without you?" I said with tears in my eyes.

"I hope we never have to find out. I know you would do the same for me in a heartbeat. Don't cry, everything will be okay. If you need me, don't hesitate to call. I'll drop everything to help you out," she said with a huge smile.

"Thanks, Jay. I guess I'll be going home so I can give Omar the big news," I said, hugging her once more before I left.

As soon as I shut the front door I heard the babies crying. I started to turn around and go back to help her but I was in no mood to deal with babies. I drove home in a daze. As soon as I sat down on the couch my cell phone started ringing. I looked at my caller ID. Damn, it was Omar. I wanted to talk to him, but now was too soon. "What should I do?" I wondered. Might as well get it over with.

I answered the phone sounding exactly how I felt, downright miserable. "Hey, Omar, what's up?"

"Nothing much, just called to see if you wanted to go out for dinner. Is something wrong? You sound sad," he asked, heavy concern in his voice.

"Actually, there is something we need to discuss. How about you pick me up for dinner and I'll tell you all about it."

"It sounds serious. Are you sure you don't want to tell me now? I have about thirty minutes left on my break," he said, trying to get me to open up.

"No, I'd rather tell you in person. Plus, I'm tired. I think I'll take a nap. What time are you coming?"

"I'll pick you up around seven, and Skye, if it's about school, I'm sure your grades will improve," he said, trying to comfort me.

"Thanks, sweetie. You always know exactly what to say. I feel better already."

I hung up the phone and went upstairs to my room. I flopped down on my queen size bed with the black marble headboard.

In the midst of my anxiety, I must have fallen asleep. I awoke to my mother yelling "Skye... Skye, are you in there sweetie?"

"Yes Mom, come on in," I said, still kind of groggy.

"What's the matter, honey? You look terrible," she said as she sat next to me on the bed.

"Thanks, Mom, that was a nice thing to say," I replied with sarcasm and a smile.

"Sorry, honey. I'm just used to you caring about your appearance. Plus I haven't seen you smile in days. Is something wrong with you and Omar? You know you can tell me anything. Well, just about anything," she said half-jokingly.

As I thought about what I had just learned, I burst into tears. My mother put her arms around me and held me close. "It will be all right, dear. Tell me what's wrong. I can't help you if you won't talk to me."

My mother looked into my teary eyes.

"You and dad are going to be real upset with me," I said, sniffling.

"Well, that may be true, but your father and I love you unconditionally. Please just tell me what's going on," she replied with sincerity.

"Mom, I'm pregnant. I don't know if I should even be telling you, because I haven't even told Omar yet. He's picking me up at seven and I'm going to tell him then. Please mom, don't say anything until I've had a chance to tell him!" I begged her to keep my little secret.

"Skye, you are a grown woman even though your dad and I sometimes treat you as a child. This is your decision, and you are responsible for telling Omar. I'm not going to say I'm happy about the situation, but I know Omar is a good man. I'm sure you both will work this out. Do you have any idea what you want to do?"

I was silent for a moment. My mother really shocked me by her response. "Well, I just found out today. I'm not sure, but I don't really want to have an abortion. Then again, I don't think I'm ready for a baby either. I'm just finding myself, and I just started school. What about college? I know Dad is going to flip out," I said as I began crying again.

"Honey, I'm sure your dad may be upset at first, but you are his little princess. He can't stay mad at you long. I'll leave it up to you to tell him. One more thing: whatever you decide, I'll support you. If you still want to go to college and have the baby, I'm sure your father and I can help you pay for daycare," my mother said as she hugged me.

"Thanks Mom, for being so understanding. I hope it goes as smooth with Dad and Omar," I said, trying to cheer up.

"Well, there is only one way to find out. You better hurry up and get dressed, 'cause it's almost six o'clock. You know Omar is always on time," she said as she walked out the door.

This was no time to be cute, but I couldn't leave the house looking a hot mess either. My mom even said I looked bad, so something had to be done. I jumped in the shower and washed my hair. When I got out, I brushed my teeth and combed my hair. I just brushed it up into a ponytail and left it wet. My hair curls up when it's wet, so I just let it do its thing. It was warm outside for early September, so I threw on a short red-and-white spaghetti strap dress made by Michael Kors and my red stiletto pumps by the same designer.

As soon as I got downstairs, Omar was ringing the doorbell. I opened the door and he was standing there with a dozen of yellow roses and a big brown teddy bear in his hands.

"Hey, baby. I bought these for you. I hope this can cheer you up," he said, kissing me quickly on the lips.

"Thank you. This was very sweet of you. Mom, I'm gone," I yelled, walking into the kitchen.

I sat the vase of roses on the kitchen table. As I put them down, I noticed a card sticking out. I opened it and it read "I don't know what's got you so down, but I'm sure we can get through this together. Just remember, I'm here for you whenever you need a shoulder to lean on. If it's too much for me, give it to the Lord. I know he can handle it. I'll pray for you. I love you very much, Omar."

"Wow, he really does love me," I thought to myself. I dried my eyes and walked out of the kitchen. I found Omar and my mom having a conversation in the living room. I wasn't worried though, I knew my mom could keep a secret.

"I'm ready whenever you are," I said, looking at Omar. We both said our goodbyes as we headed out the door. We rode in silence for about ten minutes until I decided to just let loose and tell him what was going on.

"Omar, honey, I took a pregnancy test today and it came up positive. I'm pretty sure it's right 'cause I've missed my period and I've been vomiting," I said with tears starting to form in my eyes.

"Is that what you're so upset about?" he asked, as if what I said wasn't major.

"Yeah, that's what I'm upset about. How about you? What do you think about me being pregnant? Do you want a baby?" I asked, wondering why he wasn't mad.

"Well, I'm not mad about the baby. It sure is a surprise. Well, a nice surprise, actually. Skye, I love you and I want us to be together. I know this is ultimately your decision, but I would like for you to keep the baby. You know my mom had me young, and I never knew my father. I don't want to be like him. I want my kids to know me. I want to be the kind of father that you have," he said in a sincere voice.

"I love you too, Omar, but I don't think I'm ready for this. I still live with my parents, and I don't even have a job. How will I support a child? I don't even take care of myself financially," I said, trying to reason with him.

"Do your parents know? Have you told anybody else?" he questioned.

"Yeah, I told my mom, but my dad still has no clue. And Jamyya knows, but I don't know if she told the rest of the crew yet. I wanted to tell you first, but my mom came in my room and started asking questions. I'm sorry," I said as tears streamed down my face.

"That's a'ight baby. I understand you needed support from your mother. How did she react?" he asked, not sure if he wanted to know the answer.

I told him everything my mom and I had talked about.

We finally arrived at the Cheesecake Factory for dinner. The food was exceptionally good. I was really hungry. I hadn't realized I didn't eat all day.

Over dinner Omar asked me to marry him and I said "no". Then he suggested I move in with him, since he already had a two-bedroom apartment. His roommate had just moved out because he had gotten married. I thought it over and told him I would move in next week. I still needed to talk to my dad about everything.

When I got home it was a little after nine and my dad was sitting in his black leather recliner watching TV. I went in the den and sat on the black leather love seat.

"Hi Dad, how was your day?" I asked, trying to sound chipper.

"Today was good, I can't complain. What about you? Your mother tells me we have something to talk about. What's going on?" my father asked, smiling. He then picked up the remote control and turned off the TV. "You have my undivided attention. Tell Daddy what's wrong and how much it's going to cost me," he said trying to make a joke.

"Well, Dad, it's going to cost a lot, almost as much as I did, or still do. You see, I've gotten myself into a little trouble. I'll just come right out and say it... Dad, I'm pregnant. I've already told Mom and Omar. We decided to keep the baby, and he wants me to move in with him. Actually, he asked me to marry him, but I said no," I told him, as if I had everything planned out.

"I see. Well, you know a baby is a big responsibility. I'm glad Omar wants to do the right thing. If you ever need any help don't hesitate to call me or your mom. I hope you know me and your mom love you very much and would never put you out. You are a grown woman now, so I respect your wishes. Don't be a stranger. You know you and Omar are welcome here anytime. Now, I guess little Miss Princess has to get a job," dad said laughing.

"Yeah, I guess that would be the next step. Thanks, Dad, for being so understanding. I love you too," I said, giving him a big kiss on the cheek.

"Welcome to the real world, sweetie. Do you think you'll ever marry Omar? You know, he's a fine young man. Not too many of them out here nowadays," Dad said matter-of-factly.

"That's a good question. I don't know. I just know I'm not ready right now. I'll see how things go with us living together. One step at a time. Dad, are you trying to get rid of me?" I asked, joking.

"No princess, not at all. I just want you to be happy. I know you'll need some money to help you get started, especially since you'll need a new wardrobe. I'll write you a check," he said as he got out his checkbook.

My dad wrote me a check for eight hundred dollars and handed it to me.

"Wow, thanks Dad, you're the best! I really mean it. Well, goodnight. I'll see you tomorrow," I said as I headed to my room.

"Goodnight, sweetheart."

Thank you, Jesus. Everything turned out better than I could imagine. Now I could rest and think straight. Maybe having a baby wouldn't be so bad after all. Besides, Jamyya has four, and she's doing great. One couldn't be that much trouble, plus I have my family's support. I'm one lucky lady.

***

When I first moved in with Omar, everything was great. On the days he got off early, he cooked me dinner. When he went to work in the afternoon, he cooked me breakfast. He did all the cleaning and even washed both of our clothes. I didn't work, and I dropped all my classes because my morning sickness was terrible. I was sick the majority of the time for the first four months.

Omar treated me so good. I couldn't ask for a better man. He went to all my doctor's appointments. He was so excited about the baby. He called me from work on all his breaks to check on me and see how I was doing. He always came home with a gift -flowers, candy, bears, balloons, food, something. He had something for me every day.

At first, I was flattered by all the gifts and attention, but then it became too much. When I was six months pregnant, I found out we were having a little girl. Omar was so excited, he called everyone on his cell phone while we were still in the doctor's office and told them we were having a girl. The baby wasn't even born yet. I thought I was a shopaholic, but with the baby coming, Omar had me beat. He bought stuff that the baby wouldn't even be able to use for at least six months.

My mom and Shakita went all out when it came to my baby shower. They invited everybody in Richmond. My baby shower was inside the Marriott Hotel banquet room. You know we got a discount because Omar works there. As a matter of fact, right before the baby was born, Omar got a promotion to Assistant Manager of the hotel. It was good timing, because we needed all the money he could make. You know I wasn't working.

The day had come for me to have the baby. It was April 24th at eight o'clock in the morning when Omari Janaé Rhodes was born. She weighed 5 pounds 5 ounces and was 17 inches long. Omari had a head full of black curly hair.

Omar was so wonderful when it came to his baby girl. He would wake up in the middle of the night and feed her. He changed diapers, and would keep her whenever I wanted to go out. The only problem was when I did go out with friends, Omar would magically appear. Wherever I was, he and the baby would show up. If he couldn't follow me, then he would call four or five times a day. It got so bad that I stopped answering the phone, but that didn't stop him. He would just call and harass my friends.

On the rare occasion Omar would hang out with the boys, he would still call and check up on me. He might as well stay home as much as he worried the hell out of me. Now four years later, he is still the same possessive person.

He finally got promoted to hotel manager at Marriott Courtyard. One year after Omari was born I'd gotten a job at Richmond Premier Staffing as an account executive. About three months later Omar and I moved into our five-bedroom home. He asked me to marry him again on the first night we moved in. I turned him down once again. I would think by now he would be tired of asking. As I finished reminiscing, my pedicure, facial and manicure were finished. It was time to snap back into the present.

"All done. You can pay at the front counter," Kim says in a low, squeaky voice.

"Thanks Kim. You worked a miracle on these feet," I say, giving her a tip.

"You're welcome. You know you're one of my favorite customers," she replies, grinning.

As I get inside my silver 4 door Lexus 300LS, my cell phone starts to ring. I get in and check the caller ID. Whew, thank goodness it's just Damisha.

"Hey, girl what's up?" I ask as I begin to drive off.

"Girl, where you at? I thought we were going to the mall. It's already two o'clock," Mimi states, sounding irritated.

"Damn. I didn't realize it was that late. I'm on my way to your house now. Are you ready?"

"Yeah, I'm ready. I've been sitting around waiting for an hour and a half. You could at least call and let somebody know you were running late."

"I was at the spa and didn't realize the time. My bad. Hey, why don't you call Jazz and see if she can meet me at your house?"

"A'ight, how long are you going to be? Shit, I'm hungry," she says with an attitude.

"I'm about 15 minutes away. You can get something at the food court."

"Hurry up. I'm gonna call Jazz. Bye."

Chapter Two

Damisha

Fifteen minutes, yeah right, more like thirty. I don't know why Skye is late for everything. She know damn well as soon as we get to the mall, Omar is going to start calling and acting crazy. Shit, I got a date tonight. I don't have time to fuck around wit Skye. As soon as we get to the mall, she's going to start rushing people to hurry up and buy something so she can get home to her deranged-ass boyfriend. I don't know why Omar is so damn pressed anyway. I mean, Skye is cute but she's not all that, plus she's spoiled as hell. Nobody else would put up wit' her anyway.

Finally, I called Jasmine. "Hey, can I speak to Jazz?" I ask, sounding confused. I thought I called her cell phone, but some guy answered.

"Just a minute," the deep voice replies.

"Hello, who dis?" Jazz asks in an upbeat tone.

"It's Mimi. Skye wants you to meet her over here so we can get to the mall faster. You know she got a curfew. Her dad will be calling in a minute to check up on her," I said laughing.

"Well, I told Mario he could use my car. I'll see if he can drop me off... Hold on a sec."

I can't believe my ears. Are all my friends stuck on stupid? How in the hell is somebody going to use your car and not take you where you need to go? I can't understand the mentality of this chick. Mario is Jazz's oldest sister Joy's husband. *Why can't Mario use his wife's car?* I think to myself.

"Hey, I'm back. He said he guess he got time. You want me to leave now?" she asks hesitantly.

"Please. I'm really hungry and I'm starting to get irritated," I say with a definite attitude.

"I'm on my way," Jazz says before she hangs up.

I decide to get me something to eat, because I know how them hoes are late for every damn thing.

Jasmine arrives at my house first.

"Come on in. You know Skye ain't here yet," I say as I open the door.

"Where is she coming from?"

"She said she was leaving the spa, wherever that is."

Our conversation is interrupted by somebody laying on the horn. I look out my bay window and see Skye sitting in the driveway.

"Jazz, that's her now. Come on."

We walk outside and I lock the door to my townhouse. When we get in the car, Skye wants to make small talk, like she isn't late. Lying bitch took forty-five minutes to get here. I'm so heated, I sit in the back seat.

"Hey, y'all. You look real cute, Mimi," Skye says trying to suck up.

She can tell I'm pissed by my facial expression. Even though I'm mad at her, I know she's right. It's the middle of June and hot, about ninety-five degrees. I have on a tight, white and gold Juicy Couture T-shirt, dark denim Juicy Couture mini skirt, and my metallic gold flip-flops. I put on my big gold hoop earrings, two bangles, a diamond ankle bracelet, and my gold rim Chloe sunglasses. I don't really need her compliment, because I know I look good. I'm half-Filipino and half-black, about 5'5" and a size six. I have long black hair down my back, and dark brown slanted eyes. My skin is silky smooth, and my size six feet are very pretty. The only advantage Skye has over me is her ass. She has a big butt for her size.

Unfortunately, I'm not that lucky in that department. I have what you call "nassatall," no ass at all. Even still, I pull many niggas. Shit. I know I'm fly. I'm twenty-six years old, single, no kids, and I have my own shit. I work at Virginia Dominion Power as a Customer Service Supervisor. I make sixteen dollars an hour, and I work Monday through Friday. I live by myself in a two-bedroom townhouse, and my ride is a'ight. I drive a burgundy Toyota Avalon. You could say I'm doing the damn thing.

"Don't give me that shit, Skye. You knew I would be pissed. I should've just driven my own damn car to the mall. Now you are going to be rushing to get home to Omar. I got a date tonight. I have to find the perfect outfit," I say angrily.

"Mimi, shut up. It's only a quarter 'till three, by the time we get to the mall it'll only be about three thirty. I told Omar I would be back around six. What mall do you want to go to anyway?" she asks, paying my attitude no mind.

"Let's go to Short Pump. I'm sure I'll find something there."

"Do you want to stop at McDonald's or something?"

"No. I knew you were lying, so I filled up on some chips and cookies."

It's Saturday, and the mall is packed. We have to park way in the back of the parking lot. "Let's park at Nordstrom's," I say.

"Why don't we go to Saxon Shoes first?" Skye replies.

"Okay, whatever, let's just get in the mall," I say, still mad.

"Is somebody PMS'ing today?" Skye asks, trying to be funny.

"No, but it might be coming." I had to admit I was a little snappy today.

Changing the subject, Jazz asks, "Who are you going out wit'?"

"Some dude named Chris that I met last week on my lunch break. He was at Olive Garden getting take out, and we conversed a bit while we waited for our orders."

"Where does he work at? I know he had to be fly for you to give up the number," Jazz says, being her usual nosy self.

While we are in Saxon's having our little conversation, Skye's cell phone rings. It's no surprise that it's Omar calling. I don't know why she even answered the phone. Then she has the audacity to tell him where she is. How dumb can one person be?

I find a couple pairs of cute shoes, get the salesman's attention, and ask for a size six in both pairs.

"He works at Capital One as a computer analyst, and yes he is sexy," I say with a huge grin spread across my face.

"What y'all talking about? Ooh, Mimi, I like those. If you don't get them, I want them." Skye walks over to where Jazz and I are.

"I was just telling her about this dude named Chris I met. We're going out to eat dinner, and then to the Funny Bone Comedy Club. I'm not sure which ones I like better."

"I think you should get the black Prada sandals, since you don't know what you're wearing," Jazz says.

"That's exactly my point. That's why I wanted to get my outfit first. You know Skye always does stuff ass backwards."

"Well, we can go to Nordstrom's if that'll stop your whining," Skye says, sounding snobbish.

"I have a better idea. Let's go to BeBe first, then, if I don't find anything there, we can hit up Nordstrom's."

"A'ight," Jazz replies.

As we head to BeBe, Jazz runs into a couple of people she knows. She stops to talk to them but I keep going. I don't have time for this friendly shit. Every time we go somewhere, Jazz sees somebody she knows and she can't just say "Hi" and keep it moving. Oh, no, she always got to stop and converse. Sometimes I forget she's not even from here.

When I go inside BeBe, I instantly see the perfect top. "Hey, Skye, what do you think about this?" I hold up the turquoise halter-top.

"It's real cute, but what are you going to wear with it?"

"I don't know, maybe a pair of white Capri pants or some jeans."

I grab a small and medium top to try on. The medium top fits perfectly; I think the small was way too tight. I find a pair of white Capri pants with BeBe written on the back pocket in turquoise. These are perfect. I grab my size and go up to the counter.

The short blond saleswoman rings up my purchase.

"That'll be $186.84, Ma'am."

I pulled out one hundred and ninety dollars and pay for my clothes. Skye and Jazz are still browsing the racks.

"Do y'all want to meet me at the shoe department in Macy's?" I ask impatiently. "Yeah, go ahead. I see something I like. I'm going to try it on," Skye waves me off.

"Fine," I mumble under my breath.

As I'm walking to Macy's, I hear somebody calling my name. I turn around to see Jerell coming towards me.

Damn, I haven't seen him since high school and I don't remember him looking this good.

"What's up, Damisha?" he asks, while hugging me tight like we go way back.

"Nothing much. Just doing a little shopping," I reply, batting my eyes.

"I see you still look good. Are you here by yourself?"

"No. I came here with Skye and Jasmine, but they're taking too long, so I told them to meet me at Macy's."

"Oh, my bad. Am I holding you up?" he asks hoping I say no.

"Not really, but how about we walk and talk?"

"That's cool. So what's been going on wit' you? I see you and your girls still tight. Are you married? Got kids?"

If I'm not confused, I believe Jerell is trying to holla. The funny thing is, I don't think I mind. He has grown into a fine specimen. Jerell is a redbone brotha about 5'9" with a slender frame. I can tell he has been working out because of the muscles bulging on his arms. He has pretty gray eyes and sandy brown hair that he wears in a low cut. I look him up and down and notice his Movado watch and his spanking brand new Jordan's. His other wrist is blinging wit' a diamond bracelet. I see somebody making some money. I have to pull myself together, but what should I say?

"No, I'm not married and no kids either. I'm just enjoying being single."

"I heard that. Well, I don't want to take up too much of your time. I saw you and thought I'd come over and speak. I would ask for your number so we could stay in touch, but I'm not in the mood to play myself today," he smiles.

"You just did, asshole," I thought to myself, but something about him piques my interest, so I decide to be nice.

"What about you? Do you have kids? A crazy baby momma?" I ask, laughing.

"No, not yet. I guess I've been lucky not to get caught out there," he replies, still smiling.

"Well, in that case, I don't see a problem wit' giving you my number."

With a surprised look on his face, he pulls out his Apple iPhone and I give him my number.

"Guess I'll be hearing from you soon," I say in a flirtatious voice.

"I'll holla at you, ma," he says before leaving.

Once he's gone, I turn my focus back to shopping. I rummage through a couple of shoe racks before I find the perfect shoe. It's a pair of turquoise snakeskin two-inch sandals made by JLo.

"Please, please have my size," I say to myself. I run to find a salesperson to see if they have my size.

"Excuse me, Miss. Do you need some help?" a young, tall, dark-skinned man asks.

"Yes, do you have this in a size six or six-and-a-half?" I ask politely.

"I'll go check, have a seat. I'll be right back."

While he's in the back getting my shoes, I spot Skye and Jazz.

"Over here, y'all," I yell from across the room.

They see me and come over carrying two large bags apiece.

"I see y'all finally found something."

"Girl, I found a whole bunch of stuff on the sales rack. You should've stayed with us," Jazz says excitedly.

"I'm glad I didn't, because I ran into Jerell. You wouldn't believe how cute he's gotten," I say, smiling.

"Jerell who?" Skye asks, confused about whom I was speaking of.

"Jerell Thompson who went to school wit' us," I reply, acting as if she should know whom I was talking about.

"Oh, he's always been cute, Mimi. You were just too damn fly to pay attention to high school boys," Skye says truthfully.

"I guess you're right. Anyway, I gave him my number."

"He must be making some dollars now, huh?"

"I'm not sure, but he was blinging, and the gear was tight."

"That figures," Skye and Jazz say in unison.

The salesman finally comes back out with three boxes of shoes. "Ma'am, we didn't have a six, but I brought you a seven, and I also brought the silver and pink in a six," he says with a smile.

"Thanks a lot," I reply.

I try on the seven first, because I really want these shoes. Yes, they fit. I guess they run small.

"How did you find those? They are so cute?" Skye says, screaming.

"They are, and they match my outfit perfectly," I reply, gloating.

"Are you going to get both colors?" she asks. I know she's scheming on the other two pairs.

"You can get a pair if you want, but they run small. I had to get a seven, and those are six's," I reply, trying not to sound annoyed.

She gets on my damn nerves. Why can't she find her own style and her own damn shoes?

"I'll look around first and if I don't find anything else, I'll see if they got silver in my size," she says, as if she read my mind.

Finally, everybody has found a pair of shoes. Skye decided not to get the J. Lo sandals like mine. She found a pair of Dolce & Gabbana peep toe pumps. They are actually cuter.

"I'm hungry. Let's go to the food court and eat," Jazz says, looking at me and Skye.

"What time is it?"

"About five-thirty," Skye says looking at her white leather Gucci watch.

"A'ight. I want to get something from Chick-fil-A."

"Sounds good," replies Jazz.

As we are walking to the food court, I see a tall chocolate brotha with long black cornrows. He's smiling, showing off his deep dimples. Mmm, he looks good. As people move aside, I notice him pushing a stroller with a little girl in it. Oh shit, it's Omar! I can't believe this crazy motherfucka came up to the mall. I knew Skye shouldn't have told him where we are! Engrossed in a conversation with Jazz, she must not have noticed him approaching us.

"Skye, your psycho boyfriend and baby are in the mall," I say, laughing as if it's funny. It's anything but funny, actually; it's ridiculous.

"I don't believe this shit," Skye shouts.

"Why the hell you tell him where we were, anyway?" I ask, not really wanting an answer.

"I didn't think he would come up here. He agreed to give me space. Today was supposed to be my day to be without him and Omari." She sounds mad and frustrated all at the same time.

"Hey honey, funny running into you here," Omar says, trying to make a joke.

No one laughs because this shit isn't funny. Omar's tactics have gotten old. I'm tired of it, and he isn't even my man.

"Hi, Mommy," Omari shouts excitedly.

"Hey, sweetie." Skye kisses Omari on the cheek.

"Mimi, can you watch Omari for me while I have a word with Omar?" Skye asks, looking at Omar but talking to me.

"Sure, just meet us at Chick-fil-A." I walk off with Jazz and Omari.

"Nice to see you Damisha and Jasmine," Omar says, waving.

"Whatever."

"Nice seeing you too, Omar," Jazz says laughing.

Chapter Three

Skye

"Why are you here, Omar?" I ask in a serious tone. "How many times do we have to go through this? I can't even come to the damn mall with my friends without you following me. This is not a normal relationship. You got my friends laughing at me. I will never hear the end of this shit," scolding him, not even giving him a chance to respond.

"Skye, I don't care what your friends think. It was getting late and I was bored, so I thought I would bring the baby out for some fresh air. We missed you. Omari kept saying, 'Where Mommy?' and pointing at the door, so I decided to come to the mall. I didn't expect you to still be here. You know how you do. You go to three different malls in one day," he says, trying to be amusing.

"I don't find this funny at all. I don't have time for this. I'll see you when I get home," I say angrily.

"And when will that be? You said you would be home at six; here it is almost quarter till seven. You still have to take Jazz and Mimi home. I'm not going to sit in the house and wait for you all night," he replies, sounding upset.

"Fine, don't sit in the house. I never asked you to anyway. Please go out. I want you to go out and leave me the hell alone!!" I scream at the top of my lungs.

People start turning around and looking at us, but I don't care.

"Skye, calm down, people are looking," Omar says quietly.

"I don't give a fuck who's looking! Oh, *now* you care what people think? Omar, shoot yourself! Shoot your damn self!" I scream as I stomp off.

I have lost my patience with Omar. I don't care that I just made a complete fool of myself. I try to calm my nerves.

Omar looks at me with sad puppy dog eyes. "You know what, Skye? You got your wish." He turns around and walks off.

"Where the hell you think you're going? You're leaving our daughter, jackass!" I yell as he keeps walking.

Slowly, he turns around and yells, "Find somebody else to keep her, or take her wit' you. I'm not your personal babysitter. I'm tired of you treating me like shit!"

"Fuck you, Omar."

Apparently someone called mall security, because they are quickly approaching us. "Ma'am, is there a problem?" a short, fat, old gray-haired man asks.

"No sir, the problem just left," I say calmly.

"Are you sure you're okay?"

"Yes sir, I'm fine. I apologize for the scene. It won't happen again."

After the big commotion, I was ready to leave the mall. I feel so embarrassed. I walk over to the food court to meet up with Mimi and Jazz. Omari's sitting in a booster seat eating chicken nuggets and fries.

"Thanks for watching Omari. How much do I owe you?" I pull out a chair to sit down.

"Girl, don't worry about it. Where is Omar?" Mimi asks.

"He left. We had a big argument and I flipped out on him. I'm not even hungry anymore. You guys mind if we leave as soon as y'all finish eating?"

"No, I'm good. I already got my outfit. I did want to look for some accessories, but I can drive my own car. I can tell you're upset."

"I'll be okay. He just gets on my damn nerves so much. Then he acts as if he didn't do anything wrong. Maybe I'll call my mom and see if she'll watch Omari."

"Everything will be a'ight, you just need some space. Why don't you come with me and Coco to T.G.I. Friday's?" Jazz asks.

"A'ight what time y'all going?"

"We're leaving at 10:00 P.M., and if you're not at my house by 9:55P.M., we are leaving your black ass."

We finish eating our food and leave.

I call up my mom to see if she will babysit. "Hey, Mom. Do you have any plans tonight?"

"No, your father and I are in for the night."

"Do you mind if I stop by to talk to you for a minute?"

"Sure baby, I'll be here."

Shortly after I hang up with mom, we pull up to Mimi's house.

"Thanks Skye, I hope your night goes better than your day. Don't worry about taking Jazz home, we're going to Marshall's," Mimi informs me as she and Jazz get out of the car.

"Bye, Mimi. Jazz, I'll see you later. Let Coco know I'm going too."

"Bye-bye." Omari waves her little hand. I quickly drive to my mother's house, because I need some advice.

My mother opened the door wearing a white T-shirt, a pair of blue jeans, and a pair of furry slippers.

"How are my two favorite girls?" My mom hugs me and kisses Omari on the cheek.

"Hi, Nana!" Omari happily shouts.

"You are the cutest little girl I've ever seen. Do you want Grandma to give you some cookies?"

"Yes."

"Say please, Omari," I interject.

"Please, Nana," she replies with her lip poked out.

Vivian goes into the kitchen to get some chocolate chip cookies for Omari.

"So, what's going on?" My mom crosses her legs and looks directly into my eyes.

"Well, Mom, I'm tired of Omar. Today was supposed to be a relaxing day for me, ME...by myself... without him or Omari."

Omari interrupted, "Me, mommy, me."

"Yes, sweetie, I'm talking about you," I say, smiling at Omari.

"Anyway, I went to Sylvia's Day Spa to relax. While I was there Omar kept calling. I finally answered and told him I would be home by six, just give me a couple hours of alone time. Then I go to the mall. Mom, do you know he had the nerve to show up at the mall with Omari! I flipped out on him in front of a lot of people. He got mad and left me with the baby. I don't think he is coming home tonight. Do you think I was wrong?" I wait patiently for my mother to answer.

"Honey, I don't like to interfere in other people's relationships, but I think you were wrong. Omar has feelings, and you can't keep taking him for granted. A man's ego likes to be stroked, not torn down in front of a lot of strangers. Now, I agree he shouldn't have come up to the mall, but you could have handled the situation differently. Maybe you should think about counseling. I know a good relationship therapist."

"Yeah, you're right, I did say some mean things to him that I shouldn't have, but he just makes me so mad. I know he's a good man, but I need space. I want to be able to go out without being followed or getting twenty thousand phone calls. Mom, it's just ridiculous!" I shout, getting infuriated all over again.

"Well, if you want to go out, I'll keep Omari for you. She can spend the night, and you can pick her up around five o'clock tomorrow and eat dinner with your dad and me. Honey, just try to calm down and have some fun. Things will look better tomorrow. Would you like your father to have a talk with Omar?"

"No, that's okay I'll handle it. Thanks for watching Omari. I'll see you at dinner tomorrow." I kiss my mom and Omari before I leave her house. I look at my watch; it's almost eight o'clock. Damn, time flies. I have to rush home, take a shower, do my hair, and change my clothes all by nine-thirty. I hope they don't leave me.

***

When I pull up to my house, I didn't see the forest green Escalade with twenty-two inch rims in the driveway, so I know Omar isn't home. Good, because I'm running late. I have no time for another episode of the Young and the Restless. I run into the house, drop my keys on the kitchen counter, and grab a bottle of Dasani out of the fridge. "Damn, it's hot as the Sahara Desert outside," I think.

Hunger pains begin to hit my stomach, but I have no time to eat. "You'll just have to wait until I get to Friday's," I told my growling stomach. I dashed upstairs to my room and opened up my walk-in closet. There was so much to choose from. I have designer names ranging from Baby Phat to Juicy Couture, just to name a few. Hmm ... let's see.

I begin to ransack my closet, tossing things to the side. Finally I come across a short, strapless, Michael Kors denim dress. Now, what kind of accessories should I wear? I pull out a pale yellow wide belt to go around my waist. Oh my gosh, this will match my Prada peep toe pumps I just bought. All I need now is a purse and some jewelry. I climb on top of my step stool and look on the top shelf. Aha! This will do perfectly. I pull out my yellow Prada clutch purse. This is going to be a banging ass outfit.

I hop in the shower. My hair, oh shit, what am I going to do with my hair. I plugged up the Gold N Hot curling iron and decide to put on my makeup. Once the curlers are hot, I spiral curl my long hair. I check my clock, and it's a quarter after nine. I quickly throw on my clothes. I walk over to my cream marble dresser with mirror attached and spray on my Armani Diamonds perfume. Now for the jewelry; my two karat canary diamond earrings and tennis bracelet will set my outfit off lovely. Oh, my necklace! I go back into my jewelry box dig out my twenty-four-karat gold necklace with the heart locket on it. Omar bought it for me last Valentine's Day.

Ring ... ring ... ring.

"What's up, chick?" I say as I run out of the house.

"Where are you?" Coco asks curtly.

"I'm in the car on my way to Jazz's house. I know you're not going to leave me. I'll be there in twenty minutes."

"No, you won't. You always say that shit. Twenty minutes turn into an hour. Just meet us at Friday's on Broad Street. We'll wait for you out front. Whoever gets there first reserves a table in the smoking section."

"I don't want to sit in the smoking section. You the only one dat smoke. Do that shit outside before you come in. I'm hungry as a bitch and I don't want to smell smoke while I eat," I scream, irritated.

"I'm in no mood for your stank ass attitude. Don't trip on me because Omar pissed you off. Get a grip and chill the fuck out. Just get any table, I don't even care," Coco shouts with an attitude.

I hang up and called my mother to check on Omari. My mother says she is asleep and everything is okay.

When I pull up into Friday's parking lot, it's packed. I don't see Coco's blue Ford Escape anywhere. I pull out my cell phone and call Kori. "I'm here. Where y'all at?"

"We are already here waiting up front for you."

"A'ight."

As I pass by a bunch of whack ass niggas, I hear the usual comments. "Damn baby you look good" or "you got a phat ass, ma." Tonight, however, I'm not feeling any of them. When I walk in, everybody's heads turn. *What everybody looking at? They must've never seen a fly bitch before,* I think.

"Hey girl, I see you finally made it." Coco looks me up and down.

"Yeah, I told you I was on my way."

"Yep, and it only took you thirty minutes. Not bad," Jazz says, slapping Coco five.

Coco was getting money with that outfit she's rocking. The colors look good on her milk chocolate complexion. Coco is a size eight with long legs, "C" cup breasts, and a big round booty. She can't see that good at night, so she had on her gold frame Dolce & Gabbana eyeglasses.

Some people think Coco and Omar are brother and sister because they're both chocolate with deep dimples. Since Coco does hair, of course her shit is laid. Her hair is micro braided with eighteen-inch wavy hair. You couldn't tell her nothing.

"So fill me in on what happened wit' Omar," Coco says as she sits down on the bench.

I recapped the situation at the mall.

"That was fucked up, Skye," Jazz says, throwing in her two cents.

Some guys come in and start flirting with Jasmine. Jasmine is the youngest and shortest of the crew. Jazz is twenty-four and 5'3". She's about a size ten with pecan brown skin and bow legs. Her eyes are hazel, and she wears a short layered wrap with crimson highlights.

Tonight she's rocking a bebe dress. Her ears were blinging with a pair of square two-karat diamond earrings. "It's about time," Jazz says as she checks the time on her diamond-encrusted Movado watch.

Finally our table is available in the non-smoking section. Jazz gives this guy her number, and we head in to be seated.

"I'm hungry as hell. Are y'all going to order something to eat or just sit, be cute, and order drinks?" I ask as my green eyes scan the room.

"Yeah, I'll probably get an appetizer," Coco announces while looking at the menu. The waitress comes over and takes our orders. I order some Jack Daniels buffalo wings, potato skins, and a Corona. Jazz orders the sizzling, cheesy chicken and an Incredible Hulk. Coco tries to act cute, so she orders a basket of mozzarella sticks and a frozen strawberry Margarita.

We're laughing and talking about people and having a great time until I notice a bunch of loud niggas over in the smoking section. This one dude has his back to me with this tacky skeezer sitting on his lap. From a distance I can tell he's fly. He has a bunch of hoes hanging around his table. When he gets up I can't help but notice his attire.

He has on a royal blue and gray shirt, some dark denim True Religion shorts, and gray, white, and royal blue Jordan sneakers. I can see long cornrows hanging from underneath his royal blue baseball cap. As he begins to come closer into my vision I realized this brotha I am hawking is mine.

"Oh, shit that's Omar. I can't believe this motherfucka came to Friday's and got a cheap ass hoe sitting on his lap!" I shout as I begin to get out the booth.

"Move bitch, I got to go handle this!" I scream at Jazz.

"Skye, get a hold of yourself, you are not going to embarrass us like you did yourself at the mall," Jazz replies, rolling her hazel eyes.

"Sit down, girl. I got a plan. Don't let Omar know you are here. Let's keep an eye on this chick and when she leaves, we'll leave too. Once we're in the parking lot, handle you B.I.," Coco says trying to calm me down.

Reluctantly, I sit back down and order another drink. This day has gone from bad to worse, and is about to get even crazier.

About fifteen minutes go by before I see Omar, Dontaé, Keenan, and Tyrone leaving. He must've rode with one of his boys, because I don't see the forest green Cadillac Escalade in the parking lot. It seems like it takes forever for this trick and her friends to leave.

"Come on, y'all. Looks like they finally ready to go," Coco says, getting excited.

Coco loves to fight. I guess growing up in the projects, she didn't have much of a choice. Plus she got nothing but brothers that terrorized her, so she learned to fight. Me, well, I hate fighting. I'm too cute for that shit, especially tonight. Don't get it twisted, I can throw them blows. I just prefer not to.

While following these trifling chicks to the parking lot, I overhear the tall skinny bitch that was sitting on Omar's lap say, "You know that fine chocolate one I was trying to get at? Girl, he tried to tell me he got a girlfriend and a two-year-old daughter. They living together and shit, but I gave him my number anyway. What his girl got to do with me? You know how cute niggas be anyway. Always got a busted ugly ass chick," she says, laughing while giving one of her tacky ass friends five.

"Yolanda you are too much for me "says the big booty girl that looks like a stripper.

I can't help myself. I just have to interject.

"In this case, you happen to be wrong. Because that fine chocolate brotha belongs to me, and I'm nothing but the Truth," I say with attitude.

Yolanda turns around and looks me up and down.

Damn, this bitch is fly. What can I possibly say? I know what. I bet this bourgeois bitch can't fight. I'm gone stomp the shit out her ass, Yolanda thought.

"You must not be that damn fly, 'cause your man foot the bill for all of our shit!" she shouts back at me.

No, this bitch didn't go there!

"He probably wanted you to save your money so next time you come out, you won't be rocking that cheap shit," I reply, furious at the thought this nigga spent OUR money on this bitch.

No more words are exchanged.

Yolanda's fist comes up and decks me right in the jaw. Shocked by her sudden movement, Yolanda is getting a couple of hits in. Once I regain my composure, I whoop Yolanda's ass. I punch her in the right eye, then the stomach, over and over again till she falls to the ground.

While Yolanda is on the ground, I'm stomping her with my new Prada heels.

"Skye, stop, that's enough!" Coco screams, as she sees blood shooting everywhere.

A crowd starts to form, and I know the police are on the way. One of the other girls grabs me from the back, and Coco has to jump in and beat her ass.

"Jazz, go pull the Jeep around front!" I shout.

Coco pulls me off the girl and we jump in the car.

On our way out of the parking lot, we see the police pulling up.

"I hope that bitch didn't get my license plate number. Damn, what a fucked up night," Coco huffs.

Once in the car I noticed blood on my shoes. "That bitch made me fuck up my brand new $700 Prada pumps! I should go back and whoop her ass again!" I scream from the back seat.

"You better hope that hoe don't press charges," Coco says pissed off.

"Aw, shit Skye. Look at your face!" Jazz screams.

When I look in the mirror, my left cheek is red and I have a cut above my eye. "Damn, look at this shit! What am I going to tell Omar?" I shout.

"Tell him you got it fighting at the club. Some chicks was hatin', and we had to throw down," Coco replies as if I shouldn't be worried.

"What about my car? It's still in the parking lot."

"I'll just get Jerome or Torrey to take me to get it. Give me your keys. I'll get it tonight and you can pick it up from my house. Just tell Omar you rode wit' me to the club," Coco replied.

We pull up at my house around 1:00 A.M. I get out of the Jeep. "Thanks for having my back, Coco. I love y'all. Call you tomorrow." I shut the door and go to face my doom.

I know Omar will be mad 'cause I came in late. I'm sure he called me dozens of times, but I turned my phone off so I don't know for sure.

"Now it's time to put on your game face," I mumble to myself.

I walk into the dimly lit living room. Omar is lying on the burgundy and camel print suede couch watching the flat screen fifty-four inch plasma TV. A beautiful gift-wrapped box is sitting on the glass coffee table.

"Hey, baby. I'm sorry." Omar gets up off the couch, walks over to me, and hugs me tight. "Look, I bought you something. I just wanted to apologize for leaving you at the mall with Omari." He paused and looked at my face. "What happened to you?"

"Nothing ... I got in a fight outside the club. Everything is fine except my new shoes," I respond, showing no emotion.

"Sit down and tell me what happened."

"Not tonight, I'm tired. We can talk about it tomorrow, but there is something I need to say. I shouldn't have flipped out on you at the mall. I apologize. I said some things I didn't mean, but can you please try to understand that I need a little space sometimes?"

"Okay. Skye, I'll give you some space. Before you go to bed, I'd like for you to open your gift."

I open up the neatly wrapped box; inside is a white leather Marc Jacobs purse.

"How did you know I wanted this? Thank you so much baby." I kissed his full lips.

"Because I know your style, and you're welcome."

"Do you want me to go upstairs and run you some bath water? Do you need some Advil or ice for your face?" he asks with concern.

"Ice for my face, do it look that bad?"

"Have you seen it?"

I run upstairs, go into the bathroom, look in the mirror, and instantly get pissed. The little red mark I had on my left cheek had turned into a big purple and black bruise.

"How in the hell am I suppose to eat dinner with my parents later on today!" I shout hysterically.

"Baby, calm down. Take your clothes off. I'm going to run you a hot bath and get you an ice pack."

Omar goes into the bathroom, fills the tub up with hot water and adds some bath beads. Then he heads downstairs and returns with a glass of spring water and four Advil. I slip into the steaming bath water and try to relax. He sits on the toilet beside the tub, and then places the ice pack on my cheek.

My cell phone is ringing. Who could be calling at this hour?

"Do you want me to bring you your phone?" he asks, sounding puzzled.

"Yeah, it's probably Coco calling to check up on me."

I answer sounding mad, "Hello."

"Hey, boo. I just called to tell you I got your car. Maybe I can bring it to you tomorrow or Omar can bring you over."

"That's cool. I'll call you later and let you know."

"A'ight." Coco hung up the phone.

"Who was dat?" Omar asked being nosy.

"Coco. She just call to check on me, and to tell me to see if you can drop me at her house later to pick up my car."

"I can do that, but I got some stuff to do around three o'clock"

"Well, you can just drop me off on your way."

I get out of the tub, slip on my black lace panties and my black camisole, jump in the bed, and am knocked out. Hopefully tomorrow will be a brighter day.

Chapter Four

Damisha

After Jazz and I leave Marshall's, I take her home. My feet are in need of a pedicure, so I make a pit stop at Golden Nails. I already have my outfit picked out for tonight, so I get a design to match my toes.

"Do you want eyebrow too?" the short Asian woman asks with a thick accent.

"Sure, why not? I like wax."

After my eyebrows are arched, and my pedicure is completed, I head home. When I pull up to my house, my brother Dontaé is sitting out front arguing with some girl.

"Who the hell is this, Dontaé, huh?" the girl said, loudly pointing her finger at me.

"I'm his sister, and why the hell are you in front of my house starting shit?"

"I'm so sorry! My name is Kandice, and I followed him here. I thought he might be going to one of his hoe's houses. Just wanted to catch his black ass in a lie."

"Well, Kandice, it's nice to meet you. Sorry to disappoint you, but I'm his younger sister Damisha. Now I would appreciate it if y'all could carry that drama somewhere else."

"She needs to take her ass on. I came by to visit you, not cause problems," Dontaé says, looking at me with a sly grin.

"Sorry, about that, I'll be going now," Kandice says, feeling stupid.

After she drives off, me and Dontaé go inside. "Why didn't you beat her ass?"

"I knew she was following me, that's why I came here. I knew if she came here acting crazy, you would lay her down," he explains, pissed off.

"Not tonight, big bro. I got to get ready for a date. I'm not about to mess up my hair and outfit. My shit cost too much money."

"You a trip! Do you mind if I hang out here for a while? She might come back to see if I'm still here."

"Do what you feel. Just lock my door when you leave. Oh, D, please tell me what you are doing to these girls to make them act like that?" I ask curiously. I was never one to stalk a nigga or be too pressed. Shit, they should be happy if I even call them. Ain't no man going to have me play myself.

"What can I say? They can't get enough of this ten-inch D," he replies, laughing.

"Boy, you nasty as hell."

My phone starts ringing, which cuts our conversation short. "Who dis?" I ask, answering the phone.

"This is Chris. Is Damisha in?"

"Yeah, this me. I'm getting ready now. What's up?"

"I'll be there to pick you up at eight o'clock. What's your address?"

I give him directions to my house and hang up.

"Who are you going out wit'?" Dontaé asks.

"This nigga named Chris I met at Olive Garden. He works at Capital One as a Computer Network Engineer. He getting money, and I intend on spending it," I reply, laughing.

"You are nothing nice, lil sis, not at all. Guess it runs in the family," D says, popping his collar, being cocky.

The clock read seven fifteen. If I'm going to be ready by eight, I have to get a move on.

I take a bath. A shower would've been quicker, but the steam would have messed up my curls. Coco did my hair early this morning, but it's holding up nicely. I lotion up my body with Love Spell by Victoria Secret, put on my black strapless bra and black lace thong, and go to get my outfit.

"D, can you bring my clothes to the door, please?" I yell from my room.

Dontaé knocks on the door, and I crack it slightly, sticking out my arm to retrieve the clothes. I carefully put the turquoise BeBe halter-top over my head, trying not to mess up my hair.

I hear my doorbell ring as I put on my silver hoop earrings and my white Gucci watch.

"Yo, D, get the door. I'm almost done."

"A'ight, Mimi. Do you want him to come in, or stand outside and wait?"

"Let him in, dummy, he can sit in the living room."

Dontaé opens the door and directs Chris to the living room.

"Hey, man, I'm Dontaé. Mimi, I mean Damisha's brother."

"Nice to meet you, I'm Chris."

I grab my white Coach Hobo purse, checked the mirror and was ready to go.

"Hey Chris, I'm assuming you've already met my brother?"

"Yeah, he introduced himself."

"Bye Dontaé, don't forget to lock my door."

"See ya later, Sis."

When I walk outside, I'm pleasantly surprised to see 2007 black Infiniti EX. He unlocks the doors and we get in.

"Where would you like to go eat?" Chris asks as he put in a CD.

"Red Lobster is fine wit' me."

"Cool. I was thinking we could eat, go to the Funny Bone, then chill at my place."

"Let's take it one step at a time."

As we're riding down the street my cell phone rings. Damn, that reminds me to put it on vibrate. "Yo, what's up?" I say, as I answer my cell phone.

"Hey, Mimi. Is Skye with you? She's not answering her phone," Omar asks, sounding like somebody just killed his dog.

"No, she's not with me. I'm on a date. So can you please not call me anymore tonight? She'll probably be home later."

"A'ight, sorry to bother you."

I hang up and switch my ringer to vibrate.

***

We have to wait twenty minutes for a table when we arrive at Red Lobster. We sat down in the lobby area and made small talk. This gives me the perfect opportunity to fully check Chris out. Let me see, how I would describe him? Well, he's about six-foot-one, 235 pounds of pure muscle. He has soft, black curly hair, blemish free cocoa skin, a six-pack, and the prettiest white teeth. Chris is thirty years old, and he has a son that's six. His outfit's a'ight, not the fly shit I'm use to brothas wearing. He has on a green, white, and blue plaid button up collar shirt made by Roca Wear, some Roca Wear jeans, and a pair of white and green Adidas. Don't get it twisted, there is nothing wrong with Roca Wear, but this shirt is just ugly.

"So, tell me about yourself. What you like, don't like?" Chris asks, trying to make idle conversation.

What I want to say is "I don't like this ugly ass shirt you got on", but that wouldn't be polite.

"Let's see, I like to spend money, preferably someone else's, I'm into fashion, and I love spontaneous men. I'm spoiled and like to have my way," I reply, being very serious. Chris begins laughing, as if I'm Adelle Givens doing a standup act.

"What's so funny?" I guess by the puzzled look on my face he can tell I missed the punch line.

"First of all, I don't mind spending money on a beautiful woman, but I'm not a spineless jellyfish that's going to let you walk all over me. You can't always have things your way. I love a challenge. I'm going to break you out of being spoiled."

"You think so?"

"Certain of it." We both smile at each other. This is going to be good.

Our table is finally ready. The tall brunette lady shows us to our booth in the nonsmoking section. I pick up the menu to see what I want to order.

"So, can I order whatever I want or are you putting your foot down?" I ask, trying to be amusing.

"You can order whatever your little heart desires," he replies with a huge smile.

When the waitress comes back, I order raspberry lemonade and chicken strips for an appetizer. Chris orders a root beer and cocktail shrimp. While waiting for our drinks and appetizers, Chris tries to make small talk.

"You look very lovely tonight. I'm really feeling your outfit."

"My outfit is the only thing you're going to be feeling," I reply, getting extremely irritated by his presence. Maybe Skye is right. I have been a little grouchy today, which means one thing, my period is on the way. Damn. Please not tonight, not in my new white Capri! I excuse myself, and then walk to the ladies room and check my panties. Whew! I don't see anything.

When I return, the waitress had just sat down our food. I place my order. For the rest of the meal we eat in silence. I think I hurt his feelings.

I decide to apologize, but before I can, he breaks the silence. "Would you like some dessert, or are you ready to end this date?"

The force and authority in his voice start to turn me on. Maybe he could get some after all. I like an assertive man.

"I'd prefer a Fudge Overboard. What about you?"

"I'm not big on sweets."

"Does this mean you wouldn't want to dip into my caramel?" I seductively ask, licking sour cream off my finger. "I'd like to apologize for my snide remarks. I'm not usually this feisty on the first date."

He takes a long pause. "I was wondering if you were bipolar and forgot to take your medication. You seemed so different when I met you. I guess that's how you reel them in."

"No. I just got a lot on my mind. My day has been hectic. Let's start over."

"Okay, I accept your apology. I'm going to wipe the slate clean this one time."

The waitress comes back, and I order my Fudge Overboard. Licking whipped cream off my lips, I gaze into his eyes. "You never answered my question."

"What question was that?"

Oh, now the brotha wants to play games.

"Do you want to dip into my caramel?"

"Eventually. But not tonight."

Good answer, he might turn out to be a good man after all.

"I don't mean to rush you, but its quarter till ten. The comedy show starts at 10:00," he states, looking at his platinum and diamond Rolex.

I finish off my dessert while he pays the bill. It's amateur night at the Funny Bone. The act consists of four comedians. The show's two hours long. Once we are inside the club, I decide to order a drink.

"Chris, do you mind if I order a mixed drink?"

"No baby, get what you want."

I order a glass of Hypnotic; he has a Heineken. For amateurs, the show's really funny, or maybe it's the drinks. By the end, I had drunk two glasses of Hypnotic, an apple martini, and a Corona. It's safe to say I'm lit.

"Would you like to go home, or to my place?" Chris asks as we ride down the street.

"It doesn't matter," I reply, slurring words. At 12:30 A.M., we pull up to my townhouse.

"Let me help you inside. You appear to be drunk."

Chris opens my door and pulls me out of the car. He basically holds me up as we walk to the front door. "Give me your keys. Which one is to your house?" I show him the house key, he opens the door, and we go inside.

"Damisha, are you a'ight? Do you feel sick?"

"Huh?"

"Never mind," he replies in disgust. Chris picks me up and takes me upstairs to my bedroom. He pulls off my shoes, then my pants, and next comes the halter-top. "Damn, you got a nice body, but I can't take advantage of a drunk woman. Where are your night clothes?"

"In umm ... I think they in the second drawer."

He pulls out my pink Victoria Secret's boy tank and boy shorts. I can't believe this nigga is going to dress me and leave.

"I don't want to leave you like this, you might have alcohol poisoning. Do you always drink like this?"

"Nope."

"Well, do you want me to stay here with you?"

"Yep."

"Do you even know what you're saying?"

"No."

"I thought not."

Chris takes off his clothes and lies beside me in his white T-shirt and navy blue boxers. He's actually a perfect gentleman. No touching, kissing or nothing. Hmm ... I wonder if he's gay.

When I wake up in the morning, my head's pounding. It feels like a freight train running through my head. Chris is still laying in my bed sleep. Aww, he looks so cute.

I go into the kitchen to make a cup of coffee.

"What was I thinking?" I wonder as I pop two Advil into my mouth. I sit down at the round Maplewood table, drink my coffee, and read my unopened mail. For some reason, I looked up at the clock. It's 10:23 A.M. Maybe I should wake him up. I wonder if he has somewhere to go. Before I can make up my mind, the phone in the kitchen starts ringing,

"Yo, what's up?" I ask.

"Nothing, just wanted to know how your date went," Jazz asks.

"It was nice. I got drunk as hell though."

"Well, let me tell you what went down at Friday's!"

I should've known she has to have some gossip to be calling this early. "Girl, what happened?"

"Skye saw Omar at Friday's wit' dis girl sitting on his lap. She wanted to act a fool, but me and Coco told her no, just wait. Anyway, we waited for the girl and her tacky friends to leave. When we got in the parking lot, Skye overheard the girl Yolanda talking shit, so she stepped to her. You know how Skye's mouth is. Well, the girl must've heard enough, because she straight stole Skye in the jaw. Then Skye just went to her and stomped the shit out of her."

"Wait a minute. With what shoes?"

"Girl, with the Prada shoes she just bought! They got blood all on them now. One of her friends tried to jump in, so Coco beat her ass. I went and got the Jeep. We drove off just in time, because the police was coming."

"Is Skye a'ight?"

"Except her shoes, she got a little cut above her left eye and a red bruise on her cheek."

"Well, as soon as I get myself together, I'll call her."

"A'ight. Just act like you don't know what went down," Jazz replied.

"Yeah, I know the deal. Holla back."

I hang up the phone, then go upstairs to wake up Chris.

"Chris, baby, wake up. It's time to get up," I whisper in his ear while nudging his arm.

Stretching out his arms with a big yawn, he finally sits up on the side of my queen size bed. "Good morning. Did you sleep well?" I ask, looking into his eyes. Damn, he even looks good in the morning! All I have to do is work on his gear.

"Good morning. Yeah, I slept all right, considering this isn't my bed, but I should be asking you that question."

"I'm okay, besides the migraine headache I woke up wit'. I made some coffee and took two Advil. Would you like a cup?"

"No, I'm good. What time is it?"

"Quarter till eleven."

"Damn, I didn't realize it was that late," he says, getting up, putting on his clothes.

Oh, my goodness I can't believe my eyes. Chris's package is hanging out the front of his boxers. My, my, my if it's like that soft, no telling how big it is hard.

"I'm sorry for keeping you at my house all night. I hope you didn't miss something important," I say, feeling bad about what happened.

"Oh, no baby, nothing like that. I just usually go to church. That's all. I can still make it if I leave now. I'll call you, a'ight? In the meantime, stay away from alcohol," he says as he kisses my forehead.

"Don't worry, I won't try that again. Thanks for being a gentleman. I know some men would've taken advantage."

"Yeah, they probably would have. Just be careful, and thank God it was me, not a trifling man."

"You're right. Well, don't let me hold you up."

"Do you go to church?"

"Sometimes"

"Maybe you can go wit' me one Sunday"

"Sounds good." I walk him to the door and he leaves. Hmm a church boy. What have I gotten myself into?

***

I 'm hungry, and there's no food in my refrigerator. Who can I call? I dial Coco's number.

"Hello?"

"Coco, what you doing?"

"Nothing, just chilling. Why?"

"I'm hungry and I wanted somebody to go out to eat with," I say, sounding like a little child.

"Where do you want to go? You know by the time I get me and the kids ready it will be 12:30 P.M."

"Oh, well I'll just go to Arby's or something."

"How was your date?"

"It was nice. We went to Red Lobster and the Funny Bone. I got drunk as hell at the Funny Bone, but the comedians were funny. Chris is really cute and sexy, but his gear was not on point. He brought me home, spent the night, and didn't even touch me. Then he left this morning to go to church."

"What? He seems too good for you," Coco states, laughing.

"You ain't funny. I'm hanging up, I'm hungry anyway. I'm about to go to Arby's."

"Fine, but I didn't tell you about girls' night out at Friday's," she teases.

"I already know, Big Mouth Jazz called me early this morning. But don't tell Skye."

"A'ight, catch you later."

After taking the Advil I feel a little better. I jumped in the shower, brush my teeth, and throw on a pair of Roca Wear jean shorts, a pink Roca Wear tank top, and my pink and white Roca Wear flip-flops. I look a mess, but that's okay, I'll just go through the drive thru window. I hop in my car and drive to Arby's. When I got back home, I turn on the TV and eat my roast beef sandwich with cheese fries. Guess I'll call Skye to check up on her. Ring. Ring.

"Hello," Skye says, sounding sluggish.

"Hey, Ma, it's Mimi, what up with you?"

"Nothing, just putting on my clothes so I can get my car from Coco's house. I guess you heard by now what happened at Friday's."

"I got the short version 'cause I had company when Jazz called."

"Oh, well the reason I'm mad is because this chick named Yolanda said Omar paid her bill at Friday's. At first I thought she was lying, but I checked his pockets this morning, and he had two receipts along with her phone number."

"So, it's probably a logical explanation for that. Maybe he paid for one of his broke ass friends. Who was he wit?"

"Your brother, Keenan, and Tyrone. I heard her say she slipped her number in his pocket, so I'll let that go unless he keeps it and uses it. But the receipts had two different table numbers, plus a different server's name. Explain that. They were all at the table together. Besides, none of dem niggas broke!" she shouts, sounding irate.

"You're right. Guess I can't help a brotha out this time. You should know Omar wouldn't cheat on you. Actually, he called my cell phone looking for you around eight o'clock. I told him you weren't with me, and you'd probably be home later."

"Oh, yeah, I turned my phone off last night. How was your date?"

I went on to tell Skye about my date with Chris. She asks me if I can take her to Coco's house so she can get her car.

"Give me about fifteen minutes. I'll take you."

"Thanks, boo," she says before hanging up.

After gulping down a Pepsi and eating my apple turnover, I leave my house to pick up Skye. I don't feel like getting out the car, so I call her as I approach the block she lives on.

"Skye, I'm out front," I say as I pull into the driveway.

Skye comes out the house dressed in a purple Apple Bottom tank top, Apple Bottom blue jean shorts, and a pair of white Air Force Ones. She must not be feeling well. Skye rarely wears sneakers. She opens the door and hops in the front seat.

"Where's Omari?" I ask, looking forward to seeing her cute little face.

"She's still at my mom's house. I'm going to get Omar to pick her up. I don't want my parents to see my face. I already called out from work. I'm taking three personal days. Coco told me that a little foundation should cover it after a couple of days of healing."

I turn completely around to get a good look at her face.

"Oh, my goodness, I thought you only had a little red bruise."

"Last night, when it first happened it was, but by the time I got home, it looked like this. I was mad as hell when I looked in the mirror. Omar told me to put cocoa butter on it so it won't leave a scar."

"What do you plan on doing about Omar?"

"I don't know. He never gave me a reason to think he was cheating. I'll just sit back and observe his behavior. Guess what?"

"What?"

"He apologized about the mall incident, and gave me a white Marc Jacobs bag."

"Damn, you got a good man. You cuss him out in public, embarrass the hell out of him, then he comes home with a gift and apologizes. Somebody needs to smack the shit out of you. If you're not careful, somebody's going to snatch him up. You need to appreciate Omar; there are not many men out here like him"

Skye rolls her eyes. "I'm not in the mood for your preaching. I've had enough of the Omar fan club. Let him follow you around, call all your friends, stalk you twenty-four-seven. Then let me know how much you appreciate him."

"A'ight Skye, I'll drop it." I'm in no mood to argue with this heifer.

We pull up to Coco's tan and forest-green two-story house. There are three cars in the driveway, so I park in front of the house. Coco lives in a very nice African American middle class neighborhood called Summer Hills out in Varina.

"Are you coming in?" Skye asks.

"Oh, I didn't know she was expecting us. I guess I can chill for a few."

"Yeah, I told her we were coming to get my car. I got to go inside anyway to get my keys. Plus she wants us to help her plan her birthday party."

We both get out of the car, and I ring the doorbell.

"Who is it?" Coco yells.

"Your mama, who you think it is?" I reply, being smart.

She opens the door with her hand on her hip.

"Come on in, we can go downstairs to talk."

Coco and her husband Jerome's house is banging. The family room downstairs is decorated in burnt orange, cream, and gold. The burnt orange suede couch and love seat are decorated with cream and burnt orange pillows trimmed in gold. The walls are painted cream, with burnt orange carpet. Coco has a lot of Black artwork hanging on the walls. Her gold-trimmed glass table has a beautiful flower arrangement as a centerpiece with a candle on each side. Since it's summer, the fireplace has a gold wire fence in front of it so the children won't climb in.

Coco has two children; both are boys. Her oldest son Corey is five, and we call him C. J. She had him by her ex-boyfriend André. Christian, her two-year-old, is her husband's child.

Skye and I sit on the couch, while Coco sits in a big reclining chair.

"So what's up wit' y'all for today?" Coco asks, getting comfortable in her chair.

"Nothing, I'm not going nowhere wit' my face like this. I told you I'm not even going to work. I'm going to call Jamyya and tell her to drop the kids off at my house tomorrow. She needs a break bad. Maybe you can do her hair or something," Skye says, showing her sensitive side.

Who would've thought she could actually care about somebody besides herself?

Coco looks at her strangely. "That's very nice of you, but the shop is closed on Mondays. Maybe you can keep them Tuesday, and I can give her the royal treatment then."

"You can do it here. I want her to be able to go somewhere with the girls. You're off on Mondays; everybody else has to work. You two could go out and do something. Please, for me? You know if my face wasn't a mess I would take her out. I miss her, and she deserves a day off from being Mommy."

"You're right. I'll call her later and set up something. Oh yeah, make sure y'all make arrangements for your kids, because everybody is going to attend my party. It's on Saturday, July 5th, at 9:00 P.M."

"I'll get my mom to keep Omari."

"So how are we supposed to help you plan your party?" I finally ask. I'm ready to go home and take a nap. I'm still worn out from last night.

"Well, I need to know what food to have, what kind of drinks, and an invitation list. I already rented out the top floor of Club Z. The manager wants to know what kind of liquor to stock the bar wit'. He said I can have them cater the food too. I just need to make a selection. I already decided on an all white party with gold decorations."

"You think you Diddy or something?" I ask, laughing.

"No, but my party is going to be off the chain like a Diddy party."

We all laugh. I stay about another hour helping them plan the party.

"Well, it's been fun y'all, but I got to go to work tomorrow. Good luck wit' keeping Jamyya's kids."

Somehow, the ride home seems long. My mind starts to drift off, and I don't like what, or should I say, *whom*, I was thinking about. For some reason, unbeknown to me, Jerell was on my mind. All through high school I paid him no attention, but seeing him at the mall changed all that.

I wonder how long it will take for him to call me. When I get home, it's around 2:00P.M. Maybe I'll take a nap, then go by my mom's house to see how she's doing. I doze off for what seemed like minutes.

The ringing of my cell phone wakes me up. "H-hello," I answer, sounding as if something is stuck in my throat. I clear my throat before I continue.

"Hey Damisha, this is Chris. Just called to check up on you."

"That's mighty sweet of you. I'm all better now. Thanks for staying to look after me. Did you make it to church?"

"Yeah, I got there about ten minutes late, but the important thing is I made it."

"Glad to hear it. I hope you said a little prayer for me while you were there."

"I sure did. I was wondering if you would like to go out again. I have my son next weekend, but I'm free Sunday evening."

"What did you have in mind?"

"Dinner and a movie. No alcohol this time. I really want to get to know you," he says, sounding sincere.

"Well, 6:00 P.M. is good for me, and I promise I won't drink. I work Monday through Friday anyway, so drinking on Sunday is a no-no."

"Could we make it 6:30 P.M.? I usually drop Justin off at six."

"Yeah. No problem. What movie are we going to see?"

"You being spoiled and all, I thought I'd let you pick," he replies, laughing.

"I thought you were going to break me out of it? Besides, I chose the restaurant last time. I want to see you put your foot down. Take control."

"Since you put it that way, I'll make it a surprise. I'll call you Wednesday to see if things are still on."

"Sounds good. See you Sunday," I say as I hang up, feeling better than before. Chris sure does seem like a good catch. I wonder why he's single. I better pray he's not a stalker like Omar.

I decide to stay in the house and get my things together for work tomorrow. I'm going to bed early tonight because Mondays are the worst.

I wake up at 7:00A.M. with a hurting pain in my stomach; I quickly jump in the shower and head to work. Ugh eight hours is too long to sit in here all day feeling like this. Surprisingly the day flew by and I was getting in my car at 4:30 P.M.

No sooner than I step through the door, my phone starts to ring. Damn, a girl can't have any peace. I just got off work. Shit, I thought everybody knew how rough Mondays are. To make matters worse, my period started this morning and the cramps are kicking my ass.

I answer the phone sounding pissed off. "Hello."

"What's wrong with you?" Skye asks in her innocent voice.

"Just PMS'ing. Why?"

"Never mind now. I was calling to vent but I can tell now is not a good time."

"Vent about what? Please tell me it's not Omar." I am getting real sick and tired of these same old conversations. If the nigga gets on her nerves that much, why don't she leave him? Personally, I think Skye just wants something to complain about in her perfect world.

Most women whine and nag about their man never being around. She rants and raves about him being around too much. Don't get me wrong, Omar is not one of my favorite people, but he's a good man. Like the rest, he got his issues, but you got to take the good with the bad. Skye needs to figure out if his faults outweigh the good. Frankly, I don't think so.

"No, it's not Omar. It's these damn kids. No wonder Jamyya's pulling her hair out. I don't see how she does this shit every day. I only kept them for six hours and I'm exhausted."

"I can imagine. Just think how happy you made Jamyya. She's your best friend, and you know she'll go through hell and high water for you."

"I know, that's part of the reason I did it."

"What's the other part?" I ask, getting sucked into this unwanted conversation.

"I know how it is to be fed up. Nobody understands my situation, but I can empathize with Jamyya. I'm not having any more kids. That's why I sneak and take my birth control pills, and after today, I'll never forget."

"Girl, that's why I don't have any kids. Chris called me, and we're going out Sunday evening. Maybe I can keep Jamyya's kids for a couple of hours on Saturday so you two can go out. I'll take the little heathens to Chuck E. Cheese's. They are not going to terrorize my house, it's not kid proof," I say, as we both laugh.

"Are you sure? You know you're not a children person?" she asks, sounding skeptical.

"Yeah, I'm sure. Just don't take advantage. How about I pick them up at noon and Jamyya can have them back around four?"

"Sounds good. Thanks Mimi. She'll be so excited to get out on a Saturday."

"No problem. Talk to you later."

What in the hell did I just get myself into? Jamyya has four kids, two girls and twin boys. This shouldn't be hard... at least all of them are potty trained. They're old enough to walk and talk. A piece of cake.

***

Well, when Saturday comes, I find out why I don't have kids. Jamyya and Skye drop the kids off at my house around 10:00 A.M.

"Thanks Mimi, I really needed this day out away from the kids," Jamyya states ecstatically.

"No problem, just make sure you're back here around 4:00 P.M. to pick them up."

"I will, even if I have to drag Skye out the mall," she replies.

They leave with the quickness, eager to start their day.

"Hey, y'all, Auntie Mimi have a fun day planned for you guys," I say, looking at the kids all excited with what I came up with.

"Where are we going?" Ke'Asia asks, with her hand on her imagination, which she thought was her hip.

"First, we're going to the movies, then we are going to Chuck E. Cheese's, and if we have time, stop by the mall and do a little shopping."

"I hate to tell you this, but taking the twins to the movies and the mall is a bad idea. Especially without a stroller," Ke'Asia states matter-of-factly.

"Okay, but why not the movies?" I say, dumbfounded by what the child has just said.

"Because they ain't going to sit still that long. No wonder you ain't got any kids."

This little heifer was already getting on my nerves. What's wrong with the children these days? They too damn grown, that's what.

Being naïve, I decided to go along with my plans. We drove out to Short Pump Movie Theater and I purchased five tickets for the show. The total came to $31.50. Damn, this fun day is going to be expensive. We went inside, and they immediately ran to the concession stand.

"I want popcorn, M&Ms, and a Pepsi," Tamia says, like she has some damn money.

"Okay, this is what we're going to do. I'll buy one big popcorn, and we can all share. Everybody can get one piece of candy and their own drink," I say, trying to exert control.

"You can get me a fruit punch and some Skittles," Ke'Asia replies.

"What about y'all?" I bend down to ask the twins.

"I want dat one," Keontaé says, pointing to a Reese's Cup.

"You can get them the same thing, and they can't have soda," Ke'Asia announces.

"Thanks for the info." I step up to the cashier and order a box of M&Ms, Skittles, and two Reese's cups, Sour Patch Kids, and jumbo buttered popcorn. Then I have to get drinks.

The awkward-looking pimple-faced teenager looks at me. "Ma'am, that'll be $34.75."

"Excuse me?"

"Your total is $34.75," he replies, getting impatient. I pull out forty dollars and pay him.

We walk into the theater and sit down near the front. At first, everything's cool. Everybody's eating popcorn, candy, and drinking their juices. In the middle of the movie, Keontaé gets up and runs down the aisle. Then Dontaé decides to follow. After chasing them down and putting them back in their seats, Tamia has to use the bathroom.

Since Ke'Asia appears to be grown, I tell her to take her sister to the bathroom. Minutes later they came back, then the twins have to go. I guess I'll have to take them. Finally, the movie is over and we are headed to Chuck E. Cheese's. Yes, this should be good. They can run and play all they want. Perfect. As soon as we pull up to Chuck E. Cheese's, the kids start yelling and screaming with excitement. We walk in, get our hands stamped, and then I approach the counter.

"Hello, may I help you?" a small black woman asks.

"Yes. I would like to get a large cheese pizza, a large pepperoni pizza, five drinks, and five hundred tokens," I reply, pulling out my wallet.

"That comes to $69.48."

I pull out seventy dollars and notice I only had a fifty dollar bill and two twenties left. Damn, kids are expensive! No wonder Jamyya stays in the house. I get a table in the middle of the games so I can sit and watch the kids. I divide the tokens into four cups.

"A'ight, Ke'Asia, you take Keontaé, and Tamia, you can watch Deontaé. Y'all go ahead and play. I'll call you when the pizza comes."

Ke'Asia rolls her eyes. "I thought you were supposed to watch us? Come on y'all, and you bet not be bad either."

Somebody needs to slap her grown ass. Thirty minutes later the pizza arrives. I walk around looking for the kids. Finally I find them, escort them to the table, and we eat. These kids can eat; they all have two slices apiece and want more.

"Can we go back and play now?" Tamia asks timidly.

"Yeah, we can stay a little while longer," I reply, smiling.

She's nothing like her older sister; she's quiet and sweet.

The time has come for us to leave, but we can't find Deontaé. I look everywhere. Keontaé has to pee, so I take him to the ladies room. Coincidently, Deontaé is already in there using the bathroom.

"Come on, let's go," I say grabbing both of their hands.

"We got to get prizes first," Keontaé says, looking up at me innocently.

"A'ight, then we're leaving."

We turn in the tickets, and all the kids go to pick out prizes.

"A'ight y'all, time to go," I say, checking to make sure everybody is accounted for.

We leave Chuck E. Cheese's about 2:30 P.M., and I decide to stop at Marshall's. I know by Keenan being the only one working that they don't have a lot of money. Jamyya always buys the kids stuff first, so I think it will be nice to pick her out an outfit and buy the kids one too. Marshall's got baskets, so I put the twins inside one and get another basket for the clothes.

"Ke'Asia, can you please push one of the baskets?" I ask.

"Yeah, are you going to buy us something?" she asks.

"Yes, I'm going to get everybody something, plus a gift for y'all to give your mom."

"Okay, that'll be nice. Can I pick mine out?"

"Of course."

"Me too?" Tamia asks.

"Yeah."

We stroll over to the children's department first. I find two of the same Roca Wear jean shorts with a gray and blue Roca Wear T-shirt for the twins. Ke'Asia picks out a Baby Phat jean skirt with a light pink Baby Phat halter-top. Tamia finds herself an Apple Bottom sundress that's lime green and light blue.

"Now it's time to pick out something for mommy," I say, moving over to the Junior's department. I plow through racks and racks of stuff, but nothing jumps out at me. I turn around to see a sales associate pushing a rolling rack over to where I'm standing.

"Do you mind if I look on here?" I ask, already eyeing a piece on the rack.

"Sure, I was just about to put it on the racks. This is our new stuff we just got in yesterday," she replies, smiling.

I skim through the rack of clothes like a mad woman. A-ha! I come across the perfect outfit. Hmm, maybe I should get this for me. *No. Okay, focus. You're supposed to be shopping for Jamyya,* I think. I pick out a large lime-green halter-top Baby Phat dress. The bottom has ragged edges with a cling waist. Then I come across a yellow Baby Phat tube top with a rhinestone cat logo on the front and a washed denim Baby Phat skirt. Oh, this one is mine! Yes, they have a small top and a size six skirt.

When we get to the counter, I look up at the clock. Oh, my gosh, it's quarter till four! I use my credit card to pay for the purchase. I push the cart to the car and quickly place the twins in their car seats. I drive recklessly down the highway, trying to make it home by four. I don't want Jamyya to have an excuse not to get her kids back.

Whew, we made it to my house at 4:10 P.M.! As we're getting out the car, Skye and Jamyya pull up. *Just in time,* I think.

"I hope they weren't too much trouble. Thanks a lot, Mimi," Jamyya says, hugging me.

"They were a'ight. Spent up all my damn money, though."

"Girl, you don't have to tell me how expensive kids are," she says, laughing.

The kids run to Jamyya, yelling, "Mommy, we missed you!"

"We got a gift for you, Mommy," Tamia says, handing the bag to Jamyya. She opens the Marshall's bag and sees the lime-green Baby Phat halter-top dress.

"Oh, my, this is so cute. Mimi you didn't have to buy me anything! Keeping the kids was enough," she says with tears in her eyes.

Jamyya is always melodramatic.

"I wanted to, plus I got each of them an outfit. We had a good time. Now it's time for y'all to go," I reply, trying to get rid of them.

"You're tired, huh?" Skye asks.

"Hell, yeah!"

"Well, we are leaving right now. Thanks Mimi, you're the best," Skye says as they get in the car.

"Yeah, well just make sure you get somebody else to keep them for Coco's party," I yell at Jamyya as they pull off.

"I will. See ya."

***

After dealing with them kids, I need a nap. I wake up about 6:30 P.M., and I'm hungry. I jump in the shower, brush my teeth, and put my black-and-gold Baby Phat robe on.
Ring. Ring. Ring.
I look at the caller ID, but don't recognize the number.

"Who dis?" I ask as I pick up the phone.

"Hey, Ma, it's Jerell."

"Oh, what's up?"

"That's what I want to know. What you doing tonight?"

"Nothing. Probably go to Applebee's to get some take out."

"So, you don't have a date tonight?"

"Nope. Rolling solo."

"It just so happens that I'm hungry too. How about we go together?"

"That sounds cool. What time you want to go?"

"How long will it take you to get ready?" he asks.

"I'm already dressed. Give me about a half hour. I'll be ready."

"A'ight, Ma, I need your address."

I give Jerell my address so he can come pick me up. I have to hurry up and get dressed. Good thing I already took my shower. I pull out my Marshall's bag and put on the Baby Phat outfit I bought earlier. Then I look under my bed to find some shoes. I come across a pair of white Baby Phat flip-flops and slip them on. Jerell pulls up in his white Mercedes Benz C300 with tinted windows.

My cell phone starts ringing. "Yo. What's up?" I say, running down the steps.

"Come outside, Ma."

"A'ight."

I grab my white Coach bag and head out the door. When I get in the car, he has the music blaring.

"Damn, you looking good tonight."

"Thanks," I reply smiling.

We drive to Applebee's in silence, bobbing our heads to the music. It's Saturday night, so Applebee's is off the hook. People are standing around because all the seats are taken. I peep a couple of chicks checking Jerell out. Shit, I can't even front, I am too. He is looking good in his indigo-blue and chocolate-brown Black Label shirt, with his blue jean shorts and white Air Force Ones. Those eyes - mm, mm, mm. His eyes appear to be gray with a hint of blue, but I can tell they change colors, 'cause when I saw him at the mall, they were dark gray.

We wait for what seems like forever before we are seated. A small-figured, light-skinned waitress approaches our table.

"Hello, my name is Tonya. I'll be your server this evening. What would you like to drink?" she asks as she drools all over Jerell.

"Let me get lemonade," he says, smiling.

"I'll have a Dr. Pepper."

"Would you like any appetizers?"

"Yeah, give me an order of buffalo wings," Jerell says, looking the waitress up and down.

"Hot or mild," she asks, being flirty.

"Mild."

"Anything for you, ma'am?"

"A chicken Caesar salad with Italian dressing will be fine," I reply trying to be polite.

I can't believe they have the nerve to be flirting with one another right in my face. We eat our food and make some small talk in between. I decide to start my interrogation. I am very curious to know how Jerell got so much money, or should I say appears to have money.

"So. Where do you work?"

"I'm an accountant for Coca Cola," he simply states. "What about you?"

"I'm a Customer Service Rep for Virginia Power."

"Do you like your job?"

"Its a'ight; the customers get on my nerves the majority of the time, but I like my check."

"I know that's right!"

"Why don't you have a girlfriend or any kids?"

"I had a girlfriend, but she acted a fool and broke my heart. I'm not ready for kids yet. I should be asking you the same questions. You all fly and everything. Why you don't have a man?"

"Because I can't find one that knows how to act. None of them have the whole package. For example, if he has a good job, then he's crazy, or if he's nice and sweet, he don't have a job, or he's got a crazy baby momma. Just too much drama. Worst case scenario he's no good in bed. I can't stand awful sex."

He looks at me and smiles. "Well, you don't have to worry about that with me. I got a good job, no kids, no drama, and I haven't had any complaints in the bedroom."

"Is that so?"

"Yeah, it's so. I make sure I take time to please my woman."

The waitress interrupts our conversation and places the appetizers on the table. "Are you ready to order?"

"Yes" Jerell replies handing the menu to the waitress

After ordering our food we continue our conversation.

"Are you seeing anybody?" I inquire.

"To be honest wit' you, yes. I got a friend or two that I chill wit'. It's nothing serious, they both know I see other people. I'm not ready for a committed relationship right now."

"Oh, I see, you're a playa. I got you."

"No. I'm just chilling. I'm sure I'm not the only one you're seeing."

"You're right."

"That's what I thought."

The waitress comes back to bring the bill. Jerell slides the bill over to me. "So, are you paying?" he asks.

"I didn't plan on it, but I can." I reach into my purse and pull out a fifty dollar bill.

The nerve of this motherfucka! How in the hell is he going to invite me out, then ask me to pay? I knew something had to be up with him. That's probably why his ex-girlfriend acted crazy. Cheap bastard. After I finish

cussing Jerell out in my mind, I hear him say, "Ma, I was just joking I got it."
He pulls out a small stack of money and peels off three twenty-dollar bills.

The waitress returns. "Do you need change?"

The bill is only $42.08. What the fuck do she mean, do you need change?
Who in the hell tips that much? To my surprise, Jerell does.

"No, ma, you can keep it for your tip."   Mad can't describe how I feel.
"Why did you leave her that much money?" I can't help but ask.

"Because I used to be a waiter in college. I know how it is to get stiffed. If
people don't tip you, you don't get paid. Don't tell me you're one of those
people who don't tip," he replies, shaking his head.

"No. I leave tips every time I go out. Just not seventeen-dollar ones."

We get into the car, he looks at me and says, "Do you want to go somewhere else, or are you ready to go home?"

Even though I'm enjoying his company I'm tired and my feet hurt.
"Well, I'm having a good time with you, but I've been out all day. My feet
are starting to hurt. I just kind of want to go home and relax. You're welcome
to come in, if you want."

"Do you have some movies that we can watch?"

"No, I don't stay home much, but when I do, I'm usually asleep or talking on the phone. I got a DVD player though; maybe we can stop by Blockbuster and rent some movies."

"Good idea," he says, grinning from ear to ear.

We run into Blockbuster to get some DVDs. We get three videos.

"Do you want some popcorn or candy?" Jerell asks, placing the movies
on the counter.

"Yeah, I'll take some popcorn and Snickers."

He pays for our purchase, and we are on our way out the door when I
heard a woman's voice calling. "Jerell, hey baby, what's going on?"

"Oh, long time no see. Nothing much, just chilling. Excuse my manners.
Karen, this is Damisha. Damisha, this is Karen. We went to college together."

"Nice to meet you," I respond, not showing my jealousy.

"It was nice running into you. If you see your boy, tell him I said what's
up."

I give her a fake smile, grab Jerell's hand, and walk out the door.

Jerell is so sweet; he rubs my feet while we watch the movie. Every now
and then, we make small talk. He's so easy to talk to, plus he smells so good.
He's wearing Unforgiveable by Sean John.

Why did the night have to end so soon?

"It was nice chilling wit' you, Ma, but it's getting late. I got a lot of stuff
to do tomorrow."

Looking into his beautiful eyes, I quickly kiss his lips. "I had a good time
too. Thanks for the foot rub."

***

"No problem. I'll hit you up later. Goodnight."

I walk him to the door, and then lock it. Well, I guess I better get some sleep, 'cause tomorrow I got a date with Chris. I went from no man to two!

I sleep till nine o'clock. I wanted to sleep later, but my brother wouldn't let me. He called me early because he wanted us to go to Shoney's together.

Something has to be up with him. I know my brother. He wants something. Once we get our table at Shoney's, I cut right to the chase.

"So, Dontaé, what do you want?"

"Why I got to want something just because I want to take my sister to breakfast?" "Because I know you."

He looks at me smiling, carefully choosing his words. "Well, I have a friend whose cousin looks a hot mess. I wanted to know if you could give her a makeover. She's from out of town, and he got stuck hanging out wit' her. We can't take her out with us looking like that. I need your help bad."

"How bad?"

"I'll give you a hundred dollars if you do this for me."

"What exactly do you want me to do?" I ask as I fill my plate at the breakfast bar.

"Take her shopping; get her a couple of new outfits. Do her hair and makeup. You know, make her look cute."

"Damn, D, how ugly is she?"

"She's not ugly, just very plain and tacky as hell."

"A'ight, I need to get an outfit to wear on my date anyway. Plus Coco got to do my hair, so she can roll wit' me. Drop her off at noon. I'll call you when we're finished. Don't be all day, because my date is at six."

"Thanks, Mimi. Who you going wit'? That same nigga I seen at your house last week?"

"Yes, nosy."

I go home to call Coco. Now I got to sweet talk her into doing this chick's hair. She really didn't want to do mine, but I begged her.

She said, "Since everybody's being so nice lately, keeping Jamyya's kids and all, I guess I can do your hair on my day off."

Let me call and see if she's still in the giving spirit.

"Hello," Coco answers on the third ring.

"It's Mimi. Can you do me a huge favor? I'll pay you for it."

"What?"

"I got a chick that needs her hair done bad. Can she come wit' me and you do hers too? Please. I'll owe you one."

"Damn right you will! How she want her hair?"

"It don't matter, just something fly. I'm supposed to be giving her a makeover. It's a favor for Dontaé."

"You haven't seen her yet?" Coco asks, sounding skeptical.

"No. But D said she ain't ugly."

"A'ight, come at two o'clock, because I got other shit to do. Oh, you can come to my shop Saturday and be my shampoo girl for a couple of hours."

"Okay, Ma. Thanks," I say before hanging up.

Think, think. Where I can go shopping at with only two hours to spare? Oh, yeah, I'll just go to Citi Trends and Exit 94 inside Fairfield Commons!

Five minutes till twelve, and Dontaé is just pulling up. Thank you, Jesus! I'm glad he's on time. I close my curtains and run to the door to meet my project.

"Hey, Mimi this is Lori. Lori, this is my sister Damisha, but everybody calls her Mimi.

"Nice to meet you," Lori says, staring at me.

I look her up and down. Dontaé was right, she is tacky and plain. Lori stands about 5'5" with a pecan-brown complexion. She appears to have a thin frame under her baggy clothes. Her shoes are black with a chunky heel. The gray shirt she has on appeared to be two sizes too big, along with the floor length skirt she's rocking. She has on no makeup, and her eyebrows looked like Gargamel off of the Smurfs cartoon.

"Well, come on in so we can get started."

That's not all. Her hair is an ugly dirty brown color, and she needs a perm bad.

"Do you have money to go shopping?" I ask her, trying to figure out what to do with her until I get her some new clothes.

"Yes, I got four hundred dollars," she replies with a deep southern accent.

"Where are you from, and how old are you?"

"I'm twenty-one, and I'm from Columbia, South Carolina."

"Oh, do you know what size you wear?" I ask her that question because her clothes don't fit at all. I hope she's about my size so she can wear one of my outfits to the mall.

"I guess I'm about an eight," she replies, shrugging her shoulders.

"Well, I'll leave you two alone. I'll be back around five," Dontaé says as he turned around to leave.

"A'ight, big bro."

"Oh, here's the money so you can get you something nice." He hands me a crisp one hundred dollar bill.

"Thanks, D. See ya later. I got work to do."

I go into my closet and find an old pair of shorts I had gotten when I gained weight. They are a size 8. Then I found a large white-and-blue Gap T-shirt somebody bought me for my birthday. I think it was one of my co-workers. I give Lori the blue jean shorts and the Gap T-shirt.

"Here, try these on."

She put on the clothes, and they fit perfectly.

Now for her hair. "Are you tender-headed?" I ask as I get out a big bush comb, some grease, and a brush.

"No" she replies.

"Good, 'cause I need to do something with this." I struggle to comb out her hair and apply lots of grease. I put a little gel on it too. I brush it up into a ponytail.

"Okay let's go. I'm pressed for time. We got a hair appointment at 2:00 P.M."

I dash out of the house with Lori right behind me. We go to Citi Trends first. Lori's face lights up like a child on Christmas. I find her two outfits and a purse. Then we go across the mall to Exit 94. I buy me two outfits and Lori gets an outfit and two pairs of shoes. We still have a little bit of time left, so we stroll down to Peebles. I take her straight to the cosmetic counter. She buys lipstick and eye shadow from Fashion Fair.

"Are you hungry?" I ask her as my stomach starts to growl.

"Yes, I'm starving."

"Well, there's a McDonald's, Arby's, and Burger King across the street. Where would you like to go?"

"Um…McDonald's is fine."

"A'ight, McDonald's it is."

Being that I'm in a hurry I go through the drive thru. "You can eat in the car as long as you don't drop anything," I say.

"Okay."

We get our food and head to Coco's house.

"Hey, girl this is Lori. Lori, this is Coco, she's the one that's going to do our hair," I introduce them as Coco opens the door.

"Nice to meet you. Thank you for doing my hair on such short notice," Lori says.

"You're welcome. Which one of y'all wants to go first?" Coco asks, looking back and forth between me and Lori.

"Do Lori's first so I can eat my food," I suggest, stuffing French fries in my mouth.

"A'ight, what you want me to do to it, Mimi?"

"She needs a perm, and I don't like the color of her hair. Just give her a perm, dye it, and then cut it in an asymmetrical bob."

"Do you have a perm and color wit' you?"

"No, I thought you had that shit. You are the hair stylist."

"Yeah, but everything is at the shop except the stuff I need to do your hair. I know you didn't need a perm, so I didn't bring it. Maybe Jerome can go get one from Sally's while I start on your hair."

"A'ight. Can you ask him please?" I reply in a baby voice.

Coco goes upstairs to ask Jerome to go to Sally's for her. He says, "Yeah, baby, what you need?"

Aw, how sweet. While Jerome is at the store, Coco washes my hair and rolls it with spiral rods. I sit under the dryer and read a Vibe magazine. Finally, Jerome comes back with a Silk Elements perm and a Jazz rinse called Rich Auburn.

Coco works her magic on Lori. She perms her hair, gives her a semi-permanent color, cuts it, and wraps it. After Lori's hair is finished, Coco arches her eyebrows. Wow! She looks nice! What a difference a hairdo and some new clothes can make. Coco takes the rollers out of my hair and sprays me down with oil sheen.

I look in the mirror; it's gorgeous. I have long, cascading spiral curls.

"Thanks girl, how much do we owe you?"

"I can pay for my own, Mimi," Lori says in her light Southern voice.

"Okay," I reply. I'm not one to push when it comes to spending my money.

"Mimi, yours is twenty and Lori's is thirty-five."

We pay Coco and are about to leave.

"Thanks for everything, Coco, my hair is absolutely beautiful," Lori says, beaming from the inside out.

We rush home to meet Dontaé. He has a key to my apartment, so he is chilling in the living room when we arrive.

"Damn, Lori you look good." Dontaé says, spinning her around.

"Yeah, she does. Mimi, you worked a miracle," Mike says. Mike is Lori's cousin.

"Thanks, y'all," she replies.

They take Lori's bags to the car and leave.

I wave bye and yell, "Good Luck, Lori. Don't hurt those Richmond boys."

***

My phone rings, and it's my mom. I talk to her for a few, then go to get dressed. I decide to wear the strapless pink-and-gray dress. My pink Miu Miu sandals with the tiny straps would go perfect with this dress.

This time when Chris comes to pick me up, he greets me with a dozen pink roses. "Oh, Chris, these are beautiful."

"They're almost as lovely as you."

"Thank you, sweetie." I kiss him on the cheek.

"Are you ready to go?" he asks.

"Yep."

We arrive at the Cheesecake Factory in Short Pump. "I hope this is okay with you," Chris says as he parks the car.

"It's fine; I like the food here, especially the cheesecake."

"Good."

This time I don't order any alcoholic beverages. Chris and I are having a wonderful time.

"How was your weekend with your son?" I ask, striking up a conversation.

"It was fun. We went to the park to play football, and I took him to Chuck E. Cheese's today. He also got to visit my parents."

"That's nice. I went to Chuck E. Cheese's on Saturday. I took my friend Jamyya's four kids."

"Wow, you kept four kids by yourself?"

"Yep, and the boys are three-year-old twins."

"You are a really good friend to do something like that."

"Thanks, but that's how we roll. We help each other out."

"That's how friendship is supposed to be."

I have two slices of cheesecake, then we make our way over to the movies. It's a very good movie. I'll have to get that on DVD when it comes out. I invite Chris into my house.

"I can only stay for a little while. I have to be at work early in the morning," he states.

"Okay. I have to work tomorrow as well."

Chris is looking good tonight, and his outfit is so much better. He has on a pair of khaki pants with a short-sleeved green-and-tan button up shirt, and his shoes are a pair of brown Prada loafers. Much, much better. He sits on the couch next to me, and we cuddle while watching TV. One thing leads to another, and suddenly Chris is on top of me, kissing me passionately on the lips. His hands begin to go up my dress, and he pulls off my lace pink panties. Then he pulls my dress over my head, slinging it to the floor. My heartbeat begins to quicken as a pool forms between my legs. I haven't had sex in three months, so I am willing and ready. He then twirls his tongue around my nipples, causing them to harden. I can feel his dick growing inside his pants.

As I reach down to unzip his pants, he freezes. Chris slowly gets up and says, "I'm sorry I lost my cool. We shouldn't be doing this."

"Why not? I got condoms upstairs, plus I'm on the pill."

"That's not it. It's too soon. We just met. I think I better be going." He gets up and walks to the door. Slowly, he turns around with his hand on the doorknob.

"I'm sorry, Damisha. I'll call you soon."

Just like that, he's gone. What the fuck is going on? I can't believe this shit. I never got left naked, untouched on the couch. I was a willing participant. How in the hell can he pass that up? I do the only thing I know how. I go upstairs and get my trusty dusty. You got it - my vibrator. I use it til the batteries get weak. I take a hot shower, then go to bed. So much for a good night!

Chapter Five
Coco

Today's Thursday, July 3rd. The shop is packed. Everybody crowds into Diva Style to get their hair done for the Fourth of July. I own the shop, so I have the first chair in the window. There are eight stations in my shop. I have four shampoo bowls, six hairdryers, and one nail table for my nail tech, Chantel.

My seven stylists are Mikiya, Tayanna, Danielle, Latoya, Ashley, Tashema, and Kim. Next to me, Tashema and Danielle have the largest clientele. Mikiya only does braids, and she is better than the Africans. Diva Style has it going on. We are located on Broad Street, in Downtown Richmond.

Since my birthday party is on Saturday, I decide to take off. This means I have to fit all my clients in today. I guess it's going to be a late night. I usually come in at 9:00 and leave around 6:00 P.M. Shit, I got a family to take care of, I can't be in here all day and night.

As I look around the crowded room, I spot my 10:00 appointment. "Shayla, girl, come on over here so I can get started. What you getting today?"

"Just some fish tails up into a spiked ponytail."

"A'ight. Mimi, can you wash and condition her hair?" I yell, pointing at Shayla.

Mimi owes me a favor, and now it's time to cash in. She was supposed to come on a Saturday, but you know Mimi, she got an excuse for everything. So when Jazz accidentally told me she was off today, I jumped at the chance to get her in here. With all the clients I have, I need an extra shampoo girl.

Skye and Jazz are coming to get their hair done at 1:00. Then my girl Alana has an appointment at 3:00.

Alana and I have a unique friendship. My oldest son Corey's father, André, cheated on me with Alana. Little did I know Alana was pregnant at the same time I was. André and I were living together, but he found plenty of time to cheat. I found out about Alana, and her daughter Brianna, about a year after her daughter was born. Normally, a chick would flip out finding out such news. Trust me; I lost my damn mind at first.

Let me tell you what happened. One day I decided to look through André's stuff. He had been acting strange for the last few months, and his money was always low. Well, you know what they say, seek and you shall find. I found a lockbox under the bed. Me being from Creighton Court, it was nothing to pop the lock. There were all kinds of papers stacked up in the box. I dived right on in, and pulled out paternity test results, child support papers, and his check stubs.

The DNA test concluded that André Kendal Smith was 99.99% the father of Brianna Latrice Woods. As my raging eyes scanned across the child support papers, it became painfully clear why he was low on money. This bitch was getting eight hundred and twenty five dollars a month out of his check. "Oh, hell no!"

I looked up to the top right hand corner where the entire mother's information was. Her name was Alana Shanaé Woods, she was twenty-two years old, and her address was 9820 Ridgefield Drive. Hmm ... I didn't know where that was; maybe I could go to her job.

A-ha, she worked at DTLR inside Virginia Center Commons! I thought I'd go pay her a visit. I called up Skye and Mimi on three-way. I frantically ran down the events that just happened.

Skye said, "I'm due for a mall trip anyway. Give me a minute to change my clothes, just in case we got to stomp a bitch's ass."

"You know I'm down for dat," Mimi chimed in.

It was a Tuesday evening, so the mall was dead. We got a front row parking space. I dashed through the mall like I was Flo Jo running a marathon.

"Wait up, Coco, damn! The store is not going anywhere," Mimi screamed, exhausted.

"I can't wait to see this bitch." Little did I know it was the same girl I had seen him with almost two years ago at a VCU basketball game.

As I entered the store, I tried to calm myself. I looked her up and down. She was shorter than me, about 5'3", with a golden-bronze complexion. Her hair was in two-layer cornrows, which were curled at the ends. She was a little thicker than me, about a size 10, with some big-ass titties.

"Hello, welcome to DTLR. My name is Alana. Can I help you with anything?" she asked, oblivious to whom I was.

"Yeah, let me get both of these in an eight?" I asked, shoving two pair of sneakers at her. She came back out with both pair and placed them beside me. She walked a few inches away to straighten up a clothes rack. Well, she pretended to straighten it. I'm not stupid, I know the deal. They always watch to make sure you don't steal anything.

I directed my attention to Skye, and tried on the shoes. "So, do you think these are cute enough to wear on my date with André?"

"André who?" Skye asked, playing along with my little scheme.

"André Smith, you know, the one that works at Nabisco," I said extra loud so Alana could hear me. The look on her face told it all. She stopped fixing the rack abruptly and quickly walked up on me.

"Did you say André Smith?"

"Yeah why? You know him?" I asked with a smirk.

"Hell yeah, that's my baby daddy! That nigga ain't shit. He denied my daughter for nine months until we got a blood test. Then he still didn't want to take care of her, so I took his trifling ass to court. Later on he told me he had a girlfriend, they living together, and they got a little boy. So he decided to stay wit' her and keep me a secret. I don't even talk to his black ass. You better watch out 'cause he ain't shit. He probably still got a girlfriend or two," she said, rolling her eyes.

"So you didn't know he had a girlfriend?"

"Nope. Not until I took him to court. I had to send the papers to his job 'cause I didn't have his home address. That's when he told the judge he couldn't get legal papers at his address 'cause his girlfriend would put him out. Then, he thought by telling the judge he had another child, they wouldn't make him pay as much. Cheap bastard!"

"Oh, that's some foul shit! I guess I won't need this after all. Thanks for the info."

I gave her the shoe boxes, got up to leave then I heard her say, "If you talk to that sorry motherfucka, tell him Alana said what's up!" She turned around, laughing.

We left the mall and I wasted no time getting home to confront André.

"Hey, baby. How are you?" I asked André as I sat down beside him on the couch.

"I'm cool. What's up?"

"Have you been cheating on me?" I looked into his eyes. Instantly he began to tell a lie.

"Wh-why would you ask me that?"

"'Cause I want to know." I was getting madder by the minute.

"A long time ago, but I've changed. What's brought this about?"

"I met your baby momma, Alana, today."

"Huh … h-how did you find out?"

"'Cause you, my dear, is a dumb ass nigga. Get all your shit and get out!"

"Baby, let me explain. That's in the past. We can work this out."

"Whatever. Work your way out my damn house."

Needless to say, I put André's cheating ass out. Unfortunately, two weeks later, he moved back in. We went on like this for another year or so, until I finally got fed up. André had an addiction to women and the Internet. He was on Black Planet day and night, like they were paying him money. No matter how many times I caught him, he continued to cheat. One day, I just gave up.

Still to this day, his freaky ass is still on the Internet plotting on naïve women. His newest victim is Tyesha. For some strange reason, she thinks she has a prize. I don't know why. André lost his job at Nabisco, totally lost his raggedy ass car, and lives with her. He ain't got a pot to piss in. So, you tell me why she thinks I still want his trifling ass?

My husband Jerome is nothing but the truth. He's a fine chocolate brotha about 5'9" with a pretty smile. His muscles are impeccable, and that washboard stomach is to die for. Jerome is thirty years old. He works at Long and Foster as a real estate agent. My baby pushes a cherry-red Lincoln Navigator.

I finish all my clients' hair at about 8:30 P.M. Mimi and I was the only two left in the shop.

"Girl, I'm tired as hell. Just come to my house at ten o'clock tomorrow, and I'll hook your hair up," I say, yawning at the same time.

"That's cool, 'cause I'm tired too."

***

I wake up happy because today is my birthday.

"Mommy, happy birthday. How old are you?" Corey asks, jumping on my bed.

"I'm twenty-eight, baby. Mommy's getting old."

"No you're not, honey, you're getting better," Jerome says, kissing me softly on my lips.

"Yuck," Christian says, making an ugly face.

"Come here, boy, and give your mom a birthday kiss."

"No." Christian takes off running down the hall. Before I can chase him, my phone rings.

"Happy birthday to you," a deep baritone voice sings. It's Torey, my twin brother.

"Same to you. Are you ready for the cookout? Do you need me to bring anything?"

"No sis, just bring the family."

"Oh, well the kids are not coming. Corey's going to André's house, and Christian's going to Jerome's mom's house."

"A'ight, just bring Jerome and your girls."

"A'ight, I got to go, my line's beeping."

"Holla," I click over to receive the rest of my birthday wishes.

"Hey, girl. How does the big twenty-eight feel?" Skye asks, laughing.

"Ha, ha! I'm only a year and a half older than you! Well, can't talk long, got to get ready to do Mimi's hair."

"A'ight, heifer, catch you later."

Jerome and the kids come in holding a small round Ukrop's cake with a two and an eight candle on top. They start singing "Happy Birthday".

"Thanks, boo." I blow out the candles.

"Jerome, why would you give the kids cake this early in the morning?"

"Because it's a celebration, honey. They ate breakfast first. Would you like me to fix you something?"

"Sure. I want some French toast, cheese eggs, and four pieces of bacon."

"I'll get right on it," he replies with a smile.

I've got the best husband ever. The only problem is his psychotic baby momma, Shameka. This bitch is always causing problems in our relationship. She does it in such a subtle, sneaky way that Jerome doesn't see it, or maybe don't want to see it. They have a seven-year-old daughter together named Jermeka.

No sooner did I finish eating than Mimi is walking through the door.

"Honey, Mimi is here, and I'm leaving to drop the boys off. André said he would meet me at the mall," Jerome yells as he runs down the steps.

"Bye, honey. See you later," I yell back as he shuts the front door.

"Happy birthday, girl!" Mimi shouts, hugging me.

"Thanks, let's get started so I don't be late to my own cookout."

"I got you a gift, but I figured I would save it for the party."

"Yeah, do that. Bring all the gifts to the club Saturday."

Mimi wants two strand twists in front with flip curls in the back. While she is under the dryer, I iron my clothes and take a shower. The cookout starts at four o'clock. I curl the back of Mimi's hair and spray oil sheen and spritz on it.

She looks in the mirror. "Damn, girl, you did it again. This is so cute! Since it's your birthday, I'm going to leave you a tip." Mimi pulls out forty dollars and places it in my hand.

"Thanks, Mimi, but you didn't have to do that." I hug my best friend, then she leaves.

Today is going to be a good day. I called up Jazz to see if she was coming to the cookout. "Jazz, what's up? Are you coming to Torey's cookout?"

"Yeah, I'll be there. Do you mind if I bring somebody with me?"

"No. The more the merrier. Who you bringing?"

"Shawn, the brotha I met at Friday's. We've been kicking it ever since."

"Let me find out Jazz got a new man," I begin teasing.

"Girl, you so crazy. Oh, shit, I almost forgot. Happy birthday!"

"Thanks. The cookout starts at 4:00. It's at Dorey Park."

"A'ight. See ya there."

I don't feel like doing my own hair, so I just twist my micros up into a big twist and stick a banana clip on it to hold it in place. Now, for my outfit. Since it's the Fourth of July, I decide to be festive. I get dressed in my short, red, BeBe skirt along with a red, white, and blue midriff T-shirt with BeBe written across the chest, and my white-and-red Nike sneakers. The cookout is at the park, so sneakers are the sensible thing to wear.

Jerome comes back with just enough time to take a shower and change clothes. After he gets dressed, he pulls out a big gift bag.

"I know your party is tomorrow, but I wanted to give you a gift on your actual birthday too."

Excited, I dig into the bag. Wow, it's a pair of gold Jimmy Choo sandals, along with a gold Furla purse!

I jump up into his lap and plant a long kiss on his full lips. "Thank you, thank you! You really know me, huh? This is just my style."

"I know, I thought you might need something to wear for the party. Seeing that your colors are gold and white, I bought you the gold."

"Good job, now I don't have to go to the mall tomorrow."

"I'll believe it when I see it. You know all your girls are going shopping, and they are going to drag you with them." He's laughing so hard, I think he's going to choke.

"You're right, but they won't even have to drag me. Let's get going. I want to be early in case Torey needs some help."

***

We arrive at Dorey Park around ten to four.

"Hey, Sis. I guess y'all the only ones who know how to be on time," Torey says, giving Jerome a pound.

"Yo, man, happy birthday," Jerome says.

"Oh, honey, can you go get the gift out of the car?" I ask Jerome. I bought Torey a Palm Pilot with a leather Coach carrying case so he can keep up with all his hoes. Jerome comes back with the neatly-wrapped silver package.

"Here, my man, this is from your sister and me."

"Y'all ain't have to buy me nothing. Thanks. I'll open it later when everybody gets here. Oh yeah, mom should be on the way. I'll give you your gift tomorrow."

"You better bought me something good," I say smiling.

"You know I got you, lil sis. I know your style."

"Lil sis? Please, you're only older by four minutes!"

Me and Torey start setting up for the cookout while Jerome fires up the grill. A little after four, people start pouring in. My mom Gina finally shows up with my Aunt Denise.

Two days ago, I received a birthday card from my father. He's in prison serving a fifteen-year bid. He was indicted when we were sixteen for selling drugs, tax evasion, and illegal firearms. My brother and I go visit him every other weekend. Of course my mother moved on with her life, but she accepts his calls and sends him money. She says he was a good father and he did what he knew best to take care of us.

Leon, that's my dad's name, was no fool. He stashed away $500,000 and gave it to my mom when he got sentenced. My mother bought me and Torey cars and paid for me to go to cosmetology school. For my graduation gift, she bought me my own hair salon. Torey wanted to be an electrician, so mom paid for his schooling as well. The rest of the money, Mom used to buy a house so we could get out of the projects. Plus she went to nursing school and became a LPN. She works at Henrico Doctor's Hospital.

"Hey, birthday girl. Come give your mom a hug," Gina says, smiling.

"Mom, now you know you're too old to dress like that!"

"Girl, I'm only sixteen years older than you! Shit, I still look good. I am pulling the men your age. Where's your brother?" she asks, looking around for Torey.

She's right. She does look young for her age. Most of the time people see us together, they think she's my older sister.

"Ma, he's around here somewhere."

People are dancing, singing, drinking, eating, and just having a good time. Torey has pulled out all the stops. He has ribs, chicken, steak, hamburgers, hotdogs, and Italian sausage on the grill. My Uncle Tommy is frying fish in the gas lit deep fryer. For side items, there is corn on the cob, potato salad, pasta salad, macaroni and cheese, deviled eggs, coleslaw, and seafood salad. There are four trays of fruit and two vegetable trays with dip. Another table holds the snacks and a full-size sheet cake that reads "Happy Birthday Kori and Torey". The cooler is stocked with a wide variety of canned sodas and fruit punch. Here comes the alcohol, and there's plenty of it. Torey bought the hard liquor. My mom likes wine coolers, so she brought a ton of those with her.

All of my friends show up; Skye, Alana, Jamyya, Jazz, and Mimi. Of course, Skye brought Omar and Omari with her. Alana comes solo. Jamyya comes with the Brady Bunch. Jazz brings her new man, Shawn. Damisha comes with Chris. It's nice to meet the new boyfriends.

Takori runs up to me. "Hi, Auntie, where are my cousins?"

"Hey sweetie. Corey went to his dad's house and Christian is at his grandma's."

"Oh, well happy birthday."

"Thank you, baby."

Torey has a four-year-old daughter with his girlfriend Chantel. He named her Takori after me and him. My brother loves me so much. But seriously, we are really close.

"Coco, I've been trying to catch up with you all night. I want you to meet Shawn. Shawn this is the birthday girl, Kori," Jazz said showing all her teeth.

"Nice to meet you," I say, shaking Shawn's hand.

"Same here. Happy birthday."

"Thanks. I hate to run, but I got to go mingle."

I walk over to the back table to talk with Jamyya and Skye. "Hey, what y'all up to?" I ask as I sit down.

"Nothing. Just girl talk, Ms. Birthday Girl," Jamyya says.

"Oh, so somebody's keeping secrets?"

"No, nothing you don't already know. The same ole Omar drama." Skye lets out a huge sigh.

"What happened this time?"

"He was sitting outside your shop yesterday, I saw him when I was leaving. Then he followed me to Jamyya's house and the mall. He must not have realized I saw him, 'cause he called my phone talking to me like he didn't know where I was."

"I don't know what kind of root you put on his ass, but you need to reverse it! I can't imagine nobody's pussy being that good to make a nigga act like that," I say, clapping hands with Jamyya.

"Mine is!" Mimi chimes in.

Where in the hell did Ms. Ill Na-Na come from?

"So you've told us, time and time again," Skye replies.

"Jamyya, do you have a babysitter for my party? Because no kids are allowed."

"Yeah, Jamesha is going to stay home and keep them for me."

"That's good. Are you bringing Keenan?"

"I don't know, I was thinking about hanging out without him. Is he not invited?"

"Oh, no, he can come. I'm just trying to get a count. Who I really don't want to come is Omar, but no use in that, 'cause he always shows up where he's not wanted.

Alana walked over and joined the conversation. "Hey, everybody! What's going on?"

I look at her. "Nothing, have a seat. We're just having girl talk."

"Oh, a'ight. Count me in."

At first, my friends couldn't understand how I could hang out wit Alana. But I explained to them how André tried to play us, so in return we did the opposite of what he wanted. We became friends so we could jointly give him hell. It's been working out good so far. Alana was a very sweet person once I got to know her.

Jerome leaves the cookout early. "Baby, I'm about to leave. I'm kind of tired. You think you can catch a ride home?" he asks with a tired look in his eyes.

"Well, I can leave with you. It's Torey's cookout. I don't have to stay."

"I'm not rushing you, baby. Stay and talk with your family and friends."

"Are you sure?"

"Yeah, I'll be home when you get there."

Kissing him softly, I say, "A'ight honey. See you later."

The girls and I continue chatting until Torey announces we were having a dance contest. We all get up to dance, including the kids. One of Torey's friends named Crystal wins. She danced just like the singer Ciara.

It starts getting dark, and the park is about to close. Everybody sings "Happy Birthday" to me and Torey. We both blow out the candles. He allows me to cut the cake and serve the guests.

At last it's time for him to open his gifts. He gets a lot of stuff. My mom gave him a seven day, six night vacation to Cancun, Mexico. Damn, I hope she's that generous at my party! Chantel gave him an YSL outfit and a pair of shoes to match. All the rest are birthday cards with money…what could be a better gift? I must say, he racked up, getting $1000 in cash. I'm so looking forward to tomorrow!

Alana, my mom, and Aunt Denise help me and Torey clean up the mess. Damn, I'm dog tired. I can't wait to take a long hot bath and jump right in the bed.

Alana drops me off at home. "Thanks, girl, for dropping me off," I say.

"No problem chick, I'll catch you tomorrow."

***

I open the door, dashing up the steps two at a time. As soon as I open the bedroom door, my mouth drops open. No wonder he left early! He came home to set everything up. Jerome is lying on a bed full of pink rose petals in his black silk boxers. Beside the bed on the night stand are two champagne glasses, and a bottle of Moet on ice. The room is glowing with pink, scented candles lit everywhere. There are white-and-pink balloons all around with one huge Happy Birthday helium balloon decorated with Betty Boop, my favorite cartoon character. On the chaise lounge sits a giant white teddy bear holding a little black velvet jewelry box.

"Surprise!" Jerome yells in his deep, sexy voice.

"Yes, and what a great surprise it is. Let me take my clothes off and take a hot bath. I promise not to take long."

"Take your time, baby, we got all night." He winks at me, smiling. Oh, it's like that.

Hurriedly, I take my clothes off and run into the bathroom. The tub is already filled with hot water and bubbles. I get in and yell "How did you do all this? The water is still hot."

"I had a little help from your friends. Alana sent me a text message when y'all got to the corner."

"That little sneak!"

"Yep, I was hoping I could convince you to stay at the cookout, so I could set things up. You know it's rare we have the house to ourselves."

"You're right about that."

I wash my whole body in a matter of minutes. I think this is the fastest bath I ever took! When I come into the bedroom wrapped in a towel, Jerome is standing in front of me, his arm stretched out holding a short, black, silk night gown.

"Honey, put this on."

"Why?" I ask. It's about to come off soon.

"Please, just cooperate"

"Okay, darling."

I slide into the black negligee. There is no need for undergarments. When I sit on the bed, I notice a tray of fruit with chocolate and caramel sauce. To my right, the two champagne glasses are now filled, and a bottle of whipped cream is now beside it. Oh, he must've thought of some more shit while I was in the tub.

Jerome slides over next to me and begins to feed me strawberries dipped in chocolate. I feed him apple slices covered in caramel. After we eat the fruit, he proposes a toast. "Let's toast to you seeing another glorious year. I love you, and I hope your birthday was all you wished for."

We clink glasses. "Thank you, honey. It sure was."

He brings the teddy bear holding the small black box over to me. "Open it." And so I do.

Tears begin forming in my eyes. "Wow, baby, this is beautiful! I know exactly how to thank you."

I can't believe it; I have a two-karat pink marquise cut diamond ring from the David Yurman collection. Ouch. This had to be expensive.

I push him back gently and straddle him. I kiss his lips then begin to work my way down. When I get to his stomach, I pull his boxers off, and continue on. I suck his growing manhood like it's a Popsicle about to melt.

He gently pushes my head away. "No baby, this is your night, let me please you."

We quickly switch positions. Now he is on top of me. He pulls off my gown, and begins to nibble on my soft, perky breasts. His hands explore every inch of my body. Jerome's long, flickering tongue devours my secret garden. My body begins to shake as I scream, "Yes, right there baby! That's the spot!" An ocean begins to spill from my pussy.

"Are you ready, baby?" Jerome whispers in my ear.

"Y-yesss." He inserts his thick, chocolate, ten-inch dick inside of me. My body starts to grind to his rhythm as he goes in and out. Long, deep strokes I can feel up in my abdomen.

"What's my name?"

"Jerome!" I scream.

"Is it good to you?"

"Y-yeah." We switch positions and I mount him like a jockey mounts her horse, and I ride that sucker to town. We both climax at the same time. The way my body shakes, you would've thought I had an epileptic seizure.

"Thanks baby, this is a night to remember. We should do this more often," I say, breathing hard.

"Yeah, this was fun. How about round two? This time let's use some whipped cream."

"A'ight, stallion."

I sleep later than usual, due to the wild escapade I had last night.

***

"Good morning, honey." I greet him with a warm kiss.

"Good morning to you. What time do you need to be at the club?"

"At nine o'clock. Skye, Mimi, and Alana are coming to help me set up the decorations."

"Okay, I just thought we would ride together."

"You can help too, that way we won't need a ladder."

"Just be ready to leave at eight-thirty."

It's time to get my gear into motion. I have several things to do before the party starts at ten. First, I need to go to Ukrop's to pick up my birthday cake. My next stop is Party City; they sell everything you need for a party. I buy all my plates, napkins, balloons, etc., from there.

Jerome rushes me to get ready. "Honey, you look fine. Hurry up so we can go set up."

"Thanks, Baby." I look at myself in the full-length mirror one last time. Tonight, I have on a shimmering gold halter-top with a pair of tight white Capri pants with a slit on the bottom of each side. The gold shoes and purse Jerome gave me yesterday match perfectly. My party is an all-white affair, but being the hostess, I want to stand out. That's why I'm wearing gold.

Jerome pulls me from in front of the mirror. "I'm going to leave you. Let's roll."

"I'm ready."

When we arrive at the club, I am pleasantly surprised to see Skye. She's never on time for anything.

"Hey, girl. Is it a full moon tonight? How did you get here before me?"

"Omar dragged me out the house."

I turned to look at Omar. "Thanks, you truly worked a miracle."

"It was nothing. I don't believe in being late. By the way, you look very pretty."

"Thank you."

Skye interrupts, "Something strange is definitely going on. You two rarely get along."

"I know. I think I'm just in a good mood tonight."

I hold out my hand to show her my new ring.

"Oooh, it's beautiful. Did Jerome give you that?"

"Yes," I say excitedly.

The rest of the crew arrives, and we begin setting up. Omar and Jerome do the heavy lifting. I meet with the club manager to make sure everything is straight with the food, bar, and DJ. He says, "Everything is under control. I got my best worker posted at the door with your guest list in hand. Another copy is wit' the guy working the door on this floor. I hope everyone brought their ID."

"Yes, sir. I made them aware of that. Thanks so much."

"You're welcome. If you need anything else, let me know. I'll be in my office." Then he walks off.

The DJ comes in, walks up to me, and introduces himself. "What kind of music do you want me to play?"

I give him a weird look. "Rap, reggae, and some up-tempo R & B would be fine. It's mostly a young crowd, between the ages of twenty-three and thirty."

"In that case, I'm going to rock it for you. I got all the hot shit." He continues setting up his turntables and equipment.

Soon after, people start to roll in. There are a couple of people my brother Torey invited that I don't know. Our mom and two of my aunts show up. They are the oldest people here, trying to be young again.

Damisha is the only one who changed dates. She brings Jerell with her this time. She tells me that since Chris was into church, this probably wouldn't be his scene.

I peep Omar walk over to Mimi and Jerell. "What's up, Mimi? I see you change men like you change your shoes. That's why I don't like Skye hanging out wit' you."

"Mind your damn business, stalker. If Skye knew any better, she would change men too. Go find somebody to follow. Jackass."

I can tell Mimi is pissed by her body language. I hope Omar ain't trying to start shit. I make my way through the crowd. "Skye, go get your crazy ass boyfriend. He's over there fucking wit' Mimi."

Out of breath, she asks, "What did he do?" She continues dancing.

"I don't know, he probably said some slick shit. Just keep his ass tame," I say, getting angry.

After I walk around and mingle with everybody, it's time for me to have fun. I grab Jerome by the arm and lead him to the dance floor. "Come on, baby, dance wit' me."

Gina, my mom, looks at me. "Do it, baby! You see she get that from me," she says, talking to the crowd.

The food is set up buffet style, so people can serve themselves. The bartender works at the club. He came with the fee I paid for renting the space.

Torey and Chantel dance their way over. "Nice party, Sis. I brought your gift this time."

"Thanks. I'll open them later."

"You look real cute, Coco," Chantel says, looking me up and down.

"Thanks, girl."

I turn to Jerome. "Damn, boo, it's hot in here. I'm going to get a drink."

"A'ight."

I walk over to the bar and order an Incredible Hulk. Damisha is sitting at the bar taking shots. "Slow down, Mimi. I hope Jerell is driving."

"Yeah, we rode in his white Mercedes C300."

"Oh, homeboy got it like that?"

"Yep, and soon enough I will too." She thows back another shot of whiskey, laughing. *That bitch is an alcoholic.*

Time is rolling by; I check my watch and its 1:30 A.M.

Torey grabs the microphone. "We have about thirty minutes before the club closes. Before we leave, I want everybody to sing "Happy Birthday" to my sister Kori. I love you, boo. Anybody else got some shout outs?"

"Yeah!" my mother screams. "This is to both of you...Kori and Torey. I love you very much, and I wish you the best on your twenty-eighth birthday. May you have many more. I know your father wishes he was here to see you grow up. Let's make a toast to my twins. May your birthday wishes come true." My mother hangs up the microphone and hugs both of us.

"We love you too," Torey and I say in unison.

The crowd assembles around the table to sing "Happy Birthday". Cameras are flashing as I cut the cake and open gifts.

My mom gave me an all expense paid trip to Montego Bay for a week. Torey bought me a five-piece Louis Vuitton luggage set. The rest of my gifts are gift cards and money. I racked in $800 cash.

It's now 2:00 A.M., and the club is closing. As we are coming out of the club, somebody is arguing across the street. At first, we pay them no mind, and then the screams become louder. Four shots ring out. People start running wild, knocking people over and trampling one another. The short black man runs past us, firing back. Bullets are flying all around me. I feel a hand snatch me to the ground. "Get down!" Jerome screams.

My body freezes. I'm in a state of shock. Everything was going so perfectly. We hear police sirens in the distance along with an ambulance. The crowd quickly disburses.

I get up off the ground and was startled when Jerome yelled, "Baby, are you okay? Oh my God, you've been shot!" I look down at my outfit. I'm covered with blood, but I don't feel anything.

"Baby, calm down. I don't think it's mine."

We turn to my right, and a man had been shot in the shoulder that was standing right next to me.

"Honey, he's hurt. Get the paramedics over here!" I yell to Jerome.

Upon further inspection, the man's leg is shot too.

The ambulance wheels off three people on a stretcher. Thank God it was no one we knew. On the way to the car, everyone is calling my cell phone to make sure we are all right. The night has not turned out how I had expected, but the beginning was great. Better luck tomorrow.

***

It's Sunday evening. I'm sitting in the family room watching TV when I receive a disturbing call.

"Hey, girl, what's up?" I knew it was Alana by the ring tone.

"Girl, you must have not picked up Corey yet, 'cause you sound way too calm."

"No, he's not here. Jerome just left to go meet André at the store. Why? What's going on?"

"Do you know this bitch Tyesha cut my child's hair? Brianna told me she took Corey to get his hair cut too. Plus she beat both of them for no reason and wouldn't let them watch TV, play, or do nothing the whole time André was gone."

"What do you mean she cut Brianna's hair? How short? Maybe she just clipped the ends. I don't think she's that crazy."

"Oh, obviously she is. I'm coming to your house so you can see this shit. Just wait till Corey comes home. Your ass is gone be mad too."

"A'ight, calm down. Come on over and let me look at her hair. If what you say is true, then we'll just have to make a trip to André's house and beat her ass."

"I'm down wit' that."

Before I can utter another word, Alana hangs up. The things Alana told me disturb me, so I try calling Jerome's cell phone, but he doesn't answer. Damn, I ain't in the mood for this shit.

Alana rings the doorbell like she lost her damn mind. As soon as I open the door, she starts screaming, "Look… Look at this shit!"

"Oh, my goodness," I say with my mouth wide open. I can't believe my eyes. Brianna's shoulder length mane is now up to her earlobe.

"This bitch is about to get her ass beat! Wait til I find her dirty ass!" Alana rants and raves.

André thought he was a slick nigga. He doesn't want me and Alana to know where he lives because he thinks we are "crazy." Well, today he is about to see crazy up close and personal. He would always pick the kids up or have somebody meet him at the mall or some kind of store parking lot.

"Damn, I wish I knew where his trifling ass lived," Alana says angrily.

"You know what, I can probably find out, but we'll have to wait until tomorrow. Jerome's sister Lisa works at DMV. I'll ask her to pull up whatever address André has on file. I know his license plate number, but I don't know Tyesha's. Hopefully, he updated his address since he's been with her for two years." I say, trying to think with a cool head.

"I hope so, but if not I'll ride around Richmond till I find his ass. He probably still hangs out at the libraries. When I catch his black ass, I'll follow him until he goes home. That's my word."

Our conversation is interrupted when Corey and Christian come running into the room.

"Hey, mom. Guess what? I got a haircut. I told Ms. Tyesha you were going to be mad, but she said you told her to take me. You like it?" he asks, smiling.

"Hell no, boy, I don't like it! Where is Jerome?" I scream.

Oh, now I'm really heated, this bitch done fucked up now! When Corey left my house Friday, he had long, straight back cornrows. Now he got a very low even Steven.

"I'm sorry, Mom. I told her not to take me," Corey says, crying.

"Mommy is not mad at you. I'm sorry for yelling. I'm mad at Tyesha and your dad. Now where is Jerome?"

"He dropped us off and said he'll be right back."

Christian just stands there looking at me as if I'm crazy.

"Oh, Jerome thinks he slick. He knew I was going to hit the roof, that's why he didn't answer his damn cell phone. I got something for his ass too," I tell Alana.

"I wish we could get to that bitch tonight. Oops, sorry kids." Alana covers her mouth.

"Well, you know I don't work on Mondays, so I'll call Lisa tonight and fill her in on what's going on. Then bright and early after the kids are at school, we can stop by DMV," I say.

"A'ight, I guess that will have to do for now. Just call me as soon as you find out something. I'ma go home and cook dinner. See you tomorrow."

"Okay, girl. I got some business to handle with my husband. Talk to you later," I say as I close the door.

I look at Corey and Christian. "Are you boys hungry?"

"Yes," they both reply.

"Mommy, can we go to Cici's Pizza?" Corey asks with a big smile.

"That's a good idea. Come on, let's go." Now I don't have to worry about cooking.

On the way to Cici's Pizza, I try calling Jerome again. Of course he did not answer. This time I decide to leave a message. "This is your wife, and if you plan on keeping it that way, I suggest you call me back pronto." Click. I hang up. Boy, am I pissed! I can't believe Jerome has the nerve to hide from me. As soon as Corey got in the car, he should've called me to let me know what happened. Sometimes Jerome just gets on my nerves. He always tries to avoid confrontation. I try to tell him you can't please everybody.

While we're sitting down eating pizza, my cell phone rings. Hmm…wonder who this could be? You guessed it, Jerome. I quickly answer, "Where the hell are you?"

"I—I'm at my sister's house."

"Why haven't you been answering your phone?"

"Because I knew you were going to fly off the handle. I'm not in the mood for this shit today. Especially after what happened last night. You probably wanted me to beat André's ass."

"That would have been a good idea, but I'll handle it. I'm at Cici's Pizza right now. I suggest you be home by the time I get there so we can talk."

"All right, baby. Just calm down. It's not that serious."

"Don't give me that bullshit. Oh, you know what. Let me speak to Lisa real quick."

"For what?"

"Just give her the damn phone." I can hear him yelling for Lisa.

"Hey, girl, what's up?" Lisa says with a bubbling attitude.

"Did Jerome tell you what happened to Corey?"

"Yeah, that's fucked up. His girlfriend is one crazy bitch."

"She sure is. Well, I need a really big favor. I was wondering if I give you André's license plate number, can you run it through your computer at work and give me his address?"

"Yeah, do you know her information too? You know André move so much, his information might not be accurate."

"I just know her name is Tyesha Stone and she drives a silver Toyota Camry. I don't know the license plate though."

'Okay, well I'll work with what I got. I'll call you tomorrow around 9:00 and let you know what I found out."

"Thanks a lot, Lisa. Please don't tell Jerome."

"Girl, I won't. I know how Mr. Holier-Than-Thou is," she replies, laughing.

"Thanks, I appreciate it. I look forward to hearing from you in the morning."

We finish eating and head home. Damn, I must have the hot line! Since I'm driving, I don't bother to look at the caller ID. "Hello," I answered politely.

"Hey, Ma. What's up?" Skye joyfully asks.

"Nothing, girl. Just trying to calm down."

"What's wrong?"

"Tyesha, that crazy bitch, cut Brianna and Corey's hair. Then she was purposely being mean to them. She beat them with a belt, and wouldn't let them watch TV or play."

"You've got to be joking!"

"No, I'm serious."

"So all of Corey's cornrows are gone? Why would she cut a little girl's hair?"

"I don't know. She's just crazy. Brianna's hair is up to her earlobe now."

"I know you and Alana are pissed, what y'all going to do?" Skye pries.

"Lisa is going to get their address when she goes to work Monday. Then Alana and I are going to kick some ass. This bitch is going to get a free haircut from the Queen Bee herself – me!"

"Do you need some backup? I can call Mimi and we both can come too," she offers.

"No, we'll be fine. I think Alana can take her by herself."

"Yeah, I'm not worried about Tyesha. What about André?"

"His punk ass ain't gone do shit. He probably won't be there anyway. If he is, we will just have to beat his ass too. He deserves it anyway."

"I know that's right! Call me if you need me."

"Wait a minute. Why did you call?" I yell, trying to catch her before she hangs up.

"Nothing, I just wanted to talk."

"About what? Let me guess. Omar."

"Yeah. I don't know what to do with him. Like earlier, Jazz and I went to breakfast at IHOP. Of course Omar magically appeared as always. This shit is getting old. I can't even have breakfast without him."

She sounds so frustrated. Poor thing, I really don't know what to tell her.

"Well, maybe you need a vacation."

"You know, that sounds good. When are you going on your vacation to Montego Bay?"

"I don't know. Probably in a couple of months when the children go back to school so I won't have to take them."

"Are you going to take Jerome?"

"I'm not sure. I think I need a break from him and his baby momma drama. I already got enough to deal with André's crazy ass. Not to mention Tyesha. I just need to escape from everybody," I reply. It's the truth. I've been really stressed lately.

"Well, if Jerome doesn't go, can I go wit' you? I'll buy my own ticket."

"Sure. When I plan it all out, I'll let you know."

"Okay, it could be a girl's trip. Maybe Mimi, Jazz, and Jamyya could come too."

"Maybe. Look, I just pulled up to my house, me and Jerome got some things to talk about. I'll call you tomorrow evening and fill you in on what happened wit' Tyesha."

"A'ight. Bye."

I go into the house and give the kids a bath.

"You two go in your rooms and play. Mommy needs to talk to Daddy," I say to the boys.

"Okay, Mommy."

I walk into the family room. Jerome is lying on the couch watching TV.

"Excuse me. I'm home" I say, slinging his legs off the couch and then sitting down.

"So I see. What do you want to talk about?" he asks with an attitude.

"I know you're not going to get an attitude with me! You were dead wrong, and you know it. How are you going to ignore my calls and just drop the kids off as if nothing happened?" Trust me, I have an even bigger gripe.

"First of all, don't take your anger out on me. I'm not the one who cut his hair. He's a boy anyway. It will grow back; it's not the end of the world. I'm not in the mood for this shit. I already had one fight with Shameka today. I'm not going for round two."

"What in the hell do Shameka got to do with this? She always starts drama anyway. Fuck her!"

"She was mad because I didn't get my daughter this weekend, because it was your birthday. I didn't spend time with my child since I was trying to give you all my love and attention, but do you appreciate it? No, no you don't, as always."

"Don't try to make me feel bad about you not getting Jermeka; that was your choice. You didn't have to come to my party. Secondly, Corey is my child, so somebody doing anything to him without my permission is serious.

How would you feel if I cut Jermeka's hair or beat her for no reason?" He is really starting to push my buttons.

"You can't believe everything a child tells you. He's only five years old. He might think what he did was nothing, but that may not be the case. You need to call André and talk to him to see what really happened. As for you cutting Jermeka's hair, of course I would be pissed, but her mother would be even more. You are a hairstylist, so maybe it needed a trim."

"There is no use talking to you. You are so damn naïve. André is nothing but a big liar. Lastly, I do appreciate you, but if you are going to throw shit you do in my face, then don't do it. I've had enough. Goodnight."

I stomp all the way up the steps. Fuck him too! I'm going to bed.

That night, Jerome slept on the couch and I really couldn't care less. That wasn't the first night, and surely not the last.

***

When I woke up this morning, Jerome had already left for work. I woke the boys up and got them dressed for summer camp. On the way back from dropping them off, Lisa calls my cell phone.

"Girl, I got the information for you. Her address is 5320 Thornhurst Court, Apt. D."

"Thanks, Lisa. I guess I'll just plug the info into my GPS. Do you have the zip code?"

"Yeah, Richmond, VA 23225."

"Well, let me call Alana and tell her the good news."

"Don't hurt her too bad."

"I'll try not to," I say, telling a boldfaced lie.

I call Alana and tell her to meet me at my house. As soon as I walk through the door, I run downstairs and jump on the computer. I had already printed out the directions. I was dressed in a T-shirt, sweatpants, and sneakers. I wrap my micro braids up into a tight bun and place a scarf around my head. That bitch is not going to pull my micros out!

Alana arrives and we hop in my truck. "I'm ready to kick that bitch's ass," Alana says.

"I hope she's at home. I don't know what time she goes to work."

I start getting anxious. Tyesha lives over Southside. It takes us about thirty minutes to get to her apartment. Today is our lucky day. I spot her silver Camry parked right in front of her building.

"How do we get her to come out?" Alana asks, looking at me.

"I don't know. She sure as hell not going to open the door for us." Think. "What can we do?" I look at Alana.

"We need a plan."

"I know. Give me a minute, let me think."

"You know what? My girl Mimi is real grimy, let me call her and see what she suggests."

"Good idea."

I call Mimi but she doesn't answer her cell, so I leave her a message explaining my situation.

I look at the clock; it's 11:00 A.M., hopefully Mimi will have a break soon. I know she's at work. Five minutes later, I receive a text message telling me to go buy some flowers and pose as a delivery girl. Since she has never seen me up close, I decide to play the role. Most of the time, Jerome drops off Corey and picks him up.

I share the plan with Alana.

"Good one, but she really is stupid if she thinks André is going to send her flowers." We both bust out laughing.

I drive around the corner to Strange's and pick out a cheap little flower arrangement.

"This should do," I say to Alana.

"Yeah, it's good enough. Maybe she can use it at the hospital too."

"Girl, you crazy as hell!"

We hurry back to Tyesha's place to put the plan in motion. I walk up to the door with the flowers and Alana hides behind me. I knock three times, then she opens the door.

"Delivery for Ms. Stone from André Smith," I say, placing the bouquet of flowers in her hands. The look on her face tells me she's a stupid bitch. Her face lights up and she smiles so big, I thought her face would hurt.

"Thank you, so much," Tyesha replies.

Before she can close the door I hit her with a right hook, then catch her with my left. Alana jumps out and punches her in the stomach three times. I hit her in the head, causing her to fall to the ground. I pull out my scissors and try to cut her bald.

"That's for messing with my son, bitch!" I yell while still cutting her hair.

Alana kicks her in the back while yelling, "Fuck wit' our kids again, and we'll be back!" People start coming out of their apartments. This one woman downstairs yells, "I'm calling the police!"

We dash down the steps and jump into my Jeep. We drive off so fast, my tires screech.

Once we are safely down the highway, I speak. "Girl, all that fighting done made me hungry. You want to go get something to eat?"

"Yeah, let's go to Roma's and get some steak and cheese subs."

Before going to my house, I stop to get gas and get our food from Roma's. We are in my house for about thirty minutes when I hear a knock on the door.

"I wonder who that could be?" I ask aloud, walking towards the door. I peep out the little hole in the door.

"Oh, shit it's the cops!" I open the door slowly. On my front porch stand two male cops from the Richmond City Police Department.

"Hello, we are looking for Kori Jaliyah Knight and Alana Shanaé Woods." the young white officer states.

"I'm Kori Knight."

"Is Ms. Woods here with you?"

"Yes, sir, she is."

"We need both of you to come downtown with us. I have a warrant for both of y'all arrests."

"What are the charges?" I ask as if I don't know.

"Assault and battery on Tyesha Stone, and trespassing on private property."

"Alright, well I'm ready when you are."

Alana comes to the door and we both leave with the officers. They take us down to the police station on Ninth Street. This is the first time either of us has been arrested. Once we are booked and fingerprinted, we see the magistrate. The magistrate gives both of us a $2000 bond. If we use a bail's bondsman, we only need $200 apiece. I don't want Jerome to know, plus I am still mad at him. I decide to call Skye; shit, she always has money.

The officer gives each of us one free phone call.

"Thank you for calling Richmond Premier Staffing, how may I direct your call?" a pleasantly chipper voice answers.

"May I speak to Skye Jordan, please?" I try to sound professional.

"Just one moment," the lady responds.

"Hello, this is Skye."

"Hey, Skye I need a really big favor. Alana and I are down at the city jail on Ninth Street. Can you come bail us out? I'll give you the money back when I get home."

"Let me guess. Y'all beat the hell out of Tyesha. How much is the bail?"

"You're right. The bail is $200 each. Alana already called a bondsman, so you can just meet him here."

"Okay, I'm on my way. Don't drop the soap," Skye says, laughing.

"That shit ain't funny. Hurry up, this place is disgusting."

"All right, I'm leaving now."

This is a new record for Skye. She gets here in thirty minutes, but it takes nearly two hours to release us. They give us some legal papers, and we have to show up in court tomorrow at 9:00 A.M.

We get into Skye's car. "Thanks, girl, I owe you one. You won't get in trouble, will you?" I ask, concerned.

"No, they love me. I told them it was an emergency and I'll be in tomorrow."

"Yeah, Skye, you are a life saver. Just stop by Bank of America so I can get your money," Alana states

"Okay, no problem, girl. So tell me, what happened?" Skye says excitedly. I go on to tell her about the fight and the charges.

"Punk bitch, she need her ass beat again for pressing charges!" Skye screams.

"I know, but that's okay, I got something for both of them," I say.

"Isn't that Omar behind us?" Alana asks, pointing to a green Escalade following us.

Skye looks in her rear view mirror, and by the face she makes, I know it's Omar. "He gets on my damn nerves. How in the hell did he find me?" she screams.

"I think he got a damn tracking device on your car," I reply, laughing.

Skye begins driving like a madwoman, dodging from lane to lane, speeding up then slowing down.

"Skye, what the hell are you doing?" Alana yells, holding on to the door in the back seat.

"I'm trying to lose Omar."

Finally, we lose him or just can't see him. Alana gives Skye her $200, and I pay her when I get home.

As I get out the car, I turn and say, "Thanks a lot. Please don't mention this to Omar. I don't want Jerome to know."

"I sure won't. You're welcome; what are friends for? Just do me a favor and hurry up and plan this trip!"

"Will do."

Alana walks over to her car. "Guess I'll see you in court tomorrow. Are you going to hire a lawyer?"

"Yeah. I'll probably look for one tomorrow. He can probably represent both of us."

"Okay, just let me know."

"A'ight girl, see ya."

***

I go into the house, jump in the shower, and take a nap. The next day me and Alana go to court for our arraignment. Our next court date is set for September 25th at 10:00 A.M. When I get home, I thumb through the Yellow Pages looking for lawyers. I find one named Richard Allen who works for Mason, Adams, and Associates. He says he will represent me and Alana for $225 an hour. Fine, whatever, I tell him.

I'm already late for one of my clients due to going to court this morning. I don't have time for idle chat with a lawyer.

Two weeks pass by. Then I find myself in yet another altercation.

Shameka, who is Jerome's baby momma, decides to test my patience. This bitch came to my shop purposely to piss me off. Actually, she needs to get her hair done, but what she ends up getting is embarrassed.

She parks right in front of my shop with Jerome's truck. I know that black Infiniti truck anywhere! She walks in. "Hey, Coco. Do you think you could squeeze me in? Jerome and I have a date tonight at seven. I want to look nice for him. I can't wait too long, though, because I got to pick him up at five from work."

Everyone in the shop turns to look at me, waiting for my response. "Shameka, honey, I am a hairstylist, not a miracle worker. It will take at least three hours to make you look halfway decent. You need a complete makeover, and I don't have time for that. But I hope you and Jerome have fun on your date."

"You're just jealous because I got my man back. I hope you know that you were just a rebound chick. He has never stopped loving me, and now we are rekindling our relationship."

"Good for you. Hopefully one day you'll wake up from that delusional world you live in. Jerome married me, and we've been married for four years now. Tell me, what kind of man marries his rebound chick and stays with her for four years? Since he loves you so much, why didn't he marry you? Oh, yeah, you must have forgotten, he dumped your dumb ass."

The whole shop starts laughing. Shameka's face turns red.

"Laugh now, bitches, but I bet you'll be the ones crying later!" She storms out of the shop, knocking shit off the reception's desk.

"Bitch," I reply out loud.

After I put my client under the dryer, I call Jerome to see why this bitch has his truck. Ring…ring…

"Hello," Jerome answers.

"Why in the hell do Shameka have your truck?"

"Because her car is in the shop. She needed to take Jermeka to get her hair done, and get her an outfit for her dance recital tonight."

"Oh, so that's the date she was referring to."

"Coco, what are you talking about?"

"That little bitch came to my job starting shit. Why didn't you tell me about the recital? So, I guess you two are going to ride together."

"Yeah, how else is she supposed to get there? If you were talking to me, maybe I would have told you. Plus, Shameka already told me how you embarrassed her at the shop. All she wanted was for you to do Jermeka's hair. That's real foul, what you said about my daughter."

"Jerome you are so stupid. She didn't even have Jermeka wit' her. That's exactly why I'm not talking to you, 'cause you are so fucking gullible! Go to your little family thing. Just do whatever you want."   I give him much attitude.

"Look, you can go if you want to, but I'm going to support my daughter whether you like it or not."

"Hell, no, I don't want to go! What you need to do is tell that trifling bitch to get a rental car, or get a man with his own damn car."

"I'm at work. I don't have time for your petty nonsense."

"Fuck you, Jerome, fuck you!" I slam the phone down in his ear. I'm really getting fed up with him taking her side all the time.

Chapter Six

Yolanda

It has been six weeks since the fight. My stitches have healed, but the memory is still fresh, as though it happened yesterday. I had been scheming to break up Omar and Skye since that night at Friday's. Now it's time to put my plan into action.

While looking through the Sunday's newspaper, The Richmond Times-Dispatch, I notice a job opening for a front desk clerk at the Marriott Courtyard. It's the same one Omar works at. I get so excited. I quickly dress, dash out the door, and head straight to the hotel to fill out an application.

Most of my information about Omar comes from my friend Star. Star hooked up wit Tyrone that night before the fight happened at Friday's. Tyrone and Omar are best friends, so he tells Tyrone everything.

My girl Star is a stripper at Sugar Daddy's Palace, so you know she ain't a joke. Star is twenty-four, brown skin, and don't have any kids. Her stomach is flat as a washboard, and she has shapely hips, a firm butt, and D-cup breasts. She wears all different color weaves and wigs.

Anyway, Star has a way of getting anything she wants out of a man, including Tyrone. Her friendship is very beneficial to my plan. Star has a beautiful face to match her Coca Cola body. She has a beauty mole right above her lip with almond shaped light brown eyes and full lips. That's exactly how she hooks them. Her game is tight, and so is mine.

I go after what I want. And right now I want Omar. I check my mirror to make sure my appearance is up to par. My scars healed up well. Thanks to that chick Skye, I lost twenty-five pounds because I had to have my mouth wired shut. My size-twelve frame became a curvy eight.

I don't think I'm bad looking at all. I'm a red bone sister, with a few freckles on my face. My dark brown eyes are mesmerizing, and my legs are beautiful. I'm about 5'6", and usually a good fighter. I still can't believe that snooty bitch beat my ass. But we will see who will get the last laugh!

Since I'm applying for a job, I decide to wear a tan pants suit with a white blouse and brown pumps. My hair lies in a wrap almost to my shoulders.I stroll over to the front desk.

"Hello, how may I assist you?" a young lady asks.

"I would like to fill out an application."

She hands me an application, and I walk over to a table, sit down, and fill it out. I also brought my résumé as an added bonus. When I turn in the application, I ask, "Is the manager available?"

"Just one moment, let me check," the woman at the desk replies. Her name tag reads "Sherri".

Omar comes out of the back smiling. "How may I help you?"

"Well, I just filled out an application for a full-time front desk clerk. Here is my résumé. How soon will you be getting back to applicants?" I try to appear calm, but being this close to him makes me a nervous wreck.

"Umm, I have a few minutes, if you would like to have an interview now."

"Sure, that's fine."

"Follow me." Omar escorts me into his office.

"Have a seat, Ms. Winston. Give me a minute to review your application."

He scans my application and résumé, then begins asking me several questions. When the interview is over, he says, "Thank you for coming in. I have a couple other interviews throughout the week. I'll let you know something by Thursday, because I need someone to start next Monday."

"How many positions do you have open?" I ask, hoping he will hire me for one.

"I have two full-time and one part-time front desk clerk, but I'm also hiring two housekeepers and a shift supervisor. Looking at your résumé. I see you have management experience. Would you be interested in a shift supervisory position?"

"Yes, I certainly would."

"Okay, let me check your references, and I'll get back to you."

"Thank you so much, Mr. Umm."

"Oh, I'm sorry Rhodes. My name is Omar Rhodes." Good, he didn't remember me.

I drive all the way home with a smile on my face. When I get in the house, I call up Star.

"Hey, hoochie, what up?"

"Nothing, just waking up. What are you so happy about?" Star asks.

"I just came from filling out an application at the Marriott Courtyard."

"The one Omar works at?"

"Yep, he gave me an interview. He didn't even remember me."

"That's good. Do you think he'll hire you?"

"I hope so. If he doesn't call by Thursday, I'll call him Friday to see what's up."

"Well, I hope you get the job so you can start to execute your plan."

"Job or not, I'm still going to get my man."

"I heard that. Look, I got to go run some errands. I'll holla at you later."

"Cool." I hang up, feeling better than before.

***

It's Thursday evening, and I have not heard anything about the job position from Omar. I hope he calls soon, because I already turned down two other jobs I had applied for. This just has to work! I need this job for two reasons: one, I need the money, since because of the fight, I've fallen behind on all of my bills; second is Omar. I want that man some kind of bad.

Since the day I laid eyes on him, I knew I had to have him. I don't even mind that he has a daughter, but his spoiled, ungrateful girlfriend has got to go. Star told me all about his relationship, how Skye belittles him and treats him like dirt. He needs a real woman like me to cater to his needs. I would love for him to spend all of his free time with me.

My thoughts are interrupted when my phone rings.

"Hello?" I try to sound professional.

"May I speak to Yolanda Winston?" a deep voice responds.

"This is she."

"I'm glad I could catch you. This is Omar Rhodes, manager of the Marriott Courtyard. I wanted to know if you were still interested in the front desk position. I decided to promote from within. Sherri is going to be my new shift supervisor, but I wanted to offer you the full-time front desk clerk position."

"Yes of course, I'm still interested. I'll take it." I state, full of excitement.

"Good. The position pays $10 an hour with benefits. Your schedule will be flexible, some days, some nights, and of course weekends. Are you able to work such a shift?"

"Yes, sir, I am."

"Great. Can you start Monday at 9:00 A.M.?"

"Yes."

"Bring your social security card, a picture ID., and wear black slacks and a white button up shirt with a collar. Your shoes also need to be solid black. When you come in, I'll order you a uniform. Welcome aboard Ms. Winston. I'll see you Monday."

"Thank you, Mr. Rhodes. I'm looking forward to it."

"Yes, yes, yes!" I scream. I got the job! Now it's time to celebrate.

I call up my girl Diamond. She works at Jazzy Cuts and Curls.

"Hey, Diamond, I got the job I wanted working with Omar! I start Monday. Can you squeeze me in Saturday? I have to look nice on my first day of work."

"Congratulations! You can come around eleven o'clock in the morning."

"Thanks, girl. Come up with something really cute."

"You know I will. I got you," Diamond replies.

This calls for a shopping trip. I don't want to go alone, so I call Charmese. I knew she would be home. She doesn't have a job 'cause she has three kids that she gets child support for, plus her boyfriend, Danger, is a big time drug dealer - or so he thinks. Anyway, he gives her money left and right, so she has no need to work.

"Hey, girl, do you feel like going shopping today?" I ask, already knowing the answer.

"Yeah, I'm always in the mood for shopping. What are you so happy about?"

I tell her about the new job I'm starting on Monday. She already knows about my plans for Omar.

"What time are you coming? You know I got to have dinner ready for Danger and the kids. That's how I get my money," she says, laughing.

"Well, start cooking now. I'll pick you up at seven."

"Perfect timing. I'll be ready."

Charmese doesn't have a car because neither she nor Danger has a real job. He said it would look suspicious if they bought one. Other than that, she had everything she wanted. Her two oldest children are by this man named Charles Haynes, who is a well established pediatrician. She gets $2500 a month in child support. Her youngest son Damon is by this wealthy white lawyer named Brian Osborne. She gets $3000 a month for him. Now, I guess you see why she doesn't work.

Her house is laid. She lives in a beautiful subdivision called Autumn Leaves way out in Chesterfield County. Her two-story house has five bedrooms, three full baths and a half, a large eat-in kitchen, a laundry room, a playroom, and a family room with a fireplace. She has a sunroom with a Jacuzzi inside. Her patio has a spiral staircase that leads to a basketball court and an in-ground pool.

The majority of her money goes to bills and the kids' education. All of her children go to private schools. I believe Charmese told me her mortgage is two thousand dollars a month. Then she has to pay her utilities and the kids' tuition, which is three thousand dollars a month. Money goes so fast, that's another reason why she doesn't have a car.

I pull up to Charmese's house five minutes after seven. I don't want to get out, so I beep the horn of my gold Honda Civic EX. Charmese comes running out of the house with her long, cinnamon-brown, wavy hair swinging, and her size eight frame stuffed into a pair of Apple Bottom shorts with the T-shirt to match. All of my friends have nice bodies, including me. It's just amazing how Charmese has three kids and a flat, stretch-mark-free stomach.

"Hey, girl, what mall are we going to?" she asks as she gets in the car.

"Umm…let's go to Short Pump. I want to get some new shoes from Baker's."

"Where did you get money to shop from? You haven't worked in nearly two months," Charmese states the obvious.

"I know that. I got what you call credit cards. Buy now, pay later."

"Hell no, you know that's how people get in debt! You're already behind on your bills as is. I'll tell you what. I'm going to give you five hundred dollars. Just think of it as an early birthday gift."

"I can't take your money. I'll be fine."

"Yes you can. I'm giving it to you. You know, what you need to do is find you a nice-looking rich man and have you some babies. Then if he doesn't want to marry you, take his ass to court for child support. Shit, that's how I got all my nice things!" She pauses for a second. "Guess what, yoyo? I'm getting a car this weekend!"

"About time! What kind are you getting?"

"I don't know. Nothing extravagant, probably a Toyota Camry. I like those. Since the kids are getting older, they want to go to public school. So, I decided to let Romell go to a public middle school this year."

"Does his dad know?"

"Yeah, I talked to him about it, and we both decided that if his grades drop, or he gets into trouble, he's going back to Luther Memorial Preparatory Academy."

"Oh, so you can use the extra money for the car."

"Yep. I'm tired of depending on somebody else to take me places or borrowing someone else's car."

"I know that's right! Well, thanks for the money, 'cause I need it."

"You're welcome. If you need some money to pay your bills until you get on your feet, just let me know."

"I'm okay in that department. Star loaned me fifteen hundred so I could pay my rent and car note."

"That was nice of her. How is she anyway? I haven't talked to her much."

"She's fine, just spending a lot of time working and trying to please Tyrone."

"That's good they are still together."

"Yeah, she's helping me with Omar."

We park in the Nordstrom's parking lot because Charmese wants to check out the shoes. We are in the store for about fifteen minutes when I hear a voice I could never forget. Damn, it's Skye! I haven't seen her since the fight. That little smug bitch! I turn towards Charmese. "That's the little bitch I got to fighting with, right over there," I point. Charmese wasn't with me the night of the fight. It was just me, Diamond, and Star. Star was the one that jumped in to save me. Diamond thought she was too cute to fight.

"Which one, the light or dark skinned one?" she asks.

"The light skin one, but the other one is the one that jumped Star."

"Damn, funny running into her! Do you think she will recognize you?"

"Probably, I damn sure remember her."

We sit down and waited for the salesman to come back with Charmese's shoes. Skye and her friend Coco, I believe that's her name, walk past.

"I know that's not little Miss Kmart sitting up in Nordstrom's trying to buy some style," Skye snaps as she's walking past. "You can shop all you want, but you'll never look as good as me," she chuckles.

"Do I detect a bit of jealousy?" I ask.

"Never that boo. I see you healed up nicely. You should be thanking me for helping you lose weight."

"Oh, I do. I thank you every day and I can't wait to repay you."

I get up and walk off. This bitch got some nerve. I am proud of myself though, I think I handled things very well. Charmese finally catches up to me with a bag in her hand.

"What is with her? You aren't even ugly. I think she's just jealous."

"Maybe. But of what? She's got everything, a man, a baby, a house, and tons of clothes."

"So, something's missing or she wouldn't act that way."

"Yeah, I guess."

"Don't worry, I'm going to hook you up and you are going to get that man. Mm-hmm, *her* man." We both laugh as we head to the next store.

Now I have to admit that I am one that's not big on fashion. As long as I'm clean, I'm fine. But Charmese is different. She's more on Skye's level of fashion. She helps me pick out some cute clothes to fit my new shape. She also gives me some old clothes she doesn't want any more out of her closet. Some of the stuff still has tags on it.

She says, "If I haven't worn it by now, then I'm never going to wear it. Take it, put it to good use."

"Thanks for everything, girl. I'll pay you back as soon as I get myself together," I tell her on my way out of her house.

"It's an early birthday gift. No need to give anything back."

Early isn't the word. My birthday isn't till November 5th and its only August 7th. Oh well, I'll take it as a blessing.

***

Monday doesn't come fast enough. I spent all day Saturday sprucing myself up. Charmese told me about a place called Lola's House of Beauty. I went there and got the works. I had never been to a spa before, so all of this was new to me. I got my legs waxed, my eyebrows arched, and a facial. After I was finished there, Diamond hooked my hair up. She added a few honey-blonde extensions to my dark brown hair. My hair was fixed in cascading spiral curls. A girl in the shop named Shannon does really good designs on nails, so I decided to get a full set of nail tips and a pedicure. I picked out a cute pink and white design for my nails and toes. I even went as far as buying some green contact lenses.

Thinking back to that night, if I would have worn my glasses, I wouldn't have gotten my ass kicked. I was cursed with my family's bad eyes. My vision is 20/60, and I have astigmatism.

It's my first day of work, so I wake up extra early so I won't be late. Star calls me to wish me good luck. I get dressed in the new black slacks I bought. I also purchased a new pair of black Prada loafers. I already had tons of white dress shirts, so I had three of them pressed at the cleaners.

Today is special, so I take my time putting on my makeup. Usually I walk around with a plain face, but today I'm hoping to hook a man. That man is Omar. I walk in the hotel with my head high.

"Hello, I'm here to see Omar Rhodes."

"Just one minute," Sherri replies.

I notice her name tag now reads "Sherri" with the words "Shift Supervisor" printed underneath. "Ms. Winston, he's waiting for you in his office."

"Thank you, Sherri." I smile and head into Omar's office.

He looks at me and stands to shake my hand. "Good morning, Ms.Winston, have a seat."

"Thank you. May I ask you a question?"

"Yes, go right ahead."

"Are you on a first or last names basis with your employees?"

"Oh, I'm sorry, we use first names here."

"Good, because I prefer for you to call me Yolanda."

"Hmm…that sounds familiar. Do I know you?" he asks with his eyebrows raised.

"You sure do. I'm Yolanda, Star's best friend."

"Oh, okay. Yeah, you're the girl from Friday's I met a couple months back."

"Exactly, how are things with you and your girlfriend?" I ask as if I care.

"We're doing good. Well, let's get started. Did you bring your ID and Social Security card?"

"Yes, here they are." I hand him my driver's license and Social Security card. He gives me a stack of papers to fill out.

"After you finish these forms, I'm going to show you a video. Then we can get started with the more interesting part, which is on the job training.

For the next couple of days, I'll be working with you until Sherri finishes training. Then next week, she will assist you. After that, you're on your own."

"Okay. Is the training hard?"

"No. Just learning the different screens takes some getting use to."

My first day goes by fast. Before I knew it, it's lunch time.

"Yolanda, let's take an hour lunch break. I'll see you back here at two o'clock."

"All right."

I go to the restroom because I have to pee some kind of bad. Then I check myself in the mirror. Sherri scares the shit out of me when she says, "You look fine. So how do you like it so far?"

"I think I'm going to like it here once I get used to the computer."

"Yeah, Omar is a really nice manager. Sometimes people take advantage of him. Are you on a lunch break?"

"Yeah, it just started."

"Would you like to eat lunch together? I don't have to come back until two o'clock."

"Okay, let me go get my keys, I left them in Omar's office."

When I walk to his office, the door is slightly ajar. I overhear him talking to someone on the phone. "Why don't you want to have lunch with me? I miss you, baby. We can go wherever you want," he says in a whining voice. "Fine, but you never have time for me. I just thought we could spend some time together. Just you and me. You know I have to work late tonight."

What a shame, I think. He wouldn't have to beg to spend time with me! I lightly knock on the door. "Omar, I need my keys." He hangs up the phone and looks at me with tears in his eyes.

"Is something wrong?" I ask, pulling out a chair.

"No, I'm fine. Why aren't you at lunch?"

"Oh, I forgot my keys. Would you like for me to bring you something back?" I ask, grabbing my keys off the desk.

"No, thank you, enjoy yourself. I'll be in here when you get back."

"A'ight." I walk out of his office. Sherri and I decide to have lunch at Quizno's. "Sherri, how long have you worked here?"

"For about two years, and I love it. I like seeing different people, plus the discount is good. You can use it for any Marriott, even in another state."

"That's good to know. Are you close to Omar?"

"We're cool, why?"

"Nothing. Well, I probably shouldn't mention it, but he had tears in his eyes when I went to get my keys. I asked him what was wrong but he said he was okay. I was just wondering if you knew what was bothering him?"

"Oh, probably just his spoiled-ass girlfriend. She gets on my nerves. She treats him so bad, and he is such a good man."

"Why doesn't he just leave her?" I ask.

"Because he loves her, plus they have a two–year-old daughter together. He wants to marry her, but she always turns him down."

"Really? Well, if I had a man like that, I would appreciate him. He wouldn't have to ask me twice to marry him."

"I know that's right," Sherri replies, slapping my hand.

Mmm-hmm, seems like Sherri got her eyes on my man Omar. We will see about that! Sherri seems like a nice person, but if she gets in my way, I'll have to get rid of her along with Skye.

When I return from my lunch, Omar is still sitting in his office sulking. When he sees, me he smiles. "Come on in. How was your lunch?"

"It was nice. Sherri invited me to tag along with her."

"That was nice. Sherri is a wonderful person. I'm sure you two will get along fine."

"Yeah, I think we will too."

Omar gives me a tour of the hotel and introduces me to the other staff. The only person I remember is the Assistant Manager Michael Taylor, and that's because this brotha is fine. He almost makes me lose my cool. His smooth pecan-brown skin is covered with muscles. He stands 6'2" with a shiny bald head, and he has deep dimples. I gasp as I take in everything this 250-pound man has to say. Yeah, he's perfect for Sherri. I'll just have to play matchmaker.

Before my shift is over, I slide a little note into Omar's jacket. He gives me my schedule for the rest of the week and I go home. I hope Skye finds the note first.

Without even taking my purse off, I pick up the phone to call Star. "Girl, guess what? That bitch almost had my baby crying at work today. Can you talk to Tyrone and find out what's going on?"

"Yeah, he's coming over tonight. I'll see if I can squeeze some info out of him."

"Thanks, girl."

"So, how was your first day?"

"It was nice. Omar and I got along good. I planted the note in his jacket pocket."

"For real, you better hope he don't find it first."

"I know, but I doubt he will go in there. He didn't have anything in it at first."

"Hopefully, things will turn out just how you want them."

"Yep. Well I'm good and tired. Call me when you get the 411."

After I hang up with Star, I doze off. When I wake up I'm surprised to find out it is 7:00 A.M. the next morning. I don't have to be at work until nine. Then a bright idea hits me. I'll stop by Krispy Kreme and buy two dozen doughnuts. I hope Omar likes them.

***

When I arrive at work carrying the two boxes of doughnuts, I make friends instantly.

I clock in and head to Omar's office with one dozen. The other I leave at the front desk with Sherri and the others.

Knocking softly on the door, I peep in. "Omar, is it okay to come in?"

"Sure, what you got there?"

"Some fresh hot doughnuts. I hope you like Krispy Kreme."

"Are you kidding? Who doesn't?"

"I bought them for you, help yourself." I sit the box on the desk and pull up a chair. "So, what will I be learning today?" I asked enthusiastically.

"Today, I'll show you how to make reservations, cancel them, and total out the bill. You will also learn how to answer the phone and check for available rooms."

"Wow, sounds like fun."

"No, not really, but it's what you need to know. Here, I know you're going to eat some. They're good."

"Oh, none for me. I'm on a diet. I'm trying to watch my figure."

"Nonsense, you look great! I don't see anything wrong with your body."

"Thank you. In that case, I guess I can have just one." I smile as I picked up a glazed doughnut.

I'm making progress; he actually thinks I look good. See, losing weight actually paid off. I sit in Omar's office for about fifteen minutes talking to him. He shows me pictures of his girlfriend and daughter. His daughter is so cute, she looks just like him. I wonder how our children will look.

My thoughts are interrupted by Omar's voice. "Enough chit chat, let's get to work."

We walk out of his office and go to the front desk where he begins to train me. There are two computers up front, so we practice on one while Roger assists customers on the other. I spend the whole day smelling Omar's cologne; it smells so good.

"What's that cologne you're wearing?" I finally ask him.

"Jean Paul Gaultier, why, you don't like it?"

"Oh no, I love it. It smells really good."

"Thanks, I got it from Macy's. Maybe you can get some for your man."

I start laughing. "I don't have a man in my life right now."

"What? I'm very surprised. You seem like a nice young lady. Then again, the pretty ones are usually crazy." He then begins to laugh.

"What about your girlfriend? She's pretty."

"Yeah, she is, but she has an attitude that's anything but." A moment of silence passes. "Let's get back to work. Before I forget, Sherri is going to train you tomorrow, because I'm off. Don't worry, you'll be in good hands."

"Yeah, I know. Sherri's a sweet person."

Damn, why did he have to take tomorrow off? I was having such a good time working side by side with him.

The day flies by and it's time for me to leave. "Goodnight, Omar, I guess I'll see you Thursday."

"For sure. See ya Thursday at noon. Remember, that's our late night."

"Oh, yeah, I almost forgot. Thanks for reminding me." I smile and give him a wave goodbye.

Damn, my feet hurt from standing up all day. Hopefully, this job will pay off sooner than I expect. Now it's time to move on to plan B. Skye won't know what hit her!

Chapter Seven

Jamyya

"It's been two months since I've been out wit' the girls. I'm tired of sitting in the house all the time. I want to hang out wit' my friends too," I whine to Keenan. He's getting ready to go out with the boys.

"Look babe, I've been working all week. I need to relax, plus its Tyrone's birthday. I won't be out too late. Maybe you can hook up with the girls Sunday."

"Oh, so you are going to watch the kids on Labor Day weekend? Great, 'cause I'm going to the beach."

"Whoa, the beach! No, that's too much. I was saying maybe you could find somebody else to keep the kids. I got plans all weekend. Don't you need to help them get ready for school?"

"I've already took them school shopping. Who else do you think I'm supposed to ask to keep them? Huh, who?" I am now yelling.

"I don't know. How about Jamesha? What does she have to do?"

"My sister has a job. She's working, trying to make money to buy her own clothes. You know this is her senior year. This is important to her. Anyway, these are your kids not hers."

"I know who kids they are. Look, I got to go. We'll talk about this later. Bye." He kisses me on the lips and then runs out the front door. Damn him!

I'm sick and tired of sitting in this damn house with these kids every day. Oh, I can't wait till school starts on Tuesday! I decide to call up Skye. I need somebody to listen to my ranting and raving.

"Skye, are you busy?"

"No, girl, just enjoying having the house to myself."

"I guess Omar is going to Tyrone's little get-together."

"Yes, and I couldn't be happier. This gives me a chance to get rid of him for a couple of hours."

"Well, I'm mad 'cause Keenan went. I'm sick of keeping these damn kids. I want to go out."

"Where do you want to go?"

"I don't care, anywhere, but I don't have a babysitter."

"Maybe Coco can watch them. She owes me a favor. Do you want me to ask her?"

"No, she has her own problems. She probably already has plans anyway. Shit, it's Friday night."

"Yeah, you're right. Well, how about my mother? I'm sure she's not busy?"

"Then who is going to keep Omari? Don't you think leaving her with five kids is a bit much?"

"Oh, Omari is at Omar's sister Kenya's house. She's spending the weekend with her Auntie."

"That's nice. I'm glad somebody's family keeps kids."

"Look, hold on a sec, I'ma call my mom on three-way."

Skye asked her mom if she could keep my kids. Surprisingly, she said, "Yes, just be back by midnight."

What am I going to wear? I search through my closet frantically. Being a stay-at-home mom certainly has its disadvantages. I seemed to have gained ten pounds since Coco's birthday party. Finally, I find a pair of Baby Phat capri pants. Oh, I hope they still fit! To my amazement, they do. Good, now all I need is a top and some shoes. I quickly put my clothes on and gather up the children so I can drop them off at Mrs. Vivian's house.

When I get to her house, it is already eight o'clock. Boy, time goes by fast!

I call Skye to see if she is ready. "Skye, I'm on my way to your house. Are you ready?"

"I will be by the time you get here. I'm putting on my makeup now."

"Okay. Where are we going?"

"To Friday's on Broad Street. After I hung up with you, Coco asked me if I wanted to go wit' her. I told her that me and you were going to hang out, so I figured we all would just go to Friday's together."

"Oh, yeah, that's cool. Are Mimi and Jazz coming?"

"Damisha's coming, but Jazz is busy hanging out with Shawn."

"That girl loves that man."

"She sure does. Now look, I got to go if you want me to be ready."

"A'ight. Gone."

Five minutes later, I pull up in my royal blue Nissan Altima. I get out, 'cause my common sense tells me Skye isn't ready. I ring the doorbell twice before she answers, out of breath. "Girl, come on in. Coco and Mimi are going to meet us there."

"A'ight, I'm hungry, could you hurry up? Your mom said be back by midnight."

"Yeah, I know, but once they go to sleep she'll call and say just come get them in the morning. She doesn't like people dragging sleepy children out late at night," Skye explains while primping in the mirror.

"You look cute. Now let's go."

"All right, already. Come on." She has some nerve getting an attitude when she's the one who's always late.

When we get to Friday's, Mimi and Coco are on their way to the table. "Hey, y'all wait up," I yell.

Mimi turns around. "Hey, boo. You look cute. How did you make it out tonight?"

"Mrs. Vivian is keeping the kids."

"That is so nice of her."

"Mm-hmm, sure is!"

We sit at the booth and order some drinks. "So, let's have some girl talk. What's going on in everybody's world?" I ask, excited to be out with my friends. Of course Skye has to be the one to talk first.

"Y'all will never believe this."

"What?" everyone asks.

"I think Omar is cheating on me." We all bust out laughing. "No, seriously, just listen. A couple of weeks ago, Omar asked me out to lunch. As usual I said no. Instead of him coming by anyway or calling he did neither. When I got home that evening, he had his jacket on the sofa. When I snatched it to hang it in the closet a letter fell out and I read it."

"What did it say?" Mimi asks.

"It said 'Thank you for lunch, it was wonderful.   I had a great time talking to you. I'm sorry you and your girlfriend are having problems. I hope you can work it out.'"

"You have got to be kidding! Did it have a name or signature on it?" I inquire.

"Nope, but that's not it. A week later when I got in his truck 'cause we were having dinner at his mom's house, I found an open condom wrapper in between the seat and the arm rest."

"Did you ask him about it?" Coco shouts.

"Yeah, I asked him about it, and he said Tyrone had borrowed his truck because his car was in the shop. He must have left it in there by mistake, but I never mentioned the letter."

"Well, he's probably telling the truth, 'cause Keenan had to take Tyrone to work one day last week," I add.

"Yeah Skye, I mean, everybody knows Tyrone is a hoe. Omar doesn't seem like the cheating type," Mimi states.

"Yeah, I don't think he is either, but his behavior is changing. Like tonight, for example, he left at six o'clock to go over to Tyrone's party, and he hasn't called me once. It's going on nine-thirty. Usually, he would have called twice by now."

"Maybe he's tired of you cussing him out. You told him you needed space. Now you got it," I remind her.

"Yeah, I guess you're right."

"Well, anybody else got news?" I ask, looking at Coco and Mimi.

Mimi clears her throat. "Yeah. I got some drama. Chris is so nice. He takes me out, spends time with me, he even took me to church, but he won't have sex with me. Then there's Jerell. He has a good job, we get along fine when we are together, and the sex is bum. Mmm, mmm, mmm, so good! Anyway, he rations out his time to me. I'm not used to that shit. I've always been number one or the only one. This shit is starting to get on my nerves."

"So, Jerell is seeing other people?" Coco asks.

"Yeah, too damn many. I just see him and Chris. I don't know for sure how many, but it's more than two."

"I hope he is wearing a condom."

"Oh yes, every time. I'm not that damn stupid. I like sex, but I don't want to die from it either."

"Girl, I know that's right!" I add.

"The problem is, I'm really starting to catch feelings for Jerell. I want to settle down, you know, have a monogamous relationship."

"Well, have you discussed this with Jerell?" Coco sighs.

"Yeah, but he keeps telling me he's not ready right now. He told me to be patient."

"Please girl, you need to just move on. What's wrong with Chris?" I want to know.

"Nothing. I just think he's too good for me, plus he has a son. I'm not trying to compete with his son for his time. That's one competition I will never win. Let's talk about something else."

"Well, I just want to say, I miss hanging out with you guys. Y'all know my mom is getting out of prison next week."

"For real, I didn't know Rhonda was coming home," Skye says, surprised.

"Yep. She's going to be staying with me until she gets on her feet."

"Have you told Jamesha yet?"

"Yeah, she knows, and she is not happy about sharing a room with her either."

"You know what? Maybe she can get a job working at the Marriott with Omar. He says he still needs to hire a housekeeper."

"Oh, yeah, that would be great! Tell him to hold the position for her. The sooner she gets herself together, the faster she can get out my house. I'm sure y'all know Keenan doesn't like my mom."

"Yeah, we know," everyone states.

"Anyway, I'm just so tired of sitting in the house with the kids every day. I'm glad school starts Tuesday."

"You and me both," Coco replies.

"You know I can always send you on an assignment, Jamyya, if you want to work," Skye says.

"Yeah, but Keenan doesn't think it's a good idea. He claims daycare is too expensive, and that it's just cheaper for me to stay at home."

"Whatever, that's just his way of controlling you," Mimi huffs.

"It's true," Coco says, adding her two cents.

We eat and have a few more drinks. Before I know it, it's eleven o'clock. Right when we are leaving the restaurant, Mrs. Vivian calls. "Honey, the kids are asleep, you can just pick them up in the morning."

"Thanks, Mrs. Vivian. You are a life saver."

"You're welcome, honey. Anytime, just enjoy yourself."

"Goodnight."

Hmm, a night to myself. What can I get myself into tonight?

After I drop Skye off, I go home to relax. Keenan is still at Tyrone's party, so the house is empty. I stretch out on the green Italian leather sofa in the family room. As I pick up the remote control to cut on the TV, I hear voices. Hmm, I thought I was here alone. Oh, Jamesha must be home. I get up and knock on her bedroom door.

"Yes?"

"It's me, open the door," I demand.

"A'ight. Just one minute." I hear a lot of commotion

"Girl, if you don't open this damn door right now, I'm going to tear it off the hinges!"

"I'm coming!" she yells.

Jamesha opens the door wearing only a T-shirt with her hair all over her head.

"What the hell are you doing in here?"

"Nothing. I didn't know you came home."

"Mm-hmm. Who's in here wit' you?"

"Nobody. Why you say that?"

"Oh, I'm not stupid! I heard a man's voice. Where is he?" I yell while looking under the bed and opening the closet door. Not surprised at all, I find a medium-build, mocha-complexioned brotha standing in his boxers shaking.

"Hello, Devin. Why are you half-naked standing in my sister's closet?"

"Hey, Jamyya. I just, um, dropped her off after work. Then she invited me in. I didn't know you were coming back so soon," Devin says, trembling.

"Yeah, I bet y'all didn't expect me. I hope y'all are using protection! I'm going to close the door, and you have five minutes to get dressed and leave my house."

"Okay, sorry, Jamyya," he says solemnly.

"Yeah, yeah."

A mother's job is never done. Who would have known Omar's little brother would be in my house having sex with my little sister? After Devin leaves, I feel me and Jamesha need to have a talk.

"So, how long have you and Devin been together?"

"For about two-and-a-half months. I met him at work."

"So are you on birth control?"

"No, but we use condoms."

"Well, I think you should get some pills, a patch or something. We'll go down to the clinic Tuesday when you get out of school."

"Okay."

"You know mom is coming home next Monday."

"Yeah, I know, but why she gotta stay here?"

"Because she doesn't have anywhere else to go."

"She can stay in a shelter or something. I don't want to share my room with her. I don't even want to see her."

"Well, you don't have to. Keenan said it would make more sense for Tamia and Ke'Asia to share a room. Then mom can stay in one of their rooms."

"Wow, that's great! I hope she's not here long. Look Jamyya, I'm sorry about having Devin in your house, but I'm really tired. Can we talk about this tomorrow?"

"Yeah, goodnight."

I go up to my room and get into bed. Jamesha doesn't like our mom very much. She is still upset about how she left her to chase after drugs. Our mom, Rhonda, has been in and out of jail ever since Jamesha was five years old. I guess some people hold grudges. I don't condone my mother's actions, but I forgave her a long time ago. All of this shit is giving me a headache. I'm going to sleep.

***

Thank goodness it's Tuesday. I wake up bright and early so I can get the kids off to school on time. Ke'Asia's now in the fourth grade and Tamia's in the second. At least I can get rid of two of them for the day. School lets out at 2:30, so I have time to clean up.

"Keenan, honey, I need you to come straight home from work today. I have to take Jamesha to the clinic, and I don't want to take the kids. We won't be long. It's really important."

"Okay, baby, I'll be home at noon. I'll take a half day. I need to start moving Tamia's stuff into Ke'Asia's room anyway."

"Thank you, baby."

"Sure. You know what, honey? I'm sorry for not helping you with the kids more. Maybe you can go have lunch with one of your friends when I get home," he says with a smile.

"Are you serious?"

"Yeah, you can take the rest of the day off when I get home."

"You're the best husband ever!"

"Yeah, well, I try."

After Keenan and everybody leaves for school, I start my daily chores. I fix the twins some oatmeal, eggs, and bacon. They sit in front of the TV and watch Blue's Clues. Nickelodeon has become my best friend. Watching TV is the only thing that occupies the twins longer than ten minutes. When I get done cleaning, it's about 11:30.

I put the twins in their room for a nap. My five-bedroom house is about to become a war zone. Keenan doesn't care for my mom much either. So between him and Jamesha, Rhonda doesn't stand a chance. Even though no one else is happy, I am.

On Monday, I'm planning to have a surprise dinner for my mom. I already called my brothers James and Jamal. They both live on campus, but they agreed to drive down for mom's party on Monday.

Oops, I almost forgot to call Skye to see if she's free for lunch.

Ring...ring. "Hello, Richmond Premier Staffing, Skye speaking, how may I help you?"

"Hey, girl. What are you doing for lunch?"

"Nothing much. Probably just go to Pizza Hut for the lunch buffet."

"Do you want some company?"

"Yeah, are you going to bring the kids?"

"No, Keenan is taking a half a day at work. He's getting off at noon 'cause I have to take Jamesha to the clinic."

"For what?"

"I'll explain at lunch. Do you want me to meet you at Pizza Hut?"

"Yeah, meet me at Broad Street Pizza Hut around 1:00 P.M."

"Okay, see ya later. I got to get dressed."

By the time I'm ready to go, Keenan's walking through the door. He rarely ever takes off work, so I know he had to sense my frustration. I've been really cranky lately. Keenan is the Quality Control Manager at Phillip Morris. He has been working there for five years now. He makes good money, but I feel like I should be contributing to the household as well. Shit, even my sister has a job at McDonald's making her own money.

"Hey, honey, I'm going to meet Skye for lunch. Then I'm going to pick up Jamesha from school. The boys should be waking up soon. Please fix them some lunch. I gotta go before I am late." I kiss my husband and run out the door. I'm so excited to have a break. I don't want him to change his mind.

When I pull up at Pizza Hut, I see Skye's Lexus parked out front. Oh, so she can be on time for something!

"Hey, girl, sorry I'm late," I say, smiling.

"No problem, I got time. I have to go visit a client at 2:30, so I don't have to go back to the office after lunch."

"Good. Are you ready for this? My sister is going out with Omar's brother Devin."

"Get out of here! How did you find out?"

"I caught him in her bedroom hiding in the closet wit' only his boxers on. That's why I'm taking her to the clinic, for some birth control."

"Oh, my goodness! I wonder do Omar know?"

"Probably not. She didn't know who he was, and neither did he."

"Mmm, mmm, mmm, I'm glad Omari is still a little girl. 'Cause I'm going to have a shotgun ready right along with her daddy."

"Girl, I know, but Jamesha's seventeen. She has probably been having sex for awhile."

"Probably so."

We get up and serve ourselves off of the buffet line. I look at Skye with admiration. Sometimes I'm jealous of her. She's so pretty and skinny. Her mother is wonderful, and she actually knows her father. My father is Italian, or so my mother says, but truth be told, she don't really know who any of her children's fathers are.

"Skye, I'm getting fat. How do you stay so damn skinny?"

"'Cause I work and stay active. What you need to do is say 'fuck you' to Keenan and get a job. Put the twins in daycare and get a life."

"Yeah, I know, but I don't have any money to pay for it."

"Look, I can find you a job that you can work Monday through Friday from nine to one. That way, you only have to take the twins to daycare for half a day."

"That sounds good. I'll talk to Keenan about it."

"A'ight, just let me know."

"Well, what time did Omar come home from the party?"

"Girl, let me tell you! Please don't tell anybody else."

"Of course not. I can keep a secret. What's up?"

"Omar came home around 1:00 A.M. with a hickey on his neck and a condom wrapper in his pocket."

"Stop lying!"

"No, I'm serious. I acted like I was asleep. When he got in the bed, I rolled over and saw a red mark on his neck. Now, I didn't put it there. Then when I knew he was in a deep sleep, I went through his pants pockets. That's when I found a gold Magnum condom wrapper, the same kind that was in his truck. Explain that shit!" Skye says angrily.

"Did you ask him about it?"

"I didn't want him to know I went through his pockets, so I didn't mention the condom, but I asked him about the mark on his neck."

"What did he say?"

"He said that he got drunk and some stripper was giving him a lap dance. He thinks she must have put it there."

"So you mean to tell me that he let some skank-ass stripper suck on his neck 'cause he was drunk?"

"Yep, that's what he said."

"Damn, you're taking it well. I guess I should be checking up on Keenan then, since they all hang out together. I knew it was a reason I didn't like Tyrone's nasty ass!"

"Well, I can't blame Omar's actions on Tyrone. For some reason, I blame myself for pushing him away. Jazz said that she thinks he is just trying to make me jealous. She doesn't think that he's cheating on me."

"You know what? That may just be it. Do you want me to ask Keenan about it? Maybe he might tell me something."

"No, you know them dogs all stick together. Even if he did know something, he wouldn't tell you 'cause he know you will tell me."

"Yeah, girl you're right. Well, it's time for me to go. I'll call you later, okay?"

"Bye, have fun at the clinic."

"Yeah, right." I roll my eyes and leave.

I figure it would be quicker for me to pick Jamesha up from school, and then head straight to the clinic. We have to wait thirty minutes before they call us back.

"Hello, Mrs. Brown. What can I do for you today?" the nurse asks.

"Well, my sister Jamesha is having sex, and I would like to get her some birth control."

"Okay, what kinds of birth control are you interested in, Jamesha?"

"I guess the birth control patch or something that I don't have to remember every day."

"That's fine. Now let me ask you a few questions. Do you have more than one partner?"

"No."

"Have you ever had unprotected sex?"

"Yes."

"Have you ever had a sexual transmitted disease?"

"No."

"Well, that's good. What I'm going to do is give you a pap smear, draw your blood, and take a urine sample. I'm going to check for any sexually transmitted diseases, including HIV, and make sure your cervix is normal. When was your last menstrual cycle?"

"Umm, I don't really remember. I'm usually irregular, so I don't really keep track."

"Okay, well I'll give you a pregnancy test as well, but by you being irregular you may want to try birth control pills. They will help regulate you."

"A'ight."

"I'm going to step out here with your sister, please get undressed from the waist down." The nurse closes the door. "Mrs. Brown, you can have a seat in the waiting room until the exam is finished?"

"Thank you."

I sit in the waiting area for what seems like hours. Finally, the nurse comes to get me. "Mrs. Brown you can come on back. This is Dr. Nelson; she wants to speak to both of you."

"Hello, Doctor. Is something wrong?" I ask with a perplexed look on my face.

"Not exactly. I've already told Jamesha that birth control at this time is not necessary because she is already pregnant."

"What?" I scream.

"Calm down, Mrs. Brown, your sister is six weeks pregnant. Her due date is around May 10th. Now I gave her some pamphlets on different choices she can make. There is still time to make a decision."

"Thank you for the information."

"You're welcome. I also gave her some prenatal vitamins and a list of OB-GYNs in the area. Good luck."

Yeah, right! What in the hell am I going to do now? I don't even know what to say to her. We walk to the car in silence. Once we are halfway down the street I speak. "Jamesha, what do you plan on doing about this baby?"

"I don't know. I need to talk to Devin about this."

"Okay, well let me know what you decide, because you know your decision affects all of us."

"Yeah, I know. I'm sorry Jay, I didn't mean for this to happen. We only did it twice without a condom. I thought he knew how to pull out."

I start laughing.

What's funny?" Jamesha asked baffled.

"You just remind me a lot of myself. That's the same thing I said when I got pregnant wit' Ke'Asia."

"For real?"

"Yep, I told Mom the exact same thing. I guess Devin and Keenan got something in common."

"I don't know how to tell him. What should I say?"

"Just tell him the truth. You got the papers to prove it. I don't know Devin that well, but you know Omar is his brother and he is probably just as nice. How does he treat you?"

"He's cool. He always brings me home and he buys me stuff to eat. We went out to the movies a couple times. We haven't had any major problems, but we've only been going out since the end of June."

"Well, if you want to, you can invite him over for dinner and then y'all can go to your room and talk."

"Are you sure?"

"Yeah. He can't do much else to you."

"Thanks, Jay."

"You're welcome. Dinner is at six."

Damn, what else can go wrong? When we walk in the house, the kids are running wild.

"Hey, Ma," Ke'Asia yells.

"Hi, Mommy," Deontaé says, running to hug me.

"Hello, little children. Why are y'all running around like you lost your mind?"

"'Cause Daddy let us," Tamia replies.

"Well, Mommy is home now, and I don't go for that, so stop. Go to your rooms and play."

"Yes, ma'am," they all reply, going in their rooms.

"Keenan, why in the hell are you letting them run wild?"

"Sorry honey, I didn't know you were back. They were just having a little fun."

"Let them have fun tearing up their own rooms."

"How did it go at the clinic?"

"Not good. Jamesha's pregnant."

"What?"

"Yep. By Omar's brother Devin."

"Get the fuck out of here! How did that happen?"

"Don't be smart!"

"You know what I mean. How did they hook up?"

"He works at McDonald's with her. They have been dating since June."

"Oh, really? Well, what did he have to say about her being pregnant?"

"She didn't tell him yet. We just got back from the clinic. I told her to invite him over for dinner so they could discuss it."

"Oh boy, another baby in the house. Is she going to keep it?"

"I don't know. She didn't say"

"Well, we are going to need a bigger house, or your mother will have to stay somewhere else."

"Somewhere else, like where?"

"I don't know. She'll probably go back to jail soon anyway."

"Keenan, that wasn't called for."

"I'm sorry, baby, but you know how I feel about your mom."

"Yeah, I know. You and Jamesha both."

"Well, I'm about to cook dinner. What do you want to eat?"

"Umm. Lasagna sounds good, with some garlic bread and a salad."

"Okay, well I better get started. I might need you to run to the store for some ingredients."

"All right, just make a list."

Jamesha calls Devin, and he says that he will come over for dinner. I hope he is a good man like Omar, or should I say how Omar use to be. I just can't believe the things that have been happening lately. Well, no time for that right now, I have to cook. Jamesha helps the girls do their homework while Keenan occupies the twins.

Devin finally arrives, and we sit down for dinner.

"Thanks for inviting me over, dinner was great," Devin says, wiping his mouth with a napkin.

"You're welcome," I reply.

"So, what are your plans for the future?" Keenan asks Devin.

"I want to go to college. I'm thinking about Morgan State. My major is going to be graphic design."

"Good goals. I see your brother taught you well."

"Yeah, he stays on me about school."

"So you got your own car?"

"Yeah. Omar gave me his old Honda Civic."

"That was nice of him"

"You know Omar always giving somebody something."

"Well, I'll leave you two alone to talk," I say, clearing the dishes.

"Jamesha, you can take Devin in your room so the kids won't disturb you. I'll help Jamyya clean the kitchen," Keenan says, giving me a wink.

"Okay. Thank you for everything," Jamesha says.

Jamesha and Devin go into her room to talk.

Devin and Jamesha stay in her room for over an hour. When I see Devin leave, I go downstairs to talk to Jamesha.

"Mesha, can I come in?" I ask while knocking lightly.

"Yeah, come on in."

"So, how did things go?"

"They went good. We decided to keep the baby. He said he would help me even if we broke up."

"That's good to hear. I'm sure he's a man of his word."

"I sure hope so. He's going home to tell his mom. He said he would call me to let me know how she handled it."

"Knowing Shakita, she won't be too rough on him."

"Yeah, he'll be okay. I'm kind of sleepy. I'm about to lie down. I got a long day tomorrow."

"Do you go to work?"

"Yep, for the rest of the week. I'm not off till Sunday."

"I hope you took Monday off. You know I'm having a big dinner for Rhonda."

"I know, and I'll be here even though I don't really want to."

"Thanks. Just be good for me. You don't have to stay long, but this would be a nice time to introduce Devin to the family."

"Who's coming?"

"Everybody: James, Jamal, Aunt Brenda, Angie, and Pam, Uncle Marvin, Grandma Sabrina and Grandpa Otis."

"Damn, that's a lot of people!"

"Wait, that's not all. I also invited my friends, and everybody will probably bring their spouses."

"You must be going to cook all day."

"Yeah, it seems that way, but Aunt Brenda is bringing dessert, and Grandma is bringing the fried chicken and potato salad. I should be okay cooking the rest."

"I can't wait to eat some of Brenda's cake!"

"I know. She bakes the best cakes. Get some sleep, I'll see you in the morning. Oh, yeah, go ahead and invite Devin and Shakita"

"A'ight, goodnight," Jamesha says before I shut the door.

What a day! I'm glad Devin didn't act a fool.

I go upstairs to put the kids to sleep, but Keenan has already done it. I kiss him on the lips passionately. "Honey, thanks so much for the help! I really appreciate it."

"You're welcome, but no thanks is needed. It's my job, and I've been slacking lately. I'm sorry. You know what? Maybe you should start working, since your mom is going to be staying here, and now that Jamesha's having a baby we could use another income."

"Are you sure?"

"Yeah, I'm sure. Just give me two weeks to get together some money then you can enroll the twins in daycare."

"Thanks, baby. I'm sure it won't take me long to get a job. Skye can always find me something."

"I know honey, you will do fine."

"How about I show you how much I appreciate you?"

"Are you trying to get freaky wit' me?"

"I sure am."

"Come on wit' it."

"Boy, you so crazy," I say as I jump on top of him, ready for an all-night lovemaking session.

***

The days fly by, and now it's Monday. I have to drive to the Greyhound bus station on the Boulevard to pick my mom up. She has been in Goochland County prison, this time for four years. Her charges were intent to distribute, grand larceny, and assault. Rhonda is a breed of her own, is what my grandma used to say. Out of all of her kids, my mom is the only one on drugs. She tries to stay clean, but it only lasts for a couple of months. Hopefully, this time she will change. I'm willing to help her all I can. This time she took a program called T.C. It stands for Therapeutic Community. I sure hope this program works, 'cause I can't stand another disappointment. I haven't seen my mother in so long; I hope I recognize her.

I stand in the middle of the bus station, looking around frantically, when I finally spot a familiar face. The woman has dark-brown hair in cornrows with a scarf on her head. Her complexion is like hazelnut coffee, and her eyes are light brown. She has tiny freckles on her nose. Her waist is small, but her hips and butt are big. She has on a small white shirt and a pair of blue jeans. I can tell she's looking for someone, so I call out, "Rhonda? Over here."

"Hey baby, is that you? Oh my God, Jamyya you've gotten fat girl!"

"Well, I've had twins since the last time I saw you."

"Oh, that's right. How are my grandkids?"

"They are fine. Come on, let's get you out of here," I say, escorting her to my car.

"How are my other kids doing?" Rhonda asks.

"They are fine. James is in his senior year at Virginia State and Jamal is a junior at Hampton University. Jamesha is about to graduate from high school this year. I guess you could say everybody doing well."

"That's good to hear. I'm glad none of you turned out like me."

"Me too."

"You did a real good job of raising your brothers and sister. I'm really proud of you. Maybe now I can help you with your kids."

"That would be nice, Mom, but first just concentrate on getting your life together. You remember Omar, Skye's boyfriend? Well, he is the manager at the Marriott, and he said he would hire you as a housekeeper for the hotel. All you need to do is fill out the application. I can take you down there tomorrow."

"Oh yeah, honey, that will be great! Because I don't want to cause no problems for you and Keenan. I want to make my own money so I can get my own place."

"That's good to hear. Where would you like to go eat at? I'm sure you're hungry."

"I sure am. Anywhere is fine wit' me."

"A'ight. Let's go to Applebee's it's not that expensive."

"Sounds good to me."

"Mom, I'm glad you are home." I smile at her and she smiles back.

My mom and I have a great time at Applebee's. We talk for an hour while we eat our food. She looks into my eyes, "It feels so good to eat real food and have a conversation with my daughter."

"Yeah, I missed you too. Sorry to rush you, but I have to be home when the kids get off the bus. Plus I have a lot of cooking to do."

"You're cooking dinner? Well, I can help you."

"No, Mom today is your day. I'm having a party for you. You can't cook for your own party."

"Why can't I?"

"'Cause I said so. But you can watch the kids while I set things up."

"Deal. Where are the kids now? I know they don't go to school yet?"

"No, the twins are only three. They will be four in November. Keenan's mom Sandra was off today, so she is keeping them. I told her I would be back by two o'clock."

"Okay, let's roll. I'm ready to see my grandbabies."

I speed down the highway to Sandra's house. The last thing I want to hear is how ungrateful I am being late trying to take advantage of her kindness. Sandra never liked me because I come from a poor family and my mom was a dope friend. She also didn't like the fact that I got pregnant at fifteen and Keenan married me at eighteen. She wanted him to go to college and have this fancy life, but instead he had two kids by the age of eighteen. Keenan did, however, go to ECPI for two and a half years. He got his Bachelor's degree in Electronics Engineering. To me, Keenan turned out just fine. He has a good job paying $65,000 a year. We have a beautiful five-bedroom house in Lakefield Hills, and we have two cars. I drive the Altima and Keenan drives the Jeep Cherokee.

We live pretty well for a couple that's not even thirty.

I pull up in front of Sandra's house just in time. Whew, it was 1:55!

"Mom, you can stay in the car, I'll be right back."

"Okay honey, just leave the music on. I promise not to steal the car." She laughs. I really don't think it's funny. My mom's crazy like that; I don't put anything past her. I remember the time she sold my clothes I had just bought for school. I was about sixteen, and I was working at Burger King trying to make some money. While I was at work, my mom stole my school clothes. You wanna talk about somebody being heated! So you see, she would do some low-down stuff like steal your car. She also stole from her own mother on occasion. My grandma would have to watch her like a hawk when she came to her house. What a shame. I shake my head as if to erase the memory.

"Thanks, Sandra, for keeping the boys, but I gotta run. Ke'Asia and Tamia will be coming home soon, and I need to be there to let them in."

"Okay, drive safe. Tell my girls' Grandma says 'Hi'."

"I will, thanks again."

For somebody who doesn't like me, she damn sure talks my head off every time I see her. I guess I've grown on her over the years.

As I'm driving down the street, my cell phone rings. "Hello? Oh, hey girl."

"Guess what? I got some good news for you," Skye says.

"What? Spit it out."

"Well, I just got a promotion to branch manager, which means I will be running the whole agency. I will be in training for three weeks until the branch manager, Cynthia, leaves to go to another job she got. Actually, she's moving to Florida to help her mom and dad out. They are both getting old. Anyway, I need somebody to fill my position. So I was wondering if you want my job, 'cause I get to do the hiring now."

"Really? Congratulations girl. Hell yeah, I want your job."

"I thought you would. The only thing is, I need you to work nine to five Monday through Friday. No holidays or weekends. I can start you off with twenty five thousand a year plus commission."

"Oh, hell yeah, that's just what I need! When do you need me to start?"

"Next Monday if you can, so that way when you finish training, Cynthia will just be leaving. That way I won't have to do both jobs."

"A'ight. Let me talk to Keenan. I'm sure he can put the kids in daycare by Monday, and if not, I'll see if my mom can keep them."

"Oh, that's right, she came home today."

"Yep. Are you coming over tonight?"

"Yeah. Omar and I will be there. I heard about Jamesha being pregnant by Devin."

"I guess Omar told you."

"Yeah, Devin called Omar because he didn't know how to tell Shakita. Omar told him he would help him figure out how to go to college and raise a baby. Does your mom know?"

"No, not yet. I guess everyone will find out tonight. I'll talk to you then."

"All right. What I'm going to do is bring all the paperwork to you tonight. Then you can fill out the application and everything and give it to me. When I get to work tomorrow, I can fax everything to corporate and we can do your interview by phone."

"Sounds good. Thanks a lot, Skye."

"Bye girl, good luck with Keenan."

Today was turning out to be a good day. Now all I got to do is sell Keenan on the idea of sending all the kids to daycare.

Mom is a big help. She plays with the twins and answers the thousands of questions Ke'Asia and Tamia ask her.

"Mom, I'll take you shopping for clothes tomorrow. We can also go to Wal-Mart and get whatever stuff you need," I yell from the kitchen.

"Okay baby, I got a check for $950. You know I worked in the laundry for three years making a dollar an hour. So, I can buy my own stuff. I just need you to take me to the bank to cash it."

"Is this check legal?" I ask with suspicion.

"Yes baby, it's real, the prison gave it to me. You can call and ask them. I got all my paperwork."

"Okay, I believe you. I'm glad you got your own money, because things are kind of tight for us right now. Keenan just spent $1200 on a bedroom suit for your room. I hope you like it. Whenever you move out, you can take it with you."

"That was awful sweet of him. I'll have to get him a gift when we go shopping," she says, smiling.

"Oooh, Grandma, can you buy us something too?" Ke'Asia asks.

"Yeah, sweetie, Grandma is going to buy everybody something, including Jamesha, that hateful child of mine. Where she at, anyway?"

"She doesn't usually get home til four. She should be coming now," I say, looking at the clock.

Jamesha comes home and goes straight to her room. I go and knock on her door. "Mesha, are you going to come out and talk to Mom?" I ask in my sweet motherly voice.

"Yeah, I just got in, let me get myself together. You know Devin and his mom is coming. I have to look nice. This is my first time meeting her."

"A'ight, but don't take too long."

Long would be an understatement. Jamesha doesn't come out until Devin and his mom shoed up.

"Hello, Shakita and Devin, come on in," I say, escorting them to the family room. My brother James had just arrived minutes ago.

"Shakita, this is my mother Rhonda and my brother James. Mom and James, this is Devin, Jamesha's boyfriend, and his mom Shakita."

"Nice to meet you" James says, shaking Devin's hand and kissing Shakita's.

"Same to you. Where is this girl that been messing round wit' my baby?" Shakita asks, looking around.

"Mom, stop being so embarrassing," Devin says through clenched teeth.

"Boy, shut up! I just want to meet the girl. After all, she's having my grandchild. Your ass should have been introduced us."

Rhonda and James both look at me with a scowl.

"Jamesha is pregnant? Why didn't you tell me?" James shouts.

"Because she was going to tell everyone tonight," I say with an attitude.

"Oh, so that's why she's been hiding in her room," Rhonda says.

"No, she's only six weeks. She ain't even showing yet. She just doesn't want to see you," I reply.

Shakita looks confused. "Y'all, I'm so sorry. I thought everybody knew the chile was pregnant."

"Let me go get her. Everybody just calm down and have a seat." I go to get Jamesha out of her room, but the doorbell starts ringing.

"Keenan, can you please get the door?"

"Yeah, honey, I got it."

"Thanks. Everybody is in the family room."

I knock on the door hard this time. "Jamesha, bring your ass out here. Devin and his mom are here."

She opens the door. "Okay I'm ready." Jamesha looks really pretty. She has a very light, pale complexion with gray eyes. Her hair is sandy-brown with deep waves in it. She is about 5'5" and a size six. Her hair hangs down her back. Like I said before, none of us knows our fathers, but my mom claims he was Italian or white.

From our looks, people would agree that we were mixed with something. She walks into the room. "Hello, Ms. Rhodes. How are you?"

"I'm fine, boo. It's nice to finally meet you. You are a pretty little thing. Call me Shakita. No need to be so formal. Sit down, let's chat." Shakita starts patting the cushion beside her.

"Hey, Devin and James. How are y'all doing?" Jamesha inquires.

"I'm fine, after I damn near had a heart attack finding out you're pregnant," James says.

"Sorry, I was going to tell everybody tonight."

"You're pregnant?" Aunt Brenda shouts.

"Oh, hi Aunt Brenda, I didn't see you. Yeah I'm pregnant."

"Well, I be damned! I guess all y'all want to be like your momma."

"Not all of us. I know who my baby daddy is, and I'm not a damn dope friend. I'm going to take care of my baby, not run the streets tricking and getting high," Jamesha snaps.

"The nerve of you, little girl! Somebody needed to raise you better than that! Your mother is the only disgrace in this family, and it looks like she sprinkled it down onto her kids," Brenda replies angrily.

"Now, wait just a damn minute! I think Jamyya did a good job raising us. I'm a senior in college, and Jamal is in his junior year at Hampton University. Neither one of us has kids, and even if we did, it wouldn't make us any less of a person. At least Jamyya finished high school. Some girls don't even do that. As for Jamesha, she might have slipped and made a mistake, but she has a job and a 4.0 grade point average in Honor's classes. So you are dead wrong. We're nothing like Rhonda," James barks.

"Tell her ass off!" Jamesha yelled.

"Well, umm, I'm sorry. I guess you're right. I just wanted so much more for your sister, that's all. Having a baby will change her whole life. What about college and her future?"

"She can still go to college. I'll make sure of it," James announces.

"Me too," I co-sign.

"Everybody just calm down, more guests are coming. We can do this another time," Keenan says, running to answer the door.

"Who is it, honey?" I yell.

"It's Skye, Omar, Jamal, and Aunt Angie."

Aunt Angie is my favorite aunt. She let me come live with her when I was pregnant with Ke'Asia.

Angie has a twin sister named Pamela. Well, really her name is Angela, but we call her Angie and Pamela, Pam. My Uncle Marvin is the oldest, then Aunt Brenda, then my mom, and the twins are the youngest. Everybody was surprised that I had the twins. Angie's daughter, Lisa, and Pam's daughter, Jessica, both have kids. So automatically, everyone thought one of them would have twins. But nope, it was me. Brenda seems to be the only asshole in the family that thinks she is better than everybody else.

People begin to come in, so I start serving drinks and hors d'oeuvres. My Grandma Sabrina and Grandpa Otis come right when dinner is being served. For some strange reason, my Uncle Marvin bought all types of liquor with him. Everything's going good until my mom starts drinking.

"Mom, don't you think you should slow down on the drinks?" Jamal asks.

"Hell no, I've been locked up for four years now, it's time to let loose," Rhonda shouts while dancing to the music.

My cousin Jessica was the one who thought it was a good idea to play some music, since it was a party. "Come on, girl, dance wit' your momma," Rhonda says to Jamesha, grabbing her by the arm.

"No. I don't feel like dancing. You drunk anyway. Just leave me alone."

"Oh, you think you grown now 'cause you pregnant. You ain't grown. You don't feel like it, huh. That's what you should have told that raggedy ass little boy when he pulled his little dick out. Just 'cause you gapped dem legs open don't make you no woman!" Rhonda yells.

"Now you done gone too damn far! I'll be damned if I let you talk about my son like that, or your daughter! You are a fucking embarrassment. You need to concentrate on fixing your fucked up life and stop picking on everybody else. I raised my son right, and he is going to take care of his responsibility. I'ma make sure of it. And if this girl needs anything, I'm gonna try my best to give it to her!" Shakita yells back.

"Mom I think you've had enough to drink. How about you go in your room and lay down?" I say, trying to defuse the situation.

"Why I got to go in my room? It's my damn party. Tell this bitch and her home-wrecking son to go home," Rhonda slurs, holding a glass of E & J.

"Now, Ms. Rhonda, I understand you've been drinking, but I can't let you disrespect my mother like that. Even though my mom had me young, she still took care of all her kids. My mom raised me to be a gentleman, so I'ma ask you nicely to refrain from calling my mom out of her name. As for my brotha, he's going to do the right thing by Jamesha," Omar explains.

"Fuck you and your mom! Just get the hell out, all of you!"

"I'm sorry, everybody, maybe it's time for everyone to go. I apologize for Rhonda's behavior," I say, embarrassed.

"It's okay honey, I know it's not your fault. Call me if your sister needs anything," Shakita says as she and Devin leave.

My Uncle Marvin looks at Rhonda with disgust. "You just don't know how to act. You ain't shit, and never going to be shit if you keep this up. Get some damn help before you ruin these kids' lives. I'm gone y'all. I can't take this shit no more. Jamyya, you know I'm here if you need me."

"Thank you, Unc. I'll call you tomorrow."

Everybody starts leaving my house, shaking their heads. I think my grandparents are the most disappointed. They have often wished that mom would get her act together. So much for that! I'm determined to stick by her. Maybe I can make a difference. Keenan will never let me hear the end of this.

"Goodnight, sis. Next time Mom gets out of prison, don't call me. I have no words for her. Bye Jamesha, keep your head up. Let your big bro know if you need something. I'll holla at y'all later," James says before making his exit.

"Sorry, James, but I'ma do my best and finish school. I can still go to college, even if it's part-time," Jamesha replies.

"Yeah, I know, sweetie. You have a lot of support, so use it, but don't abuse it," he smiles.

"I gotta get going so I can get up for my classes in the morning."

"Bye, James. I love you," I say.

Jamal doesn't have no words; he just leaves shaking his head with tears rolling down his face. "I love you too, Jamal," I yell at him.

"I love both of y'all, take care and good luck with trying to reform Rhonda." Jamal hugs me and Jamesha, then disappears.

"Mesha, why don't you go on ahead to bed. I'll clean this mess up. I know you're tired." I take the trash bag from her shaking hands. "Everything will be all right."

"Yeah, whenever she leaves. See you in the morning." Jamesha goes in her room and locks the door.

Keenan comes to help me clean up. "Where she at now?" I ask.

"Probably passed out in her room somewhere. I told you this was a bad idea. I don't like her staying here. Jamesha shouldn't be stressed in her condition, and the kids shouldn't witness such behavior."

"I know, honey. I promise I will talk to her tomorrow. Just give her a couple days. If she don't change or she fucks up again, I'll put her out. Okay?"

"Mmm. If you say so."

"Well, I have some good news. Skye just got a promotion to Branch Manager, and she wants me to take her old job as Account Executive. She's going to pay me $25,000 a year plus commission. The only thing is, I need to start Monday. I'll work Monday through Friday from nine to five. No holidays or weekends. So what do you think?"

"I think that's great! Call around and find a daycare. I'll give you some money Friday to register them. Find something close to home, but not too expensive. I'm happy for you, honey."

"Thank you. But you know Tamia and Ke'Asia will need after-school care too. I got to find a daycare that can pick them up from school."

"Yeah, that's true. Well, we will figure it out. Just enroll all of them."

"I love you, honey. Thanks for giving me the opportunity to contribute to the household."

"I love you too. And you contribute a lot, just not financially. To tell you the truth, you have the hardest job, and you do it so well."

"Thanks, honey."

I go to bed relieved. I'm glad I get to start in the workforce. My mother's homecoming did not go as planned, but I'll work with her until she gets it right. Hopefully it won't take her whole life.

Chapter Eight

Omar

I still can't believe the shit that's been going on lately! How in the hell did I end up with a hickey on my neck? Even I don't believe the story I told Skye, but it was the truth. For some reason, I don't remember much that happened at Tyrone's birthday party. I know some strippers were there, and from what I heard, one was all over me. The strange thing is why didn't I stop her. Hmm, must have been the alcohol and that blunt I smoked.

Damn, I don't really feel like going to work today. I have a lot on my mind. My little brother Devin got his girlfriend pregnant, and she happens to be Jamyya's little sister. Small world, I guess. On top of that, me and Skye are having problems. She's suspicious of my every move. This is the first time we've had trust issues. Time to put on my game face.

I walk in to the Marriott, smiling like my life is perfect.

"Good morning, ladies."

"Good morning, Omar," Sherri replies.

"Hey, boss," Yolanda says, smiling.

"So, Yolanda, how was your first day working on your own? I'm sorry I couldn't be here with you."

"That's okay. Everything went smoothly. I really like working here."

"I'm glad to hear that. Do you mind if I borrow Sherri for a moment?"

"Nope, I can handle things by myself"

"Thanks a lot." I escort Sherri into my office.

"So how are things really going with her?"

"Good. She's a fast learner. I really do like her. She's really friendly. I think she has a crush on you."

"Oh, you do? What makes you think that?"

"'Cause she smiles and laughs at everything you say. Anytime someone mentions your name, her eyes light up. She always tries to be near you."

"I hadn't even noticed. I guess it's nice to have somebody want me."

"What is that supposed to mean?" Sherri asks, looking confused.

"Nothing, just thinking out loud. Well, you can get back to work. Call me if you need me."

"Sure thing."

"Oh, one minute, Sherri. A lady named Rhonda is supposed to come in around 2:00 P.M. Give her an application to fill out, then let me know she's here."

"Certainly. Anything else?"

"No, that's all for now."

Sherri shuts my office door and returns to the front desk. I shouldn't even hire Rhonda after that shit she pulled last week. Good thing I love Jamyya like a sister. I'm only doing this for her. If Rhonda messes up just one time, I'm firing her trifling ass!

I pick up the phone to call my girl; maybe we can have lunch together. "Hey, Skye, what time are you going to lunch?" I ask.

"Why?"

"I thought maybe we could meet somewhere and have lunch together. We haven't spent much time together lately."

"Okay. Where do you want to meet?"

"How about Olive Garden?"

"What time?"

"I don't know. I have an interview at 2:00 P.M. Maybe around noon."

"That's good. You're right, we need to talk. I'll see you there."

"I love you, Skye."

"I love you too. I gotta go. Talk to you soon."

Wow! I can't believe she agreed to lunch so easily! Maybe the guys were right. Dontaé told me to give Skye space, stop calling and following her, then maybe she will miss me and want to spend time together. Looks like his plan might work. I quickly turn my attention back to work. The day whisks by; it's a quarter till twelve already. I shut down my computer and exit my office.

"All right, ladies, I'm off to lunch. I should be back around 1:30. If you have any problems, Michael will be in at noon. See you later."

"Bye Omar, have a nice lunch," Sherri says.

When I arrive at Olive Garden Skye isn't there, so I ask the hostess for a table for two. As I sit at the table waiting for her to arrive, I contemplate what to say. My thoughts are interrupted by a sweet, gentle voice.

"Hey, baby, sorry I'm late."

"No problem, I haven't been here long." The waitress comes over and takes our orders.

"Let me cut right to the chase. Are you cheating on me?"

"No, I would never do something like that. I can understand why you would ask, but I only desire you. You've been telling me to back off, to give you space, so that's what I'm trying to do. Skye, I love you, and I want our relationship to work."

"Me too. I didn't want to believe that you would cheat on me, but your behavior lately has gotten me suspicious. I'm glad you've decided to back off. I appreciate the space."

"You're welcome. By the way, congratulations on your promotion. I'm very proud of you. Maybe we can celebrate this weekend. My mom can probably keep Omari."

"Sounds good. How about Friday night? Me and the girls planned on celebrating Jamyya's job on Saturday night."

"That's fine, 'cause I get off at six."

"Good. It's a date. Sorry to rush off, but I got a meeting in a half hour. See you when I get home."

"Okay, have a good day."

"Thanks baby." Skye kisses me and rushes off. I pay the bill and head back to work.

***

"Did you have any problems while I was gone?" I ask as I walk in.

"No, everything is fine," Yolanda replies.

"Where is Sherri?"

"She went to lunch. I'm going to go when she comes back."

"Okay, buzz me if you need help."

"Omar, what's got you in such a good mood?"

"I just had lunch with my girlfriend. She always brightens up my day."

"That's really nice. I'm glad you're happy."

"Yeah, me too. I'll be in my office if you need me."

"Okay."

I go in my office and start processing the payroll. Hmm…I still need to do performance reviews before the end of the month.

Knock, knock. "Come in!" I yell.

"Omar, Rhonda Carter is here to see you," Sherri says.

"Okay, send her in. Did she fill out an application?"

"Yes, she did."

I stand up to shake Rhonda's hand. "Hello, Ms. Carter. Please have a seat." She hands me her application.

"Omar, I would just like to thank you for this opportunity to prove myself. I'm sorry about the things I said to your mother. I was drunk and out of control. It won't happen again."

"I hope not. I'm giving you one chance, Rhonda, just one. If you mess up one time, you're fired. Do you understand?"

"Yes, I do. I promise I won't let you down."

"All right, this is what the job entails. I need housekeepers to work from 8:00 A.M. until 2:00 P.M. Now, your days off will rotate, 'cause everyone here works weekends, including me. Basically, what you will do is clean the rooms, change sheets, towels and so forth, then vacuum, dust, and clean bathrooms. We have gloves for you to wear, and cleaning supplies. We'll supply you with a uniform, but you need to buy your own all-black shoes. The pay is $8.00 an hour with benefits. Do you have any questions?"

"Yes, when can I start, and will someone train me?"

"Good questions. Yes, someone will train you for three days. That's usually as long as it takes. You can start tomorrow if you want. We get paid every two weeks on Fridays."

"Okay, I want to start tomorrow."

"Okay. Come in at 11:00 A.M. until 4:00 P.M. I don't come in until 11:00 tomorrow, and I need to do your paperwork. Bring your Social Security card and ID."

"I have them with me. Can we fill out the paperwork now?"

"Yeah, I suppose we could."

Her enthusiasm about the job surprises me, but I'm glad she's ready to work. Before picking up Omari from daycare, I decide to buy Skye some flowers. I go inside a small boutique called Xpressions. They have all types of gift baskets, candles, flowers, and gifts. I find a candy bouquet and a card. Yeah, this is perfect! It looks like a flower arrangement, except it's made with candy, how interesting. Skye's going to love this. I hurry home to make dinner.

When Skye walks in, she smells my famous grilled salmon cooking.

"What's the special occasion?" she asks.

"Nothing, just wanted to show you how much I love you." I hand her the Hallmark card and candy bouquet.

"Aw, thanks sweetie, this is beautiful! Where's Omari?"

"She's in the living room watching her Dora DVD."

Skye goes into the living room. "Hey, how is mommy's baby?"

"Shh. I watch TV," Omari says with her pointer finger on her lips.

"Well, excuse me! I guess I'll just go upstairs."

While I'm cooking, the phone rings.

"I'll get it, Omar."

"A'ight."

"Honey, it's for you. Do you want me to tell Devin to call you back?" Skye yells from upstairs.

"No, I'll talk to him."

"Okay."

I pick up the cordless phone. "What's up?"

"Everything. I need some advice," Devin says.

"About what, the baby?"

"Yeah, I'm not ready for this. I just turned eighteen. I wanted to go to Morgan State. How can I do that with a baby?"

"What do you want to major in?"

"Computer Graphic Design."

"Okay, well you know ECPI or ITT Tech has those classes. Plus you'll finish a lot faster if you go to a technical school. You can go full-time and still work a couple of hours a day. You know me and mom will help you."

"Yeah. I hadn't thought of that. That's a good idea."

"Yep. That's what brothers are for."

"I just hope I can be as good of a dad as you."

"I raised you. I'm sure you'll do fine. If you need some advice, you know who to call. I hate to cut you short, but I'm in the middle of cooking dinner," I say while taking the pan out of the oven.

"Good looking out, bro, talk to you later."

I continue cooking the vegetables and setting the table. I notice Skye's purse sitting on the table. I look inside to check her vitamin bottle. Mm-hmm, just as I thought, she's still taking the pills. When I found out Skye had hidden her birth control pills in a vitamin bottle, I decided to switch them with fertility pills. My boy Tyrone works as a pharmacist at CVS, so he hooked me up with a bottle. Since she's still taking the pills, she must have not noticed the difference.

"Honey, the food is ready," I yell.

"Okay, I'll be right down."

Skye comes in the dining room wearing a black and hot pink Baby Phat tank top with matching boy shorts.

"Damn, you look good! I guess I'm getting lucky tonight."

"You might, but don't say that in front of Omari."

"Oh, my bad. Daddy's sorry, honey. Don't say that, okay, it was a bad word."

Omari looks up at me with those beautiful hazel eyes. "Okay. Eat, eat Daddy."

"I think she's ready to eat." Skye says, placing Omari in her booster seat.

"Voila, the food is now being served." I hand Omari her plate first.

"Thank you, Daddy," Omari's little baby voice says.

Our dinner is interrupted by the phone. I get up to answer it. "Hello."

"Hey, baby, what you doing?" Shakita asks loudly.

"Nuttin Ma, eating dinner. What's up?"

"I was just calling to invite you to your sister's engagement party next Saturday at 4:00 P.M."

"Who's getting married?"

"Kenya and Keith. Oh, by the way, can we have the party at your house? You know mine is too small for everybody. Damon and Tyquan are coming down for it."

"Yeah, Mom. Y'all can use my house. Do I need to reserve any rooms for the guests?"

"Just three rooms, one for Damon, one for Tyquan, and one for your Aunt Markita. Everybody else lives here."

"A'ight, Ma, when are they coming?"

"Next Friday afternoon. Just book the rooms for Friday through Monday checkout."

"Okay, Ma. Can you keep Omari this weekend? Me and Skye want to go out to celebrate her promotion."

"Yeah, baby, just bring her over Friday around 7:00. I'll be here playing Grandma's Daycare."

"Thanks a lot, Ma."

"You're welcome; now go finish your dinner. Tell Skye I said hey and kiss my lil grandbaby."

"I will. Bye."

I hurry up and hung the phone up. Damn, my mom sure could talk a nigga's head off! After dinner, I give Omari a bath, then read her a bedtime story. Skye comes in to kiss her good night and tucks her in.

Now it's time for the grown-ups to play. I hop in the shower. The water is steaming hot, just like I like it. When I come out of the bathroom, I'm wearing only a towel. I snatch the towel from my damp body and begin to dance naked for Skye. My big, thick, long chocolate dick slaps against my thighs as I gyrate my hips.

"Boy, you are a damn fool. Come over here and give me some special attention."

I walk over to the bed, and my strong hands quickly pull off her boy shorts and tank top. She's wearing nothing underneath. I start at her neck, planting soft, wet kisses all the way down to her navel. My hands grab her firm, perky breasts as my tongue twirls around her clit. She lets out a soft moan. That's my signal to keep going. I bury my tongue inside her warm walls. I suck and lick like a baby nursing a bottle.

"Mmm. Omar, that feels so good."

"You like it, baby?"

"Yeah, I love it!" she screams while holding my head in place. After thirty minutes of licking her pussy, she came all over my face.

Now it's time for the real party to start. I climb on top of her and insert my nine-inch throbbing penis inside her slippery pussy. I start off with slow, deep strokes, then my pace begins to quicken as Skye forcefully pumps back. The rhythmical motion is causing the headboard to bang up against the wall. "Don't stop, don't stop!" Skye screams as she digs her nails into my back.

"Whose pussy is it?"

"Omar!"

"Say it again."

"Omar!"

We switch positions. Now she's in control. She climbs on top of me, kissing my lips passionately. She grabs hold of my dick and places it inside of her. She winds her hips like she's dancing to a reggae song, but no music is playing. Her movements become faster and faster. She leans her head back and I yank her by the hair. Her body begins to shake as if she's having tremors. Seconds later I explode, leaving all of my little soldiers inside of her.

"Damn, baby, that was some good shit," I say, exhausted.

"Mm-hmm. It sure was."

"We should do this more often."

"You're right. I'll start making more time for you."

She rolls over and looks into my eyes. "Baby I really do love you, it's just sometimes you smother me. I can't deal with the constant following. It makes me think you don't trust me."

"I do trust you. I just don't want to lose you to another man."

"Don't worry, baby, I'm not going nowhere." She lays her head on my chest to listen to my heartbeat.

Mmm…just like old times. I've never felt closer to her. I'm going to sleep good tonight.

"Goodnight, honey. I love you," I whisper as my hand strokes her hair.

"I love you too."

Wow! What a perfect night.

"Omar, wake up. What time do you go to work today?" Skye asks, nudging me in the arm.

"At eleven. Why? What time is it?"

"Oh, it's only seven-thirty. I'ma take Omari to daycare this morning, go ahead, sleep in. I probably won't see you til late tonight. You know I'm going out wit' the girls."

"Oh, yeah. I don't get off till eight. Do you mind picking Omari up from daycare, and then dropping her off at my mom's house at seven?"

"That's fine. I wasn't meeting them till 8:00 P.M. anyway. I guess I won't see you until I get back. Why don't you go out wit' your friends?"

"Yeah, I'll probably hang out wit' Dontaé and Keenan. We'll find something to do. Have a good day honey."

"You too," she says, leaving the room.

***

I sleep for another two hours. On my way to work, I call up Dontaé to see what's going on for tonight.

"Yo, D, what's up for tonight?"

"Same ole same ole, we probably going to John's Sports Bar and Grill. You know, get a couple drinks, shoot some pool, mack on some hoes. The usual."

"A'ight. I'ma roll wit y'all 'cause Skye is hanging out wit the girls tonight."

"Dog, meet us at my house around nine-thirty. We can all ride together. I think it's going to be me, you, and Keenan."

"Cool. See ya tonight. I gotta get to work."

"Gone"

Well, at least I got something to keep me busy so I won't follow Skye around.

I'm greeted by Michael, my assistant manager. "What's up Omar?"

"Nothing, just pay day."

"I know that's right."

"How's everything going? Is the new housekeeper, Rhonda, doing all right?"

"Yeah, she's cool, but I really like that new chick Yolanda. Her body is hot. Have you seen that booty? Mmm…girl makes me drool."

"Is that right?"

"Yep. Don't tell me you haven't noticed? I know you got a girl, but you still got eyes."

"Yeah, she's cute, and her body is very nice."

"Mm-hmm I know. You think she got a boyfriend?"

"No, last time I spoke wit' her she didn't. Maybe you could ask Sherri, they seem to be getting kind of tight."

"Good idea, O. I'ma go to lunch. Be back in an hour."

"A'ight."

I chat with Roger, one of my front desk clerks, for a couple of minutes, then go to check the banquet rooms. It's time for my monthly inspection of the whole hotel. On my way back to my office, I spot a redbone young lady with a long, sandy-brown wrap. Her body is shaped like an hourglass. She has on a pair of tight Dollhouse jeans with a black and gold long sleeve shirt, and gold pumps. Her ass is so round and firm. Damn, somebody sure is lucky! She turns around as I get closer. Oh, shit, it's Yolanda! I guess Michael was right, but I never noticed all that before. This was only my second time seeing her in street clothes. Mmm…looks like she's lost some weight.

"Hey, Yolanda, what are you doing here on your day off?" I play dumb as if I didn't know she came to pick up her check.

"I came to get my check."

"Well, do you always dress this nice to pick up money or do you have plans for the day?" I ask as I walk to my office with her following

"No, I don't have plans until tonight. I just threw this on to run some errands."

"You look nice. Have you lost some weight?"

"Thank you. Yes I have, I'm surprised you noticed. You don't seem to pay too much attention to me."

"I'm your boss, I notice a lot, I just might not mention it. Like the fact that you're doing an excellent job. I appreciate you coming in on your day off last week."

"No, problem. Glad I could help." I hand Yolanda her paycheck.

"Don't get too skinny on me. Men like a woman with some thickness."

She blushes. "Oh, I'm not trying to lose anymore. I like my size six. I'm happy now. See you tomorrow."

"A'ight, don't hurt nobody."

She laughs. "I'll try not to."

Damn, that goes to show what clothes will do for you!

"I think I like your real hair better. You should keep it that way. It looks nice."

"Oh, so you like your woman real?"

"Sure do. There's nothing fake about me, so I like my woman the same way."

"Guess I shouldn't wear these green contacts anymore, huh?"

"Nope, I'd like to see your real eyes."

I can't believe it. She takes the contacts right out and throws them in the trash.

"How about that?" she asks.

"Beautiful, your brown eyes are perfect."

"Thank you, Omar. I gotta get going."

"Bye."

What in the hell am I just thinking? Oh well, she gives me compliments all the time. It's purely innocent. I rush home so I can take a shower and change clothes. I hate being late for anything. Skye, on the other hand, doesn't care one way or the other. It's eight-fifteen when I pull up in my driveway. Skye's already gone. I call her just to make sure everything went okay.

"Hello," Skye answers.

"Hey baby, how was your day?"

"Good."

"Did you drop Omari off already?"

"Yes, baby, I'm on my way to Jazz's house."

"A'ight, I'm going to John's Sports Bar over Southside wit' Dontaé and Keenan. I'll be home around one."

"Okay, sweetie, have fun."

"I will. Be careful out there. I know how men look at beautiful women. And I can imagine what you're wearing."

"I'm fully dressed, but fashionable of course. It's getting too cold outside to wear hoochie gear anyway."

"Good. I'll see you when you get home."

"Bye, honey."

I look in the full length mirror; my gear is tight. I decide to wear my burnt orange and brown True Religion shirt, 'cause it's long-sleeved but lightweight. My dark denim True Religion jeans with my wheat Timberland boots match perfectly. Mm...but my hair looks terrible. I am in desperate need of some new cornrows. I grab my brown hat, and I'm ready. Sometimes I wish Skye could braid hair. I haven't had time to go to the shop. Maybe I can catch up with my sister Tamara so she can hook me up.

When I get to Dontaé's house, I see Tyrone's car parked out front. What a pleasant surprise. I haven't seen him since his party. Tyrone got a new girlfriend named Star. He has been so busy with her, I haven't seen him much. I knock on the door.

"Hey, O, what's up my nigga?" Tyrone asks, giving me a pound.

"Nuttin', surprised to see you here. I thought you might be chilling with your girl. When I spoke to D earlier, he didn't mention you were coming."

"Yeah. It was kind of last minute. Star had to work tonight, so I figured I would hang wit' the boys."

Dontaé walks in the room. "Keenan just called, he's going to meet us there. So we can leave now, if y'all finished wit' the reunion."

"Ha ha, very funny mister comedian!" I say. "You're a smart ass just like your sister."

"Yeah, Mimi told me how y'all be beefing and shit. Don't pay her no mind. You know how women are."

"Actually, I don't. Skye is so sometimey. One minute she wants me around her, then the next she needs space. I don't get it."

"Well, you're not the only one. Women are a different species altogether. We don't think nothing alike. Whatever you think she wants, just do the opposite. That usually works for me," Tyrone suggests.

Keenan is already at John's Sports Bar when we get there.

"Hey, cuz, how long have you been waiting?" Dontaé asks.

"About five minutes. How did y'all get Omar to let go of Skye's titties long enough for him to come out?"

"Oh, everybody wanna be Chris Rock tonight. Your ass ain't funny. You know Skye and Jamyya went out to celebrate her promotion."

"Jamyya ain't going out tonight. She was still in the house lying in the bed when I left," Keenan says.

"Stop joking!"

"I'm not playing. The kids are there and everything. Plus Jamesha is at work, and who the hell knows where Rhonda is."

"Why should Skye lie to me?"

"Maybe she went out with everybody else. She might've just assumed Jamyya was coming," Dontaé states.

"Yeah, I guess you're right. She did say she was going to Jazz's house when I talked to her earlier."

"That explains it then," Tyrone adds.

We play a couple games of pool and order some drinks.

"Man, I can't get drunk like I did at Tyrone's party. I went home wit' a hickey on my neck and a condom wrapper in my pocket. And I still don't know how I got either one."

"Well, the hickey came from that fine ass stripper you let suck on your neck," Dontaé says.

"Well, I won't let that happen again! Can you explain the condom wrapper?"

"That, my friend, is a mystery. I don't remember seeing you fucking nobody or going in the bedroom, but then again I was drunk too." We all laugh.

I go to the bathroom to call Skye, but I don't tell the fellas that.

"Hello?" Skye huffs.

"Hey baby, where are you?"

"Why you wanna know? Aren't you out wit' your friends?"

"Yeah, I am, but Keenan is here wit' me, and he said Jamyya's in the house asleep. I thought y'all were celebrating her job?"

"Oh, yeah, we were, but she couldn't find a babysitter, so we came without her. It's just me, Jazz, and Coco. Mimi had a date with Jerell."

"Oh, all right. Have fun. I won't call you no more."

"Okay baby, see you later."

When I come back to the table, everybody is whispering to one another.

"What's going on?"

Dontaé looks at me. "Man, some fine ass broads just walked in. It's three of them too. But that redbone one right there really caught my eye with that plump ass. Damn, make a nigga wanna reach out and touch somebody!"

"Man, your ass is crazy," I say, sitting down.

"I like the chocolate sister to her right," Tyrone says, staring hard at the women.

There's something vaguely familiar about this one woman. When she walks over to the bar, I see her face. Oh, shit it's Yolanda! Funny seeing her here. She changed her outfit, but her hair's the same. Now she's wearing a pair of tight red pants with BeBe on the back pocket. The red, white, and black striped v-neck shirt shows off her cleavage. I can recognize a pair of

Prada pumps anywhere, and that's what kind of shoes she is wearing. Damn, she does look good.

"Shit, the girl even got Omar speechless," Dontaé says, laughing.

"No, dog, I know her. She is one of my employees."

"Call her over here so we can meet her friends. What's her name?"

"Yolanda, and I'm not calling her over here."

"I knew you would say that. So I'll do it myself."

Dontaé begins to yell. "Hey, Yolanda! Over here!"

"Damn, you get on my nerves!" I slap Dontaé upside the back of his head.

Yolanda spots me, then sashays her way over to my table.

"Hey, Omar. Funny seeing you here. How's it going?"

"Fine, yeah, small world I guess. Let me introduce you to my friends. This is Dontaé, Keenan, and Tyrone. Everybody, this is Yolanda."

"Nice to meet you," Dontaé and Keenan say.

"I know you; you're one of Star's friends." Tyrone looks her up and down.

"Yeah, Star is my best friend. You must be THE Tyrone, the one who's stealing all her time."

"Yeah, that's me. Who you got wit' you?"

"My girls, Charmese and Diamond. Star had to work, so she couldn't come."

"Yeah, I know."

"Well, it was nice meeting y'all. Omar, I guess I'll see you at work tomorrow."

"Sure thing. You look nice. Enjoy your night."

"Thank you. You do the same."

Yolanda goes back over to her table.

I walk over to the pool table to shoot another game. As I'm setting up the table, Yolanda walks over.

"Can I play a game of pool wit' you?" she asks seductively.

"Umm...sure. Do you know how to play?"

"A little bit. Maybe you could teach me."

"All right. I'll try."

I go over and grab her hand. "You got to hold the stick like this between your fingers."

"Oh, okay."

I move behind her, but not too close, to help her guide the stick to hit the ball in the corner pocket. I have a really good time. Yolanda is a cool person to hang out with. We pay our tab and are about to leave.

"I had fun, Yolanda; you're a really cool chick. See ya later," I say, smiling.

"Thanks for the lesson. Maybe next time I'll beat you."

"You are on."

When we get in the car, everybody has something to say. "I can't believe you out flirting with your employees, even if she does look good. Skye is going to kill you," Keenan snaps.

"No, she's not. It was completely innocent," I reply.

"Yeah. Leave the man alone. Let him have a little fun," Tyrone defends.

"Look, but don't touch. Ain't that right, O?" Dontaé says, giving me pound.

"Yep. That's right," I nod my head.

"Whatever," Keenan says dryly.

"He's just mad 'cause he is the only one married wit' four kids. His playing days are over with a capital 'O'," Tyrone teases.

"For your info, I'm happily married, and I love all my kids." Keenan's getting defensive.

I step in, "Leave the man alone. He has a beautiful wife and family. I would be married, too, if Skye would stop turning me down."

"Thanks for having my back, Omar. These dogs will calm down one day - I hope."

"Yeah, one day," Dontaé says sarcastically.

It's about twelve-thirty when everybody decides to leave. When I get home, Skye still isn't back.

I call her cell phone. "Hey, baby, when are you coming home?"

"Oh, I'm on my way now. I just got to get my car from Jazz's house 'cause I rode wit' her."

"A'ight. I might be asleep when you get here 'cause I gotta go to work in the morning."

"Okay, goodnight."

I take off my clothes then climb into bed. The last thing I remember is my head hitting the pillow.

I am tired as hell the next morning. I pour me a cup of coffee and sit at my desk trying to collect my thoughts. Me and Skye are supposed to go out tonight. I wonder where I should take her? Hmm, I got it - I'll take her to Kabuto's for dinner, then we can catch a movie.

I want to leave work early so I can get my hair braided, 'cause it's fuzzy. Well, so much for leaving early! Three people call in sick, and the hotel is busy for some reason today. I also got a wedding reception going on in the banquet hall.

I bump into Yolanda. "Hey, how's it going?" she smiles.

"Everything is fine. It's been busy today, makes the time go by."

"Yeah I know, of all days, it would be busy today. I wanted to leave early," I say, frustrated.

"You got something important to do?"

"Not really important, I need my hair cornrowed. Skye and I are going out tonight, and I want to look nice. Plus, I need to wash it, it's really dirty. By the time I leave here, all the shops will be closed. I should just get a haircut."

"No, don't do that. I like your cornrows. I can braid it for you. I'm not doing anything when I get off work. I don't mind. You can come to my apartment; I live about five minutes down the street."

"Are you sure it won't be too much? You probably will be tired when you get off."

"I'll be fine. Besides, I'm off tomorrow, I can relax all day."

"A'ight. Do you mind if I wash my hair at your house?"

"No. It's fine. I got a blow dryer, grease, and a comb."

"Okay. I'll just follow you home then."

"Fine with me."

***

I don't leave work until six o'clock, an hour later than scheduled. Yolanda left at five, but she gave me directions to her house. I make a quick stop at Burger King 'cause I'm hungry, then proceed to her house. Yolanda opens the door wearing a white T-shirt, gray sweatpants, and black fluffy slippers.

"Hey, Omar come on in."

She leads me into her small, neatly-kept living room. Her taste in furniture is nice. The couch, love seat, and chair are peach with speckles of cream mixed in. The material as soft, like suede. Her carpet's thick and fluffy and also cream.

"Do you mind if I eat first? I'm starving," I ask, taking a sip of my soda.

"No, go right ahead. I'ma go get you some towels and shampoo."

She has the TV on watching *Paid in Full*. Oh, shit that's my favorite movie!

"Is this on TV, or are you watching a DVD?" I yell.

"It's a DVD. You can watch something else if you want. I don't mind."

"No, this is fine. Matter of fact it's my favorite movie."

"Get out of here! Mine too." She comes back in the living room and starts taking my cornrows out.

"I thought you could use some help."

"Thank you," I reply.

I go into her bathroom and wash my hair. Her shampoo smells good. I look at the bottle - it's Pantene Pro-V for women of color.

Yolanda greases my scalp and blow dries my hair. Skye never would do my hair. She barely combs Omari's. When Yolanda is finished, I get up to look at my hair in the mirror. Damn! My shit look good. She braided just like the Africans.

"Thanks, girl. This looks really good. How much do I owe you?" I ask, reaching into my pocket for some money.

"Boy, I'm not going to charge you! I volunteered my services. Put your money back."

"Do you do hair professionally on the side or something?"

"No, not any more. I used to, but I don't have the patience to do it all day, every day. I don't mind doing it every once in a while, you know, for my friends."

"Oh well, I thought I had found me a new stylist," I laugh.

"Whenever you need your hair braided, I'll be more than happy to do it for you. For free. You got good hair, so it doesn't take long anyway."

"I might have to take you up on the offer the next time I can't make it to the shop. I better be going. It's getting late. Thanks again. If you ever need a favor, don't hesitate to ask."

"I won't. Have a good time on your date."

"I will. See ya."

My cell phone starts vibrating as soon as I step outside. "Hello?" I answer, not recognizing the number.

"Hey bro, what's up? Did I catch you at a bad time?" Tyquan asks.

"No, you cool. I didn't recognize the number. What's going on wit' you? How's school?"

"I'm good. ODU is a good school wit' some fine sistas. I just got to tighten up though. I'm going to pledge."

"Really? That's cool, I'm proud of you."

"Thanks. I just called to check up on you. I heard Devin got a baby on the way and Kenya's getting married. So what's the news wit' you?"

"Same ole shit. I ain't getting married and no baby on the way. Just working and being Daddy. You don't have any babies coming, do you?"

"No, I make sure I stay strapped. I ain't got time for that. Shakita ain't going to beat my ass. I guess she told you to reserve me a room. I'm coming down Friday around 4:00 P.M."

"Yeah, I got you, bro. Damon coming too."

"Yeah, I know. He's bringing his girlfriend Latrice wit' him so everybody can meet her."

"A'ight. Well I'll catch you later. I'm about to take Skye out to dinner."

"Okay, see ya Friday. Kiss my niece for me."

"Will do. Holla."

I run into the house. "Hey, what's up, babe?"

"Nothing, just waiting for you." Skye's sitting on the couch flipping through a magazine.

"I'm sorry, honey. Three people called in sick so I had to stay an extra hour. Then I went to get my hair braided. See?" I say, pointing to my head.

"Yeah, it looks nice. Now hurry up and get dressed. I already ironed some clothes for you to wear."

"Thank you. It won't take me long."

Over dinner, I tell Skye about Kenya's engagement party and that it was going to be at our house. I wait for her to snap.

"That's fine. Should we hire a caterer?"

"No, honey, they have it all under control. She just needed a place to have it. If you prefer, I can reserve the banquet room at the hotel. I think it's still free."

"No, it's fine. She can use our house. You know I like your sister. I'm happy for her."

"Thanks, babe."

"You're welcome."

The rest of the night goes smoothly. We even have sex twice tonight. Mmm, mmm, mmm, it's off the chain, too! I scheduled myself off this weekend so I could hang out with my brothers and help my sister set up for her party. I planned an outing for us guys to go on Friday night when they got in.

Damon and Tyquan live in Norfolk, so I don't see them as much as I used to. I called Damon. "What's up, lil bro? How about hanging out wit' me, Tyquan, and Devin?"

"That's cool, but I don't want to leave Latrice in the room alone all night."

"Oh, yeah, I forgot about her. Maybe Skye can take her shopping or something. Hold on, let me ask her."

I go downstairs. "Hey, honey. Damon brought his girlfriend Latrice with him, and we want to go out, just us guys. Do you think you could hang out wit' her? Take her shopping or something."

"Yeah, Omar if she's not busted, she can roll wit' me. If she is ugly, I'll just bring her back here and we can watch movies or something," Skye says.

I kiss her. "Thanks, honey, but I doubt she's ugly."

I get back on the phone. "Yo, Damon, Skye said she'll chill wit' her."

"I'll be at your house in an hour."

"Cool, I'll tell everybody to meet here."

I call up Devin and Tyquan and tell them to meet here. We decide to go to Buffalo Wild Wings.

***

When Damon and Latrice walk in, I'm speechless. Latrice is what I would call "ghetto". She's about 5'7" with a long black wavy weave with blue highlights. Her chestnut skin is flawless, but she has an earring in her eyebrow and under her lip. Her teeth are pearly white, except for the two crowns she has on her two front teeth. Then there's her outfit - I know Skye will have a fit! Latrice has on a black spandex cat suit with a big silver belt around her waist and silver three inch pumps on her feet. Her ears are covered with different size hoop earrings. It looks like she has six holes in her ear. It's safe to say my brother found him a straight hood girl. She reaches to shake my hand, and that's when I notice her SWV nails. They are about four inches long and have a picture airbrushed on them.

"Nice to meet you, Omar. I've heard a lot about you. Good things, of course," Latrice says.

"Yes, it's nice to meet you too. Umm, well, we better get going. Don't want to be out too late. You girls have fun."

I snatch Damon and Tyquan. "Come on, y'all, we'll catch Devin outside."

"What you do that for?" Damon asks, dumbfounded.

"You know how picky Skye is. No offense, but your girlfriend is straight up ghetto."

"Yeah. She is a hood chick, but she's sweet, and the pussy is out of this world."

"Thanks for sharing," I say, disgusted.

"Hey, Devin, hurry up and hop in, we gotta go, I'm on a mission."

"Yeah, you know damn well Skye will be calling in a minute, 'cause her and Latrice got to fighting. Skye may be cute, but she's a beast," Tyquan says.

"She sure is. She thinks she's a miniature Laila Ali," I reply.

Hanging out with my brothers is fun. We haven't done this in a long time. I call Skye to see how things were going with her and Latrice.

"Honey, we're fine. Take your time coming back."

"Baby, are you all right?"

"No, she's a real cool person. Her blue hair is a bit much, but Coco will fix that for her."

"Don't tell me you're giving the girl a makeover?"

"Yeah, she can't meet your momma looking like this. Don't worry, she's in good hands."

"A'ight babe. See ya later."

I turn to Damon. "You will never believe this."

He looks scared. "What happened?"

"Skye is giving Latrice a makeover. She said her blue hair had to go. No telling what you will be coming home to."

"I trust Skye. She looks nice, I'm sure she'll do a good job."

"What in the hell is going on here? I feel like I'm in the twilight zone."

"Omar, what are you talking about?" Tyquan asks, confused about what's going on. I explain to them about the condom wrappers, the hickey, and Skye's sudden behavior change. Skye has been very nice lately - so unlike her.

"Maybe she realizes that she might lose you, so she decided to straighten up her act," Damon suggests.

"Maybe. Who knows with her? Her moods change from day to day."

"She might be bi-polar," Tyquan states.

"She ain't bipolar; she's just moody, that's all. Plus she's a spoiled brat," I reply.

"Yeah, definitely," Damon agrees.

Me and Damon have a couple of drinks. Tyquan is twenty and Devin is eighteen, so they have soda.

Damon says, "Tyquan can be our designated driver." Damon is twenty-four and a high school football coach in Norfolk. He really wanted to play pro ball, but it didn't happen, so coaching is the next best thing for him.

When we get back to my house Skye and Latrice are sitting in the living room chilling and watching TV. Latrice gets up and runs over to Damon

"Look! Baby do you like it?"

"Yeah, it looks real nice."

Latrice's black and blue wavy weave was replaced with a softer black, more natural-looking weave that's cut in a long bob. There are burgundy highlights throughout, but not too drastic. Her six silver hoops were replaced with small diamond studs. Only one pair of hoops remained.

Of course, her cat suit had to go. Now she's wearing a pair of Baby Phat jeans, a burgundy Baby Phat shirt, and a pair of Baby Phat ankle boots.

"Yeah, you look really pretty," I say. "Well, I mean, you were cute before but this is a little more subtle."

"Thanks. I know what you meant," Latrice says, smiling.

Everyone leaves happy. "See y'all tomorrow," I shout.

Skye walks over and puts her arm around my waist. "I couldn't get her to lose the eyebrow and lip ring, but it's an improvement. I had to beg her to cut them nails down. Now she has a French manicure - so much better! Where does your brother get these girls from?"

"I don't know, but thanks for giving her a makeover. My mom would have laughed at the girl so hard."

"I know. I didn't want Shakita to act up on Kenya's day, 'cause it's no telling what Keith's family looks like."

"Ain't that the truth." We both laugh.

Today's the day of my sister's engagement party. Kenya, Tamara, and my mom come over at one o'clock to set up everything.

"Hey Kenya, do y'all need some help?" I offer.

"Yeah, you can hang up this banner and get the card table and folding chairs out of my trunk. Oh, Mom has some in her car too."

"A'ight. I'm really happy for you, Kenya."

"Thanks, Omar. Your turn will come soon enough."

"I hope so. By the way, where are you getting the food from?"

"Oh, I ordered food from Ukrop's, and the cake. Keith is going to pick it up. He should be here around three."

"Good. I thought you let Mom cook." We all start laughing.

"You ain't funny, boy. My cooking has gotten a lot better," Shakita says with her hand on her hip.

Keith finally arrives with the food and drinks. Everything is set up perfectly. The guests start to arrive exactly at four. I'm really excited to see my Aunt Markita. She is my mom's oldest sister. Her and my mom are really close, but she moved to Atlanta two years ago 'cause of her job. My nieces and nephews also came. Kenya's kids Kayla and O'Ryan are dancing and playing, making themselves the center of attention. Kayla is eight and O'Ryan is six. Tamara's son Kemonni is five. Omari is the youngest grand-child - well, until Devin and Jamesha have their baby.

The house is packed with people. Kenya invites her friends from work and Keith's family and friends came as well. Maybe I should have rented out the banquet room.

Kenya comes over to me. "I'm sorry Omar. I didn't think everybody would show up."

"It's okay, as long as they don't mess up my house."

Damon introduces my mom to Latrice. "Nice to meet you, Ms. Rhodes."

"Oh, baby, call me Shakita.I ain't that old; I'm not even fifty yet."

"I'm sorry. I'll call you Shakita."

"Thank you. So how did you meet my son? Do you have kids?"

"No, I don't have kids. I met Damon at a football game. I went to see my lil brother play. He's a senior in high school, he's the star quarterback."

"Oh, do you have a job?"

"Yeah, I work at a shoe store part-time, 'cause I'm still in college."

"What is your major?"

"Fashion Merchandising, this is my last year. When I graduate, I want to be a buyer for a major department store like Macy's or Nordstrom's."

"That's good, you have nice goals. Your hair is cute too. It suits your face well. You are a pretty girl. Why in the hell did you put them earrings in your face?"

"Umm, Mom, come over here, I would like you to meet some of Keith's family," Kenya says, dragging my mother to the other side of the room.

Devin invited Jamesha so he could introduce her to my grandparents, brothers, aunts and uncles. The party turns out well. Damon makes a toast to Kenya and Keith, then we eat the cake.

Kenya's engagement gets me thinking about me and Skye's relationship. My Aunt Markita came up to me. "So, Omar, when are you and Skye going to tie the knot?"

"I don't know. She keeps saying she's not ready."

"How long have you two been together?"

"Four-and-a-half years."

"Well, don't waste your whole life away waiting for her. She may never be ready. Just think of other options. There are a million girls out there who would love to marry a man like you."

"Thanks for the advice, Auntie."

"You're welcome, baby."

After all the guests leave, my mom, Kenya, Tyquan, and Keith stay to help clean up. While we're cleaning, I suddenly become depressed. I'm happy for my sister, but I want the same commitment. I decide to ask Skye to marry me again. I wrote her a poem awhile back, but never read it to her. I pull out the ring from the previous proposals, and I read her the poem, then I pop the question. "Skye, will you marry me?"

"I knew you were going to start with this shit again. Just because your sister is getting married, don't mean we need to. I'm just not ready, Omar. How many times do I need to tell you this? Just when everything was going good, you had to go and fuck it up. Goodnight. I'm going to sleep." She rolls over and pulls the covers over her head. Well, damn, you would have thought I asked her to have a ménage à trois or something outrageous! Same ole shit.

Chapter Nine
Coco

Since the fight, I haven't let André see Corey. About a week ago, I received a summons on my door for me to appear in court for visitation. The nerve of that bastard, thinking he's going to see my son! Hmm, not as long as he is still living with that bitch!

Of course, Alana called me yelling and screaming 'cause she received the same bullshit. I can't wait til we go to court, because I'm requesting sole custody with supervised visitation. I already hired me a lawyer, even though the court date isn't until December 19th.

I'm not mad at Jerome right now, but something is bound to happen that will make me upset with him. Shameka will make sure of that.

Well, today is Wednesday, one of the least busiest days at the shop. Jazz calls me for an emergency appointment, and since my chair is free, I tell her to come on.

"Hey Jazz, how have you been? I haven't seen much of you lately." I wrap the towel around her neck then put the black cape on her.

"I'm great. I've just been spending all my time with Shawn. He's such a good boyfriend. I finally introduced him to Joy and Mario. They both like him."

"That's good, but you still need to hang out wit' the girls sometimes. How are you getting your hair?"

"Just some twists in a bun. Nothing too fancy. I can't keep curls in my hair because Shawn is a sexaholic. He's like the Energizer bunny. He keeps going and going."

"Girl, you are crazy as hell!"

"Why didn't you go out with us to celebrate Jamyya's new job and Skye's promotion?"

"I didn't have a babysitter. You know I don't let Corey go over André's house no more."

"Oh, yeah, that's right. I'm looking for a new job so I can get my own place. I'm tired of living wit' Joy and Mario. They got too much drama for me. I need a bigger income."

Joy is Jazz's oldest sister; she's thirty. For some reason, she thinks she is Jazz's mom. Their parents died in a car accident when Jazz was ten years old. Mario is Joy's husband. They've been married for eight years, but they don't have any kids. Mario is sterile, for some unknown reason.

"What's going on wit' them two?" I ask.

"Same ole bullshit. Joy is still cheating on him, taking a whole lot of business trips, so she says. I don't know why he don't just leave her dumb ass."

I am not trying to touch that one, so I decide to change the subject.

"Oh. Where are you trying to get a job at?"

"Probably an elementary school. I want to be a teacher. You know I majored in Education."

"Yeah, I remember, but I thought you were a teacher at the daycare?"

"No, I'm an assistant teacher, but I don't make any money. I only get paid $11an hour."

"That ain't shit. You know what, maybe you should open up your own daycare? You know plenty of people who got kids, plus I know some people who need a job."

"That's a great idea, but I don't have any money to start a business. I don't even have my own place."

"You know, maybe Jerome could find you a big house for a good price, then you could start off with a home daycare, then branch off to a building. I'm sure if you do good in the house, you could get a small business loan. I would let you keep Corey and Christian, and I'm sure Skye and Jamyya would give you business too. Plus there are my niece and Omar's nieces and nephews."

"Well, check into it for me. Tell Jerome to give me a call if he can get me something that rents for $700, no more than $850."

"A'ight. I'll talk to him when I get home and let you know."

"Thanks Coco. How much should I charge?"

"Daycares are usually expensive. It depends on the ages. Probably sixty-five for two years and up and ninety-five for children under two"

"Yeah. I'ma do some research and come up with a business plan. In the meantime, I'll be saving up some money. I can check the rates at the daycare I work for."

"If you want to, I could use some help on Saturdays. You could be my shampoo girl. I usually pay $3 per wash, and $5 for washing perms and color. I'll pay you cash, tax-free money."

"Oh yeah, that would be great. Can I start this Saturday?"

"Sure, come at nine o'clock."

I twirl Jazz around to see her hair. "This looks so good! Thanks, girl." She hands me twenty dollars.

"See ya Saturday."

"A'ight, chick," I say, waving bye.

I close up the shop at five, then stop by the Chinese restaurant to pick up some take out. Tonight, I'm not in the mood for cooking.

As soon as I walk through the door, Christian comes and hugs me.

"Hi, Mommy."

"Hey, sweetie, how are you?"

"I fine."

"Good, let go of Mommy's leg so I can put the bags down."

"Okay."

Jerome walks in. "Hey, baby, guess you're not cooking tonight."

"No, I bought some Sweet and Sour Chicken, Shrimp Fried Rice, and Egg Rolls."

"Mmm, smells good! I'll set the table. Go get relaxed."

"Thanks, honey. Where is Corey?"

"In his room playing video games."

On my way to my bedroom, I peep inside Corey's room. "Hey honey, go get washed up for dinner."

"A'ight, Mom, guess what?"

"What?"

"I got an 'A' on my science project!"

"Very good! I'm proud of you."

I go into my room and change my clothes. I throw on my pajama pants and a T-shirt. Then I slip my aching feet into my pink fluffy slippers.

"Come on, honey, the food is going to get cold!" Jerome yells.

"I'm coming, boo."

While we eat dinner, I decide to talk to Jerome about finding Jazz a house. "Honey, do you think you can help Jazz find a house? Like a rent to own for about $700, no more than $850?"

"First, I would have to pull her credit report. If her credit is good, and she has a nice down payment, I can probably find her something for eight hundred. How many bedrooms does she need?"

"I'm not sure. She's going to be living by herself, but she wants to run a daycare out of it."

"Really? Sounds good. Let me look into some stuff when I go to work tomorrow, and I'll let you know."

"Thanks, baby. Whenever she gets it started, I'ma let her keep Christian and Corey."

"Sounds good. I may have some cheap commercial properties she might be interested in too. How was your day?"

"It was slow. I had a couple appointments. I made a little dough."

"Well, I'm sure you're booked for this weekend."

"Yeah, I'm swamped."

"Guess who called me today and gave me some interesting information?"

"Who?"

"André. He told me how you and Alana beat down Tyesha. And how Tyesha pressed charges against y'all and you go to court tomorrow. Why didn't you tell me about this?"

"Because I didn't want to hear your mouth. I knew you wouldn't approve."

"Either way I was going to be mad, but even madder that I had to find out from somebody else."

"Don't act like you don't do shit with Shameka and hide it from me! You don't ever consult me when it comes to her or Jermeka."

"No, you're not going to turn this around on me! Shameka has nothing to do with you keeping secrets from me. Anyway, I got a lawyer, and he says I'll be fine. So be mad if you want, I'm going to bed. I got to get up early, but then again you already know that. One last thing: don't take Corey to André's house, and I mean what I say. Let me find out he has had contact wit' André! All hell is going to break loose. Goodnight."

"I'm sleeping in the guest room tonight."

"Do what you feel."

I go into my bedroom and slam the door. I try to go to sleep, but toss and turn for two hours until I quit trying. I turned on my flat screen TV. The cable box reads ten o'clock. Shit, it's still early. I picked up the phone and call Damisha.

"Mimi, are you busy?"

"No, just waiting for Jerell to call. What's up?"

"Nuttin'. I had a fight wit Jerome now I can't sleep."

"Again? What y'all fighting about this time?"

"Well, you know I gotta go to court tomorrow for assaulting Tyesha. Jerome didn't know about it until André told him tonight. Now he's pissed at me 'cause he thinks I'm keeping secrets."

"Damn, André did that shit on purpose just to start drama."

"Yeah, I know. So what's going on wit' you and your two men? Are you still seeing Chris too?"

"Mm-hmm. I like both of them, it's hard to choose. Jerell is real cool to hang out wit', and the sex is off the chain, but he's a straight hoe. Chris is very sweet, but he won't have sex wit' me, plus he has to spend time with his son. I just wish Jerell had more time for me. Sometimes I think I want to settle down, but Chris seems too good for me, and Jerell isn't interested in a relationship."

"Nonsense. Chris is not too good for you. Maybe he is just the thing you need to calm you down. You just want a bad boy. That's why you are so into Jerell, and I'm sure the bomb ass sex has something to do wit' it too. You just like the chase. You want Jerell 'cause you can't have him, but as soon as you get him, you ain't going to want him no more 'cause the chase will be over."

"You think that's what it is?"

"I know so. What time do you expect him to call?"

"I don't expect him to call at all, just hoping. If he do, it will probably be after midnight."

"A late night booty call, huh?"

"I guess you could call it that."

"Call it what you want, but that's exactly what it is. Don't put too much energy into Jerell 'cause he might be the one to turn the tables on you and break your heart. You know how hard you are on the guys - love 'em and leave 'em. Payback's a bitch"

"Thanks for the advice, Coco. Are you going to be okay with court tomorrow? Do you need me to go wit' you?"

"No, girl, I'm cool. I'll call you if they lock me up, but I doubt it. My lawyer seems confident that I'll get off."

"Hold on a minute, I got a beep."

Mimi clicked over. "Girl, that's Jerell, call me when you come from court and make me an appointment for two o'clock Saturday."

"A'ight, I gotcha."

Time to get some sleep. I turn off the TV and lie down.

***

Tyesha shows up for court looking a hot shitty mess. Her size 24 frame is stuffed in a too-small pair of black slacks. She wears a black-and-white striped button-up shirt with some black turned-over shoes. I would say she's about 5'6", 306 pounds with a medium-brown complexion full of acne. She needs to let me do her nappy ass hair that she tried to brush into a short ponytail.

Mmm, mmm, mmm, what in the hell do André see in her? Her ass is as flat as a pancake, and her stomach rolls over her pants three times. Yuck! That's not all. Her teeth are yellow with spaces in between each one, and her dark brown eyes look like they are going to pop out of her head.

I walk past her and whisper, "Tacky bitch." She just looks at me and smiles, showing those dirty-ass teeth.

My lawyer and Alana walk in at the same time. He quickly briefs us, then the trial begins. The judge calls Tyesha to the stand first. She tells her version of the story, then me and Alana tell ours. Actually, for the first time in court, I tell the whole truth. The judge gives both of us the same sentence. He drops the trespassing charge and sentences us to three months and anger management for the assault and battery charge. He suspends all three months, contingent upon completion of the anger management class.

Whew, that was close! Alana and I go out to lunch to celebrate. "Girl, where do you wanna go eat at?" I ask.

"How about O'Charley's? We haven't been there in a while."

"Good choice! My treat. Do you just wanna follow me there?"

"Yeah, it would make more sense for me to follow you instead of leaving my car here then coming back to get it."

"A'ight, but you better keep up, 'cause I'm hungry."

"Girl, I ain't getting no ticket fucking around with you!"

I get to O'Charley's first. I'm seated in the non-smoking section in a booth by the window. I call Skye, Jazz, and Mimi to tell them what happened in court. I leave a message on Mimi's voicemail, 'cause she was the only one that doesn't answer. I debate on whether or not I want to call Jerome. No, he can wait till I get home. He gets on my damn nerves anyway.

Alana finally shows up.

"What took you so long?"

"Girl, I had to stop by the bank and cash my check, then I called Jason to let him know I wasn't in jail."

Jason is Alana's boyfriend. He's Puerto Rican and fine as hell. The brotha even has a good job. He owns a construction company that builds commercial businesses. Jason got loot and no kids, which means no baby momma drama.

Damn, sometimes I wish I would've left Jerome alone when I found out Shameka was crazy! Too late now, I'm stuck wit' him. "I told you I was paying. You so damn hardheaded," I scold.

"That's fine, but I still needed to cash my check. I got bills to pay."

"Oh. Is Brianna's hair growing back yet?"

"I think so, I let this girl at work cornrow it, and she got beads on the end. Brianna loves it, so at least she's happy."

"That's good. I'ma let Corey's grow back out, and I dare somebody to cut it again. Do you know Jerome had the nerve to talk to André? He pissed me off so bad last night. He always takes everybody else's side, and I'm supposed to be his wife."

"That's fucked up. What did André have to say to him?"

"He called to tell Jerome how we beat up Tyesha and asked him to bring Corey over to his house while I was at work. I told Jerome if he takes him over there, it's going to be hell to pay."

"I know that's right!"

We order our food, eat, and leave. The food was good, but I'm getting tired of eating out. I think I'll cook dinner tonight for the kids. I stop by the grocery store before I go home. My brother calls me while I'm shopping, "Hey, Torey. What's up?"

"Just calling to make sure your ass isn't in jail. What happened?"

"I got three months with three months suspended, and I have to complete an anger management class."

"So you got off easy?"

"I guess you could say that. Oh, I got to pay her $2000 for her hospital bill and pain and suffering."

"Damn, two g's, that's a lot! You must've really fucked her up."

"Actually it's $4000, but Alana has to pay the other two grand. But yeah, we tore her ass up," I laugh.

"I see you still nice wit' dem hands. Look, I need a favor. Can you keep Takori for me tonight, please?"

"For how long?"

"Just for three hours. I want to take Chantel out on a surprise date. I can drop her off around five, and be back at eight, no later than nine o'clock."

"A'ight, bring her little bad ass on."

I buy some snacks and stuff to make dinner with. I think I'll make barbeque ribs, mashed potatoes, corn on the cob, and collard greens. I buy some Nestle chocolate chip cookie dough so me and the kids can bake them for dessert. Oops! I forgot the milk. I run back to the dairy section and bumped into Shameka, of all people.

Not today, please not today! I don't have time for this shit. She looks up at me "The word is excuse me. You need to watch where you're going."

"Oh, I got a few words for you, but I can't say them in public. Why don't you just do yourself a favor and kick rocks?"

"How about I just kick your ass?"

"Only in your dreams, boo. I would hate for Jermeka to visit her mom in intensive care. I'm not in the mood today." I push past her, grab a gallon of milk, and walked off. Good girl.

I have to pat myself on the back for that one, 'cause I wanted to punch her dead in the face. For some strange reason, Shameka decides to press her luck. She gets in line directly behind me on purpose. I hear her talking loudly on her cell phone. "Oh, hey Jerome, are you still getting Jermeka this weekend? Uh huh, okay...sounds good. I'll be waiting. Love you too."

No, this bitch didn't just go there! Now I know damn well Jerome didn't tell her that he loved her. I don't have time for the childish games, so I simply ignore her. I have only a few items, so I carry my own bags to the car. Just so happens that I pass Shameka's blue Nissan Sentra. Now what I did was mean, but she deserved it.

I take my car key and scratch up the whole passenger's side. Ah, I feel much better!

***

When Jerome gets home I had finished cooking, given the kids baths, and was setting the table.

"Hey, Coco. What happened in court? I guess they didn't lock you up."

"I got to pay her $2,000 and take an anger management class. He gave me three months, but he suspended all of them. I have to be good for two years."

"You need an anger management class. I hope you take it seriously. When do you have to pay her?"

"The judge gave me ninety days. I got some money in the bank; I'll pay it next month sometime."

"Well, I got some money if you need it."

"Thanks, but I got it covered. I cooked, why don't you get yourself together so we can eat dinner?"

"A'ight, it smells good too. I'll be there in a minute."

Me and Jerome talk and eat dinner like nothing happened last night. I decide to be the bigger person and apologize. "Honey, I'm sorry for not telling you about my charges. I shouldn't keep things from you, but can you please try not to act like my daddy? I need a husband, some support. You always take someone else's side instead of mine. Even if I'm wrong, you should at least try to see my point of view."

"If you can try to control your temper, then I can work on supporting you. Maybe we should go to marriage counseling. I think they can help us communicate better."

"Let's wait on that for a little while. I can only do one self-help class at a time. Once I finish anger management, we can look into it."

"Deal, don't forget you said it!"

"I won't."

***

Saturday is busy as hell in the shop. I'm glad I hired Jazz to help my other shampoo girl. Damisha comes in for her appointment, but I'm still finishing up Bonita's hair.

"Mimi, have a seat I, got one more person in front of you," I say while still curling Bonita's hair.

"A'ight. I'ma just sit and look at some magazines."

While waiting to get her hair washed, Mimi overhears two of Mikiya's clients talking. One girl's name is Keema and the other is Tonya. "Girl, Jerell gets on my damn nerves, he's always at work! He don't never spend time wit' me. We were supposed to go out last night, but he was so tired from working he fell asleep," Tonya complains.

"What you mean he fell asleep?" Keema inquires.

"I called him twice and he didn't answer, then the third time I called him he answered the phone sounding like death. My baby works too hard. I told him I'll just see him Sunday night."

"You know the boy gotta go to work so he can pay for that white Benz he got."

"Yeah, I know, but he needs to take a vacation, my pussy is going through withdrawal."

It didn't take a rocket scientist to figure out they were talking about Jerell Thompson. Yep, the one Mimi is so in love with. I look at Mimi to see what she will do.

"Excuse me. Do I know you from somewhere? You look very familiar," Mimi asks Tonya.

"Um, I don't know. Do you come here often?"

"Yeah, but it's not from here. Where do you work at?"

"I work at Applebee's, I'm a waitress there part-time, plus I go to VCU. Are you in college?"

"No, I graduated already. It was probably Applebee's. If you don't mind me asking, how long have you been going out wit' that guy you were talking about?"

"Oh, for a little over a month. Why? Do you think he's cheating?"

"It depends on what type of job he's working. What does he do?"

"He works at Coca Cola and cleans buildings at night."

"Oh, well if he has two jobs, I'm sure he's busy working, but he still has time to see other people."

"So you're saying you think he's seeing somebody else?"

"If his name is Jerell Thompson, light skin wit' gray eyes, then he's seeing a lot of other people, including me," Mimi smiles.

"So, you mess with Jerell too?"

"Yes ma'am, for about three months. I remember you were our waitress at Applebee's back in June. When did y'all hook up?"

"He comes to Applebee's all the time, and one day we started talking and I gave him my number. We've been kicking it ever since."

"Oh, well when I met Jerell, he told me that he had other friends, so I'm not surprised he's seeing you. He said he's not ready for a relationship. What did he tell you?"

"Nothing, I just assumed I was the only one, but I guess I was wrong."

"Do me a favor; don't mention our little conversation to Jerell. I would greatly appreciate it."

"No problem, I don't think we will be talking any more. I'm not in the mood to deal wit' this shit."

I call Mimi over to my chair. "Girl, I'm ready for you. How do you want your hair?"

"Just wash and roller set. Did you hear my conversation with that girl?"

"Mm-hmm, I sure did. So what are you going to do about it?"

"Nothing. What can I do? He already told me that he was seeing other people. I'ma wait and see if he lies to me about what he's doing on Sunday. He always tries to say I come first, so I'ma see about that."

"You're just as dense as that chick sitting right there. You know as soon as she leaves here, she's going to call Jerell and ask him about you."

"I don't care. That's on her. In a way, I want her to confront him, 'cause I wanna see how he's going to handle it."

"Go over there and let Jazz wash your hair. She's my new shampoo girl."

"Yeah, I heard, who keeping your kids today?"

"Jerome got both of them, but he's getting mad 'cause he got shit he wants to do. I told him to do it on Sunday when I'm off. I'll probably get my mom to keep Corey next Saturday."

"I'm thinking about going to the club tonight, you wanna come?"

"No, but I do want to go to the concert that's coming in October. The one wit' Keyshia Cole, Mary J. Blige, Alicia Keys, and J. Holiday."

"Oh yeah, let me know when you are going to buy the tickets, I'll go wit' you."

Mimi finally goes to get her hair washed. "Hey, Jazz. What are you doing tonight?"

"Me and Shawn are going out to the movies and stuff. Why?"

"'Cause I'm bored as hell. Jerell will probably be busy tonight, and Chris has his son this weekend. I wanted to go to the Hyperlink."

"Call Skye and Jamyya, they might wanna go. You know since Rhonda came home, Jamyya gets to go out more, and Skye never has a problem with somebody keeping Omari."

"Yeah, I'll call her later on to see what's popping."

I finish Mimi's hair then I go to Lee's Chicken to get something to eat.

"Anybody want something from Lee's Chicken? I'm leaving now." I take a couple of orders and leave.

Jerome calls me pitching a fit. "I'll be off by six o'clock, Jerome," I say very curtly.

"That's not why I called. André wants to see Corey. You already beat Tyesha's ass, so I doubt if she does anything to him. Why don't you just let him go over there?"

"'Cause I don't want to. He lost his visitation privilege when he let that bitch torture my son and cut his hair. It's no point of him going over there if André ain't going to be there with him."

"Well, I have things I want to do too. Don't get me wrong, I love Corey like my own son, but I'm tired of keeping three kids every weekend."

"Fine, when I get home, you can go wherever you want. I'll find somebody else to keep him next Saturday. If that's not good, enough pack him some toys and drop him off at the shop. I'll keep my own damn child," I respond with attitude.

"A'ight. I'll be there in thirty minutes."

"Mm-hmm." I hang up.

He gets on my damn nerves! Jerome just wants to be nasty; he got Christian and Jermeka, so I don't know where the hell he thinks he's going. I go back to the shop pissed off. I sit down and eat my food, trying to calm my nerves. Nothing seems to work.

"Anybody got a Newport?" I yell.

"Girl, I thought you stopped smoking," Tashema says, digging in her pocket for a pack of Newports.

"I'm trying, but today I just gotta have one."

She hands me two cigarettes.

"Looks like you need more than one. What's wrong?"

"Jerome getting on my damn nerves. You know the usual."

Before I can finish my statement, Jerome walks in with all the kids. He has Christian, Corey, and Jermeka.

"Hey, Mom," Corey says, waving at me.

"Hey baby, you can sit up front, watch TV, and play with your toys. Here is some money for the snack machine."

I give Corey three dollars, and Christian takes off running behind him.

"Hello to you too, Christian. You're not speaking to Mommy today?" I go behind him and pick him up.

"Hi Mommy, I want down. I go wit' Corey."

"A'ight, go with Corey."

Jermeka walks up to me. "Hi, Coco. Can you do my hair? It looks a mess."

It sure does. Now I have two options. One, be nasty and say no, or be nice and say yes. Saying no would piss Jerome and Shameka off, but doing her hair really cute would piss Shameka off even more and make Jerome feel bad.

"Yeah, baby, I'll do your hair, but I got to finish my clients first. Ask your dad if you can stay here with Corey and I'll do it later."

Jermeka looks at Jerome with puppy dog eyes. "Daddy, can I please stay here and get my hair done?"

"Yeah baby, just call Daddy when you are finished."

He looks at me smoking my cigarette. When Jermeka leaves to join her brothers, he shakes his head.

"I thought you quit smoking. You were doing so good. What happened?"

"Stress happened. I'll just bring Jermeka home with me, unless I finish her hair early and she wants to leave."

"A'ight. I'ma drop Christian off at Lisa's house. I'll be home later."

"Fine. I don't mind watching the kids. All the kids."

"I'm not going to argue with you. We can talk when I get home. Bye." He kisses me quickly then leaves.

After I put my clients under the dryer, I do Jermeka's hair. I wash it myself since she isn't a paying customer.

"How do you want your hair?" She looks at me with those big brown eyes.

"Twists in the front with curls in the back."

"Okay, sweetie." I twist her hair and sit her under the dryer. I look at the clock; it's five o'clock. Hopefully, I can be outta here by seven.

Tayanna yells, "Phone, Coco!"

I answer the phone. "Diva Style, Coco speaking."

"Hey, boo. I need to get my hair done Tuesday evening. You know I'm a working girl now," Jamyya says.

"I know. What time do you wanna come?"

"Around 5:30P.M.?"

"A'ight. So how do you like your job? Is Skye a cool boss?"

"Yeah, I really like it. I'm so glad to get out of the house and work! Now I've got my own money."

"Ain't nothing like having your own. How is your mom doing? I heard she got a job working for Omar's crazy ass."

"Actually, my mom has been great. She goes to work on time every day, helps me with the kids and house work. She hasn't acted like a fool since her party. Even her and Keenan are getting along a little better."

"Did he ever find out you went out that night?"

"No, but it was a close call. What's up with you for tonight?"

"Nothing, keeping the kids. I can't go nowhere, but Mimi wanted to go to club Hyperlink."

"For real? I'ma see if I can get out tonight. You should try too. I know your mom or somebody will keep the kids."

"Yeah, I could ask my mom. Let me call her, then I'll hit you back when I get off work. I got two more heads to curl before I can leave."

"A'ight. Let me know, I'ma call Skye to see if she wanna go."

"Okay, holla."

I curl my last customer's hair then do Jermeka's.

She looks so cute and happy. I'm glad she looks like her dad, 'cause Shameka ain't all that cute. I turn her to the mirror so she can see her hair.

"Ooh, thanks Coco, it's so cute! I like it a lot."

"You're welcome, sweetie. Come on, let's go."

I go to the front to get Corey, and he's asleep on the couch.

"Corey, wake up baby, let's go home."

I don't feel like cooking, but I'm hungry as hell. I call Jerome to see if he's home.

"Hello," Jerome's deep baritone voice answers.

"Hey, it's me. Did you and Christian eat yet?"

"I fed Christian, but I'm still hungry. Why?"

"'Cause we are on our way home and none of us has eaten. Can you call Pizza Hut and order a couple of pizzas with some buffalo wings?"

"Yeah, I'll call now. See you when you get here."

I'm tired as a dog. Even if I could get a babysitter, I don't know if I want to go out. My feet hurt like a runaway slave's. The pizza delivery truck is parked in front of the house when I pull up. Good, perfect timing. Everybody's hungry; we eat both large pizzas, Buffalo wings, and cinnamon sticks. I put a scarf on Jermeka's hair, and the kids go to bed.

"Thanks for doing Jermeka's hair. It looks really cute. I know you were mad at me. I appreciate you not taking it out on her," Jerome said.

"Yeah, like you did to Corey?"

"Why can't we just have a good night? One without confrontation."

"You're right, 'cause I'm too tired to argue with you. You don't have to thank me for doing her hair. I did it 'cause I wanted to."

I call Jamyya and tell her I'm too damn tired to party. I take a long hot shower, then crawled into bed. Jerome tries to make nice, so he massages my back. He probably thought he was going to get some pussy, but I fall right asleep. Oh well, better luck next time.

***

I wake up feeling refreshed. I can smell bacon and blueberry muffins. Jerome must be cooking breakfast. Thank you Jesus, 'cause I'm hungry! Jerome comes in carrying a tray of food with a glass of orange juice.

"Good morning, sweetheart, I made you some breakfast. Eat up."

I smile. "Thank you, baby. That was very thoughtful of you."

See, today is going to be a good day. Even though me and Jerome have problems, we normally work through them. I love him so much, even when he gets on my nerves.

"Honey, let's take the kids to Chuck E. Cheese's today," I say excitedly.

"You can take them. I had plans to go to the gym. What time were you planning on going?"

"I don't know, maybe around two o'clock. Go ahead with your plans. I'll call Skye and Jamyya, maybe they will want to go take their kids too."

"Good idea. Just be back by five so I can take Jermeka home."

"Okay."

I haven't seen Alana lately, so I call her first.

"Hey, Alana, what are you doing today?"

"Nuttin', just chilling. I will probably wash some clothes, do a little cleaning, and cook dinner. Why? Do you have something in mind?"

"Yeah, I'm going to Chuck E. Cheese's at two o'clock. Do you want to bring Brianna and chill with me?"

"Yeah, she would like that. She misses her brother. Just call me when you're on your way. I'll meet you up there."

"A'ight. I'ma call Skye and Jamyya. They might come too."

"That's what's up! See y'all later."

I call Jamyya, then Skye. They both said they would come. Good, a girls' day out with the kids! I hope I got some coupons. I went to go tell the kids the good news.

"Hey y'all we are going to Chuck E. Cheese's today. Here is what I need you to do: clean your rooms, take a bath, brush your teeth, and put your clothes on. I'll pick your clothes out and iron them. Any questions?"

"What time are we going?" Corey asks.

"At two o'clock, so you need to get busy."

"Coco, can I go too?" Jermeka asks.

"Yes baby, everybody is going except your dad." I smile at her then go into my room.

"Jerome, can you help me get the kids ready before you leave?"

"Yeah, baby. What do you need me to do?"

"Iron the kids' clothes while I give Christian a bath"

"Sure."

Since I'm going to be dealing with kids today, I decide to wear my pink-and-gray Roca Wear sweatsuit with my new pink-and-gray Nikes. When I get on the highway, I called Alana so she can meet us there. Alana lives about ten minutes down the street from Chuck E. Cheese's. She has a nice 3-bedroom apartment in London Towne. Brianna is her only child, so she likes to play with Corey.

Jamyya is sitting at the table by the door waving when we walk in. "Hey, Coco, over here!"

I have to snatch Christian by the hand, 'cause he's headed straight for the games.

"Christian, wait a minute! We have to buy some tokens first. Let's go say 'hi' to Jamyya."

He looks at me with his lips poked out. "I wanna play, Mommy. Me go over there!" He points his little finger at the sliding board.

"Okay honey, just one minute."

I sit down at the table. "Hey, where are the kids?"

"Playing. They couldn't wait. I already bought tokens."

"Oh, a'ight. I got some coupons. I'm going to order some pizza, 'cause I didn't feed them yet."

"Well, we can all put up. Skye and Alana just walked in. Here, give them some of these tokens until we figure out what we want to do."

"Good idea." I give Corey and Jermeka some tokens.

"Y'all go play."

Christian looks at me. "I want some."

"Okay, baby." I give him two tokens.

"I'll take him over there with Ke'Asia so he can play with the twins," Jamyya says, holding Christian's hand.

Skye comes and sits down with Omari. "Hey, girl. Where's Jamyya?"

"Taking Christian to Ke'Asia, so he can play with the twins."

"Oh, okay."

"Hey, Coco and Skye," Alana greets us warmly.

"Hey, girl," Skye replies.

"Here, give these to Brianna so she can go play. Omari can go with her," I say.

Alana gives Brianna the tokens, and she and Omari leave.

"So, what's up with y'all?" Alana asks.

"Nothing much, trying to figure out what to order. We're going to need another table."

"Yeah, I'll sit over here to save this table for the kids."

"So what should we order?" I ask.

We end up using all four of the coupons and ordering two baskets of buffalo wings. Those kids eat like they are starving! All four large pizzas are gone. They go back to play more games while we have girl talk.

"I have a problem, y'all," Skye huffs.

"What's new?" I reply.

"Nothing really, just the same ole stuff, but listen anyway. You know me, Jamyya, and Mimi went to the Hyperlink Saturday night. Tell me why Omar was there too! I didn't even drive my car, so I want to know how he knew I was there? When he called my cell phone, I didn't answer. He's been acting crazy since his sister Kenya had her engagement party. He wants to get married, and I'm not ready."

"You know what? Dontaé might have told Omar where you were. I think Mimi tells her brother stuff sometimes, not thinking that he will tell Omar," Jamyya says.

"I never thought about that. His crazy ass got mad 'cause I was dancing with some dude. We weren't even close. I could see if we were all up on each other. At least I didn't come home with a hickey."

"What did he do?"

"He came over and grabbed my arm, looked at the dude, and said 'This is my girlfriend; you need to step off before a problem arises. I'd hate to beat your ass in front of all these people.' Then the dude just walked away sucking his teeth. He lucky the nigga ain't want to fight. One day Omar is going to find somebody crazier than him."

"You ain't lying," Jamyya chimes in.

"Has anything else strange been going on with Omar? By strange, I mean not his normal behavior," I ask, being humorous.

"You ain't funny. Yeah, he had lipstick on his collar, and I could smell perfume on him too, one day last week. He had a story for that too."

"What was it? I'm dying to hear this shit," Alana says.

"He claims that the girl from work must have gotten her lipstick on his shirt by mistake when he hugged her cause she was crying. He was trying to comfort her because her grandma died. The perfume must have rubbed off on him too."

"That's some bullshit!" I yell.

"Yeah, well, I asked Rhonda and she confirmed that this girl at work, her grandma did die, but she didn't see them hugging or nothing."

"Mm hmm...that could be his cover up. You know what; you should follow him to see what he is doing. If he thinks you are always cheating, it's probably because he's the one doing it," Alana replies.

"I hate to admit it, Skye, but she has a point. When a man starts acting different, something is wrong. All of these coincidences don't add up," Jamyya says, taking a sip of her soda.

"I just can't believe Omar would cheat on me. When would he have time? He's always up my ass," Skye retorts.

"She's right about that," I comment.

"Let's talk about something else," Jamyya insists.

"Well, Kenya wants me to be a bridesmaid in her wedding. She also want me to help pick out the dresses," Skye explains.

"That's nice that she wants to include you. What's the problem?"

"Omar is the problem! He's having a tough time dealing with her getting married. The night of Kenya's engagement party, he proposes to me again. As usual, I said no."

Before Alana can ask why she said no, guess who appeared? You got it, Omar! He walks in looking around the room until he spots us.

"The stalker is here," I sneer.

"Speak of the devil," Alana says, laughing.

"See what I'm talking about?" Skye snaps.

Omar walks up to the table smiling at everybody. "Hey, how are y'all lovely ladies this afternoon?"

Everybody looks at him and says, "Fine," in an exasperated tone.

"Why are you here, Omar?" Skye asks, trying to remain calm.

"Oh, I just stopped by, I thought y'all might need some help wit' the kids."

"Actually, we do. They are over there. Go check on them and help them win some tickets. Here, take these tokens with you," I hand Omar a cup of tokens.

Jamyya smiles at me. "Yeah, let's put his ass to work since he came to help."

"Good idea, we can wear his ass out," Skye replies.

Poor Omar, we have him doing everything! He takes the twins to the bathroom, plays games, chases after them, and takes them to pick out prizes. Finally, all the tokens are gone and it's time to go. I check my Kenneth Cole watch; the time is now four-fifteen. Good. By the time I get home it will be naptime. I can wash clothes then cook dinner while Jerome takes Jermeka home. I'm glad Jerome is not as possessive as Omar. I couldn't take him showing up everywhere I go. I know Skye's pissed - shit, I am too, and he ain't even my man! That shit is just flat out embarrassing.

When I get home, the house is spotless. I hear the washer and dryer running. I yell, "Jerome, where are you?"

"Upstairs, in the kitchen."

I got upstairs while the kids go to their rooms.

"Hey baby, thanks for cleaning up. I was going to wash clothes and cook when I came back."

"Well, you can cook. One less thing for you to do. Did the kids have a good time?"

"Yeah, they did, and we had a nice girls' talk until Omar showed up. As usual, he pissed everybody off. So that broke our spirits."

"What the hell is wrong with him? Skye must have put a root on him or something. That brotha is sick. That's exactly why I don't hang out with him."

"I know. I'm glad you don't act like that."

"If I ever do, please shoot me! I don't want to live acting a damn fool. What are you cooking for dinner?"

"Cheesy chicken and rice casserole, and I will probably make a cheese-cake for dessert."

Jerome rubs his stomach. "Mmm, I'm getting hungry just thinking about it."

"You better make a sandwich or something. I'm not cooking until quarter till six."

"I'll just grab something from McDonald's. I'm not messing up my clean kitchen. It's time for me to take Jermeka home anyway."

"A'ight, see ya later."

I lie down to take a cat nap. I'm awakened by the phone ringing. I wonder who this could be? I had just left from talking to the girls. Maybe it's Jazz or Mimi. I snatch the phone off the hook.

"Hello," I answer groggily.

"Who in the hell gave you permission to do my child's hair? She is only seven years old; you got her looking like a project-ass teenager! I know you didn't put a perm in her hair either!"

"I know you must be good and crazy to call my house, waking me out of my sleep for some bullshit. First of all, her hair looked like shit when she came to my house. If you didn't want anybody to touch it, you should've done it yourself. Second, I didn't put a perm in her hair. I just know what I'm doing. That's why it looks so good. Lastly, her father gave me permission to do her hair. If you don't like it, take it up with him. Now I suggest from now on, you call Jerome's cell phone. Don't call my house with no foolishness. I would love to kick your ass, but we both know it would make Jerome mad. That's the only reason why I haven't done it yet," I slam the phone down in her ear, then cut the ringer off. No more disturbances.

I wake up around six-thirty when Jerome comes in slamming the door.

"What the hell is wrong with you?" I scream.

"That's the same thing I was going to ask you! Shameka called me and said that I can't see Jermeka no more 'cause you threatened her and you permed Jermeka's hair. Now all of it is going to fall out."

"You and that bitch both are crazy! I didn't perm her hair, all I did was flat iron it then curl it. Her hair is not going to fall out. She took her to the shop before. She's just mad that I did it. Yeah, I did tell Shameka that I would beat her ass if she keep calling here with dumb shit. That bitch woke me up out of my sleep, and so did you."

"All you care about is sleep, when I'm telling you that I can't see my daughter no more."

"She just said that shit, she don't mean it. Even if she do, just take her to court for visitation like André is doing me. Fuck her. She'll get tired of keeping her every weekend. Now this conversation is over."

I get out of bed and go into the bathroom to get myself together.

Now it's time for me to make dinner. Jerome's mad at me again, so he refuses to eat. He moved some of his stuff into the guest bedroom. I don't really care, he'll get over it soon enough.

I call Mimi to see if she wants to come over for dinner. "Hey, chick, what you doing?"

"Nothing much, about to get dressed so I can go out to dinner."

"Who you going out wit'?"

"Jerell, so I guess Tonya won't be seeing him tonight."

"So you don't think she told him about what happened?"

"She probably did, but he ain't' going to let me know. He's going to try to play it cool. Girl, I know the game. I'm in love, not stupid."

"I'm glad to hear that. I just called to see if you wanted to come over for dinner, but I see you've got plans. I'll just catch you later. Have fun."

"Oh, trust me I will. I'ma have loads of it."

"You are so damn nasty. I'm surprised you ain't got twelve kids by now."

"That's 'cause I keep it safe. If it ain't wrapped up, I don't want it. Same thing goes for gifts. I'll talk to you tomorrow. I got to finish getting pretty."

"'Bye, chick."

I decide to go downstairs and watch a movie. I pop some microwave popcorn, get my ice-cold Pepsi, and sit on the couch. I turn on the TV and surf the channels until I find something to watch. I think about my marriage and the problems we have been having lately. I decide I will sign up for my anger management class tomorrow, since Mondays are my off days.

I start taking my micro braids out. I had them in forever; it's time for a new hairstyle and a new attitude. The faster I get finished with my anger management classes, the quicker we can get marriage counseling. I hate to admit it, but we need professional help. Maybe Skye and Omar can get some couple's counseling. I'll call her tomorrow to tell her about it.

Hopefully, I can get all this shit out of my head by tomorrow morning. I have an appointment with the Africans to get some Senegalese twist. I usually always keep my hair braided. Doing other people's hair everyday makes me hate to even think about touching mine. Everybody always thinks my hair is short, but actually, it's pretty long. It comes down to my shoulders. Maybe for Christmas, I'll wear it in a wrap or something.

I call my mom to see if she can keep Corey and Christian on Saturday.

She said, "Yes, I'll be happy to keep them. I haven't seen my grandbabies in awhile. Matter of fact, just pack them a bag, they can spend the night. Just drop them off early Saturday morning. I'll feed them breakfast."

"Thanks, Mom, I appreciate it. I'll pick them up Sunday around six," I tell her.

Hmm, maybe I should go to church next Sunday,' cause my life is sho nuff falling to pieces. I'm tired of the roller coaster ride of this relationship. I'm going to bed.

Chapter Ten

Jasmine

Shawn has been the love of my life these past couple of months. We spend all of our free time together. I'm tired of living with Joy and Mario. I'm twenty-four years old. I should have my own place.

Last week, I went down to Long and Foster Realty. That's where Jerome works at. He said my credit was good, but I don't make enough money to qualify for a loan. He suggested that I get another job, then re-apply in six months. So now I'm on a job search.

Damisha told me that she would let me know if they start hiring at her job. I went to the public library and checked out four different books on home daycare centers. I think Coco had a great idea, so I'm doing some research on it. I'm lying on my bed taking notes from the book I'm reading called <u>Everything You Need to Know about Starting a Home Daycare</u>.

My phone rings. I look at the caller ID; it's Shawn. A big smile comes across my face.

"Hey, baby. How are you?"

"I'm fine. What's up wit' you today?"

"Not much, just doing some research on starting my own daycare business."

"Would you like some company? Maybe we can go out to eat or something later on."

"Yeah, you can come over. Nobody's here but me."

"A'ight, I'll be there in thirty minutes."

"Okay."

My boyfriend Shawn is so sexy. He's 6'2", brown-skinned with light brown eyes, and built with muscles. He works at Hewlett Packard on the first shift, and he drives a Chevrolet Malibu. I guess 'cause he's single, he doesn't feel the need to have his own place. He and his best friend Dwayne live in a two bedroom apartment around Treehouse Apartments. Shawn is twenty-seven years old with no kids. Thank God for that, 'cause Coco goes through too much drama wit' Shameka and André's crazy-ass girlfriends!

Me and Shawn have been together for almost four months now. I already introduced him to my sister Joy and her husband. Maybe if we are still together around Thanksgiving, I'll introduce him to my aunt, brother, and little sister.

My parents died in a car accident when I was ten years old. My mother's sister Linda raised us. I was born and raised in Philadelphia. I moved to Virginia when I was sixteen. My sister Joy moved to Virginia to go to college. She graduated from Virginia State University. After she graduated, she got married to Mario and had a job here, so she stayed. I was getting into too much trouble up in Philly, so I moved to Richmond to live with Joy. My brother Justin and my sister Jalisa still live in Philly. Justin has two little boys. Jalisa goes to Temple University. She's in her junior year. Jalisa doesn't have any kids yet. I go to visit my family in Philly every couple of months. I plan on going up there for Thanksgiving.

My research is interrupted by somebody ringing the doorbell. I answer the door wearing my white T-shirt with my M & M pajama pants.

"Hey baby, come on in."

"Aw, don't you look cute," Shawn says, looking me up and down. We go into my bedroom and sit on the bed.

"So, what do you want to do?" I ask.

"Well, if you wanna go out, you need to put some clothes on first."

"Where are we going?"

"Where do you want to go?"

"I don't know. Let's go to Ruby Tuesday to get something to eat."

"A'ight, well get dressed so we can go."

"Okay," I whine. I didn't really feel like going out, but we didn't have shit else to do.

I comb my hair, throw on a pair of Seven jeans with a white-and-red long-sleeved shirt, and slip on a pair of red-and-white Adidas.

"I'm ready, let's go," I nudge Shawn.

"Who's driving, me or you?"

"You are."

We get in Shawn's car and head to Ruby Tuesday on Mechanicsville Turnpike.

While we are eating, Shawn's cell phone keeps vibrating, but he doesn't answer it. I stare at him suspiciously. "Are you going to answer that, or act like you don't know it's vibrating?"

"It's not important, I'm with you. I don't need to talk to nobody else."

"Whatever." I give him much attitude.

"Don't go catching an attitude. Come on baby, let's have a good night."

"You're right. I'll calm down."

We finish our dinner and head back to my house. When we pull up, I notice the lights are on and Joy's car is in the driveway. I unlock the door, and Shawn follows me in.

"Hey, Joy what's up?" I say, walking towards my room. She's lying on the sofa in the living room.

"Hey, Jazz and Shawn," Joy replies, sitting up.

"Hello, Joy, how are you this evening?" Shawn's deep voice asks.

"I'm just fine. Enjoying watching TV by myself."

"Sounds fun. See ya."

Shawn follows me into my room. I turn on some slow R & B music to set the mood. Then I light the scented candles that are sitting on my cherry wood dresser. Shawn starts taking his clothes off.

"Wait a minute, baby, let me lock the door," I whisper.

After locking the door, I dim my lights and begin to strip to the music. I twirl my shirt above my head before throwing it to the floor. Shawn is only wearing his navy blue Sean John boxers. I stand in front of him, wearing my red silk bra and red silk thong. With his hand rubbing on his growing manhood, he says, "Damn, baby, you look good! Stop teasing me. Come over here and give me some of that juicy stuff."

I blush. "I'm on my way."

I unsnap my bra and slide down the red thong. I climb on top of him and stick my tongue in his mouth. As we kiss, his big masculine hands rub my voluptuous derrière. His warm hands glide up and down my body. He rolls me over so he can take control. Shawn begins to kiss my stomach on down to my love nest. He puts my golden0brown legs on his broad shoulders, then he begins to lick my clit with his long tongue. As he twirls his tongue around, tasting my sweet nectar, I start to moan. Shawn ignites a liquid fire inside of me that can't be extinguished.

"Not yet, baby, I'm not finished," he says in his sexy voice.

I'm trying so hard not to cum, but it isn't working. He gets up and pulls a condom out of his pants pocket. He quickly slides it on, then he slowly pushes himself inside of me. The first couple of times we had sex, it hurt my poor little coochie, but now I can handle all that he's got to give.

As he strokes my treasure box, I feel immeasurable bliss. I'm in paradise! My moans become louder and louder. The bed starts squeaking from all the rapid motion. We change positions. Shawn's favorite position is doggy style. I have to make sure he puts it in the right hole. For some strange reason, he always tries to stick it in my asshole. Nigga, please, the sign on my ass says *Do Not Enter!* I'm not that big of a freak. I wish I could say the same for some of my friends. I'm not saying any names, but you probably can guess which ones.

Shawn slams into my ass so hard, I think I see stars. "Is it good, baby?" he yells, still stroking me at a rapid pace.

"Yeah, it's good, boo."

"Can you handle this big dick?"

"Yeah baby, I got it under control."

"I don't know if you can handle all this," he says, shaking his head. He begins pushing his whole dick inside of me. I think he's going to rip out my insides.

"Fool, are you crazy?" I scream.

He starts laughing. "I told you, you couldn't handle it."

I don't see a damn thing funny.

"Let's try something else, let me get on top."

I get on top of him to show his ass a little something. We are going to see who can handle what! I climb on top of him with my back facing him. I bend over slightly and begin to bounce my ass up and down. My ass makes a smacking noise every time I slam down on his thick, brown dick.

"Oooh, damn girl, this pussy is so good!"

"Yeah, nigga I know!" I wish he would just shut the fuck up and bust a nut. Five minutes later, I end up making my own self have an orgasm.

"Whew, that was some good shit," he compliments.

"So I've heard."

"From who?" Shawn sits up fast.

"You, boy!"

"Oh, let me find out you cheating!"

"Never that, boo. You're all the man I need. Let's get in the shower." We are both sweaty, and my sheets are wet like somebody pissed on them.

After we take our shower, I'm tired and hungry. I slip on my sweatsuit and sneakers. "Baby, I'ma run to 7-Eleven real quick to get something sweet."

"You just had something sweet," he grabs his crotch.

"Yeah, but now I need some chocolate. You want something?"

"Yeah, bring me a Black & Mild and an Icehouse."

"You got some money?" I ask with my hand out.

"Look in my pocket."

I pick up his pants and go into his pocket.

This dumb ass gets up and goes into the bathroom to pee while I'm digging in his pocket. Now I'm not a thief, but I am nosy. I pick up his cell phone and forward his last three text messages to my phone. I take a twenty dollar bill from his little stack of money. This broke nigga only has a hundred dollars in his pocket! No wonder he isn't worried.

"I got twenty dollars. I'll be right back," I yell, walking out of my room.

While I'm out, I decide to stop by Taco Bell too. I call him from my cell phone. "Shawn, I'm at Taco Bell, do you want something to eat?"

"Get me three Taco Supremes."

"A'ight."

While sitting in the drive thru, I read the text messages. The first one reads: Hey boo. What's up for tonight? I miss you. *Please find some time for me in your busy schedule. Love you boo.* The next one reads: *Why aren't you answering your phone? Call me back when you get this message. I know you ain't at work.* The last one says: *Oh, you must be wit' her. You get on my damn nerves. Tonight was supposed to be my night. Please call me; I need some of that good dick, baby. Holla at your girl.*

I wonder who the fuck that is texting my man? I look at the phone number, but it only shows Shawn's. Damn, I should have remembered the number! Now I'm pissed, but I can't tell Shawn, 'cause he'll know I went through his shit. Lying, cheating-ass bastard! Men ain't shit! I don't know why I thought this one was different.

Shawn's lying in the bed fast asleep when I get back. Poor thing, I must have worn him out. I push, him trying to wake him up. "Get up, boo. I'm back with your food."

"What took you so long?"

"Taco Bell had a long line. You know only the drive thru was open. Sorry, here is your Black & Mild and your beer."

"Thanks baby, I'm starving."

He eats his food, smokes, drinks the beer, and goes back to sleep. I fall asleep soon after; I have to get up early for work in the morning.

Shawn doesn't usually spend the night on Sundays. Maybe I'll wake him up early so he can go to work. When I wake up, Shawn's not in bed, then I hear the shower come on. I decide to go through his cell phone to see who's sending him the text messages. I press the button, but all the messages are deleted. Damn him, slick bastard.

I decide to confront him when he gets out of the shower. When he comes out of the bathroom with the towel wrapped around his waist, it's hard for me to stay focused. Why does he have to be so damn sexy? I divert my attention to the TV.

"Shawn, can you please get dressed? We need to talk," I say in a serious tone.

"Sounds serious. What's up?" he asks while putting on his uniform.

"Who was blowing up your phone last night?"

"Come on Jazz, it's too damn early for this shit. It wasn't anybody important. Just one of my boys wanting to borrow some money. Now can you drop this?"

"No, 'cause I don't believe you. How do you know what he wanted if you didn't answer?"

"'Cause he wasn't calling me, it was a text, smart ass. I read it last night while you were gone for damn near two hours. I should be asking you questions. It doesn't take that long to get something from Taco Bell and 7-Eleven."

Oh, now I know his ass is lying! How is he going to try to flip this shit on me, like I did something wrong? See, the old me would have fell for this shit, but today is a new day. Damisha taught me well. Plus, his dumb ass don't know I read all his text messages, and none of them said anything about money. When did fucking another woman become your homeboy asking for money? Nigga thinks I'm stupid!

"Don't try to turn this shit around on me. I'm asking the questions. I did exactly what I said I was doing. I'm not a hoe. You of all people should know that! I just finished fucking you. I only do one dick a week, a'ight!"

"That's nice to know. So who you doing next week?"

"You ain't funny! The question is, who are *you* doing next week? If this shit keeps up, it won't be me. If you got somebody else, let me know, 'cause I can step off. I was fine before you, and I'll be even better without you. Now, I'm going to work. Think about what I said, you know the number."

I throw my Dooney & Burke purse on my shoulder and walk off. Hold up, this is my damn house!

I go back. "Shawn, it's time for you to go. I'm leaving now, and so are you."

"Baby, don't go to work mad! I'll call you later. You know you're the only one for me. I love you." He kisses me on the cheek, 'cause I turn my face away from his lying ass.

"A'ight, see ya," I respond, throwing my hand up.

I hope them kids don't get on my damn nerves today!

***

Work goes well as usual, I love kids, 'especially 'cause they are not mine. I can leave them at work and go home to peace and quiet. Well, most of the time, that is, if Joy and Mario aren't acting like fools. They need to get a divorce.

As I'm leaving work, my cell phone rings. I thought it might be Shawn, but when I look at the caller ID, it reads "Justin". I start getting excited; I haven't talked to my brother in almost two weeks.

"Hello," I say excitedly.

"Hey, lil sis, what's going on? Are your fingers broke?"

"No, I've just been busy. I got two jobs now. I'm trying to get my own place."

"I feel ya on that one. You only got a couple more months till you're twenty-five."

"So what does that have to do with anything?"

"Nobody told you about the trust fund Aunt Linda set up for us? You get to get it when you turn twenty-five. When Mom and Dad died, we got

Social Security checks every month until we turned eighteen, plus they had life insurance. Linda used the Social Security money to send us to college, and put the life insurance money in a trust fund for each of us. We each get $75,000 dollars when we turn twenty-five. How do you think I bought my car?"

"I didn't know your car was paid for. So I can use that money to start my daycare business?"

"Yep, that's a good idea. I kind of blew mine on the car, the wedding, and fixing up the house. Anyway I was calling to see when you were coming up for a visit. You know Jayden's birthday is in two weeks. His party is on October 18th, and he wants his Aunt Jasmine to come."

"I wouldn't miss it. I'ma try to take the 16th off so I can come up that day, and I can spend all day Friday, Saturday, and Sunday, 'cause I want to go shopping while I'm there."

"I figured that. Well, I'll let everybody know you're coming. Do you think Joy and Mario will come too?"

"I don't know. Call and ask her. I'ma stay at a hotel, 'cause I might bring a couple friends with me."

"Cool, just call and let me know when you get here."

"Will do, I love you, and tell everybody I said hi."

"A'ight ma, I love you too. See ya in two weeks."

That's just what I needed, a getaway. Me and Shawn have been spending too much time together anyway.

I call Mimi to see if she wants to roll.

"Hey, boo. Would you like to go to Philly with me on October 16th? My nephew Jayden is turning six and wants me to come to his party. I'm going to come back Sunday night, but I'm leaving early Thursday morning."

"Yeah, I'll go. I'ma put in for the 16th and 17th off. If it gets approved, I'll go with you. Can we go shopping?"

"Hell yeah, why you think I asked you to go? I'ma call Skye to see if she wants to come too. Since she's a manager now, she can probably take off."

"Yep, it can be a girls' weekend. Maybe we can get Rhonda to use her discount to book our room, 'cause if Omar does it, he will be up in Philly with us."

"Ain't that the truth? But I think Omar has to book Rhonda's reservation for her. I'll just pay full price so Omar doesn't find us."

"I know that's right! We can just get one big suite and split the cost three ways. How are things with Shawn? I'm surprised you're not taking him."

"He's cheating. I'm still trying to figure out how I want to handle it. I found some text messages on his cell phone, but he doesn't know I saw them. The only reason I went through his phone is because we went out to eat last night, and his phone kept vibrating but he ignored it. That shit made me curious."

"Girl, I know the feeling. Jerell has been acting strange lately. He calls me every day, and he even sent flowers to my job. I think that girl Tonya told him that we had a lil conversation about him. He hasn't said anything to me about it yet. I wonder how long this is going to last. Anyway, just back off of Shawn. Give him some space; don't call him for a couple of days then we you leave to go to Philly, don't tell him you're gone. If he knows he got you, he's going to act a fool 'cause he think you ain't going nowhere. Start giving your number out. Shit, let your phone ring off the hook, then don't answer it. Two can play that game, remember."

"Girl, you crazy as hell, that's why I love you. I'm going to take your advice, and maybe you want to listen to your own."

"I'm trying, but it's hard. I do, however, always answer my phone unless I'm having sex. Jerell knows about Chris, he just doesn't care. He got too many other women occupying his time, but I'ma teach him a lesson too. Honey, don't worry, I got this under control."

"I hear ya, Ma. Well, let me call Skye to see what's up with her, so I can make reservations and shit. I'll call you back later on in the week."

"A'ight. Oh, yeah, give me your résumé so I can give it to Chris. He told me Capital One is hiring for customer account reps. He said he would recommend you if you had a résumé he could take to the lady that works in Human Resources."

"Tell Chris I said thank you. I'll bring you my résumé tomorrow on my way to work. Talk to you later."

"'Bye." Good looking out, Mimi! That's why she's my girl.

I go upstairs to take my scrubs off and relax. For some reason, the daycare I work at requires us to wear nurse uniforms. I got some really cute cartoon ones though.

Damn, I'm hungry. I bump into Mario in the kitchen. "My bad."

"You a'ight. How is everything going?" he asks.

"Fine, I guess. Justin called me today to invite us to Jayden's birthday party. Are you and Joy going?"

"This is the first I heard about it. I'll talk to Joy and see what she says."

"Okay, well, me and Mimi are going up there on the 16th. I'm about to call Skye to see if she want to go."

"What about Omar? You might as well invite him too." Mario says, laughing. That's a damn shame everybody knows Omar is a stalker.

"That shit ain't funny, Mario. Omar needs professional help, but I doubt he would come all the way to Philly."

"I don't put it past him. The brotha has got it bad."

"Yeah, he does. Well, let me know what y'all decide so I can call Justin and let him know how many people are coming."

"I sure will. See ya later."

I make me a turkey and cheese sandwich with lettuce and tomatoes, grab a soda out the fridge, and go back to my room. I have one missed call. I look on the caller ID and it reads "my boo". Hmm, that's what I stored Shawn's phone number under. I see he's not only *my boo*, but someone else's sex toy. I don't bother to call him back. Mimi was right; I've got to be strong. Instead, I eat my food and call Skye. Her drama would be enough to distract me; by the time I finish talking to her, I'll be good and tired.

"Hey, Skye, what's going on?"

"Nothing, just enjoying some peace until Omar comes home. He's working til nine tonight. I start not to answer 'cause I think it's him calling again. Knowing him, he will probably leave early if it's not busy, 'cause I haven't answered none of his calls since six o'clock."

"Damn. Well, I have a proposition for you. Me and Mimi are going to Philly Thursday, October 16th through Sunday, October 19th for my nephew Jayden's birthday. I wanted to know if you want to roll with us. We are staying in a hotel, going shopping, and just hanging out away from our men. Sounds like you could use a quick getaway."

"I sure could. Coco is taking too damn long to go on her trip to Montego Bay. I was going to go with her, I wish she hurry up."

"Ooh, I want to go too! Let's go in January for my birthday. Justin just told me that I got a trust fund for $75,000 dollars that I can get on my twenty-fifth birthday. So I can buy me a ticket to go with y'all, then start my business when I come back."

"That's very good news. We should talk to Coco about that idea. Maybe Mimi, Jamyya, and Alana can come too. What kind of business are you going to start?"

"I don't know. At first, I was going to start a home daycare, but now I think I might do something else. I got a couple of months, I'll figure out something."

"Yeah I want to go, I know I can take off work, but I got to see if my mom or somebody will keep Omari. You know how Omar gets. Sometimes when I want to go out, he don't want to keep her."

"I know, but don't ask too early, 'cause I don't want him to be able to take off work and come follow us."

"You're right. I'll just ask my mom that Tuesday before we leave. I'm sure she will do it, if not I'll ask Shakita."

"A'ight, I'ma go get on the computer and make reservations. I'll call you in a couple of days to tell you how much everything cost. We are going to split it three ways."

"Just let me know. I'll be ready. Damn, I can't wait to go."

"Me either. We are leaving at 9:00 A.M. sharp. Don't be late."

"I won't. I'ma pack my stuff Wednesday night and hide it in the trunk of my car."

"Good thinking. I'ma catch you later."

"See ya."

Good, everything is working out fine.

I go downstairs to get on the computer. I book us a room at the Hyatt Hotel on the Northside of Philly. I didn't want to take any chances of Omar finding us. I go back upstairs and take a shower. When I get out, I notice I have two missed calls. Shawn called again, and the other was from Coco. It must not be meant for me to talk to him. Every time he calls, I miss it.

I dial my voicemail to hear my messages. First message was at 8:23 P.M. "Oh, heifer, I know you didn't invite everybody to go to Philly with you and you didn't even bother to dial my number? Then you got the nerve to think you are going to Montego Bay with me. Girl, forget it! Call me back when you get this message if you can remember the number."

Well, damn, Skye must have told her. I didn't think she could go 'cause she works on Saturdays and she don't have nobody to keep them damn kids. Let me call her back. As I'm about to dial her number, Shawn calls again. Hmm, wonder what he wants? This time I answer. "Hello?"

"Hey baby, I've been trying to catch you all day. Are you avoiding me?" he asks, concerned.

"No, I'm just trying to deal with some issues, that's all. I'm really disappointed in you, so I just thought I would give you some space."

"Baby, I'm sorry if I gave you the wrong impression. I love you and I want to be with you. I don't need space. Please forgive me. I promise to be a good boy from now on. Let me make it up to you."

"How?"

"I'll do whatever you want, just name it."

"I want you to be with me and only me. Get rid of whoever the chick on the side is. What does she give you that I don't?"

"Do you really want to know the truth?"

"Yeah, I do."

"She sucks my dick and she let me sex her anyway I want. She's secure about her body. I wish you could be the same way."

"You mean to tell me you cheated on me 'cause I won't suck your dick or let you fuck me in my ass? You have got to be kidding! That's exactly why I don't do that shit, 'cause your trifling ass don't deserve it."

"Look, you asked so I told you. We never agreed to be monogamous anyway, but if that's what you want, I'll do it. I don't want to lose you. I'm sure we can work this out."

"Let me think about it. I'm glad I make you wear condoms with your nasty ass. I'll call you in a couple days to let you know what's up. In the meantime, do you think you can keep it in your pants?"

"Yeah, baby, I can. I love you. I'll be waiting for your call."

"'Bye, Shawn."

I hang up the phone in disbelief.

He is one bold man to tell me some shit like that. I'm going to keep this to myself, 'cause if I tell my girls, then I take him back, I'll never hear the end of it. After I calm down, I call Coco.

Here comes some more drama. "Hey, Coco, I got your message but can you please let me explain?"

"No need to. I know why you didn't ask me. I was just blowing off some steam. I gotta work anyway, plus Jerome is getting on my nerves about keeping the kids."

"You could take off though. We are not leaving for another two weeks. Ask Torey or your mom to keep the boys. I'm sorry I didn't ask you. I should have let you make the decision whether or not you wanted to go. Come on, it will be fun. Try to find a babysitter, that way you can get away from Jerome for a while."

"A'ight, I'll let you know. That's a good idea going to Montego Bay for your birthday. We all need to get together so we can make reservations and book a flight together. The sooner we do it, the cheaper the tickets will be."

"A'ight, well I'll plan this trip. You can call Damisha, Jamyya, and Alana to plan Montego Bay. I can go anytime after January 18th, 'cause I'm quitting my job once I get my trust fund money."

"Yeah, I heard about that. Congratulations. Now you can move out and start your daycare."

"I know, I'm so excited, but I think I might do something else besides a daycare. I'm not feeling that too much. I'm going to think about some things and do some research. I'll figure out something. So are we cool?"

"Yeah Ma, we are cool."

"Call me as soon as you find out."

"I will. I should know something by Thursday."

"A'ight chick talk to you later."

Now I'm good and tired. I go to sleep contemplating my relationship with Shawn. I wonder if he will really let his side chick go?

Over the next two weeks, Shawn went out of his way to spend time with me. He sent a dozen long stem white roses to my job. Then, the next day, he surprised me with lunch from Ruby Tuesday. Shawn bought me a card, teddy bear, and a bouquet of Calla lilies. The teddy bear was holding a pair of two-carat diamond earrings. Wow, now why couldn't he always be like this? Lately, Joy has been sick with some kind of stomach virus, so she and Mario are not going to Philly.

Coco had finally called me to let me know that she is coming with us. Since the four of us are going, I decided to rent a SUV so we can have enough room for our luggage and shopping bags. I call everybody at 7:00 A.M. to make sure they are awake and ready.

I get Mario to drive me to Enterprise Rent-A-Car so I can pick up the Ford Expedition I rented.

"Thanks Mario, I wish y'all were coming," I lie.

"Yeah, well, I'm sure Joy will be sad she missed it."

"I'll take some pictures of the party. See ya Sunday."

"Be safe. Don't go up there acting crazy."

"I won't. I better get a move on so we can get on the road. Tell Joy I hope she feel better."

"Okay, lil sis. Have fun."

I call Skye to see if she's ready. I'm going to pick her up first since she's near Enterprise.

"Girl, are you ready? I'm on my way to your house."

"Yeah, I'm packed and ready to go. Omar's at work, so the coast is clear."

"You didn't tell him you were leaving?"

"Yeah I told him, but I lied a little. He thinks I'm going to Baltimore to finish my training."

"If it works, more power to you." We both laugh.

I pull up in the driveway 'cause I know Skye will have a lot of luggage. She swings the front door open as soon as my foot hits the porch.

"Here, help me take these." Skye hands me a Dooney & Burke traveling bag with matching suitcase. She drags two rolling suitcases behind me.

"Skye, we are coming back, baby."

"I know, but you never know how the weather is going to be or where we might go."

"It's October in Philly. It's going to be cold. We are going up North where it snows a few feet in the winter."

"Oh, shit I forgot! I didn't pack a coat."

"You can buy one at the mall."

For October, it is pretty warm outside. It's only eight o'clock, and it's already sixty-two degrees.

"I'm hungry, let's stop by Krispy Kreme to get some breakfast," Skye suggests.

"Girl, that is not breakfast, it's sugar."

"I know, but I need a sugar rush to wake me up. Damisha will want some too."

"A'ight, I don't want to be in traffic anyway."

While standing in the long-ass line at Krispy Kreme, I call Mimi, while Skye calls Coco to tell them we are on the way.

"Coco said she's ready."

"A'ight. Mimi said she'll be ready by time we get there."

"I bet you five dollars that Jerell is over there. Mimi is always ready on time, she been waiting to leave for days now."

"You know what, she did sound funny when I called her this morning." Sure enough, when we pulled up to Mimi's house, Jerell is getting in his car about to leave.

"I told you!" Skye screams. "Give me my five dollars!"

"Girl, please."

I beep the horn for Mimi to come out.

"That heifer better be ready," I say, looking at Skye. Mimi comes running out the house, smiling ear to ear.

"Hey ladies, how is everybody this morning? Ooh, doughnuts, I want some."

She throws a big Baby Phat overnight bag in the back and climbs in. Now I know something is up, 'cause Ms. Diva only has one bag.

"I'm fine, but I think you've lost your damn mind. Where is the rest of your stuff?" I ask, confused.

"That's it. You said we were going shopping, so I didn't need to bring a lot. Plus, Jerell gave me $500 to shop with. I'll be a'ight. Now pass the doughnuts."

"Here girl, you must have worked up some appetite. We saw Jerell leaving."

"Yeah, I did. I'm tired as hell too. He kept me up all night," she says, smiling and taking a bite out of her doughnut.

Jerell must have put something tough on her, 'cause she's glowing. Sister is singing and snapping her fingers the whole way to Coco's house.

"I see Jerell puts it down," Skye teases.

"He sure does! My baby must've got his Doctorate degree in licking pussy, 'cause he does it so well."

"You are a nasty lil chick! It's too early to be talking about pussy," I reply.

"Oh, you just mad 'cause you ain't get none before you left."

"Damn right! We are going to go to McDonald's for breakfast after we scoop Coco."

"A'ight."

We arrive at Coco's house fifteen minutes later. Coco comes out struggling with two big Louis Vuitton suitcases. I still have to stop by my house to get my luggage. If I was thinking, I would've brought it with me.

"Are you hungry?" I ask.

"Nah, I already ate breakfast."

"Oh, well I didn't, so I'ma stop by McDonald's."

"Fine with me."

"You know what, y'all, I left my luggage at home, but I don't feel like going to get it, 'cause it's already nine. I wanted to be on the highway by now."

"Well, I can drive when we stop at McDonald's, since I already ate. I would like a doughnut, though," Coco says.

"Y'all some sweet tooth-having people. It's too early for all that sugar. I think I'll just buy some new clothes when I get to Philly. I got some money to spend since I don't need to save no more. I'ma treat myself to a whole new winter wardrobe."

"I know that's right! Make Shawn beg to have you back," Mimi says.

When we stop at McDonald's, Coco gets in the driver's seat so I can eat while she drove. That way, we can get on the highway. Skye spots Tyson's Corner, a mall in D.C., from the highway. She got eagle eyes when it comes to seeing someone or a mall.

"Can we stop and go shopping here? I got to use the bathroom anyway."

"Mm-hmm, sure you do. You can use the bathroom anywhere."

"You said we could go shopping. Plus I'll drive the rest of the way."

"Yeah, I did say that, but we didn't get to Philly yet. But I guess we can stop. What y'all want to do?" I ask.

"We can stop, I'm tired of driving anyway," Coco says.

"Good," Mimi chimes in.

Coco gets off at the exit to the mall.

As soon as we go in, everybody runs to the ladies room. This mall has a lot of expensive stores in it. Not really my style, but I know everybody else is enjoying it. I buy one outfit from Saks. It cost me $375 dollars. Oh hell no, I won't buy anything else until I get to Philly where shit is cheap and there are no taxes.

You should know Ms. Diva had three bags full of stuff. Who else could I be talking about but Skye? Her protégé Damisha doesn't do too bad, although one pair of Christian Louboutin boots cost her $675. That's probably why she only bought two outfits. Coco buys a coat and a purse. She says, "Shit, I ain't spending all my money on one thing in this expensive-ass mall!"

"I ain't either. Come on y'all let's go. Time is ticking. We got to check in before they give our room away," I plead.

"A'ight, I'm ready," Skye replies.

Skye drives the rest of the way to Philly. When we got to the hotel, it's quarter to five. I call my brother to let him know we made it safely. After I hang up, I notice I have some missed calls. The music was up loud in the truck, so I must have not heard it. Of course Shawn called; the other was from Joy, and my friend Paris from work. I call Joy back first.

"Hey Joy, are you feeling better?"

"A little better. I drank some ginger ale and ate crackers. I should be fine in a day or two. Are you in Philly yet?"

"Yeah we got here about fifteen minutes ago."

"Okay, I just wanted to make sure y'all made it safe. I love you. Don't forget to take pictures of everybody. Tell them I'll see them for Thanksgiving."

"I won't forget. Love you too. I hope you feel better."

"Thanks. Have fun. Talk to you later."

Should I call Shawn back or not? While I'm pondering that question, Skye interrupts my thoughts. "I'm hungry. Jazz, let's go get something to eat, but you are driving this time."

"Where do y'all want to go? I thought y'all would be tired by now."

"Let's go somewhere that sells subs and pizza. Like a lil Italian spot or something," Coco replies.

"Oh, I know the perfect spot. Come on so we can get back, 'cause I'm tired. I've been up since six-thirty this morning."

"Yeah, I'm tired too," Mimi adds.

"I know you are!" Skye responds.

We drive to Leo's on 25th Street. We sit in and eat our food. Everybody orders a cheese steak, 'cause Philly is known for them. The food is very good. All of a sudden, I remember I don't have any underclothes, pajamas, or personals.

"Damn y'all, I forgot I didn't bring my suitcase. We have to stop by the store. I don't have any underclothes or personals."

"Make it quick. Is there a Wal-Mart or something around here?" Mimi asks, irritated.

"No, but Target is not far from here. It'll only take me a minute. I promise."

I get on the expressway. It only takes us ten minutes to reach Target. I run in and buy four bra and panty sets, a pack of white socks, deodorant, lotion, and Dove Cucumber soap. Skye and Mimi stock up on junk food to take back to the hotel room.

By the time we get back, it's a little after seven. Everybody is beat, and we settle down to go to bed.

I call Shawn back when I wake up to go to the bathroom in the middle of the night.

"Hey, baby. Did I wake you up?"

"No, I was just lying around. What's up?"

"Nothing, I was just returning your call. I was tired and fell asleep; I just woke up to pee."

"Oh, I didn't want anything. I called to talk to you. I miss you. Are you still mad at me?"

"A little, but I miss you too. I'll call you Sunday when I get back home. I need a little more time to think about us."

"Where are you?"

"I came to Philly for my nephew's birthday and to visit my family. I'll be back Sunday night."

"A'ight boo, I'll talk to you then. Do you think it's possible for us to talk in person?"

"Maybe. I'll let you know."

"I love you, Jazz."

"I love you too. Goodnight."

I better get some sleep if I'm going to be the ghetto tour guide for tomorrow. We slept until about 10:00 A.M. I'm the last one to wake up.

***

"Good morning, sleepy head," Coco greets me with a smile.

"Good morning, ladies."

"Look, we already took showers, and we are dressed waiting on you. We're hungry as hell. Good thing I bought some snacks last night. Hurry up and get dressed," Skye demands.

"Here, somebody iron my clothes while I get dressed."

I hand my clothes to Mimi. "Thanks, Ma."

"Yeah, yeah just hurry up."

I'm glad I don't have to comb my hair; I got it braided last week by the Africans. The shit cost me $200. I'm thinking about leaving it in till it dreads up. I don't know how Coco keeps spending all that money on her hair. Seems like she keeps their lights on. Coco hates to do her own hair. She keeps some kind of braids in her hair. Right now, she got Senegalese twist. I just got some small, shoulder-length box braids. They are really neat though. Everybody says it looks good on me.

"I'm ready, let's go to Pizza Hut for lunch. "

"A'ight, then let's go to the mall. I'm ready for a shopping spree," Skye replies.

"Calm down, we are going to go shopping. Just slow your roll."

"You know I got a shopping habit."

"Yeah, we all know. I'm surprised Omar hasn't called you yet. Shawn called me yesterday."

"Oh, he called four times but I only talked to him twice. Please don't talk him up."

"No, I don't want to do that."

We eat at the lunch buffet at Pizza Hut. After everybody's belly is stuffed, I drive us to the mall. First we go to King of Prussia. While we're shopping, I run into Fatima, one of my childhood friends.

"Jasmine Taylor, I can't believe my eyes. What are you doing here?"

"Just visiting Justin, Jalisa, and my Aunt Linda. Tomorrow is Jayden's birthday."

"Oh, well, it's nice to see you again. Who are your friends?"

"Excuse my rudeness; this is Kori, Damisha, and Skye."

"Nice to meet y'all. I've heard a lot of good things about y'all," Fatima shakes everybody's hands.

"Nice to meet you too," everybody replies.

"So how long are you staying?"

"Just til Sunday, but I'll be back for Thanksgiving."

"A'ight, well don't be a stranger. Call me when you come back up."

"I will. Take care of yourself."

"Hey, what are you doing tonight?"

"Nothing, why?"

"'Cause we will probably go to the Black Club. Do you want to go?"

"Hell yeah, girl! Just call me if y'all going. I can just meet you there. Maybe Jada can come too, we can catch up."

"Okay, I'll call you later."

The look on my friends' faces scares me. "What's wrong with y'all?"

"How in the hell are you going to invite some strange hoe to go out with us!" Skye screams.

"She ain't strange, that's my friend from high school. She's really cool, don't trip."

"It's supposed to be us spending time together bonding," Mimi agrees with Skye.

"Come on, y'all are being selfish. We can see her anytime we want. Let her hang out with her friends. It's not like we ain't going with her," Coco says.

"Thank you, Coco. I'm glad somebody is understanding."

We shop for another hour, then drive around town. I show them my old high school and where I used to live. Finally, we go back to the hotel. On the way back, Omar calls Skye.

"Yes, Omar. I'm fine. How's Omari? Good…I love you too. Yes baby, I do miss you…I'll be back Sunday…mm hmm. Okay, goodnight." She blows him a kiss.

"Eww, that's so mushy," I say playfully.

"Shut up. You probably do the same thing with Shawn."

"No, I don't," I smile.

"Do y'all want to go to the club tonight or what?"

"Yeah, let's go meet some cuties!" Mimi exclaims.

"What about Jerell? I thought you were ready to settle down," Coco asks.

"I was, but he's not, so why should I sit around and wait? Jerell is my first choice, but he's not dependable. Sometimes he can be so sweet and attentive, then the next week he's M.I.A for days at a time. Now Chris is starting to get impatient with me 'cause he wants me to be with him only. I like Chris a lot, but I can't choose."

"You are just like a man. You want to have your cake and eat it too. Don't treat Chris how Jerell is treating you. You're stringing his feelings along and that's not fair." I try to show her she's wrong in a nice way.

"You're right; I'ma let Chris go when I get back. He's too sweet for me to take advantage of him."

After our little girl talk, we all take a nap. We know tonight is going to be a long night, especially if Fatima and Jada come. Fatima is sweet and gets along with anybody, but Jada is a stone cold diva like Skye and Mimi. She doesn't hesitate to say what's on her mind. And of course she thinks she's the flyest thing on this earth. Jada and Skye are going to clash. It's inevitable. Mimi, on the other hand, may be able to control herself if she finds a man she likes. Damisha loves men, and they will steal all her attention if his pockets are right.

I decide to wear my short, chocolate brown skirt, a dark purple shirt, a pair of purple, brown, cream print tights, and chocolate brown high boots made by Chanel. Damisha wears a tight, black pair of Jean Paul Gaultier pants, a silver V-neck off the shoulder sweater, and a pair of silver T-strap Jimmy Choo heels. Coco is rocking a long, black, halter-top Versace dress, a silver chain belt, with silver Versace pumps. Last but not least, Ms. Diva Skye has on a long, off-the-shoulder burgundy sweater by Just Cavalli, a pair of burgundy, tan, and navy blue print tights, and three- quarter camel boots by Michael Kors.

We all look very cute, if you want my opinion. Skye, of course, made a dress out of a shirt, something that she and Mimi do frequently. Mimi does it more in the summer time; Skye however, doesn't discriminate. Fatima and Jada are going to meet us at the club. This is about to get interesting.

We meet up with Fatima and Jada outside the club. It's cold as a bitch outside, and the line to get into the club is very long. Jada knows the guy working the door, so we bypass all of the hatin' bitches still waiting to get in.

"Thanks Jada, girl, you know I'm not used to this cold weather. It's still kind of warm in Richmond," I say, giving her a hug.

"No problem, boo, I got you. Looks like you lost some weight since the last time I saw you."

"Yeah, I did lose about ten pounds. Let me introduce you to my friends. This is Kori, Skye, and Damisha."

"Hey y'all, what's up?"

"Nothing, just trying to find some cute men with some money in their pocket," Mimi replies.

Everybody just looks at her.

Skye rolls her eyes. "I'm going to sit at the bar," she flicks her hand and walks off.

Coco follows behind her. "Excuse me, let me go talk to her. It's nice to meet you."

"Yeah, you too."

Jada looks at me. "What's up with your girl?"

"She's just a diva with a 'tude, that's all."

"Well, you should've left her stuck-up ass at home! She act like she too fly to hang out with us. Shit, I know I'ma bad bitch. She better recognize."

"Jada, please don't start, that's just how Skye is. She's probably just mad that you ain't busted. She don't handle competition well," I say.

After the last word, leaves my lips, I know I have just put my foot in my mouth. Me and Damisha are about to have it out, but it's the truth. Jada is very pretty. Her skin is silky-smooth chocolate, and she has big beautiful brown eyes. She's 5'7" with a Beyoncé-shaped body when she played in *Dream Girls*. Jada's sense of fashion is no joke. She's wearing the hell out of her red tight tube dress by Juicy Couture. Her small waist holds a gold chain belt, and her gold peep toe pumps are banging. She's wearing her hair in a very long layered wrap, and yes, it's real, as Skye would say. Her smile is beautiful with deep dimples and bright white teeth.

Mimi jumps to Skye's defense. "Skye ain't jealous of nobody, she just doesn't associate with just anybody. I can't believe you would say some shit like that."

Mimi walks off pissed.

"Damn," I say while holding my hands to my head.

"I didn't mean to cause problems with you and your friends," Jada says apologetically.

"It's all right, she will get over it. We go through our moments from time to time. Let's just have fun."

"I know that's right! They get to see you every day, we only see you every blue moon. Come on, let's dance."

Fatima pulls me onto the dance floor. We dance until I get hot.

"Girl, let's go get some drinks from the bar."

"That's what's up," Fatima replies.

On the way to the bar, I spot Mimi dancing with some tall, cute brotha. I knew all she needed was a man to satisfy her. Coco and Skye are still chilling at the bar. I pull up a stool beside them.

Coco looks at me. "Hey, Ma I was looking for you. Where you been?"

"Oh, girl, I was on the dance floor shaking my ass."

"You go, frisky momma!"

I laugh, then ordered me an apple martini.

"Skye has something to say. Don't you Skye?" Coco nudges Skye with her elbow.

"I'm sorry for being spoiled, Jazz, and Jada, I apologize for having an attitude with you. I don't even know you not to like you. Actually, I should be happy that you got style, 'cause I would hate to have to hang out with a tacky chick."

"I'll take that as a compliment, and I accept your apology. Come on out to the dance floor with us. Shit, it's time to have some fun." Jada replies.

"Okay, come on Coco. you coming too." Skye grabs Coco's hand. We all dance with each other and a couple of different guys.

One drunk-ass dude with a mouth full of fronts comes up to Jada. "Hey girl, introduce me to your friend," he demands, pointing at Skye.

"Freddie, don't nobody want to meet your drunk ass," Jada retorts.

"Girl, you don't know that. I'm the flyest nigga in Philly. You better recognize."

Skye looks him up and down. "No, actually she's right. I don't want your drunk ass. No introduction is needed." We all walk off.

Everybody's tired and ready to go, but first we have to find Mimi's hot ass.

"Where the hell is your girl?" Fatima asks.

"I don't know. I'm about to get the D.J. to page her ass," I reply.

As I am making my way to the DJ booth, I spot Mimi in the corner sitting at the table with some guy. He's very cute, but at this point I didn't care. My feet are killing me. That damn stiletto heel on my boot is wearing a sister out!

"Excuse me, Mimi, we're ready to go."

"A'ight Ma, give me a minute."

Mimi gives the dude her phone number and a kiss on the cheek.

"It was nice meeting you. Call me sometime. Maybe I'll come back up here to visit," she says to the man.

"Aight, baby, I will definitely do that." He smiles then takes a sip of his drink.

I'm glad towards the end of the night, everybody got along.

Mimi never told Skye what I said about her. Good thing, 'cause I don't feel like arguing tonight. We get back to the hotel room around 2:30 A.M. 'cause we stop to get something to eat before we go in. The music in the club was so loud that no one heard their cell phones ringing. It's too late to return calls, so we do that in the morning.

Today is Jayden's birthday party. We go to Toy's 'R Us to buy him a gift. I buy him a Transformer and Skye gets him a remote-control car. Coco and Mimi had got him an outfit from the mall that night when we went. I'm so excited to see all of my family, I run up the steps to my brother's house. I bust through the door

"Hey, everybody, Auntie Jazz is here."

Justin, Jr. and Jayden come running to hug me.

"Hey, baby, come on in here. Let Grandma get a look at you."

"Hey, Grandma. How are you doing?"

"I'm fine, 'cept my arthritis is acting up, and I got a bad case of hemorrhoids, but I'm real good. I'm so glad to see you. Give your granny a kiss."

I kissed my grandma on the cheek. "I love you, Grandma."

"I love you too, baby. You need to come visit mo' often. Where Joy at?"

"Joy has been sick lately. I think it's just a stomach virus. She said she'll come up for Thanksgiving."

"Okay, doll baby. Are you going to introduce your friends?"

"Yes, ma'am. This is Skye, Damisha, and Kori." They all go and give my grandma a hug.

I talk to my Aunt Linda and my brother Justin. They have a whole lot of food and kids running around. I eat so much, my pants can't button anymore.

Jayden opens all his gifts after we sing "Happy Birthday". I take pictures of everybody. My family really likes my friends. I'm glad Skye knows how to act around older people.

Finally, Sunday comes around and it's time to go home. We go to Atlantic City for a couple of hours before we return to Richmond. Mimi and Coco are the only two that win money. Coco wins $300 and Mimi wins $2000. All she does is buy Jerell and Chris stuff with the money.

"I thought you were breaking up with Chris when you got back?" I ask, confused.

"Yeah, I am, this will be a goodbye gift, that's all."

"How thoughtful of you," Coco says sarcastically.

"Shut up, it will be better to let him go now before he gets too attached, I really like Chris and I care about his feelings."

"I'm glad you finally care about somebody else besides yourself" I reply.

"I'm not a selfish person. I will do anything for my family and friends."

"I know, but when it comes to relationships, it's all about you."

"Yeah, you're right. If I don't love myself nobody else will."

"I feel ya," Skye adds.

I drop Coco off first, then Mimi.

"Skye, can you follow me to Enterprise so I can take the car back?"

"Yeah, no problem. I got my keys with me so Omar doesn't know I'm home."

"You know what? We can go to my house first and you can drive my car, then I'll drop you off."

"Okay, that sounds better 'cause Omar has already called me three times today since I talked to him."

We pick up my red Chrysler Sebring and return the Expedition to the rent-a-car place. When I pull up to Skye's house, we see a strange car parked out front.

"I wonder whose car that is," Skye says.

Chapter Eleven

Yolanda

I am on cloud nine today. My best friend Star just called and told me Omar's girlfriend went out of town for business. She won't be back until Sunday night. Yes, this is just what I need to accomplish my plan. I had already purchased Rohypnol to slip in his drink. Now all I need to do is get him to my house. I bought an ovulation kit to pinpoint the exact time of ovulation.

I'm going to get pregnant by Omar, and then he will be all mine. My plan has been working so far.

Tyrone confirmed that Skye and Omar have had several fights about the condom wrappers, hickeys, and lipstick on his collar. I love Star, 'cause she has really helped me pull this off. I got her to call my job a couple of weeks ago to tell me that my grandmother died. I was a very good actress, if I say so myself. Omar hugged me while I had my breakdown, and I pressed my berry-covered lips on his collar. Him hugging me felt so natural and good. I wish I could tell him how much I love him. Ever since the day I corn-rowed his hair, he has been coming back to get it done every week.

He has an appointment tomorrow, which is Friday. I'm off from work, so I'm going to cook a nice dinner for him, then slip a little Rohypnol in his drink. Then we are going to make love all night long. I'm going to put hickeys all over his sexy body. I can just tell by the way he walks that his dick is big.

I decide to go shopping for a new outfit and some lingerie. I already have an appointment to get my hair done tomorrow morning. Omar doesn't leave work until five o'clock tomorrow, so I'll be ready. I have to rush to the mall, 'cause I have to be at work by one o'clock. I make it just in time. The time clock reads 12:55 P.M.

"Good afternoon, Sherri. How are you today?" I ask, smiling.

"I'm fine, and it looks like you are doing better. I'm glad to see you smiling."

"Thanks, I feel a lot better."

Sherri is a real cool supervisor. I like her a lot, but I have to watch my actions around her. I don't want anybody to know my plan. Once I get pregnant, I plan on quitting anyway. I'ma look for another job before I start showing.

I work half my shift before I see Omar. He's walking around looking sad.

"What's wrong? You know you can talk to me about anything. I'm your friend as well as your employee." I smile at him.

"Thanks, but I don't want to burden you with my problems. I'm happy to see you back to normal. I have missed your smile."

"Thank you, but I want to be there for you, like you comforted me in my time of need. How about we have lunch together? That way we can get out of here and talk openly. I'm a discreet person, I can keep a secret."

"You know, I wouldn't mind having company for lunch. Let's go to Famous Dave's around five-thirty that way the part-time crew will be here."

"Sounds good. I'll even drive if you want me too."

"Deal. I'll pay."

It's four o'clock. I walk around 'till five-thirty, smiling so hard my face hurts. My customer service is better than normal. I can't wait to go eat.

I call up Star. "Hey girl, I need a big favor."

"What's up?"

"Omar asked me out to lunch. I need you to wait in the parking lot of Famous Dave's and take pictures of us when we get out the car."

"For what?"

"So I can prove to Skye that we went out on dates and shit. Use it for collateral."

"Oh, okay, I got to get a camera and get dressed."

"A'ight, just be there by 5:30."

"Yeah, I'll be there. I'ma park in the back, text me when y'all about to pull in the parking lot."

"Cool. Thanks boo, I owe you one."

Now my ultimate plan is springing into action. I took the ovulation predictor yesterday and I'm ovulating, so I'm going to have to sleep with Omar this weekend. Hopefully, we can do it more than once to increase my chances of getting pregnant.

Omar calls me to his office. "Are you ready to go?"

"Yes, just let me grab my coat and purse."

I start the car then type my text message to Star. When we pull into the parking lot, I hit the send button. Omar gets out and opens the door for me. He is such a gentleman! I walk closely beside him so Star can take pictures. I make myself trip so he can catch me. I hope she got a picture of his arm around my waist! I'm loving every minute of the attention. We talk while waiting for our food.

"So are you going to tell me what's wrong, or do I have to beat it out of you?" I ask playfully.

"I miss my girlfriend, that's all. She left this morning to go on business, and she won't be back 'till Sunday. We have been having some problems in our relationship. My sister Kenya is getting married, and I'm happy for her, but I want to get married too. Me and Skye have been together for almost five years; our anniversary is November 17th. Anyway, I recently asked her to marry me, and she cussed me out and said no. Do you think I'm a bad man? Am I not marriage material?"

"No, personally I think you are a great man. Any woman should be thankful to have you. Did she say why she doesn't want to marry you?"

"She just keep saying she's not ready, and that I'm too needy."

"Maybe she's keeping her options open. She might be seeing someone else."

"No. I don't think she would cheat on me."

"The ones you least expect be the ones that will fool you. Why don't you surprise her with some flowers or something nice? Have it shipped to her while she's on her trip. I'm sure she'll appreciate that."

"Good idea, I'll call and set it up when I get back. Are we still on for tomorrow?"

"Sure, I have some errands to run, but I'll be finished by four. You know what, I have an idea. How about you come over straight from work, and you can get dinner with me since your girl is gone. I planned on cooking anyway. I would hate to eat alone."

"If it's not too much trouble. I'm tired of fast food. You know how to cook real good?"

"That's what I've been told. My mom taught me how to cook when I was ten years old. What's your favorite meal?"

"Oh, I don't care what you cook. I'm not a picky eater. I pretty much eat anything. Don't go through any trouble."

I bat my eyes. "That's not what I asked you."

"Well, if you insist, my favorite food is fried chicken breasts, collard greens, macaroni and cheese, candied yams, and rolls."

"You sure do like to eat, don't you? But it's no problem. I'll cook all that and then some."

"Yolanda, I appreciate the offer, but just cook whatever you planned on cooking. I'm not hard to please. I'm sure whatever you make will be delicious."

"It sure will be! Just make sure you come with an empty stomach. I'ma even have a special surprise for you."

"Really? I love surprises."

"Good, we better get back to work. I only get an hour break. I don't want to get fired!"

"Don't worry, I'm sure your boss will excuse you this one time." He gives me a wink.

I drive us back to work and look at the clock. We have been gone for almost two hours.

Omar escorts me into his office. "Don't worry about your time, I'll fix it so you only took an hour lunch. Let's just keep this between us. Thank you for listening to my problems. You brightened my cloudy day."

"You're welcome, I'm available anytime. What time do you leave tonight?"

"At eight o'clock; I'm tired too. I've been here since eight this morning."

"You only have thirty minutes left, you can make it. Have a good night. I'll see you tomorrow."

"I'll try. Goodnight to you too."

The rest of my shift flies by 'cause my mind is on Omar. I'm so happy that he has been confiding in me and complimenting me! I'm on my way to making him mine. On my way home, I stop by the grocery store. I buy everything Omar said he wanted to eat, plus ingredients to make a chocolate cake. I also buy a pregnancy test, ice cream, and a case of Coronas.

***

I wake up Friday morning smiling. I have a nine o'clock appointment with Diamond to get my hair done. Since Omar likes my natural hair, I'm going to get spirals all over with no extensions.

"Hey, Diamond. I got shit to do, so don't have me waiting all day."

"Well, good morning to you too! What do you have to do that's so important?"

"I got a date with Omar tonight. He's coming to my house to eat dinner and get his hair braided. When I leave here, I'm going to the nail shop to get my toes and nails done. Then I got to cook dinner, clean up, and look sexy."

"Excuse me, Miss Thang! I guess you need those eyebrows arched, and don't forget to trim up your private area."

"Oh, yep, that's on my list too. Make sure you curl it tight so when my curls fall, it will still be cute."

"A'ight. You can just wrap it when the curls fall. It'll just look like a roller wrap."

"That'll work."

Diamond finishes my hair at eleven-thirty. "Thank you girl, this shit is fly."

"You're welcome. Call me tomorrow and let me know how things went. You know me and Charmese are going to the club tomorrow night, let me know if you feel up to going."

"A'ight, I'll holla at y'all later." I hug Diamond and jet off to my next stop.

When I get home, I am tired so I take a nap until three o'clock, when my phone wakes me up. Still disoriented, I answer, "Hello?"

"Hey boo, were you asleep?"

"Yeah, just taking a nap. What time is it?"

"It's three o'clock, boo. I just called to tell you I got your pictures developed. They came out good, too. I'll come by tomorrow and drop them off. I don't want Tyrone to find them."

"Me either. I didn't know it was this late. I got to go cook. I'll call you tomorrow."

"A'ight, be careful. You don't want him to know what's up. If he finds out you really like him, it might scare him off. He probably doesn't want to put himself in a situation to cheat."

"I'll be careful, but I think I got it under control."

"I hope everything goes well. Good luck, boo. If you want to call me, I'll be up, 'cause I work tonight until midnight."

"I gotcha. Now I gotta go bake my cake."

"Ooh, save me some!"

"A'ight. Gone."

I run to the kitchen to make my three-layer chocolate cake from scratch. I bought some vanilla whipped icing to go on top. Then I crushed up some Oreo cookies on top of that. Now it's time to prepare the rest of the food.

When Omar knocks on the door, I am just finishing taking the chicken out of the grease. "Come on in. You're right on time."

"Mmm ... it smells good in here. I'm hungry too. My stomach is hitting my back. I didn't eat lunch 'cause I was anticipating your meal."

"Well, sit down I'll fix you a plate. I know you don't drink sodas; would you like iced tea or fruit punch?"

"Iced tea would be great."

I fix Omar's plate with two rolls, two chicken breasts, macaroni and cheese, collard greens, and candied yams. I sit the plate in front of him. His eyes get big. "Damn girl, you sure do know how to throw down! Everything looks good."

I sit down the glass of tea.

"Thank you. Go ahead and eat up."

"I'm waiting for you to sit down so we can say grace together."

"Okay, give me a second." I quickly fix my plate. I don't put much on mine, 'cause I'm trying to stay skinny until I get pregnant.

Aw, Omar is so sweet, he even wants to say grace! I sit at the table with my fruit punch.

"Okay let's say grace." We say grace, and then the room fell silent. All I hear is Omar's fork scraping the plate.

Skye must not cook for this man at all.

"Did you like it?"

"Girl, I loved it. You're right; you can definitely burn in the kitchen. I got to give you your props. I wish Skye would cook sometimes."

"Would you like some dessert? I made a chocolate three layer cake from scratch, and I have vanilla ice cream."

"That sounds real good, but I'm full. Maybe I can eat some after you finish my hair."

"Okay, if not, you are more than welcome to take some home for you and your daughter. By the way, where is she?"

"She's spending the weekend with her grandparents."

"Oh, that's mighty nice of them."

"Yeah, Skye parents are cool people. Do you mind if I go wash my hair? I'm kind of tired, I'ma go home and relax. I probably fall asleep before I hit the bed."

"Sure, let me get you a towel."

I clean the kitchen while Omar washes his hair. Before he comes, I put the Rohypnol in his tea, that's why I didn't drink any. If I can get him to drink some more or a Corona, I'll put a little more in.

Omar takes a minute to come out, so I go to check on him. I knock on the door. "Omar, are you a'ight?"

"Yeah, I'm coming now." He opens the door yawning.

"You look tired. Are you okay?"

"Yeah just a little tired. I'll be okay."

He sits in the chair while I blow-dry his hair. Since he's tired, and I'm on a mission, I do a quick style. It's still neat and cute, but I didn't freak it like I usually do.

I give him the mirror. "Go in the bathroom so you can see the back."

He goes and looks at his hair then comes back. "This is hot. Thanks, Yolanda. How much do I owe you?"

"You know I ain't going to charge you! Put your money back in your pocket. Now come sit down and have some cake and ice cream. Maybe some cold ice cream will wake you up."

"Yeah, I got some room. Hook me up."

I cut us some cake and serve it with Breyers vanilla ice cream.

"This shit is good. You cooked all this by yourself, for real? You sure your grandma didn't make this for you?"

"I made it myself. My grandma died, remember?" I make a pitiful face and try to squeeze out some tears.

"Aw shit, my bad, I'm so sorry! I completely forgot. Maybe I should go now."

"No, don't go! I need some company just for a few more minutes."

"Okay, I really didn't mean to upset you."

"I know you didn't"

"I got to use the bathroom, I'll be right back."

While he's in the bathroom, I fix us a drink. I slip some Rohypnol in his Corona. He should start feeling something in a minute. Omar comes out and we watch a movie while he sips on his Corona. Before the movie ends, he is knocked out. I slip off his shoes and all his clothes.

Now it's time to wake his soldier up. I gently massage Omar's penis until it starts to rise. I place his thick chocolate dick into my warm, wet mouth. I suck and stroke him until his dick becomes rock hard. Damn, I never knew he was packing this much meat! I strip down butt-naked and climb on top. I ride him until we both come. After I finish, I strategically place hickeys on his neck, thighs, and chest.

I call up Star. "Hey, girl, I need somebody to put some hickeys on me so he thinks that he participated too."

"Well, come down to Sugar Daddy's. You can make some quick money and get hickeys all at the same time. He will probably be out for another four hours or so."

"A'ight, let me take a shower. I'll be right down."

"A'ight. Then when you get back have sex again. If you are lucky, he will join in."

"Girl, I hope so, 'cause he got a monster dick on him! I know he got some skills. I can't wait for him to put it on me."

"I know that's right! I can't wait 'til I get off so Tyrone can please me. Hurry up, 'cause I might leave early."

"Give me forty-five minutes. I'm coming." I throw on my new fuchsia pink lingerie that I got from Victoria's Secret that I planned on wearing for Omar tonight.

I rush down to Sugar Daddy's Palace and I give three lap dances. During the process, I get several hickeys and make one hundred-fifty dollars. I have to run out the club before Dexter, the owner of the club, sees me. He would be mad that I took his customer's money and he didn't get a cut. I ball down the street, disobeying a dozen traffic laws. I'm glad I don't get stopped.

When I walk in, Omar is still sprawled out naked on my sofa. I drink a glass of water, and then I put in a porno flick to help arouse me. I place myself on top of him again after making him erect. This time I turn with my back facing him. I lift his hands and rub my soft large breasts with them. Halfway through I hear Omar moaning. Hmm, I think he likes it. Whew, now I'm tired! I cuddle up next to him and go to sleep.

I wake up to Omar yelling, "Oh, shit what the fuck just happened? I know we didn't have sex! Tell me we didn't do what I think we did!"

Rubbing my eyes I speak calmly. "I'm sorry Omar. I guess we both got carried away. It shouldn't have happened. I'm so sorry."

I burst into tears, shaking my head. Then I run into my room and shut the door. I wait for him to come after me. Just when I'm about to give up hope, he knocks on the door.

"Can I come in?" his deep voice asks.

"Yeah," I say, still crying. I try to wipe my nose before he comes all the way in.

"I'm sorry. I didn't mean to upset you. I know it's not your fault. I don't blame you. I must have had too much to drink and lost my head. You are a very attractive woman, I guess I just needed some attention and you gave it to me. I shouldn't have taken advantage of you. Your grandmother just died and you're still grieving. I feel awful."

"No need to apologize. We are both adults. We are equally to blame. I know you have a girlfriend and a child. I don't expect anything from you. We had a li'l too much to drink, that's all. Let's just act like this didn't happen. I don't want you to think I sleep around, 'cause I don't. I'm not that type of girl. I haven't had sex for a long time, so I guess I jumped at a chance to be with you. I'm sorry for that."

"I accept your apology. But the hickeys on both of our necks won't let us forget. At least, not for a couple of days. We both can't go to work with hickeys. That shit will look suspicious, especially since Skye is gone."

"Well, can't you act sick and call in? I can go to work; no one will suspect a thing. Maybe Michael or Dana can cover for you."

"Yeah, I guess so. Can I use your phone so I can call and let them know I'm not coming?"

"Sure, it's one in the kitchen if you want privacy. I'ma take a shower so I won't be late."

I get in the shower feeling guilty for what I've done. I never wanted Omar to feel so bad about this. I need to find a way to cheer him up. I slip on my uniform and I'm ready to go to work. Omar is sitting at my kitchen table when I walk out.

"Did you have any luck finding somebody to cover for you?"

"Yeah, Michael is going to pull twelve hours then Dana will be there second shift. They don't need me on second shift anyway. I hope you have a nice day at work. I'ma go home and clear my head. I'll be back on Tuesday."

"A'ight. Please don't be too hard on yourself. I won't tell a soul. Your secret is safe with me. Skye won't ever have to know."

"Yeah, but I do, and my conscience will eat me alive. I'll figure out something. Thanks for last night. I meant the dinner and braiding my hair. I gotta go."

He looks at me then lowers his head in shame and leaves. Damn, what did I just do?

After he leaves I notice twenty dollars on my coffee table. Oh no, now he's trying to play me like a two dollar hoe!

***

I walk around work sad all day, plus I'm deep in thought. When Dana works she is never around. Her and some man she's seeing on the side go into one of the vacant rooms and have sex all night. I never snitched 'cause that was her business, and it gave me time to look through Omar's office.

I decide to call Omar to check on him. "Omar, this is Yolanda, I just called to make sure you are okay. I thought about us, and I decided to quit. I'll put in my two weeks notice when you come back."

"Yolanda, I'm feeling better, there is no need for you to quit. I'm sure we can get through this. Don't make any rash decisions. I'll call you back later when I get myself together."

"Okay, goodbye." I hang up feeling a little better.

The rest of my day at work is relaxed, and I'm off Sunday anyway. I call Star to meet me for dinner while I'm on break. She tells me Diamond is with her. I meet them at Roma's Italian Restaurant.

"Hey y'all. How are y'all doing today?" I'm smiling hard.

"I'm fine. So how did it go?" Star asks, anxious to find out what happened.

"Everything went good last night. Omar got a big-ass dick. Anyway, we had sex twice and he came all in me. The second time he started moaning and moving a little. Well this morning when he woke up naked with me laying beside him, he freaked out. Then he saw the hickeys on his neck he flipped even more. I felt so bad 'cause he was truly upset and hurt."

"What did you say?" Diamond inquires.

"I told him that I was sorry, and I started crying really hard then ran to my room. He ended up not going to work so it wouldn't look suspicious 'cause both of us have hickeys. He told me it wasn't my fault."

"If only he knew."

"Very funny! I didn't want to hurt him, I love him. I just hope he won't flip out when I get pregnant. I offered to quit, but he said no."

"You should quit, especially if you get pregnant."

"Yeah, I am I'm going to start looking for a job tomorrow when the newspaper comes. Omar will give me a good reference. I need a sit down job anyway."

"Yeah, being pregnant is hard especially in the later stage. I hope everything works out. When are you going to take the pregnancy test?"

"Probably next month, my period is like clockwork. If it doesn't come, I'll know what's up."

"Here are your pictures, dear." Star hands me the pictures.

They came out great. Anyone who sees them will think we are a couple.

"Are you coming to the club tonight?" Star asks.

"No, I'm tired; I'll catch y'all next week."

"A'ight."

"It's time for me to head back to work, catch you later. By the way, how is Tyrone?"

"He's fine. We're going out tomorrow. I think I'm falling in love. Look for a job for me too. I'ma go legit. It's time for me to have kids. Diamond and Charmese already have kids and you want to get pregnant, so I might as well jump on the band wagon."

"Girl, you crazy! We can be pregnant at the same time. I got to go before I get fired. See y'all hoes later."

"Bye, heifer," they both yell.

Diamond has a three-year-old daughter named Enyce by her boyfriend Jermaine. Enyce is so cute, she looks just like Diamond. I hope my baby looks just like Omar. I think he has strong genes, 'cause Omari looks just like him. Dana is at the front desk when I come back.

"Oh, girl, I just noticed that hickey on your neck. You must've got some on your day off."

"Yeah, I got a li'l something to hold me over till tomorrow."

"I know that's right! We can keep this between us right."

"Yeah, no doubt. What you do is your business."

"Thanks girl. You can leave early if you want; I'll clock you out at eight."

"Are you sure?"

"Mm hmm, my man is gone, plus it's slow. I can handle it. Go get some rest or do whatever."

"Thanks Dana, goodnight."

I run and get my purse out of my locker and drive home. I am really worn out. When I get home I pour out the pitcher of tea and wash the pitcher real good. I don't want to make a mistake and drink it. I've got a little left. I'm going to use it on Omar again just to make sure I get pregnant. The only problem is getting him to be alone with me again. I fall asleep trying to contemplate my next move.

When I wake up, it's Sunday morning. I wash my face, then brush my teeth. I go in the kitchen and make a cup of coffee. I go to the door to get my Sunday's newspaper. As I sip my coffee, my eyes glance over the want ads. Hmm, this sounds good. SunTrust bank is hiring for Customer Service Reps starting at thirteen dollars an hour. Oh yeah, that's just what I need, a raise. If I'm going to have a baby, I need more money. This hotel shit barely pays my bills. Luckily, I get extra money dancing at Sugar Daddy's every now and then.

I've been living in my apartment for years, so my rent is still fairly cheap. I'm supposed to be off today, but Sherri called and asked if I could come in for a few hours. I need the money, so I go.

"Girl, thanks for coming in. I can't believe three people called in today, plus Omar is not here. You can leave at two o'clock," Sherri says.

"No problem, I need the extra money."

Time goes by fast, 'cause I only work four hours, but every little bit helps.

On my way to the time clock to clock out, Michael stops me. "Yolanda, can you do me a huge favor?"

"What's up?"

"I have very important papers for Omar to sign. They have been on his desk since Friday night. I think he forgot about them. It would mean a great deal to me if you could take them to his house."

"Umm … Sure I guess I can do that. Is he at home?"

"Yeah, I just talked to him. He's too sick to pick them up."

"Oh yeah, that's right. I totally forgot. Maybe I should go so I can check on him. Where are the papers?"

Michael hands me a big manila envelope with an address on top and twenty dollars. "Here, take this for gas. Just bring me a receipt when you come back to work. The address with directions is on top."

"Thanks, I'll see you tomorrow."

I'm elated. Finally I get to go to Omar's house. He doesn't live far, only fifteen minutes away by highway. I check my hair and makeup in the mirror before I get out of the car. I ring the doorbell cautiously. Omar opens the front door looking like death hit him.

"What's wrong? I hope you are not still tripping about Friday night."

"No, come in it's cold outside."

The weather is quite breezy and it looks like it is about to rain.

"Here are the papers you need to sign. I can take them back for you if you want me to."

"Ah, that's a'ight. I'm going to overnight mail them in the morning."

"Your eyes are red. Have you been doing drugs?"

"No, I just found out Skye lied to me about her business trip. Her job doesn't even know where she is. I hired a private investigator, and he said she went to Philly with her friends. She was spotted with some man in a club. I've been crying. I can't believe this shit!" Omar begins shouting and knocking things over.

"Calm down. I'm sure it's a good explanation for all of this."

I wrap my arms around him and held him tight. I dry his tears with my hand. That's when he shocks me. Omar kisses me on the lips.

The next thing I hear is a woman's voice yelling, "What the fuck is going on here?"

I immediately pull away from him and dash past both women standing in the doorway, jump into my car and speed off. I can't take a chance of fighting and losing my baby. We were so wrapped up in our conversation, neither one of us heard the door open.

Maybe this is the chance I've been waiting for. Skye thinks he is cheating, and he thinks she's cheating. Hopefully this will break up the not so happy couple.

When I get home, my heart is still beating fast. I go in the house and try to calm down. I pick up the phone to call Star.

"Hey girl, what are you doing?"

"Talking to Charmese."

"Please tell her you will call her back, I got something important to tell you."

"A'ight, chick, hold on."

She clicks back over. "Now what's so important?"

"Skye just came home and caught me and Omar kissing. I ran out the house before she could catch me."

"How in the hell did you get to his house?"

I tell Star the whole story about what went down.

"Well damn, ain't she a sheisty bitch! Maybe now he will leave her and be with you."

"I hope so, but I can't go back to work 'cause she might try to come up there and fight me. If I'm pregnant I don't want to lose my baby."

"Yeah I know, you can come work with me until you find another job."

"No, that's alright. I'ma see if I can get unemployment or transfer to another location."

"Good idea. You know if you need me you can always call, but Tyrone is on his way so I gotta go. I'll call you if I find out anything."

"Thanks, girl."

Damn, what a day. I slip my clothes off and took a long hot bath. When I get out of the tub, I call work to let them know I wouldn't be in. Now all I have to do is find a job tomorrow. I wake up bright and early to get on the Internet. I log onto Monster.com.

I post my résumé to several customer service representative positions. Hopefully I will get a call for an interview by the end of this week. I don't feel like sitting around the house all day, so I call Charmese. I haven't talked to her in awhile anyway.

"Hello?"

"Hey girl, what are you doing today?" I ask, trying to sound chipper.

"Same ole stuff. Do you want to hang out with me? I'm going shopping and getting my nails and toes done."

"Yeah, I could use a shopping trip. I need some new winter gear anyway."

"A'ight, well I'll pick you up in about two hours."

"I'll be ready."

It's the end of October and rather breezy out, so I decide to wear my Baby Phat sweatsuit with my Nike sneakers.

On my way out of the door, my cell phone rang. Without looking at the caller ID I hurriedly answer the phone.

"Hello?"

"May I speak to Yolanda?" a deep baritone voice asks politely.

"This is she."

"Why aren't you at work?"

Oh, now the voice is familiar to me, it's Omar.

"I feel funny being around you with everything that has happened between us. Plus Skye looked really mad. I don't want her coming to your job ready to fight."

"Yeah, she was pissed, but so am I. She moved out last night anyway. I don't think she will be coming up here acting crazy. She got caught in her own little lies. Anyway, I don't want you to just quit. What will you do for money?"

"I'll be okay; I'm already looking for something else. Just make sure you give me a good reference. I hate to rush you off the phone but I was on my way out."

"Don't let me keep you. Good luck on finding a new job. I'll be sure to give you an excellent reference. Don't hesitate to call me if you want to talk."

"I'll call you back later on tonight. Bye."

Charmese looks pissed when I finally come out of the house. I open the car door to get in. "I'm sorry girl, that was Omar on the phone. You know I had to talk to him."

"Mm hmm," she says, rolling her eyes.

"Where are we going first?"

"To the nail shop. Do you have some money?"

"Yeah, I got money. I don't need you to pay for me."

"Just checking."

"You know my birthday is coming up and I want to go to New York to go shopping. Do you think Danger will let you go?"

"I can go wherever I want to. Danger ain't my damn daddy."

I know just what to say to piss Charmese off. She gets on my nerves sometimes 'cause she thinks she's better than everybody else 'cause she got money. I get a pedicure, but I leave my hands alone. I don't want to get fake nails 'cause Omar might need his hair braided. I try to make small talk with Charmese at the mall.

"So how are things going with you and Danger?" I ask.

"We are not speaking right now. I heard he got some li'l young chick pregnant that live around Fairfield Court. When I asked him about it, he didn't even deny it. He just said 'it could be mine, I don't know for sure.' I'm getting tired of his cheating ass."

"Why don't you just put him out?"

"Then I'll have to pay all the bills myself. I like to shop too much for that, plus I don't want a job. What's up with you and Omar? Are you pregnant yet?"

"I don't know. We had sex twice. I have to wait until the end of November or December sometime to tell. His girlfriend moved out, but I don't know where that leaves us."

"This is the perfect time to make your move. Don't come on too strong. Just act like a concerned friend. Then slowly move in for the kill."

"Thanks for the advice."

I buy a soft leather coat from Wilson Leather and a Deréon puff coat from Macy's. I don't have much money, so that was the extent of my shopping trip. Of course Charmese has six shopping bags full of stuff. She ends up buying me a pair of BCBG boots from Saxon Shoes.

"Thanks, Charmese. I'll pay you back one day."

"Girl, don't worry about it. I love spending Danger's money when I'm mad at him even more than when I'm not." We both laugh.

"Well, I appreciate it. Let me know if you need anything."

"I will. See ya later. Good luck with Omar."

"A'ight."

I run inside the house, 'cause it's very cold outside. The temperature changes fast. I put my shopping bags in the closet and turn on the TV. *Well, another lonely night,* I thought. Then I remember to call Omar. I wonder if he's still at work. I call his cell phone and he answers on the third ring.

"What's up?" he asks.

"Did I catch you at a bad time?"

"No, I just wanted to get some things clear between us. I don't want to treat you like a rebound chick, so I think we shouldn't see each other. I'm still in love with Skye even though we aren't together right now. I'm not trying to jump into another relationship. I hope you understand. It's not nothing that you did it's me. I need to think some things through."

"Oh, yeah I understand. Just call me if you need someone to talk to. I hope everything works out for you. Just know that you are a wonderful man, and you deserve someone who will appreciate you."

"Thanks a lot, Yolanda. Let me know if you want a transfer to another location."

"I will. But first I'ma try to find something else. If that doesn't work, I'll call you."

"A'ight. Keep in touch."

Chapter Twelve

Skye

I still can't believe Omar was lip locking in our living room with some heifer. The whole situation seems like a bad dream. After the skeezer ran out of the house, I asked Jazz to leave me and Omar alone. I had some things to get off my chest.

"What in the hell is going on up in here?" I yelled, pointing my index finger into Omar's forehead.

"It's not what it looks like. She's an employee from work. All she did was come by to drop off some papers."

"Did she drop off those hickeys too, or did some other hoe give you those. You sure have been having fun while I was gone. Huh?"

"No, but you have. I know you lied to me about going away on business. I called your job 'cause I was going to have a gift delivered to you, but no one knew where you were. So what have you been doing this whole weekend?"

I began to get irate. "Don't try to turn this shit around on me. You're the one with passion marks all on your neck, condom wrappers everywhere, and to top it off, a bitch in our house that you were kissing. I can't take this anymore. I'm moving out."

I ran upstairs and started packing Omari's clothes. I already had clean clothes still packed. I pushed past Omar and threw my luggage in the car.

"Where is my daughter?" I screamed.

"At your parents' house."

I got into my car and peeled down the driveway. I was so mad I couldn't even think straight. Instead of going to my parent's house, I pulled up in front of Damisha's townhouse. Her car was parked out front, so I assumed she was home.

"Mimi, open up it's me, Skye."

Mimi opened the door with a bowl of Byers M & M Chocolate Chip Cookie Dough ice cream in her hand. With the spoon in mid-air she managed to say, "Girl, what the hell are you doing here?"

"It's a long story. I just need somewhere to stay temporarily."

"What's wrong with your house?"

"When I opened my front door, I caught Omar and some tramp from his job kissing and hugging in my living room."

"Oh, well that explains it. Sure, you can stay here as long as you want. Put your stuff in the guest bedroom. Where's my goddaughter?"

"Omari is at my parents. I'll get her later. First I need to calm down."

"Sit down and tell me all about it."

I sat on the couch and spilled my guts. Tears rolled down my cheeks. *Why am I crying,* I asked myself? I should be happy to get rid of Omar and his possessive ways. Good luck to the poor girl that has him next.

Once I got myself together, I felt a lot better. "Thanks for listening. I better go pick up my baby before it gets too late."

"You're welcome. Here, take my spare key so you can get in and out. Chris is supposed to be coming over, but if you need me I can cancel."

"No, don't be silly. Me and Omari will stay in the room. Handle your business. I'm tired as hell anyway."

"Omar is not going to show up any minute knocking on my door, is he?"

"No, he shouldn't, but if he do, I'm calling the police. I will get a restraining order if I have to."

"I feel ya. Be safe. If you see a black Infiniti out front, you know I got company. Please don't disturb, unless Omar breaks in and is choking the shit out of you."

"Girl, you are a fool. I get the point. I'll just eat some of your ice cream and throw a pity party for myself. Catch you later."

I dread going to my parent's house when something is wrong. Maybe I can act like everything is okay. I check my mirror on the dash before going to the door. I ring the doorbell twice.

"Who is it?" I hear my mother call.

"It's me, Mom."

She opens the door with a Gucci scarf tied around her head and a black satin robe on.

"Looks like you're ready for bed," I say, laughing.

"Yes I am. This little girl right here wore me out today. I think I'm getting old."

Omari cut in. "Hi, Mommy. I miss you."

"I missed you too, sweetie."

I pick her up, then look at my mother. "You're not getting old, just out of shape."

"I still look good, for your information. Most people don't even think I'm a grandma."

"I'm just teasing, Mom. Thanks for keeping Omari. It's getting late, I better get going."

"Okay, baby. Did you have a good trip?"

"Yeah, it was really educational. I'm really tired. I'll talk to you later." I kiss my mom and picked up Omari's diaper bag.

"Where's dad?"

"Oh, he's watching the game at Al's house."

"Well tell him I said thanks. Maybe you can invite us over for dinner this week so we can talk."

"Sure honey, I'll call you Wednesday. Love you."

My mom kisses me and Omari. "Bye, Grandma" Omari waves. I managed to get out of my mother's house without discussing Omar. Whew! I am not in the mood to talk about this shit again.

"Mommy, where is Daddy?"

"Daddy is at work. You can see him tomorrow. Okay?"

"Okay."

I feel bad lying to my two-year-old, but it's too complicated to explain to her. When I pull up at Mimi's house, I know she has company, so I take Omari straight to the guest room. After I get her to go to sleep I go into the kitchen and get a bowl of ice cream.

I check my cell phone, and I have several messages from Omar and Jazz. As I go to dial, the phone vibrates. It's Omar. "Yes, what do you want?" I ask with much attitude.

"I want to see my daughter tomorrow."

"Fine, you can pick her up from daycare and she can spend the night with you. I'll get her from daycare the following evening."

"That's cool. Tell her I love her. Bye." He hangs up on me. Damn, that's a first!

Let me call Jazz back so she'll know I'm okay. "Hey Jazz, I'm staying at Mimi's house for awhile."

"Yeah, thanks for letting me know. I was starting to get worried about you. What did Omar have to say for his self?"

"Nothing I wanted to hear. I'll be fine though. He called to see Omari tomorrow, and he hasn't come looking for me, so I guess he needs space too. He found out that I was lying about going away on business."

"For real? Damn. Maybe he thought you was cheating, that's why he kissed that girl."

"I don't think so, he had hickeys all on his neck. Things have been stacking up against him since Tyrone's party. Now I know the truth. I just need time to think. Maybe we can work it out, I don't know."

"Well, if you need somebody to talk to, you can call me anytime. I don't mind listening."

"Thanks girl, maybe we can go out for a drink after work tomorrow, since Omar will have Omari."

"Deal. Just call me and let me know where."

"A'ight. I'll talk to you tomorrow."

I go to sleep with my mind boggled. I toss and turn all night. My first thought is to call in sick and stay home and wallow in self-pity, but I decide against it.

"Get yourself together, Skye. You can do this. Everything is going to be okay," I try to encourage myself. Somehow I manage to get Omari and myself dressed. I drop Omari off at daycare, then head to work. For the first time in months, I'm late for work.

I never realized how much help Omar was until now. Everything he did, I took for granted. He always gets Omari dressed and takes her to daycare. I arrive at work forty-five minutes late and pissed off. Jamyya immediately notices my fake disposition.

"Skye, honey, what's wrong?" she asks.

"A simpler question would be what's right. I don't want to get into it now. Let's talk later on after work. Me and Jazz are going to go out to Buffalo Wild Wings, do you want to come?"

"I can't. My mom got a new boyfriend, so she's never home. Keenan is not going to keep the kids, and Jamesha is at work."

"How are Jamesha and your mom doing?"

"Jamesha is fine, except she eats and sleeps a lot. Rhonda is never home anymore, so her and Jamesha just coexist basically."

"Well, I guess it's better than them fighting."

"Yeah, I guess. So, how was your trip or should I ask?"

"No, the trip was fine. It's when I got back the problem started. Trust me, I'll tell you all about it later. Please, just call Keenan and see if you can get away for at least two hours. He should understand you are a working woman now. We can leave straight from work."

"Okay. I'll call him and try, but I won't promise you anything."

"Thanks a lot, Jamyya. It would mean a lot if you could come. If not, I'll call you later and fill you in."

"A'ight. I'ma go call now. Maybe I can catch him in a good mood before he gets mad and tired."

"Good luck, ma."

I shut my office door and check my e-mails. I have enough work to do to keep me busy. Good thing I don't punch a clock no more, but I still hate being late 'cause I want to set a good example. I call Jazz to make arrangements for later.

"Hey, Jazz. How about we meet at Buffalo Wild Wings on Broad as soon as you get off work?"

"Okay, that will work. Is anybody else coming?"

"Maybe Jamyya. I don't know for sure, but if you could call Mimi and Coco for me, I would appreciate it. I only want to do this once, so it will help if everyone attends."

"Yeah, sure I'll call them now. I'll hit you back later and let you know what's up."

"Cool. See ya later."

"Hey Skye, everything is going to be a'ight. I got your back."

"Thanks, ma." I hang up feeling a little better, just a little.

I dive into my work and stay in my office for majority of the day. I don't feel like eating lunch, but I need some air so I go shopping on my lunch break instead of eating. Shopping always makes me feel better. I go to Saxon's and buy two pair of boots. I spend a total of three hundred seventy-five dollars. Then I get three outfits from BeBe. After that I am almost broke, I have $200 left.

I decide, what the hell. I go to Macy's and spend my last $200 on Omari. I get her a new coat and some Ralph Lauren outfits. I forgot all about Christmas coming. Oh, well. While walking to my car, I see a young couple with a little girl. It makes me think about my broken family and I begin to cry. I put the bags in the trunk and jump in the car.

Damn, damn, damn. Why did things have to be this way? Maybe it's my fault for constantly pushing Omar away. Why couldn't I just say yes and marry him? I know why, 'cause I knew something was wrong.

Tears burn my cheeks as snot begins to come out of my nose. My face is red and my eyes are puffy. This is a first for me. I'm used to being the one who cheats and leaves; not the other way around. I never cried over a man before.

Get it together! You are Skye Jordan, and you can have any man you want. That's right, I can! I wipe my eyes with a napkin and try to pull myself together. I decide to put a little makeup on to hide my puffy eyes. I stop by Starbucks and buy a large mocha latte. "Things will get better," I tell myself. I am not the first woman who has been cheated on, and I'm definitely not the last. The last thing I expected Omar to do was cheat on me. Shit ... were things that bad between us? I shake my head as if to clear the thought out of my mind.

Get it together, it's time to go back to work. The rest of the day goes by in a blur. I don't know what went on, really. Jamyya managed to get Keenan to watch the kids so she could go out. Jazz had called me a little before five and told me that Coco and Mimi were coming, but Mimi couldn't get there until seven, so if we left before then to call her. Mimi already knew what was up anyway, so if she missed the first half, I could catch her up later.

***

I pull up to Buffalo Wild Wings with a smile on my face. Even though I am going through it, my appearance is flawless. I took extra time to do my hair this morning. I didn't want my friends to know I was broke down inside. I have always been the rock, the one with the steady relationship no matter how psychotic it was.

Me and Omar were on our way to the five year mark. Actually, I should be relieved. I walk in smiling with my head held high. "Hey chicks, what's going on?"

"What's going on with you is the question," Coco says, with her eyebrows raised.

"I'm good. I guess you all know by now that I left Omar. I packed my stuff and I'm staying with Mimi. When I came home from our trip, I saw Omar and some woman tongue kissing in our living room. Me and Omar had some words. He found out that I lied to him about the trip. I saw hickeys on his neck and that about sums it up."

"Why didn't you put him out?"

"'Cause I didn't want the constant reminder every time I went into the living room."

"So have you talked to him since that night?" Jamyya inquires.

"Yeah. He called about seeing Omari, but strangely that's all he said, then he hung up on me."

"Really? Do you know how long he has been seeing this other woman?"

"No, I didn't care to ask. Actually, I don't think I want to know. Let's talk about something else. I know somebody else got some drama going on."

"Yes as a matter of fact I do. I don't know what to do about Shawn. He has been groveling for awhile now, and I miss him," Jazz responds.

"If you miss him, take him back. People make mistakes all the time. If he didn't really want to be with you, he wouldn't go through all the trouble he's been enduring. Trust me, he wouldn't work this hard for pussy alone. It has to be some feelings behind it."

Damn, I give good advice, if I must say so myself.

"Thanks Skye, you know just what to say. I'm supposed to be comforting you, and you end up schooling me."

"What she needs to do is listen to her own advice. You need to talk to Omar and find out exactly what happened. Who knows what he was thinking you was doing, since you lied to him too. You need to think about how nasty you treat him and how many times he has forgiven you. Maybe you do need a little time apart, but I don't think you should totally end the relationship either," Jamyya advises.

"I'll think about it, but right now I'm shocked and hurt. I plan on talking to him in due time, when I feel I'm ready."

"A'ight. Do you, but it may be too late. You think Omar is always going to cater to you, but one day he is going to get tired. I'm just telling you the truth 'cause I'm your friend."

"Thanks, I appreciate the advice. I'll consider it. Now let's talk about something else."

I've always been good at changing the subject.

"Well, everybody should know I have drama in my life. Rhonda has been going to work, which is great, but now she has met this guy name Ronald Stevens. She's never home. She comes in all times of the night smelling like alcohol and cigarettes. I just hope she doesn't start shooting up heroin again. At first, she was helping me with the kids and paying bills. Now she never has money and she doesn't clean up. Keenan is constantly fussing at me about her and it's getting on my nerves. The kids won't give me a break. As soon as I walk through the door, I'm still at work. They want this, they need help with that. I can't take it anymore. Keenan gets off at 3:00 P.M., so he has time to himself. As soon as I get off, I have to pick up the kids then come home and fix dinner. I'm really stressed. I need a serious vacation."

"I feel ya girl, you should come to Montego Bay with us. We are going to leave on Friday January 16th and come back January 24th. If you start saving now, I'm sure you would have enough to go. Especially if we get two rooms and we split the charges," Coco states.

"Yeah, Jamyya, start making arrangements for the kids now. It's going to be a week-long celebration for my birthday. We all need a break from something. Don't worry about the hotel, I'll pay for that. Just have money to spend and get a plane ticket there. I'll take care of the rest." Jazz replies, sipping her drink.

"I sure could use an escape. I need to clear my head. I haven't even told my parents about me and Omar splitting up yet. I'm so confused," I admit.

"Take your time and think things through. If you and Omar are meant to be you will get back together. Me personally, I think Omar needs some counseling. He has serious control issues. He is too possessive and sometimes it's scary. Take this time apart to reflect on you and what you want out of life. Do you really want to continue to run and hide to get away from him? You are a grown-ass woman; Omar is supposed to be your partner, not your shadow or your father. He needs to deal with his emotional issues before you can have a healthy relationship. If neither one of you change, and y'all get back together, things will go back to being the same," Coco says in a serious tone.

"You're right. Thanks for all the good advice. What would I do without y'all as my friends?"

"Live a life full of drama with a stalker."

"Girl, shut up."

It's getting late and Jamyya has to leave.

"Thanks y'all for inviting me out. Skye I'm sorry about your situation, but you know if you need to talk I'm available. I'ma start working on planning our trip, 'cause I'm going to be there even if I have to run away. Y'all take care. See y'all Saturday."

"What's going on Saturday?" I ask, baffled.

"Girls day out. We are getting our hair done, nails, and massages. It's a day of relaxation and pampering."

"And who is keeping the kids?"

"Ke'Asia is going to a sleepover Friday night, so she won't be back until 6:00 P.M. on Saturday. Tamia is staying with Jamesha, and the twins are going to Keenan's mom's house. I already have it mapped out."

"Wow, what time does this event begin?"

"At 9:00 A.M. sharp. We are going to eat breakfast first. We can go to Golden Coral, Shoney's, or IHOP."

"Let go to Denny's," Coco chimes in.

"Fine, we can go there; now I gotta go. Tell Mimi I said hey, and invite her. Holla."

About five minutes after Jamyya leaves, Damisha comes in.

"Sorry I'm late, but I couldn't get off early. What did I miss?"

I looked at her. "Not much. Same ole stuff. Just girl talk. We decided to go to Montego Bay Jan. 16th through Jan. 24th and Jamyya has planned a girl's day at the spa for this Saturday at 9:00 A.M. You are cordially invited. Breakfast will be first at Denny's."

"Wow, sounds good. Can I order some food, or is everybody about to leave?"

"No, order away. I want to hear about your breakup with Chris," Jazz says.

"Well, actually we didn't breakup. I tried to tell him how I felt, but he wouldn't let me finish. He grabbed me and started kissing me and we had sex for the first time. It was so good, and it felt so right. Now I'm really confused, 'cause I can't sleep with him then dump him. I really like him and Jerell. It's hard to choose."

"I can't believe you slept with him! Was it better than Jerell's?"

"Yeah, overall I would say it was. It was different. I felt more in sync with him. It's like we had a spiritual connection. Well, it's hard to describe, but it was more passionate and intense. I had multiple orgasms."

"I can tell. Your face is still glowing. I hope you know what you're doing," I say.

"Actually, I have no clue. Right now I'm just doing me, having fun and enjoying life. Chris knows he is not the only one. They both know the situation, so it's their choice whether or not they want to continue being with me."

"That's true. Do you girl. Just don't get hurt in the process. You might mess up a good relationship 'cause you thinking with the wrong part of your body. You need to follow your heart, and think with your head not your pussy," Coco tells her.

"Fair enough. I'll slow down one day, but today is just not the day. Men play the field all the time, and it's okay, but when I do my thing, I'm wrong. It's a double standard. At least I'm woman enough to be honest and let them both know what's going on. I'm not hiding anything from either of them. Of course Jerell couldn't care less what I do anyway. As long as I'm jumping when he says jump, everything is lovely. Chris is the only one who wants a relationship, but I feel I'm not ready to give him what he expects from me."

"I'm glad you recognize how you play yourself when it comes to Jerell. At least you acknowledge it. Now do something about it. The more he knows you want him, the more he is going to act a fool. But you already know this. Follow your own advice and leave him alone. Pay him no mind and he'll come around. Watch what I tell you."

"I know all of this, but for some reason, it's hard to do."

I interrupt. "You know why? 'Cause he got your nose wide open. This is payback for all the shit you've done to men. Now snap out of it and get back on your game. I'm staying with you now, so I got your back. We can help each other."

"A'ight, I'ma give it a try."

My cell phone starts vibrating. I wonder who this could be? I looked at the caller ID. Who else would call me when I'm out with the girls but Omar? I answer the phone, irritated as usual. "Hello."

"Yeah, I just wanted to let you know that I got Omari, and she's fine. I'm about to go over to my mom's house, so if we aren't here, that's where we will be. Are you okay wit' dat?"

"Yeah, that's fine. I would prefer it if you didn't have any female company while Omari is with you. Going to your mom's house is fine."

"I don't have any females, but that's beside the point. Are you okay with moving out? If you want, you can have the house and I'll leave. I don't want Omari to be upset 'cause her environment has changed."

"Yeah, I'm good. You can stay there, 'cause I can't come back to that house right now. I'm kind of busy right at this moment so maybe we can talk later."

"Sure, I think it would be a good idea to talk too. Just call me when you are ready. I do want to say one thing though. I'm really sorry for what happened between us. I shouldn't have had her in the house, but the reason she was there was completely innocent."

"Mm hmm. Well, we can talk more later. Bye. Tell Omari that I love her."

"A'ight, baby."

I just have to hang up. I am not ready to deal with this right now. Just hearing his voice softens my heart. He sounds like he's hurting, but so am I. I know sometimes I come off spoiled and stuck up, but truth be told, I really do love Omar. I just wish he would change some of his ways. The number one problem I have with him is his constant following. If he would stop calling me and following me wherever I go, things would be great. I know he has problems with me 'cause my attitude sucks at times, but I'm willing to work on it. Well, I guess I'm willing to start right now.

It's time for a change.

Coco continues telling us about her madness.

"I started my anger management classes last week. As of right now, they aren't helping any. Just the other day Shameka called the house to speak to Jerome. As usual she tried to start shit. She wanted him to come to her house and put together a new bed she bought for Jermeka at nine o'clock at night. Do you know his dumb ass got dressed and went over there? I was pissed as hell! She still got him wrapped around her finger. One day I'm going to just snap and beat her ass. I can't take much more. Then André is getting on my nerves, leaving stupid-ass messages about seeing Corey. He knows damn well he don't care about him. He just wants to get on my nerves."

"Well, why don't you just let him see Corey? I'm sure since you beat Tyesha's ass, she won't mess with him anymore," Jazz replies.

"Yeah, she probably won't, but it's the principle of the situation."

"I guess. Well, it's getting late. I'ma go home and call Chris. I'll see you hoes later."

"Bye," we all say simultaneously.

"I think I better get home too, 'cause me and Jerome already beefing. I'll see y'all Saturday when y'all come to get the hair laid." Coco gets up to leave too.

"Guess it's just you and me, Jamesha."

"Yeah, I'm almost finished eating. You can leave if you want."

"No, I'll stay. I don't have anything else to do."

"Since it's just you and me, tell me how you feel about Omar, for real. No bullshit."

"Well, to be honest, I'm hurt. This came out of left field. As much as Omar stayed on me, I wouldn't think he would have time to cheat. In a way, I feel it's my fault. Really, I don't know what to do. I want us to work it out, but I don't know if I could ever trust him again. Then again, he probably doesn't trust me either, 'cause he thinks I was out cheating. Who knows what will happen?"

"You know Omar is not my favorite person, but he is a good man. Yeah, he got some flaws, but under all that, he is a good person. I know he really loves you and Omari. Maybe he's just lashing out from all the rejection you keep giving him. He might be trying to get your attention to let you know somebody else is interested. You need to make up your mind whether you want your family together or not. Now, you are more than welcome to stay with me as long as you need to. I just want you to weigh your pros and cons. Sometimes time apart helps both parties realize what they were missing."

"I appreciate all the advice you guys have been giving me, but it's something I have to decide for myself."

We sit for a couple more minutes then leave. When we get in the house, I feel funny not going home. For some odd reason, I miss Omar. I decide to get some advice from someone older, so I called my cousin Trina. She's thirty-two and lives in Hampton. I haven't seen her in awhile, but call her anyway.

"Hello, may I speak to Trina?"

"This is me. Who is this?"

"It's Skye."

"Oh my God girl, what's going on? I haven't heard from you in awhile."

"I'm having a problem and I need some advice. Do you have time to talk?"

"Of course, baby, I have time for you. What has Omar done this time?"

"Well, to make a long story short, I lied to him and told him I was going on a business trip, but I really went to Philly wit' Jazz, Coco, and Mimi. When I came back, I caught him kissing some woman in our living room. After the woman left, I noticed hickeys on his neck. Now, you know about the incidents that happened last month. What do you think?"

"I think you need to leave his ass alone. Omar wants to control you. You are your own woman, and you need to let him go and move on. The ones you least expect to do you wrong will be the one that will stick it to you good. It has to be a reason you wouldn't never marry him. Maybe you felt something was wrong deep in your gut. Always go with your instincts. Enjoy some time without him breathing down your back. In time y'all can get back together. Y'all have been together so long, and both of y'all are young. Maybe a break is what y'all need."

"You sound like everybody else. So, do you think it's my fault?"

"No, it's not your fault. You may have influenced his decision, but a man is going to do what he wants to do. He doesn't need you to do something for him to cheat. Although you tend to bruise his ego if another woman wants him and knows y'all situation, she might be able to manipulate the situation in her favor. Just think about it."

"Thanks, Trina I won't keep you any longer. Maybe I'll see you on Thanksgiving. I appreciate all the advice."

"Sure honey, anytime. I'll be coming to Richmond for Thanksgiving. I'll see you then. Goodnight, sweetie."

"Goodnight."

Maybe tonight will sleep little better. I wake up to a loud banging on the door. When I roll over and look at the clock, it's 2:00 A.M.

Who in the hell could this be at the house this time of the night? I think. Me being lazy, I call Mimi with my cell phone. "Mimi, is everything okay?"

"Um, yeah, why? What's wrong?"

"I thought I heard somebody banging on the door."

"Oh, my bad, that was my bed banging against the wall. Sorry, I'll keep it down."

"You are so damn nasty! It better be Chris up there."

"Oh, yeah, it is."

"A'ight. I'm going back to sleep. For a minute I thought it was Omar outside beating on the door."

"No, crazy hasn't came over yet. Don't talk him up."

"You're right, I don't want to do that. Goodnight."

"Goodnight, ma."

The week flies by. Before I know it, it's Friday. I have been avoiding Omar all week. I text him to see if he will keep Omari this weekend. He says that he has to work, but Shakita will watch her until he gets off. Other than that, we haven't talked.

I'm surprised to get a dozen pink roses with two helium balloons and a card. The balloons read "I'm sorry". Of course when I read the card, it's from Omar. Everyone at work thinks it's so sweet, but only Jamyya knows the truth.

Around lunch time, a delivery man comes in with a big white box and a huge teddy bear. "I have a delivery for a Skye Jordan."

"That's me."

"Just sign right here. Thank you very much, and enjoy your day."

Jamyya and all the other employees gather around.

"Open it" Denise says. Denise is the receptionist.

"A'ight."

I open the box. In it was a heart-shaped chocolate-iced cake with red icing. The cake says, "I'm hurting please forgive me." The brown teddy bear has on a T-shirt that reads, "You broke my heart." The bear also has band aids on his head and arms.

"Aw, that's so cute," Denise says.

"Yeah, very," I say in disgust. I go into my office and pull out my cell phone. I text Omar to tell him thank you for the gifts. I tell him we can talk Saturday afternoon.

"What are you doing tonight?" Jamyya asks.

"Nothing. Tonight is my time to spend with Omari. I will probably play with her for awhile then read her a story."

"What about tomorrow? Are you hanging out with us?"

"Yeah. I'ma drop Omari off at Shakita's house on the way to Denny's. She's going to keep her until Omar gets off work. What about you?"

"Hell yeah, I'm going! I really need it. Of course Keenan is bitching about me spending my money, but who cares. It's my check, and I deserve to look nice. Jamesha even gave me some money for bills, 'cause she's trying to be responsible. I wish Rhonda would help out. She's still hanging out."

"Well, she has been locked up for a while. Give her time to get herself together. She just wants to have fun just like you."

"Well, she had fun all my life while I was taking care of her kids. I never got to have a childhood, and in a way I blame her. It was her drug habit that ruined all of our lives. It's time for her to grow up and face real life. She needs to be a mother and grandma."

"Have you told her how you feel? She ought to know that her behavior is bothering you."

"If she would stay home, maybe I could talk to her. Keenan is getting on my nerves about her moving out. I thought her being gone would loosen things up, but instead he complains about her running in and out. I can't win for losing."

"I sympathize with you. At least tomorrow, you get a little break from reality. So just enjoy it. Maybe we will have time to go shopping too. You know Damisha's birthday is coming, and Christmas is just around the corner."

"Yes, time flies by fast. I'll try to make the shopping trip. I do need to get some things for the kids."

"Well, I'ma go cash my check, and I'll see you tomorrow."

"Okay, wait a minute. What are you going to do about Omar? It seems like he's trying to make up."

"Yeah, it seems that way, but I'm not ready yet. If I take him back too soon, it will send him the message that if he sends me gifts, then he can do whatever he wants. That's not the case. We really need to talk so I can find out exactly what happened."

"Fair enough. You know what's best for you. See ya, boo."

I take my cake and roses with me. I don't feel like cooking, so I stop by Ukrop's, and get some fried chicken and some sides. Omari's daycare is right down the street, so I pick her up and head to my temporary home.

Omari is sitting in her car seat pointing out the window. "Mommy, I want to go home."

"We are going home. Mommy got some food for us. Are you hungry?"

"Yes."

"Okay, I'll fix you some chicken when we get to the house."

"Okay."

Damisha is still at work, so I have the house to myself. Omari notices it isn't our house and she begins to pout her lips then cry.

"Mommy, I want to go my house. Daddy house, Mommy! I want to see Daddy."

Oh shit, what am I going to do? "Okay baby, we can go home." I love my daughter and I hate to see her upset, so I put my feelings aside and drive to our house. Her little face lights up like a Christmas tree. Unfortunately, Omar is home. I don't see any other cars around, so I assume he is alone.

The look on his face when I walk through the door is of pure shock. Omari runs up to him. "Hi, Daddy! I miss you."

"Hey baby. I miss you too. How are you doing today?" he asks her.

"Fine. I hungry."

"A'ight. I'll get you something to eat. What do you want?"

"Mommy got chicken."

"Oh, okay."

I set the grocery bag on the counter. "I bought us something to eat from Ukrop's. I didn't know we were coming here. Omari started crying she wanted to come home, so here we are. I hope we aren't interrupting anything."

"Oh, naw, I wasn't doing nothing. This is still your house too. You can come home whenever you want."

"Thanks. Look, let me get her straight, then if you have time, I would like to talk to you."

"That's cool. I'll be in the living room."

"A'ight."

I sit Omari in her high chair, fix her a plate of food, give her a cup of juice, then turn on the TV to Nickelodeon. "Watch TV while Mommy goes to talk to your daddy, okay?"

"Mm hmm," she says while eating her chicken.

My baby must be hungry, 'cause she never looks up.

I go into the living room and sit in the lounge chair.

"Look, I'm not ready for us to be back together, but this situation is negatively affecting Omari. I decided to move back in, but I'll be staying in the guest room downstairs. Just act like I'm not here. She wants to sleep in her own room, and I respect that."

"That's fine with me. I understand you need time. So do I. I can't believe you lied to me! If you wanted to hang out with your friends, that's all you had to say. You had me thinking you were cheating and shit. I had a private detective follow you. He said he saw you at a club in Philly with some guy, but when he showed me the pictures, it was Damisha."

"See, that's exactly why I didn't tell you, 'cause you are always following me. If you don't show up where I am, you call a thousand times. I've told you several times to back off. You are too damn clingy. Even if you thought I was cheating, that doesn't give you the right to bring another woman to our house and do who knows what with her. Even before all this happened, your behavior has been questionable. The letters I've found, the condom wrappers, all the hickeys. I've had doubts, but I pushed them aside 'cause I just knew Omar wouldn't cheat on me. Not my man, oh hell naw, he loves me too much. Well, I guess me being naïve paid off for you, 'cause I come home to catch you in the act. Now explain that."

"On Friday, I went to Yolanda's house to get my hair braided, she offered my something to eat and drink. I must have gotten drunk and passed out, 'cause all I remember is waking up naked wit' hickeys on my neck. Because I was all marked up, I didn't go to work. I had left the payroll papers in the office, and they needed my signature so everybody could get paid. So Michael asked Yolanda to drop them off. That's what she was doing here. It was cold outside, and I asked her to come in. We started talking, and I was crying 'cause I was upset about you lying to me. I thought you were cheating. That's when she hugged me and I kissed her. Then you walked in. I admit I was wrong and I'm sorry. This is the first time I ever slept with anybody else. All the condom wrappers I really can't explain. Just know I'm telling you the truth. I know you are upset, but Yolanda doesn't work with me anymore. I know it's no excuse, but I'm tired of you rejecting me. For once, somebody paid attention to me. She wanted to be near me, and she enjoyed my company. I felt lonely and abandoned."

"I appreciate you being honest with me, but I just can't believe you slept with someone else. I know I have mistreated you, and I'm sorry you feel that way. So maybe we shouldn't be together. Even though you get on my nerves, I never once, not once, cheated on you. Now it's going to be hard for me to trust you. I'm glad you are being honest, but I can't be with you right now. So how do you feel about this Yolanda now?"

"I mean, she was a good friend, but I don't want to be with her. I told her what happened between us was a mistake, and she agreed. I don't plan on seeing her again. She felt so guilty she quit her job."

"Oh, so the only reason she doesn't work with you anymore is because she quit? You didn't have anything to do with it?"

"I wasn't going to fire her, and I won't ask her to quit either. My plan was to transfer her to another location so I wouldn't have to see her every day. This is mostly my fault, 'cause I put myself in the situation. I own up to the blame."

"And you should. I'm really pissed right now, so I have nothing else to say. I'ma go in the kitchen and eat with my daughter. If some food is left, you can have some. Other than that, I would appreciate you staying out of my way when I'm here, and I'll do the same for you."

"Whatever. You don't ever want me around anyway. I think I'll just leave for the weekend so you can cool off. I'll be staying at work. Just leave Omari at my mother's house tomorrow. I'll pick her up when I get off work. Enjoy your cake. See ya later."

Omar goes upstairs and packs a bag, then leaves. After I eat and play with Omari, I call Mimi.

"Hey girl, I just want to let you know I'm moving back home. I don't feel like talking right now. I'll tell y'all everything tomorrow. Love you, and thanks for everything."

"I hope it's not what happened last night that scared you off! I'm not use to having company. I promise to tone it down. I know kids shouldn't hear that type of stuff."

"No, no, it has nothing to do with that. It's something totally different. It has nothing to do with you. You have been a very good friend. Let's discuss it tomorrow."

"A'ight Skye, have a good night."

"I'll try to."

***

I can't sleep, so I take two Advil P.M.s to help knock me out. They work, too! I wake up Saturday morning with a smile on my face. I forget all about today being Halloween. Anyway, I am determined to have a good day. I start my morning on a positive note. I don't know if Omar told Shakita about what's been going on with us, so I decide to act as if nothing is wrong. Shakita still lives in the same house that they lived in when me and Omar first met. I knock on the door, and Devin answers it.

"Hey, what's up Skye? Hey little momma," he says to me and Omari.

"Hi, Uncle Devin," Omari says, waving.

"Hey Devin, where is your mom?"

"Oh, she ran to the grocery store real quick. She told me you were coming. You can leave her here with me. I guess I better get use to keeping kids anyway since I'm about to have one," he jokes.

"Yeah, I know. How are things with you and Jamesha? You know that's my best friend's li'l sister. I'm not going to have you dogging her."

"No, I wouldn't do that. We're cool. We're still kicking it. She's starting to eat a lot, though. I can't have anything around her. She always wants a piece. I hope she don't get real fat."

"She might. That's what happens when you get pregnant. I wish you the best of luck. I gotta run so I won't be too late."

"A'ight. She's in safe hands. We'll be cool. My mom should be back in a minute anyway."

"Okay. Well, she already ate, but if she sees you with something, you know she will want some too. Kind of like a mini Jamesha," I say, laughing.

"Yeah, you're right. See ya, Skye. Tell Omar I said he could call and check on a brotha."

"You'll probably see him before I will. He's coming to pick Omari up."

"Cool."

I dash out the house and jump in my car. Damn, my car is dirty! Well, no time for that, it's already quarter till nine. I'm going to be late as usual.

When I get to Denny's, everyone is already there.

"Sorry guys, but y'all probably already knew I would be late."

"Yeah, we did. No wonder, its cold outside. I can't believe Skye has on a sweatsuit and sneakers," Mimi says.

"Yeah, girl, do you have a fever? Are you feeling a'ight?"

"Yes, I'm okay. I knew we were shopping today, plus its cold out. I still think I look cute though."

"Yeah, you do," Jazz replies.

Usually I'm not a sneaker chick, but today I'm rocking a baby-blue-and-gray Roca Wear sweatsuit with my white and blue Jordan's. Even in my sweatsuit, I look good.

"Well, I guess you are wondering why I moved back home. It has to do with Omari. Last night when I took her to your house, she kept saying she wanted to go home. She missed her daddy and she started crying. I felt really bad, so I went back home. I'm sleeping downstairs in the guest room."

I tell them in detail the conversation me and Omar had about him and Yolanda.

"And you're okay with that?" Mimi asks.

"No, I'm not, but that doesn't change the fact that it happened. I'm just staying in the house for my daughter, but I have nothing else to say to Omar."

"I can't believe he told you that he slept with someone else," Jazz says.

"Me either," Jamyya chimes in.

"Well, it happened. Now I have to move on. Let's focus on something fun. Today I want to relax and forget about my problems."

"Good idea. Let's change the subject," Mimi suggests.

We go to Sylvia's Day Spa for our massages, facials, and nail treatments. While I am relaxing, I decide to reinvent myself. I'm going to do something different. I usually get a French manicure and pedicure, but this time I opt for color and designs. I get my nails and toes done with the same design. I pick out a bright purple, teal, and gold. The design is a flower with glitter. It's very pretty. Then when I go to Diva Style, I shock Coco with how I want my hair. I show her a picture I saw in the Black Hair magazine.

"Coco, please cut it like this. It's time for a new style. Plus I want to dye it spicy cognac."

"Skye, have you lost your damn mind? You are not Angela Bassett in <u>Waiting to Exhale</u>. Just 'cause you and Omar have problems don't mean you should go crazy and cut your hair!" Coco exclaims.

"Just do what I ask you to, or I'll get somebody else to do it. Either way, I'm getting it cut."

"Fine, I'll do it, but first you need to understand, once I cut it, it's gone."

"I know, and if I don't like it, I'll buy some weave."

"A'ight, come on, let's do this."

I sit under the hair dryer for what seems like hours. While I was under the dryer, I read a book called *When a Woman's Fed Up*. Hmm, don't I know about that! I wish I would have had time to finish it; the book is very good.

Anyway, when my hair is finished, everybody compliments me and Coco on a job well done. Finally she turns me around to look in the mirror.

"Oh, my ... this is so cute, Coco! I love it." I am absolutely thrilled.

Damisha gets her hair blown straight out and she also cuts her hair, but she gets hers in a three-layered wrap with bangs.

"What's up with everybody cutting their hair?" Coco asks.

"I'm not cutting mine," Jazz shouts. Jamyya doesn't cut hers either.

Jazz gets her hair in wild flips and Jamyya gets spiral curls all over. We all leave the shop looking absolutely gorgeous.

"Girls, when we go to the mall, we are going to be turning heads," Jamyya says.

"We sure are! Everybody looks so beautiful. Thanks guys, I needed this." Tears start forming in my eyes.

"You know we got your back. Now let's go spend some money. I got a hot date tonight," Mimi says.

"Wit' who?" I ask.

"Wit' Chris. I've been following your advice. I haven't talked to Jerell since I left to go to Philly. He called me a couple of days ago, but I didn't answer. And I didn't call him back. It's hard, but I'm doing it."

"I'm so proud of you. What mall are we going to?"

"Let's not go to the mall. We should ride down to Potomac Mills and go to the Outlet," Jazz suggests.

"Yeah, let's go somewhere different. I bet we won't see Omar there," Mimi agrees.

Too bad she's wrong. I'm walking around the mall swinging my bags, enjoying all the men staring, when I spot a familiar face.

"Now I know damn well that's not Omar! Somebody please tell me my mind is playing tricks on me!" I am heated.

"Skye, let me ask you something. Did Omar put a tracking device up your ass or what?" Mimi asks.

"Girl, I don't know, but this is ridiculous! I told you he had somebody watching me. Maybe the private detective told him where I was. Let's act like we don't notice him."

"Oh shit, he even got Tyrone and Dontaé with him. Maybe it was just a coincidence," Jazz says.

"I doubt it," I respond.

As we walk past, Dontaé grabs Mimi by the hand. "What's up li'l sis? I know you not going to just walk past me and don't speak. What, you too fly for me now?"

"No, what's up with you and your boy? Why he always following us every time we go somewhere?" she asks with an attitude.

"How we suppose to know y'all was going to be here? We came out here so we wouldn't run into y'all. Omar knew y'all were going shopping, that's why we drove way out here to avoid confusion, but I see it didn't work."

"No it didn't, 'cause we came out here to do the same thing. It's all good though. Nice to see you."

"Likewise. I see you cut your hair, I like it. It's tight. I won't keep you. I see your girl over there rolling her eyes."

Dontaé looks at me. "Yo Skye, I like your new do, it's hot."

"Thanks Dee, I see ya later. I gotta go to the ladies room."

As I walk off, Omar steps in front of me.

"Oh, so now you are going to act like you don't know me? You go get all fly and shit, now you out flaunting. You know what, fuck you Skye, you ain't shit, for real!"

Omar turns and walks off. I really don't believe this shit! I'm speechless. This nigga cheated on me, and he has the nerve to talk shit to me! I'm through. Well, this blew a perfectly good day.

Jazz comes into the bathroom behind me.

"Skye, are you alright?"

"Yeah, I'm fine. Let's just leave. I'm ready to go."

"Okay, I'll let Mimi know."

We leave the mall and ride home in silence. I keep trying to figure out how he knew where I was. No matter where I go, Omar always seems to find me. Maybe I should get a restraining order on his crazy ass. I hope he doesn't come home tonight, 'cause I'm not up for any more bullshit.

I go home and make me an apple Martini. Shit, after the day I just had, I need a drink!

Chapter Thirteen
Jamyya

Today is the day I decide to deal with my mother. Rhonda staying at my house is starting to take a toll on my marriage. Keenan never liked my mom because she neglected me and my siblings. I had to grow up fast to take care of us. Me and Keenan rarely went out 'cause I always had to keep my brothers and sister. For some reason, he can't bring himself to forgive her.

I'm sitting at the kitchen table Sunday morning, reading the newspaper and drinking a cup of coffee. Rhonda comes staggering in like nothing is wrong.

"Hey baby, what you doing up so early?" she slurs, smelling like cigarettes and cheap liquor.

"Sitting here waiting for you to come in. Mom, we need to talk. Please sit down."

"Talk, for what? Child, it's too early for all this nonsense. I'll speak to you later." She waves her hand as if to blow me off.

"You are going to sit down and listen to what I have to say. I've been putting this off long enough. Now sit down, please. This won't take long."

Rhonda finally pulls out a chair and sits at the table. I fix her a cup of coffee.

"Drink this. Mom, you know you shouldn't be drinking alcohol. It could lead to other things. I'm proud of you for going to work and keeping a job. I'm glad you've found a man to spend time with, but you need to calm down. You are disrespecting me and my house. You can't just run in and out the house all hours of the night. You need to focus on reconnecting with your family. We barely see you anymore. I thought you were going to change your bad ways. You promised me things will be different this time. You haven't cleaned up your room or paid any bills in weeks. If your seventeen-year-old daughter is responsible enough to pay bills and clean up, you are too. I'm tired of you coming in wrecking havoc on my life. You need to make a choice. This family, or drugs and alcohol?"

"See, ain't nobody doing no damn drugs! I've been saving my money so I can move out. Jamesha ain't that damn responsible, 'cause her dumb ass got pregnant. Plus I'm a grown-ass woman, and I should be able to come and go as I please. I've been locked up for four years, and all I want to do now is enjoy my freedom. It's my life. Don't be mad 'cause I won't stay home to keep your kids anymore. You're just jealous you can't hang out like I do. All my kids are grown. My babysitting days are over. I'm not an old-ass grandma that's going to sit in a rocking chair making quilts. I'm still young. Shit, I'm only forty years old."

"Damn right I'm mad! I didn't have a childhood 'cause I was busy doing your job. I was the one who raised your damn kids while you got high. You never cared about us. All you care about is yourself. You've had fun your whole life. Now it's time to grow up and face your responsibilities. I feel you owe me and yourself that much. I'm tired of taking up for you. No more excuses. So you know what you can do. Pack your shit and get out. That way you can do whatever in the hell you want to, 'cause it ain't going to happen in my house. Call me if you can ever get your shit together. I'll be glad to hear from you then. Not a minute sooner. You may not be tired, but I am. A person can only take so much, and I'm just plain fed up with you."

"Fine, I'll go stay with my man. Ronald will be happy to have me. You need to let go of the past, 'cause I can't change it. You need to move into the future and own up to your own mistakes. It ain't my fault your li'l fast ass got pregnant at sixteen. You should've kept your legs closed. Now you got four kids to raise, and you want to blame me for it. I don't think so. I don't mind helping out, but I got a life too. I wish you would realize that. Make Keenan help keep them damn kids sometimes, he's your husband. Shit, he had fun making them. Look, I got a headache, I don't need this shit. I'ma go pack my stuff and get the fuck out."

"Well, at least I know who my kids' father is. Did you ever think how that made us feel growing up without a dad? Not even knowing who he is or what he looks like. That's a hurting feeling. My having kids young is partly your fault, 'cause you didn't give me any supervision. If I would have had some guidance and love, I wouldn't have turned to men for it. You know what... this conversation is over, 'cause you don't listen anyway. Prison has taught you nothing. You need to find some counseling quick, 'cause if you get locked up again, don't call me, call your damn man or Paul Mason."

"I'm sick of your smart-ass mouth. Don't worry about me, I'll be fine. Go back to your boring little life. I've had enough of you and your husband looking down on me. Fuck both of you."

Rhonda storms off to her room, slinging boxes and bags around while packing her stuff. She calls Ronald and he came to pick her up.

Keenan tries to comfort me, but it feels more like an I-told-you-so.

"Baby, it's for the best. Rhonda is always going to be Rhonda. Ain't no changing that. She will get tired one day. You can't save a person who doesn't want to be saved. Maybe now things can get back to normal. Did you talk to Jerome about getting a new house?"

"No, I forgot all about it. My mind has been somewhere else. I think we should just stay here. Money is tight enough. I'm trying to save some money so I can take a vacation. I've been meaning to talk to you about going to Montego Bay. Jasmine's birthday is on Jan 15th and everybody's going to Montego Bay to celebrate with her. I need a getaway."

"So who's going to keep the kids while you are gone? You don't think I work hard? I deserve a break too. What about me? You know, you are becoming very selfish. You need to stop hanging around Skye. Listening to your friends is going to complicate our marriage."

"I'm not saying you don't work hard, but I do too. I'm the one always taking care of the kids and the house. I have a job now, and I'm still doing the same shit I use to. It's like I have two jobs. I'm never off. Even when I get home from work, I'm still working here. I need you to do more than just be here. You can take care of the kids for a week. Shit, I've done it for years. Maybe if you experience what I go through, you would appreciate me a little more."

"I do appreciate you. Maybe we should talk later when you calm down. Don't take your frustrations out on me 'cause things aren't working out with you and your mom."

"Whatever. You're always trying to blame our problems on someone else. My mother and my friends have anything to do with this. I have a mind of my own, and contrary to what you believe, I use it."

"I'ma go out for a little while. I don't know if you are PMS'ing or what, but I'll leave you alone for awhile. As a matter of fact, I'll take all the kids with me. We'll be back later on tonight. Hopefully you will feel better by then."

Keenan gets the twins dressed and takes the girls with him. I don't know where they are going, and frankly I don't care. Finally, some time to myself!

The nerve of him! I'm going to Montego Bay whether he likes it or not. I know Skye is going through it with Omar, so I don't know who to call. I try calling Mimi, but she is busy with Chris. Hmm, maybe Coco is available. I call Coco, but she doesn't answer. Okay, Skye it is.

Ring …ring… "Hey Skye, are you busy?" I ask skeptically.

"No, I'm just chilling. Is everything a'ight with you?"

"No, me and Rhonda got into it this morning, and I put her out. Then I told Keenan about the trip to Montego Bay, and we got into it. He took the kids and left. Now I'm home alone and I'm still pissed. I just don't know what to do. I can't seem to please anybody."

"Don't worry about nobody else. You need to concentrate on you and what makes you happy. Since the kids are gone, how about you get dressed and we go out somewhere? Just me and you. We can go wherever you want."

"Sounds good. Let's go to the Cheesecake Factory for lunch, then to the movies."

"A'ight, be at my house in an hour. I'll be ready 'cause it's just me. Omari is still wit' Omar. How about this crazy fool called me this morning and left me three messages."

"For real? What did he say?"

"Girl, hold on. I'ma let you hear them." Skye dials her voicemail number on three way.

"First message, 6:09 A.M. ... Skye, I know you see I'm calling you. Pick up the damn phone. A'ight, it's like that. Fine, be that way. You are going to need me one day. Second message, 6:49 A.M. ... Oh, you think you cute now 'cause you cut your hair and shit. You're still the same selfish bitch you've always been. I don't know why I didn't leave you a long time ago. You don't deserve me. All you are is a user, you use people. I'm through kissing your ass. Don't worry about me following you. You're not worth my time. Oh, yeah you want to go get restraining orders and shit. That's fine, oh that's fine. Play your little games. Do you, 'cause I'ma do me. Fuck you, Skye. You ain't shit. I'm tired of you mistreating me, no more. I give up on you and our weak-ass relationship. All I wanted to do is love you. You can pick up Omari at 8:00 P.M. from my mother's house. Don't worry, I won't' be there. Third message, 8:05 A.M.... You still acting like a li'l bitch. Don't answer. I'm not going to call no more anyway. I'm through trying to make up with you. Just pack all my shit and sit it outside. I'll get my brother to come by and pick it up. I don't even want to see your face. Oh, yeah, that's right, I can't come within ten feet of you. I can't believe you went to the police. You are one sneaky bitch. It's cool, mm hmm, it's cool. You are going to get yours one day. Oh, yeah, when you need something, you are going to miss me. No more ass-kissing for Omar. I'm done."

Click! The messages are done.

"Now you see what type of crazy bullshit I gotta deal with." Skye says, laughing.

I try to hold it in, but I have to laugh too. This nigga done lost his mind! Literally.

"Yeah, I see. I'm shocked too, though. I would've never thought you would get a restraining order on him."

"Girl, he pissed me off so bad yesterday, I went straight to the police station after y'all dropped me off. I'm tired of him following me. Enough is enough. He needs to go stalk that bitch he works with."

"Well, he might now, since he claims he is through with you. I'ma go get dressed before my family comes back. I'll see you in an hour. No sneakers, it's dress-up day."

"Look at you, trying to tell me how to dress! I got this, I'ma be the fly chick I always am. Trust that."

"You are so damn conceited, but I love you anyway

"If I don't think I look good, who will? I like to call it self-confidence."

"A'ight chick, go get glamorous. I'll be there in a minute."

"Bye."

I had already taken a shower, but need to get dressed. My hair still looks good from yesterday. I know Skye is going to be on her game, so I have to find something hot.

After rummaging through my closet, I decide to wear a cream cashmere Dolce & Gabbana sweater dress that is off the shoulders, a pair of cream-and-brown print tights, a wide brown belt, and my knee high brown suede Alexander McQueen boots. Oh, yeah, I have to admit I'm the shit. I drive over to Skye's house, knowing she isn't ready. I automatically get out of the car and ring the bell. To my surprise, she opens the door fully dressed with her purse in hand.

"Wow, you're actually ready! It's going to snow tonight."

"Shut up. You ain't funny. Mmm, mmm, mmm, look at you! Don't you look cute! This look like something I'd wear. Let me find out my good fashion sense is finally rubbing off on you!"

"Nope. I got my own style. I just thought this was cute. It was time to treat myself."

"I know that's right! If I knew you were going to be rocking a dress, I would've put my dress on too."

"Skye, you are fine. You always look cute, no matter what you wear. You could put on a paper bag, and people would still compliment you."

Skye really did look pretty. She had on a dark purple tight long v-neck shirt, black leggings, a long black beaded chain, and purple Jimmy Choo pumps. But I have to admit, this time, my outfit looks better. Inside, I am secretly enjoying her envying me for once.

At the restaurant, we are both turning heads. We have a great time talking, just me and Skye. We have always been the closest. Don't get me wrong, all of us are cool, but me and Skye stick together and Damisha and Jazz are tight. Coco is just mixed all up in the middle. Next to Skye, Damisha is my next favorite. I like them all for different reasons. Coco is the one who I get marriage advice from. Jazz is just fun to hang out wit'. Damisha is smart when it comes to how men think and what they want. I go to her for advice too. Skye is just a confidence-booster, she always makes me feel good about myself. She always comes to me in a crisis. I love how she values our friendship. Even though I feel Skye is wrong most of the time, I know deep down inside she's a good person.

On our way out of the restaurant, two fine men approach us.

"Hello, lovely ladies. How are you doing this afternoon?" the tall pecan-colored man asks.

"We are fine. Nice of you to ask," Skye says, flirting.

He sticks out his hand to shake hers. "My name is Jefferson, but all my friends call me Jeff. What's yours?"

"I'm Skye, and this is my friend Jamyya."

"Yes, her married friend," I respond, showing off my wedding ring. His friend begins to back off, but Jeff keeps on talking.

"Are you married too?" he asks Skye.

"No, I'm single, sexy, and free."

"You are sure right about that! Is it possible for me to get your number so we can go out sometime? You know, get to know one another?"

"Sure, my number is 555-2311. I hope to be hearing from you soon."

"Oh, you will. Y'all ladies have a lovely evening."

"You too, sweetie."

I snatch Skye to the side. "I can't believe you are out here flirting, giving out your number and stuff. What is wrong with you? You've been hanging around Mimi too much."

"No I haven't! I'm just having fun. You heard Omar's messages. We are not together anymore. I'm free to do whatever I want. Shit, he was fine. What did you want me to do?"

I pause a minute. She's right, brotha was fine. He was about 6 foot, 210 pounds with smooth pecan-brown skin. He had big pretty brown eyes, a low cut with waves, and beautiful white teeth. I guess if I was single, I would flirt too.

"You're right. Do your thing girl. He was fine."

"Exactly! I need somebody to help me take my mind off Omar. Maybe if he sees me with somebody else, he will back off."

"I don't think so. You know how over-protective Omar can be. Just be careful, 'cause it seems Omar's strings are unraveling. The boy is not wrapped too tight."

"Now you are starting to see what I'm talking about. He has always been like that, but nobody wanted to see it."

"Have you told your parents yet?"

"No. I'll probably tell them on Thanksgiving. I hope he doesn't show up at my mom's house like everything is good."

"Yeah, that would be some wild shit. Maybe you should tell them ahead of time so they won't let him in."

"It don't matter one way or another, they all think Omar does no wrong. Somebody will let him in regardless of how I feel."

"Oh, well in that case, I don't know what to tell you."

We go to the movies and have a great time. I go back home feeling like a brand new woman. Oh, please let things cool down between Keenan and me! When I walk in the house, Jamesha is cleaning up the kitchen and the house is quiet.

"Where is everybody?" I ask, astonished.

"Oh, I cooked dinner for the kids, gave them a bath, and now they are asleep. I braided Ke'Asia's and Tamia's hair. That way you won't have to worry about it in the morning. Then I ironed all the kids' clothes for tomorrow. Keenan went out with some of his friends. I told him I would watch the kids."

"Thanks Jamesha, you didn't have to do all that. The kids actually listened to you?"

"Yep, they didn't give me any problems. I'm surprised they went to sleep at eight-thirty when I told them to go to bed. I'm getting in some practice."

"I see. I'm very proud that you're taking your responsibility seriously. What did you cook?"

"Barbecue chicken, corn on the cob, string beans, and rice. It was good, too. Keenan even ate some before he left. He told me Rhonda moved out."

"Yeah, she's gone. I hope she's a'ight."

"I'm sure she is. Don't worry about her. Some people never change. You just have to learn to accept that. Devin kept his niece yesterday. He called me to tell me how he's practicing being a dad."

"That's so sweet! So I assume things are working out for you guys."

"Yeah, we are cool. Nobody at school knows I'm pregnant; we decided to keep it a secret."

"Yeah, it's probably best. Well I'ma go get ready for work tomorrow. I'll see you in the morning. Don't stay up too late."

"I won't. I'll probably go to sleep after I finish cleaning up. Goodnight."

"I love you and I really am proud of you. I'm glad you are still getting honor roll in school. You are growing up nicely."

"Thanks, I love you too. Oh, guess what?"

"What?"

"James sent me $200 dollars through Western Union so I could go shopping. He said he figured I would need some new clothes soon. Devin said he would take me Friday after school."

"That was very sweet of him."

"Mm hmm, he told me to tell you he's coming for Thanksgiving and he is bringing his girlfriend."

"I can't wait to meet her. Did Keenan say when he would be back?"

"No, but he left about an hour ago."

"A'ight. Goodnight."

***

I go into my room and pick out my clothes for work. I'm glad somebody understands a sista needs help! Jamesha is so sweet. I'ma make sure she has a nice Christmas. Keenan must've come in late, 'cause I don't even notice he's home until I wake up to get the kids ready for school.

"Are you still mad at me?" I ask him.

"No, I'm not mad. Are you in a better mood today?"

"Yeah, I'm straight. So what did you do last night?"

"I went to Leon's house and watched boxing. We had a couple beers and just talked. Nothing special."

"Oh, I just asked 'cause I didn't hear you come in. That's all."

"I got home around midnight. You must've been knocked out. Did you have a rough day?"

"No, I just chilled with my friend that you don't seem to like much. We ate dinner and caught a movie. I had a good time."

"I'm glad. It's not that I don't like her, she's just stuck on herself. She's ungrateful and selfish. I just don't like her attitude towards Omar, that's all."

"Well, you don't know everything that goes on. It's their business anyway."

"You're right, and I'ma stay out of it. Let's not argue this morning."

"Fine. I hope you have a good day at work honey." I give him a kiss.

"You too, sweetie. I love you, and we will talk later about Montego Bay, okay?"

"A'ight. See ya later, I'ma cook dinner tonight."

"Good. Oh yeah, Jamesha cooked dinner last night. It was delicious. She did a good job on the kids' hair too. She even gave them a bath. You have a good sister. I think she will be a great mom. You did a good job raising her. I hope Devin treats her right."

"Thank you, honey. I hope he does too. He's been good so far. Maybe they will end up happy like us. I know we have our problems, but I love you and I never regret marrying you."

"Me neither. Sorry to run, but I got to get to work. See ya when you get home. Oh, don't worry about the kids. I'll pick them up from daycare today," he smiles at me.

"Thanks honey, you're the greatest."

I give him the biggest hug and he leaves to go to work.

See, today brings about a whole new aura. Thank you, Jesus! I go to work with a big smile on my face.

"Good morning, everybody," I say as I walk in.

"Well, I see somebody had a good weekend," Denise says.

"I sure did."

I walk to my desk and start on my work. As the day goes by, a delivery boy comes in with a bouquet of pink Calla lilies and a teddy bear that says "I'm sorry". I know it's for Skye, but to my surprise Denise calls my name. "Jamyya this delivery is for you."

"What?" I am shocked. I sign for the delivery and open the card. It reads *I'm sorry for being inconsiderate. Please forgive me. I understand you need a break from the kids. You're right, you have two jobs and I should help you more with the kids. I love you very much. We can talk later on tonight. This time I promise to have an open mind. Love Keenan.*

I get so emotional, tears start coming down my face. Skye comes out of her office. "What's wrong? Is everything okay?"

"Yes, I'm just touched. Keenan sent me this to apologize for yesterday. Here, read this." I give her the card to read.

"Aw, he is so sweet! At least he can admit when he is wrong. I bet he'll let you go to Montego Bay."

"I hope so. He's picking the kids up from daycare today. It's a start. Oh, let me tell you what Jamesha did." I tell Skye how great my sister is.

"Oh yeah, she's going to be a great mom. I'm proud of her too. I already talked to Devin. I told him he better treat her right. You know he kept Omari Saturday. She just loves him. He's so sweet. I'm just glad he is not crazy like his brother."

"Girl, don't I know it! Well let me call my husband to tell him thank you. I'll see you at lunch."

"Okay, let's go at 1:00 P.M. We can get something from Vinny's."

"Great. See ya later."

I call Keenan at work, but he doesn't answer, so I leave him a message. I guess he's busy. My day is getting better by the minute.

I have another surprise when I get home. Dinner is already prepared. "Hey baby, I thought I would surprise you and cook dinner. Now, you know I only can cook a few things, so we are having spaghetti tonight."

"Keenan, you are so sweet! Thank you very much. Spaghetti is just fine. I guess we can eat pork chops tomorrow." I begin putting the groceries away. I went to the grocery store thinking I had to cook tonight.

"Once you get yourself together, there's something I want to talk to you about. Jamesha came up with a good suggestion. I want to know what you think about it," Keenan says.

"Tell me now. I'm all ears." I sit down while Keenan continues to cook.

"We came up with a schedule for cooking. Like I can cook twice a week and Jamesha will cook on Thursdays, so that way you can have a break and we don't have to eat fast foods. Plus, I will start picking up the kids on Mondays and Wednesdays. How does that sound?"

"It sounds great! Where is Jamesha?"

"She had to work tonight. She gets off at nine. She said she will eat at work."

"Okay, well I guess it's just us. Where are the kids?"

"Downstairs doing their homework, and the twins are watching TV."

"I can't believe it's actually quiet in here and they aren't asleep! How is it that everybody can control them but me?"

"'Cause you are too nice? You need to put your foot down. Let them know who's boss."

"You're right. I'm going to change my clothes and get ready for dinner. I'll check on the kids."

Thanksgiving is approaching and the kids are going to be out of school for a couple of days. I decide to ask Skye if I can take those days off to spend with my family. My brothers are coming to my house for Thanksgiving. As a matter of fact, the majority of my family will be at my house. My Aunt Angie is supposed to come over and help me cook. I know Grandpa Otis will bring over his collard greens and honey-glazed ham. Uncle Marvin will contribute the alcoholic beverages, and Grandma Sabrina will bring her homemade sweet potato pies. I can't wait to eat all that good food!

Coco calls me just as I am finishing dinner. "Girl, I'm sorry I didn't call you back yesterday! I was busy with the kids. Did you need something?" she inquires.

"No, I just called to talk, but since I got you on the phone, can you schedule me and Jamesha an appointment for this Saturday? She has been such a big help to me lately, and I want to do something special for her."

"Yeah, what time do y'all want to come?"

"Early, say around eight, 'cause she probably has to work and she usually goes in at one o'clock."

"That's fine, I'll pencil y'all in. Do you still want to talk?"

"Not right now, but thanks anyway. My crisis is over. I talked to Skye about it yesterday. I feel better now."

"Skye actually made you feel better? That's a first."

I laugh. "Come on now, cut her some slack. Skye is not all that self-consumed. She can be a really good friend at times."

"Yeah, I know. It was a joke. You're her favorite anyway, so she'll always make time for you. I guess I'll see you Saturday and leave them kids at home."

"Don't worry I will. Bye."

I go into the bedroom and sit down beside Keenan. "So let's talk about Montego Bay."

"You can go on one condition."

"What is that?"

"You conduct yourself as a married woman, and we will take a family vacation this summer."

"That's two…but it's a deal."

"Good. I was thinking we could take the kids to Disneyland when they get out of school, like around the end of June or maybe August."

"June would be better. We could use our tax money to go, 'cause I only have to pay for my ticket to Montego Bay. Jazz is paying for the hotel room, and I'll need a little spending money, but that's all."

"That would probably work."

"I'm happy that we could come to a mutual understanding. Compromise is a big key to a healthy marriage. We've actually beat the statistics."

"And we've proved my mother wrong. Our anniversary is April 28th, it will be six long years."

"I know. That makes me feel old. It's hard to believe Ke'Asia is about to be ten years old."

"Mm hmm. You better talk to her about them boys too. She ain't going to be bringing no babies up in here."

"I sure hope not. I'll give her the talk this weekend. Now enough talking. Let's make up properly. I'ma show you how much I appreciate you."

We lock the doors and cut off the lights. You can just imagine what happens next. We got four kids, remember?

Time flies by fast. It's Saturday already. So far, the schedule we worked out is flowing smoothly. I wake Jamesha up this morning to surprise her with a hair appointment.

"Jamesha get up. I'm taking you to Coco's shop to get your hair done."

"What time is it?"

"It's seven-thirty. Now get up and get ready so we won't be late. Do you have to work today?"

"No, I'm off."

"Good, then you can go back to sleep when we get back."

"All right. I'm up. Let me find something to wear and jump in the shower. Are you going to cook breakfast?"

"No, we can stop at McDonald's or somewhere on the way to the shop."

"Oooh, let's go to Burger King. You know I'm sick of McDonald's. I work there, remember?

"Oh, that's right. Well, get dressed and don't look like a bum either. I'll be upstairs. Try not to make a lot of noise. I don't want the kids to wake up. Keenan is keeping them until I get back."

"I'll be quiet."

Jamesha takes a shower and gets dressed in forty-five minutes. We stop at Burger King to get breakfast. Devin is right, she can eat! Jamesha orders two ham, egg, and cheese croissants, large hash browns, two cinni-minis, and a large orange juice. Then when we get to the shop, she gets two bags of chips, a pack of cookies, and a Fruit Punch out of the machine.

"Jamesha, if you don't slow down you are going to be huge. How much do you weigh?"

"I'm only one-hundred-thirty pounds. I stay hungry. That's the same thing I try to tell Devin. It's like I can't get full."

"Are you taking your prenatal vitamins?"

"Yeah, and I drink milk, eat vegetables, and fruit."

"Very good. I'ma take you to the WIC office too so you can start getting some food. That will help out a lot 'cause our grocery bill is getting high."

"I know. I'ma start buying my own food. My friend said I should apply for food stamps and Medicaid."

"Yeah, that's a good idea. We will look into it. I'll take off early one day this week and take you. So what are your plans for today?"

"Me and Devin are going to go to the movies and Golden Coral. I wanted to go to Olive Garden, but he said I eat too much. We need to go to a buffet 'cause it will be cheaper. He is trying to save money for the baby. Omar is suppose to get him a job at the Marriott downtown 'cause they pay more than McDonald's."

"That would be good. I'm glad both of y'all are taking y'all responsibility serious. It will be hard, but with help, everything will be okay. It's much easier if you have help. Children need a mother and a father."

"I know that from experience. Devin knows too that's why he's trying his best to support me."

Coco interrupts our conversation. "Nice to see you, Jamesha. How do you want your hair?"

"Umm … just give me some twist-up into a ponytail."

"A'ight, come on over to the shampoo bowl."

I decide to get a roller wrap, something simple.

I hurry home after we got our hair done, 'cause Keenan is keeping the kids and I don't want them to get on his nerves all day.

Keenan suggests that we take the kids to Dave and Buster's. They just opened one in the Westend.

***

Two weeks have passed by and I haven't heard a word from Rhonda. I wake up early this morning to prepare for Thanksgiving dinner. Jazz, Joy, and Mario go to Philly for the holidays. Skye says she will come by after she goes to her parents' house. Coco, Jerome, and the kids are eating dinner at Coco mom's house. Damisha is going to meet Chris's family. He invited her to have dinner with them. I hope everything goes well for everybody.

My Aunt Brenda comes over early to help me set up. She likes to run everything. I hope she doesn't start any mess this time!

Keenan's mom Sandra is coming over for the first time to eat Thanksgiving dinner with us. My family can be kind of crazy, so I hope everyone is on their best behavior this evening. Dinner starts around four o'clock. Jamesha invited Devin, and he said he would come after he spends some time with his family.

James introduces everybody to his girlfriend Debra. She isn't exactly what I expected. Her appearance is a bit conservative, and she looks like she is about thirty-five years old.

I'm not afraid to ask questions, so I sit beside her. "So how did you and James meet? Do you go to Virginia State too?"

"No, I graduated some years back. We work together. He's doing an internship for my company."

"Oh, do you have any kids?"

"Yeah, I have two boys. My oldest is fifteen and the other is twelve. They are with their father this Thanksgiving."

"If you don't mind me asking, how old are you?"

James interrupts, "Jamyya I don't think that's necessary. You don't need to answer that." He looks at Debra.

"Oh, no, it's fine James. I'm forty years old."

"I thought you were about thirty-five. You look good for your age."

"Thanks."

I feel really stupid after that. What is James doing with somebody as old as our mom? Eww, that's just gross. Everybody else talks and mingles. I catch up with Jamal and what's been going on in his life.

"I think she's too old for him too," Jamal adds.

"Well, I guess growing up without a mom does something to you. Maybe he's trying to make up for lost time."

"Couldn't be me. I like them young but legal."

"You are still silly."

Everybody is getting along good until my mother and her drunk-ass boyfriend Ronald show up. Nobody discussed what went on about me putting her out, so James just let her in.

"Oh, I see y'all started without me. It ain't no party until Rhonda gets here. Y'all slide over and make room. This is my boyfriend Ronald."

"Hello, nice to meet you" everybody says.

Rhonda is drunk as usual, and so is Ronald. "Damn, Jamesha, you got enough food on your plate! How many babies you got in there?" Rhonda asks, stumbling to the table. Jamesha just rolls her eyes and keeps eating.

"Would you like me to fix y'all a plate?" Aunt Brenda asks.

"Yeah. Shit, we hungry as hell. You can give Ronald a nice size plate like Jamesha got. I'm on a diet, so just fix me a little bit."

"You got two hands, get up and get your own plate," my Uncle Marvin says.

"Whoa, buddy, who you talking to like that? You need to watch your mouth. That ain't no way to talk to a woman," Ronald says.

"Shut the hell up with your drunk ass! Rhonda ain't shit, and it seems like you ain't either. Don't come up in here ruining a good family moment."

"You know what, Marvin? I'm tired of you and everybody else looking down on me. This is my daughter's house and I came to see my kids. If you don't like it, you can leave. Go to your own kids' house!" Rhonda yells.

"Rhonda, if you can't act like somebody with some sense for once, you can just leave. Stop embarrassing and traumatizing these kids," Grandma Sabrina pleads.

"You raised me, old woman. It was your poor-ass mothering skills that led me to drugs. You and that no good husband of yours."

Rhonda starts throwing food. "Fuck all y'all and this food. That's all y'all care about is eating and looking good. I don't need none of y'all."

Keenan gets up from the table. "Rhonda, it's time for both of you to go. The next time you come to my house, I'm calling the police. You are not welcome here anymore."

"I just got here, I ain't going nowhere. Kiss my ass Keenan, you ain't shit. You need to keep your damn kids instead of putting everything on Jamyya. Your punk-ass mama should've taught you how to be a man."

Rhonda sits down and starts eating. "This food is good. Who cooked this macaroni and cheese? Ain't it good Ronald?"

"Mm hmm baby, it sure is. Do y'all got some E & J or something to drink?" Ronald asks.

"I don't think you need anything else to drink. We got sodas and juice," James says.

"Did I ask your opinion? I'm a grown ass man. I can drink as much as I want. Rhonda, you need to get yo' kids in check. They ain't got no home training."

"All right, that's enough. Either y'all get out or I'ma put you out!" Uncle Marvin screams.

"Put me out, Marvin. I want you to try."

Uncle Marvin grabs my mom by the arm and Ronald jumps up and punches him in the jaw. Marvin slings my mother to the side and catches Ronald in the eye with a right hook. Keenan grabs the phone and calls the police. I am trying to get my mother off of my uncle's back. My uncle's wife Danielle pushes my mom, then the two of them are fighting.

The police come and everyone gives their version of the story. Keenan wants to press charges against my mother. We start arguing in front of the police. My Uncle Marvin takes out assault charges against Ronald. The police lock him up. They take my mother also, 'cause she is drunk and belligerent.

My night cannot possibly get any worse! Everybody leaves after all the commotion.

I know James is so embarrassed, 'cause this is the first time Debra met us. What a bad first impression! I guess by now, Devin is used to the craziness.

I lay into Keenan as soon as everybody is gone. "I can't believe you called the police! That's my mother. What were you thinking?"

"I was thinking these drunk-ass people won't go to tear up my house! Ronald assaulted your uncle. Your mother was throwing shit. Things were getting out of hand. What did you want me to do? Let them tear the house up? Your mom is completely out of control. She needs help. Professional help."

"Yeah, I know, but obviously going to jail doesn't help her. She needs support, and maybe family counseling. She just got out, now she's back already. I just can't deal with this."

"Now you won't have to. Let her stay in jail where she belongs. She has caused enough problems in our home. Just forget about her. You can't save everybody. Hopefully she will learn one day. I don't want to fight. Just calm down and relax. I'ma get a beer and watch TV downstairs."

"Whatever, Keenan. Just go away. I'll talk to you later."

I hope Skye doesn't come over, 'cause I'm not in the mood to have company. Luckily, she doesn't come. Her cousin Trina came to dinner and they hung out. She called to let me know she will see me in the morning for our Black Friday shopping trip.

I hope Omar doesn't impose this time! I wonder if Trina is coming too. Coco even takes the day off to go shopping with us.

I have to wake up at 4:30 A.M. to be ready for the early bird sales at Wal-Mart, Target, and Best Buy. I wanted to get Jamesha an iPod and a foot massager. She's always complaining her feet hurt. Ke'Asia wants a Playstation 3, and Tamia wants a Bratz stereo. The twins want everything they see on TV.

I go to Wal-Mart alone, 'cause Skye don't wake up but so early. Me and Coco meet Jazz, Skye, and Mimi at Virginia Center Commons Mall.

"Guess what, y'all? I got a date tonight with Jeff, the guy I met at the Cheesecake Factory," Skye announces.

"Really? You are one brave soul. You know Omar is going to snap if he finds out," I say.

"So? We're not together anymore. He's the one who cheated, remember?"

"It's *when* he finds out not *if*. We'll probably bump into him today. Like he always manages to magically appear," Mimi huffs.

"I hope not! Let's go to Macy's. I know they got a sale. I need a new outfit for tonight."

"I bet you do. You still got clothes in the closet wit' tags still on them. You don't need nothing else," Jazz states.

"Yes, I do. I'm going for a new style. I'm a changed woman, so I need a whole new wardrobe. I'm going to donate my old clothes to the homeless shelter and a group home. My mom's friend works at a group home for teenage girls."

"That's very nice of you. I'm glad you have the Christmas spirit."

"Yep, I do. I'm even giving some toys to the Angel Tree. I think all kids should enjoy Christmas."

"Wow, what did you have for Thanksgiving?" Coco asks sarcastically.

"The usual: turkey, stuffing, sweet potato pie, cheesecake, and macaroni and cheese. Stuff everybody always has. I talked to my cousin Trina and she gave me some really good advice."

"I'm glad you listen to somebody," Mimi replies.

"Ooh, girl, these shoes are cute. This looks just like you," Jazz says to Skye.

While we are looking around, I notice a man approaching us. My heart starts beating fast, then I realized it's Jerell. He speaks to me, then walks up on Mimi.

"Hey Damisha. Nice to see you. I guess you've been too busy to return my calls," he says.

"Yeah, I've had a lot going on these past few weeks. I'm sure you didn't miss me. You got plenty of other women to occupy your time."

"That's not true. If I didn't miss you I wouldn't have called. If don't want to kick it no more, just let me know. I won't bother you anymore."

"Nah, I'm through kicking it. I need more than that. Either I come first or not at all. I need somebody who's going to spend time with me. Not make excuses all the time for not being there."

"You're right. You do deserve more. Call me when you find time so we can talk about it. And I don't have a lot of women anymore, I let most of them go. I don't want to hold you up. I hope to hear from you soon."

"I'll think it over. It was nice seeing you though. I'm glad you're doing well."

"Bye, Damisha."

After Jerell leaves, you know we had to talk about him. "Let me find out you got a li'l Omar in the making," Skye teases.

"No, that's what is called a coincidence. He don't pop up everywhere I go. Stop saying his name before he appear like Candyman," Mimi says.

We are all laughing. Skye buys a chocolate-brown halter-top pantsuit, a gold chain belt, and gold and bronze pumps by Miu Miu.

"I hope your date goes well. Call me when you get home," I tell Skye.

"I sure will, you know you got to make sure I'm safe. I don't know him that well. He could be crazier than the one I just left."

"For your sake, I hope not. I'll talk to you later."

Me and Coco leave 'cause we rode together. On the ride home, I ask Coco for some marriage advice.

"I don't know if I'm the right person to ask. I think me and Jerome have more problems than your marriage. Tell me what's going on. I'll try to help, but my opinion may be biased," she says.

I tell her about Thanksgiving with my mom and how I put her out weeks earlier.

"Do you think I was wrong to be mad at Keenan for calling the police?"

"No. Even though she has issues, that's still your mother. But on the other hand, you need to understand his position too. They were cussing, throwing stuff, and fighting. He *did* ask them to leave and they refused. You have to admit, things did get out of hand. I guess he didn't want it to go any further. Maybe he didn't know what else to do."

"I guess you got a point, but Keenan has never liked my mom. They always get into it. It's like he has it out for her."

"That could be true. Try to work it out. Don't let your mom come between you. Your mom always puts herself first, you should start doing the same."

"That's the same thing Skye told me."

"Listen to her for once, she's right. If Skye knows anything she knows about being selfish," she chuckles softly.

"Y'all are going to stop dogging my girl."

"It's all in fun. She's my girl too, but you know better than anybody how she can be."

"Don't I! Thanks for the advice."

I go home and play with the kids. Keenan keeps his distance. I guess he called himself being mad at me. Oh well, he will get over it. Maybe we need our space. I stay upstairs. Since I woke up so early to go shopping, I take a nap. When I wake up it is 10:00 P.M.

Jamesha knocks on the door. "Jay, Skye is on the phone. Do you want to talk?"

"Yeah, I'll get it."

I pick up the phone.

"I know your date is not over that fast!"

"Oh yes it is! Let me tell you what happened. Are you sitting down?"

"Yes, what's wrong?" Skye is making me nervous; I can hear the frustration in her voice.

"Skye, did he attack you or something?"

"No, Omar showed up. Do you know this nigga came and pulled up a chair and sat at our table? Jeff looked at me and asked who he was. Then Omar stuck out his hand and introduced himself. Then he said he was my boyfriend. Jeff said he wasn't aware that I had a boyfriend, and I said I don't, and told Jeff that Omar and I had broken up about a month ago. I told Jeff to ignore Omar because he was delusional and he must have forgotten about the restraining order I have against him. The waitress came, and Omar had the nerve to place an order as if he was staying. Then he looked at me calmly and said he didn't give a fuck about the restraining order, and then asked Jeff if he was fucking me? I got up from the table, grabbed Jeff's arm, and told him let's go. I told Omar he needed serious help, and the only reason I didn't call the police is 'cause I didn't want Omari to visit her dad in jail, but next time I won't be so nice. When we left, Omar just sat at the table laughing. He smelled like weed and liquor. I think he has completely lost his mind."

"I can't believe this shit. Your situation is just as bad as my mom. What are you going to do?" I ask.

"Girl, I don't know, but Jeff told me not to call him anymore. So I'm alone again. One for Omar, but I'ma get him back some kind of way. It's time to even up the score," Skye says in a serious tone.

"Don't get hurt, be careful. Omar is definitely not working with a full deck. You might want to change your locks."

"Good idea. I'll call a locksmith first thing tomorrow. Thanks for listening."

"No problem. I always got your back. Goodnight. Please be safe. Call me when you get to Mimi's."

Chapter Fourteen

Shawn

"Man, I don't know what's up with this chick! It's like she has gone insane or something! I told Joy from the beginning I wasn't leaving Jazz. Now she's calling me four or five times a day. She even showed up at my job."

Dwayne shakes his head. "Ain't she married? You should have known something was wrong with her. Who sleeps with her sister's boyfriend in her sister's bed? That's just plain fucked up."

I had told Dwayne about Joy sucking my dick and me fucking her in her ass that night when Jazz had gone to Taco Bell to get us something to eat.

"I know. It was both of our faults, but now I want to let it go, and she can't seem to understand that. I figured out that I really do love Jasmine. I don't want to lose her. Now Joy claims she's pregnant. What am I going to do?"

"Maybe she's lying. She probably just said that to get you back."

"No. I think she's telling the truth, 'cause Jazz even told me she's been sick. Plus she's been eating a lot. She brought the pregnancy test to my job."

"Maybe it's not yours. Is she still sleeping with her husband?"

"Yeah, but he's suppose to be infertile. They've been trying to have kids for years. I wanted her to get an abortion, but of course she said no. I just hope she doesn't tell Jazz."

"That's why you didn't go to Philly with her? Well, if Joy is already pregnant, you might as well keep hitting it."

"But I don't want it no more. If I don't see her, she says she will tell, but I think she's bluffing. 'Cause she know Jazz will never forgive her."

"I hope you're right. I told you, you were playing with fire. Maybe it's not yours. She could be sleeping with somebody else."

"That's a possibility. I hope it's not mine, 'cause I can't deal with her crazy ass. She wants everything her way."

My cell phone starts vibrating. "Speaking of the devil. Should I answer it?"

"Yeah, see what she wants. If you don't answer, she just gonna come over anyway."

Dwayne is right. "Hello. What do you want?"

"I want to come see you. We need to spend some time together. Me and the baby miss you. Where are you?" Joy asks cheerfully.

How can she act as if nothing is wrong? "I'm busy right now. I really don't think it's a good idea for us to see each other anymore. We've already been through this numerous times. I'll give you child support or whatever the baby needs, but we can't be together. We are through."

"No we are not! I'm carrying your baby! Now unless you want our little secret exposed, you will do what I tell you. It's not over until I say so. Now I suggest you get home if you're not already there, 'cause I'm coming over."

"If you come over here, I'm calling the police. I'm not joking. This stalker crazy shit has got to end! Calm your nerves. I don't want you. Nothing you can say or do can change that."

"Like I said, I'll see you in thirty minutes." She hangs up.

This bitch is really crazy! My dick done got me in some deep shit this time! Sure enough, thirty minutes later Joy is knocking on my door. She has the nerve to show up on time like we have a date. I ponder whether or not to open the door. She continues to bang on the door. I jerk open the door. "What?" I yell.

"Hey honey, did you have a rough day? No need to yell. Calm down. I brought us something to eat, but I left it in the car. Can you go get it?"

"No, why didn't you bring it with you?"

"'Cause I didn't know if you were going to let me in or not. Plus it's heavy. I shouldn't carry heavy things."

"What is it?"

"A big pan of lasagna, some garlic bread, and some chocolate chip cookies. I made all of it from scratch, except the bread. Now go get it before it gets cold."

"A'ight, give me your keys."

Against my good senses, I go to Joy's car. I make sure I take my keys with me just in case she tries to lock me out. Surprisingly, she does have food in the car. When I come back in, she has set the table for two with champagne glasses and candles.

"I need you to go back and get the grocery bag too," she says, smiling.

"Can I put this down first?" I ask with an attitude.

"You are so cute when you're mad!"

I go back out to the car to get the rest of the stuff. I ain't making no more damn trips to the car! This time when I come back, she's sitting at the table wearing a red lace corset with red lace thongs.

"What happened to your clothes?" I ask while setting down the bags.

"I thought I would slip into something a little more comfortable. Sit down and eat. I can cook very good."

She didn't lie about that! The food is good.

I try not to talk much, but she keeps asking questions and trying to seduce me. She twirls a cherry around her tongue, dips her finger in whipped cream then licks it off.

She gets up from the table. "Are you ready for dessert? I have a special treat for you."

"I'm full. I don't need anything else. Isn't it time for you to go home? Mario is probably looking for you. I don't want you to be out too late. It isn't good for the baby. You need your rest."

"You're right, but first I need some love. Mario will be a'ight. He thinks I'm visiting a sick friend. Taking care of people takes time. And I plan on taking care of you."

She kisses me on my lips. I try to turn my head.

"Leave now, or I'm calling the police."

"Stop acting like a little punk! Just give me what I came for, and I'll leave. It's very simple. Do what I say and we will get along fine."

"You are one crazy chick! I'ma blame it on the hormones. Have you gone to the doctor yet?"

"No, I have an appointment in two days at three o'clock. Are you going to go with me?"

"Yeah, I want to go. Now please leave. Dwayne will be home soon, and he doesn't like drama. You are going to piss him off. Just go, I'll see you Thursday."

"I miss you, baby. Make love to me. I'm already pregnant. What else could happen? Give me some of that good stuff."

"Go get it from Mario. I'm tired; you know this psychotic relationship is not going to work. You can't make me be with you."

In the middle of my sentence, my phone starts vibrating.

"Who is that calling you? Answer it!"

"It's none of your business and I'll call them back later. You're really starting to get on my nerves. My patience is wearing thin."

Joy starts taking off the lingerie. She stands in the dining room buck bald naked. Seconds later, Dwayne comes in. He drops the whole pizza box. "Oh, shit, I didn't mean to interrupt!" He covers his eyes with his hands.

"You didn't interrupt. We haven't got started yet. Shawn is trying to act like he is scared of the pussy. He used to want it. What's wrong with it now? Do you see anything wrong with me Dwayne?"

"Um I – I uh, no there is nothing wrong. I'ma go to my room."

Dwayne picks up the pizza and runs to his room. I have never heard him stutter before. Joy is out of control! I wrap a blanket around her.

"Joy, please go home. You have just embarrassed me and yourself. You have no class. This is why we can't work. Jasmine is a lady. You are just a hoe - pure trash. Now get the fuck out before I put you out! I don't want to hurt you, but I'm fed up, and you need to go now. If you have plans on keeping that baby, you need to leave."

I speak with authority, and I am dead serious. I guess she got scared, 'cause she puts her clothes halfway on and leaves. This shit has gone too far. My mind is so boggled, I can't even call Jasmine back. I text her and tell her I will call her tomorrow. I make up a story about being drafted to work a double shift. I feel bad lying to her, but I can't tell her the truth. Not now, but I know she will find out eventually. Everything you do in the dark will one day come to light.

***

Today I'm leaving work early to be at Joy's doctor appointment. I want to know if she's really pregnant. I talked to Jazz yesterday, but my guilty conscious wouldn't let me see her. We made plans to be together this weekend. Joy wants us to ride together, but I choose to drive my own car. Her doctor's office is at Henrico Doctor's Medical Center. The doctor's name is Karen Hoffman.

"Mrs. Allen, you can come on back," the nurse says.

Joy grabs my hand, and we go into the exam room. The nurse takes her blood pressure, temperature, weight, and has her urinate in a cup. She weighs 125 pounds at 5'5".

"Dr. Hoffman will be in shortly," she says.

The doctor comes in smiling. "Congratulations, Mrs. Allen, you are indeed pregnant. When was your last period?"

"Um … I think it was August 25th. I know for a fact it was the end of August."

"Okay, let's see here. We need to do a pelvic exam and withdraw some blood. Come into the lab, then when you get back, get undressed from the waist down."

"All right. Thank you," Joy replies.

After the doctor leaves, she looks at me and smiles. "I told you we were having a baby. Isn't this great? I'm so happy!" She hugs me. "I'm going to the lab, I'll be right back."

I just want to cry. Why is this happening to me? I hope this is somebody else's baby. But deep down I know she wasn't sleeping with no one else but her husband. Jazz had told me when we first met that Mario couldn't have any kids, and Joy was sad about it.

Damn. Why did she have to be pregnant now? Maybe she will have a miscarriage.

After her examination, the doctor says, "You are eight weeks pregnant. Your due date is June 30th. Everything looks good, except your iron is a little low. Here are some prenatal vitamins, they should help. Also increase your intake on food high in protein. I also have a mother-to-be package for you. If you don't have any questions, I'll see you next month."

"No, I'm too excited to think of any. Thank you Dr. Hoffman."

"You're welcome. Take care of yourself and that baby. Nice to meet you, Mr. Jackson."

"Same to you," I reply.

Outside of the doctor's office, I tell Joy, "Look, your behavior is not healthy for the baby. You need to calm down. That shit you pulled at my apartment the other day was uncalled for. We need a break from each other. I'll call you when I'm ready to talk. See ya next month."

"What do you mean next month? You only want to come to my doctor's appointments. What about us? I need to feel you. I want us to have a physical and emotional connection."

"There is no us. I really don't want to come to your appointments either. So if you feel some type of way, I won't come at all. Honestly, I hope you have a miscarriage," I scowl.

"Fuck you, Shawn! You are a selfish bastard." She starts crying, but I don't care.

"That's exactly what you're not going to do anymore. I'm done. Leave me alone."

I walk off and get into my car. When I pull off, Joy is still standing in the parking lot crying. I hope I hurt her feelings bad enough for her to leave me alone!

Before going to the doctor's office, I had stopped by Strange's and had flowers delivered to Jazz's job. I hope she likes them! While sitting in the Wendy's drive thru, Jazz calls me. "Thanks for the flowers baby, they are so pretty. What are we doing this weekend?" she asks.

"I'm going to reserve us a hotel room at the Embassy Suites so we can be alone. Just you and me. We can do whatever you want?"

"Hmm … Whatever I want. That could get a li'l wild and kinky."

"That's how I like it," I tease.

"Oh, before I forget. Damisha is having an all-black birthday party on Dec. 6th, which is next Saturday. She's going to be twenty-seven. I want you to accompany me. So clear your calendar."

"A'ight, but why all your friends have color coded parties? Why can't I wear what I want to?"

"Boy, shut up and get an all-black outfit. That shouldn't be hard to do. Now I got to go back to work. I love you. See you tomorrow night."

"I love you too. I'll call you later with the room number."

"Okay. Bye sweetie."

I ain't that stupid, 'cause Joy won't be popping up this weekend acting crazy while Jazz is over here! Oh, no, it's not going down like that. I hope Jazz don't tell Joy where we are going. I call the Embassy Suites and make reservations for a honeymoon suite. I go all out when it comes to setting things up. After a lot of hard work and begging, I got Jazz back. Now I'm scared of losing her again.

I buy her a long, black, satin gown from Victoria's Secret with a pair of black mesh panties. I set a vase full of red and white roses on the table along with scented candles, a bottle of cold Hypnotiq, and strawberries with whipped cream. I look at the menu and order room service to be delivered at seven-thirty. I had also picked up a gift basket filled with Victoria's Secret lotion, body wash, perfume, and lip gloss.

I want tonight to be special. This will be our first time having sex since we've been back together. After I get everything set up, I take a long hot shower, spray on some Unforgiveable by Sean John, and slip into my black silk pajamas. When Jazz knocks on the door, I light the candles and turn on J. Holiday's CD.

She walks in with a pleasant but shocked look on her face. "Is all of this for me? It's not my birthday, so what's the occasion?"

"Appreciation Day. I want you to know how lucky I am to have you in my life. Sit down and relax."

I take her shoes off and begin to massage her feet.

"How was your day at work?"

"It was fine. The kids were a little hyper after lunch, but it went okay. I love my job, but I'm looking for more. I'm thinking about opening my own business. I just want more out of my life."

"What kind of business do you want?"

"I'm still debating. It's between a twenty-four hour daycare and boutique of vintage shoes, accessories that sort of thing. Once I decide on what I want to do, Jerome is going to help me find a location. Also, I'm moving out in February."

"You are? Where are you moving to?"

"Probably the Westend. I need my own space. I want a three-bedroom townhouse. Something along the lines of how Damisha's is."

"Don't you think starting a business and moving at the same time is going to be expensive? Are you getting a small business loan or something?"

"Yeah, and I'm applying for a federal grant. I've been saving up some money too. I know it will be tough at first, but I'm almost twenty-five. I need my own place."

"That's true. We do need some privacy. This room is costing me a fortune, but I'll gladly do it because I love you. We need quality time together."

"Yes we do. Can we get something to eat? I'm starving."

"I already ordered us some room service. They should be coming any minute."

"What did you order?"

"Grilled salmon, garlic mashed potatoes, broccoli and cheese, and glazed carrots. For dessert, I got a three-layer chocolate cake with chocolate icing."

"Ooh, sounds good! I can taste it already."

"Here, let me feed you some strawberries until room service comes."

I feed her and we continue talking.

"You know what I love about you? Your ambition, talent and drive. You are such an intelligent woman. Whatever you decide to do I know you will succeed. If you need any help doing anything like moving furniture or decorating, I'll help."

"Thank you, baby. I'll be sure to take you up on that offer."

Room service finally comes and we sit at the table to eat. I pour both of us a glass of Hypnotiq. "Let's make a toast to a long lasting relationship. May we grow together and one day become inseparable," I say. We clank glasses.

"Everything is so beautiful. You make me feel like a special lady. I love you Shawn." She kisses me seductively on the lips.

"Wait, there is more."

I go into the bedroom and retrieve the gift basket and wrapped gift. "This is for you as well. A token of my love for you. Open it."

She rips the paper off the box then pulls the black gown out. "This is beautiful, Shawn. I like the gift basket too. Let me get in the shower and use my new stuff, then I can model the gown for you."

"Don't take too long. I can't wait to see you in it."

Jazz goes into the bathroom and gets into the shower. I check my cell phone and notice I have four voice messages, four text messages, and six missed calls. All the calls are from Joy except two. One is from Dwayne and the other from Mike. Mike is my friend from work. I check the voicemail first.

"Hey, Shawn this is Dwayne. Man, that crazy bitch keeps coming over here looking for you. She knocked on the door like the police. I told her you weren't here so she sat in the parking lot. Then when Gabrielle came over, she came barging in with her. Gabrielle almost hit her, but I told her she was pregnant. You need to call and get your bitch in check before she gets hurt or goes to jail! The neighbors are complaining. I'm not trying to get put out. Do something."

Beep. "Shawn. Where the fuck are you? I know you with my sister. Go have your fun now, but remember I'm the one having your baby. You can fuck her, but not me? We both know I'm better anyway, that's why you cheated on her. You better get your shit together. I would hate for something bad to happen to you. I want our baby to have a father. You better find time to call me back, or you'll be sorry. You may think I'm weak 'cause you made me cry, but I'm stronger than you think. I always get what I want, and I want you. Don't fuck with me, Shawn! I swear you will regret it! I demand respect. If you can stop making love to me, you can stop giving it to her too. If I can't have you, no one will."

Jazz comes out, so I hang up the phone fast.

"Who was that?"

"Oh, just checking my messages. It was Dwayne, see." I show her the caller ID.

"Oh, what's up with him? He sure did call a lot. Is everything okay?"

"Yeah, he was looking for something. I called and told him where it was. Now enough of that. Come over here and give me some of that good stuff."

"Oh, it's good huh? Do you really think so?"

"Of course I do. I can show you better than I can tell you."

I pull her down on the bed and climb on top of her. My hands caress her silky smooth skin. I remove her gown then kiss every inch of her body. She turns over and lies on her stomach. I pull out my hot massage oil and rub her back intensely, down to her feet. My tongue teases the lips in between her thighs. As I bring her to ecstasy, I begin to hear Joy's voice echo in my ear. I stop for a brief moment.

"Baby what's wrong?" she asks.

"Nothing, I'm okay. I guess I'm a little tipsy, that's all. Maybe you should take over," I suggest.

"Sure. I'll be happy to please you."

For the first time ever, Jazz grabs my dick and places it in her warm, wet mouth. She sucks it like a pro; I am shocked! Either she's a natural, or she's been lying to me. She climbs on top of me and does her thing. I'm pleasantly shocked.

"Damn baby, that was great! I really enjoyed it. You've really out done yourself."

"I'm glad you liked it. Maybe next time we can try something else new. I'm coming out of my shell."

"Oh, yes you are! You should feel comfortable to open up to me. We're in a relationship. We should know one another intimately."

"I'm working on it. Just give me time. It's hard to put all your trust into a person. I've been hurt too many times before. Work with me. I'll make it worth your while."

"I know you will," I reply.

"You wore me out. Let's go to sleep so we will be refreshed for tomorrow."

"Good idea. I am tired."

When we wake up in the morning, Jazz is smiling wide. "Good morning, sleepy head. What are we getting into today?"

"Umm … let's get breakfast first, then we can do whatever you want. The day is yours to plan."

"We can eat breakfast at Silver Diner. I'm in the mood for something different. Then we can go Christmas shopping, plus we need outfits for Damisha's party. Later on we can go bowling. Why don't you call Dwayne and see if he and his girlfriend want to go?"

"No, boo. I want it to be just me and you."

"But it will be more fun with other people."

"You are right. But I see Dwayne all the time. It's your day, invite one of your friends and their man."

"Okay, I'll call Mimi to see what she's doing."

"I'm surprised you didn't pick Skye."

"Oh, her and Omar broke up. He cheated on her while we were in Philly. She found out about it and she left him."

"I'm sorry to hear that. They seemed like a happy couple."

"Well, looks can be deceiving. Now he's stalking her and shit. He even left her several messages on her voicemail cussing her out. The nigga done lost his mind."

"That's sad. I hope she's okay."

"Yeah, she got a restraining order against him, but he still follows her. That piece of paper don't work. He started acting crazier when she got it. Hopefully, he will get tired and calm down. But enough about that madness, let's focus on us. Come take a shower with me so we can go eat."

"A'ight, do your sister know where you at? 'Cause you ain't been home, she might be worried about you."

"Please, Joy only cares about herself. I'm grown, I don't have to check in with her. She probably figures I'm with you anyway."

"Excuse me, miss grown-ass."

We get dressed then go to eat. Damisha agrees to meet us at the bowling alley at four o'clock. Jasmine is a shopaholic. We go to two malls and three different shopping centers. She buys three different black outfits, 'cause she doesn't know which one she likes best. Then she buys a birthday gift for Damisha, and Christmas gifts for everybody and their momma.

Finally I say, "Baby, I'm tired. If you try on one more shoe, I'ma fall out. Can we please go now? I refuse to ever go shopping with you again. This is ridiculous. You need your girlfriends for this stuff."

"I know. You're no fun. We can go, 'cause I'm sick of your complaining. Stop whining like a baby. I should buy you a pacifier."

"Ha ha, very funny! Aren't you a regular little comedian?"

"Oh, you throwing around short jokes now! Don't be mad at me 'cause you hit your head every time you walk through a door. It ain't my fault you're a giant."

"You cracking on me now? Umm hmm, I should leave your ass here. Come on now, I'm getting cranky."

"So I've noticed. Let me pay for these, then I'm ready. Why you rushing anyway? I thought we were going bowling."

"We are, it's already two-thirty. I need a break, and I'm hungry. I want some pizza. Let's go to Pizza Hut Italian Bistro."

"You're greedy. We just ate breakfast."

"No we didn't, that was five hours ago. If you stop trying to be cute, you would be hungry too."

"Aw, the big baby is hungry. Is that why you're so snappy?"

"Yeah, I guess. I didn't mean to be rude. I'm just not into shopping. I'm tired. I just need a break."

"A'ight baby, come on, let's go," she says.

I wonder where Jazz is getting all this money from. It's none of my business, so I don't ask, but lately she has been throwing out bills. We meet Damisha and her boyfriend Jerell at the bowling alley.

"Shawn, this is Jerell, you already know Damisha," Jazz states.

"What's up, man?" I give him dap.

"Nothing much. Y'all ready to bowl?"

"Yeah."

The girls do more talking than bowling, but I have a good time anyway. Jerell seems like an a'ight guy. Jazz doesn't seem to like him too much. She tells me that they all went to high school together.

When we get in the car, Jazz snaps, "I can't believe she brought him with her! She done lost her damn mind! I can't wait to tell everybody about this."

"Why she can't go out with him? He seems cool. Is he married or something?"

"No, he's a gigolo. He got too many women and he don't treat her right. He thinks she's a booty call, but she wants more. She supposedly broke it off with him, but I see they are back together."

"Did you ask her about it?"

"Yeah, she said they talked and they agreed to work it out. I don't buy it."

"Jazz, you can't control other people's lives. Think about it, your friends probably didn't want us back together. I know Skye don't like me. Damisha has to make her own decision. You never know he might change. I did. If you really love someone and you are afraid of losing them, people tend to shape up."

"How did you get so smart?"

"From experience, I've been through a lot. Trust me, Damisha knows what she's doing. I thought you said you get good relationship advice from her."

"Yeah I do. You're right she will be fine. She's older than me. I guess she knows what she is doing. I have an idea. Stop by my house real quick so I can get my bathing suit. I wanna go swimming."

"Just buy one from the store."

Shit, she must be crazy, I ain't going to that house. Joy is off the hook! No telling what her psycho ass might do.

"Baby, it is the middle of winter. Bathing suits are not in season. I didn't see one when we went shopping earlier."

Damn, that's right, it's cold as Alaska outside.

"Come on, please? It won't take me long. You're about to go right past the exit to my house anyway. Let's have some fun. You said it was my weekend, remember?" Jazz whines.

"A'ight, and you better make it quick."

"I know exactly where it is. You can stay in the car, I'ma run right in. I'll be back in a flash."

Damn, I hope Joy ain't home! So much for that scenario. Joy is home, but so is Mario, maybe she won't act crazy since her husband is here. She might not know I'm outside.

"Hurry up, Jazz, ain't that much gas in the car. You know I gotta keep the heat on 'cause it's cold."

"I know. It will be quick, I promise."

Jazz gets out of the car and goes inside. She doesn't come back fast enough. Joy must have looked out the window and seen me, or Jazz told her I was outside. This crazy bitch comes outside in thirty-five degree weather with a pajama pant set on and slippers. Her hair is in rollers with a scarf tied around it. She walks up to my window and knocks hard.

"I knew you was out wit' her! Didn't you get my message? Why haven't you called me back? Something could've been wrong with the baby. You didn't know what I wanted."

I interrupt her ranting. "Look Joy, I'm not going to be with you, you just need to accept that. If something was wrong with the baby, you would have said so in the message. I'm warning you, don't come to my house anymore, Dwayne is going to call the police or Gabrielle is going to beat your ass. Now go in the house before you get sick. It's cold outside. Get a grip."

"I need you Shawn, baby, I miss you so much."

"A'ight. This is what I'ma do. If you be good and leave me alone this weekend, I'll spend time with you all night Monday. But the phone calls, text messages, and stalking need to stop. Okay. Stop it now."

"I agree, and you better not be lying either. Make sure we have sex this time, 'cause I'm ready."

"We will, now go in before somebody gets suspicious. I love you." I give her a quick kiss on the lips. I knew that would calm her crazy ass down and make her go in the house.

"I love you too, baby. See ya Monday." She skips her deranged ass back in the house. Whew, that was close! As soon as she leaves, Jazz comes out.

"What was Joy doing out here?"

"I don't know, she looked like she was looking for something in her car."

"Oh, well I'm ready. Let's go."

"Now we have to stop by my house so I can get my swimming trunks."

"Mm hmm. Do you know where they are?"

"Yeah, you know me, I'm Mister Organization. My closet is neat. I know where everything is. Dwayne, on the other hand, can never find anything. I'll be quick."

"Good, 'cause I don't feel like getting out of the car."

"Fine. Just lock the door until I come back."

I go in the house, hoping Dwayne is too busy to start shit with me 'cause I never called him back. I tiptoe into the house. When I get to the living room, I hear some loud moaning. I know at that moment Dwayne is busy. Good, one plus for tonight. I go into my closet and get out my Polo swimming shorts and my Polo flip-flops. I rush back to the car. "See, it didn't take me long. I was faster than you."

"So what?"

We go back to the room and change into our swimwear. I'm not big on swimming, but I would do anything for my baby. We were the only two people in the pool. I guess most people aren't big on swimming in the winter. We race and splash until our skin is wrinkled. Back up in the suite, we made love again. The weekend goes by fast. Before I know it, it is Monday.

***

I don't even begin to know how to handle Joy. My first thought is to hide from her - not go home at all. But I spent all my money this weekend. I am dead broke. Hmm… I go shopping with my last twenty dollars. I buy Joy a "Congratulations, you're pregnant" card and a small white teddy bear. I have to do something to calm her down, so I decide to play her little game.

"Hey baby, I'm so happy to see you," Joy says she hugs me tight and kisses me.

"I'm happy to see you too. Sit down, I got something for you."

"For me? A present? Wow. What is it?"

I bring the gift bag out.

"Here, open it."

"Oh, baby, I love it. Thank you. I knew you would come around."

"Yeah, I owe you an apology. I'm sorry. This is an exciting time for you, and I need to support you. I want to be here for you and my baby. But you need to calm down. Stress will hurt the baby. You want the baby to be healthy, don't you?" I rubbed her stomach.

"Yes, of course I want a healthy baby."

"Look, we need to be really careful so we can keep this under wraps. We don't want Jazz or Mario to find out. I'm going to spend time with you, but when you act crazy, that shit turns me off. Now I'ma tell you now. Me and Jazz got plans this weekend and I'm working overtime to save money for the baby."

"So you're saying you won't be able to spend much time with me?"

"That's right, but I'm here now, so let's make every minute count."

I kiss her and begin to take her clothes off. I finally give her what she wants, *the dick.*

Joy snuggles up next to me. "Shawn, that was great. You always make me feel so good. Only you know how to satisfy me. I love you."

Damn, here she goes with this love shit. "Yeah, I love you too. Look, I got to wake up early tomorrow; I have a twelve-hour shift to work. It's getting late; shouldn't you be on your way home?"

Joy turns to look at the clock, "Oh, I didn't know it was this late. I should get going. I don't want to worry Mario. I'll talk to you later."

She jumps up and wiggles into her clothes. "I'ma take my teddy bear to work and sit it on my desk. Thanks again, baby. Have a good night's sleep."

I look at her and smile. "Oh, I will, you wore me out."

I hate to admit it, but Joy is still good in bed. She knows just what to do. Even though I had a good time tonight, I still felt guilty about sleeping with her, but things are so much easier for me to just appease her. Actually, Joy is not a bad person. We used to have fun together until I broke it off. It's tragic what a breakup does to people. Maybe her hormones are out of whack 'cause she's pregnant. Who knows?

I hope Joy doesn't come up to my job, 'cause I'm not working overtime. I just want to keep her away from me. My goal is to spend as little time with her as possible. Damisha's party is this Saturday, so I have to get ready for that. I go to get a haircut Friday and buy a new pair of shoes. I even decide to buy Jazz and Joy a gift. I get a gift basket full of candy delivered to Joy's job since she's been such a good girl this week. Jazz gift is a little something I know she likes. I buy her an Ashanti CD. That's her favorite singer.

Since Joy isn't acting crazy anymore, I felt it's safe to let Jazz come over. I haven't had sex with Joy since Monday, but had lunch with her Thursday. I popped up at her job and surprised her. I'm trying to keep her happy. She called and thanked me for the gift basket.

Damisha is having her party at a club called the Black Tie. Jazz comes over to my house so we can ride together.

"Damn baby, you look good, turn around. Let me get the full effect." She spins around and does a runway walk. Everything about her is gorgeous. She's wearing a black, strapless, long Dolce & Gabbana dress with a high side split. She completes the look with silver dangling earrings, bracelets, and belt, black J. Lo stilettos, and a black wrap around her shoulders.

"You don't look too bad yourself, and you smell good. Is that new cologne," Jazz replies.

"Yeah, it's Jean Paul Gaultier."

I am wearing a black Roca Wear sweater, black Roca Wear jeans, with my black Timberlands. With all this black on, you would think I'm about to commit a robbery.

"Are you ready to go?" she asks.

"Yep, I hope this party ain't as wild as Coco's party was."

"No, this is at a different club, plus Damisha deals with a different set of people."

"Good, 'cause I don't feel like running tonight."

Chapter Fifteen

Damisha

I take today off 'cause it's my birthday. Today I'm twenty-seven years old. Yep, Damisha Monaé Miles was born on December 5, 1980 in Richmond, Virginia.

I have so much stuff to do for my party I'm having at the Black Tie. Coco had an all-white party, so I decide to have an all-black party. Everyone has to wear all black with the exception of silver, white, or gold for their accessories, but the majority of the outfit needs to be black. For the party, I'm wearing red and black, and so is my date Chris. My dress is a red, short, strapless, satin dress made by Zac Posen. It has a black bolero trimmed in red and a skinny, black patent leather belt. The dress fits snug to my body. It is so cute. My shoes are red satin peep toe pumps by Christian Louboutin. Oh yes, they were expensive. They cost me seven hundred fifty dollars.

I helped Chris pick out his outfit. He's wearing a black Armani suit with a black button-up collar shirt and red silk tie. His shoes are by Ferragamo. Chris is going to look so good! I can't wait to see him.

My phone has been ringing off the hook all morning with birthday wishes.

Who could this be? I answer quickly, "Hello."

"Good morning, birthday girl, what's up with you today?" Coco asks.

"Nothing much, just getting some last minute stuff for my party. Jerell is taking me out tonight for my birthday. I don't know where we are going though. Thanks for doing my hair tomorrow. I really appreciate it. I know; it's supposed to be your day off."

"Yeah, but you're the birthday girl, so I don't mind. I'm surprised Chris is not taking you out. And how did Jerell get back in the picture? Who's coming to the party?"

"Well, Chris has his son this weekend, so we are going out for lunch. Chris's mother is going to keep him so he can come to my party tomorrow. Me and Jerell are going out later on tonight. He's coming to the party too. I started seeing Jerell again after we bumped into him at the mall. He's been making more time for me lately. I'm giving him another chance. It seems like things are reverse now. Chris is always busy with his son lately."

"How is that going to work with both of them at the party? I can't wait to see this. This should be good. You really think you're a player."

"No I don't! At first, Chris was my date, 'cause I wasn't dealing with Jerell no more. Then Jerell came back into the picture, so he basically invited himself. He said he would play the background and not start no shit, so I said he could come. He knows Chris is my date."

"So who is he supposed to be, your cousin or something?"

"No, he's a friend from high school, and that's the truth. I just hope Shawn don't say nothing, 'cause me and Jerell went bowling with him and Jazz last weekend. If he sees me with Chris, he will probably be confused. Oh, is Jerome coming?"

"Yeah, he said he was. Torey wanted to come too. I was telling him about it."

"Yeah, he can come. I just hope Dontaé don't bring Omar, cause Skye is going to have a fit if he does."

"Tell him not to, he should respect that."

"It's not that simple. Omar already knows about it. Dontaé said he's going to come with or without him, but he promises not to bother Skye. I told him, yeah right, I'll believe that shit when I see it."

"All hell is going to break loose. I hope Omar doesn't ruin your party."

"Me too! Well look, my line is beeping I'll just see you in the morning."

"A'ight, come to the shop. I'll be there at nine-thirty."

"Okay, chick see ya."

I click over to answer my other line. It's Skye, "Happy birthday, old lady. What you got planned for today?"

"Chris is taking me out to lunch, then Jerell is taking me out tonight, but it's a surprise."

"Go 'head, playa. Can't do nothing with you. So who's your date for the party?"

"Chris is, but Jerell is going to stop by."

"That's going to be something. Is Omar coming?"

"Yeah. I'm sorry Skye, I didn't invite him but you know that never stops him. Dontaé said he promise to leave you alone and not start any shit."

"Mm hmm, then why is he coming? He should know you don't like him. He just wants to irritate me, that's all, but I'm not going to allow it. I'ma wear the baddest outfit I can find. He is not going to ruin your party or my night."

"I'm glad you have a positive attitude, but you can't look better than the birthday girl, it's against the rules," I joke.

"I'm not going to show you up, I'm just going to look good. We can both be fabulous together."

"I know that's right! I'll see you tomorrow then. I got to get ready for my nail appointment."

"A'ight, ma. Talk to you later."

"Wait. Do you already have your outfit?"

"Yeah, I got two. I haven't decided which one to wear yet. Why?"

"Is it all black? I know how you don't follow directions"

"Yes, I do! I wore all white to Coco's party. Yeah, it's all black, and my accessories are white or silver depending on the outfit."

"Good, I gotta go; I'll see you at the party. Don't forget my gift."

"I won't. Bye."

I drive to the nail shop to get my nails and toenails designed. I also get my eyebrows arched. Talking on the phone threw me off schedule. I have to rush home to get ready for my date with Chris. When he comes to pick me up, he greets me with a dozen pink roses, a card, and three helium balloons.

"Happy birthday, baby. These are for you. Now I know what you're thinking, but I'm saving the real gift for tomorrow."

"That's not what I was thinking. I'm happy with this. Now let's go eat, I'm starving. Oh, thank you, baby." I kiss Chris and hug him tight.

"Mmm Mmm Mmm... I wish I could be with you tonight, but I got to spend some time with my son. He has been acting out in school. I'm going to have a talk with him."

"Baby, it's okay. I understand that you are a parent first. That's good, no one should come before your child. I'll have you tomorrow night, you can make it up to me then." I smile at him.

"I sure will. I'm looking forward to it. Where would you like to go for lunch?"

"Let's go to Olive Garden, since that's where it all started."

"Great choice. I had a taste for some Italian food."

We have to wait awhile for a table 'cause we're there during the lunch rush. I have a great time though. Chris drops me off 'cause he has to go back to work. I hope he doesn't try to surprise me tonight and pop up over my house!

I still have a lot of time before Jerell's coming to get me, so I call up the club to make sure everything is straight. Then I take a nap 'cause I'm bored. Everybody else is at work and I finished all my errands earlier. When I wake up, I watch TV for awhile then take a long hot bath with bath oil beads. It makes my skin soft and smooth. I shave my legs, armpits, and trim up my treasure chest. I know sometime tonight me and Jerell will wind up in the sack.

Even though I like Chris a lot, it's just something about Jerell that I can't get out of my system. I don't know if I have bad boy syndrome or not. Hopefully, things will work out at the party. I don't expect Chris to act jealous. I hope Jerell don't cross the line. I find a cute outfit to wear to wherever we are going.

Jerell calls me at six-thirty. "Hey, birthday girl. Are you ready?"

"Yeah."

"Well, I'm outside. Pack a bag real quick, I want you to spend the night with me."

Oh, my goodness, this is a shock! I have never been to Jerell's house. I was starting to think he's married or has a girlfriend.

"Give me five minutes. I'll be right out."

For some reason, I get butterflies in my stomach. Damn, after all these months, he still excites me. I feel like a lovesick teenager. I run out the house and hop in the white Benz.

"You look beautiful as usual. So what has the birthday girl been up to today?" Jerell asks, looking at me with those pretty gray eyes.

"Thank you. I went to the nail shop, picked up some party decorations, and ate lunch at Olive Garden. Today was a good day."

"Who did you have lunch with?"

Hmm... should I lie or tell the truth? I opt to be honest. "Chris took me to celebrate my birthday."

"Oh, I see. How else did y'all celebrate?"

"Do I detect a bit of jealousy?"

"No, it was just a question. Don't sweat it, it's not that serious."

"We didn't have sex, if that's what you were referring to."

I am smiling in the inside. I can't believe he's jealous.

"Where are we going?" I ask.

"To my house."

I instantly catch an attitude.

"You mean to tell me I got all dressed up to go sit in your damn house? Are you serious? Where are we going after that?"

"Calm down. Why are you tripping? I got something special planned. If you don't like it when we get there, then we can do something else. You are so damn spoiled."

"Whatever." I cross my arms and pout the whole way.

Jerell lives in a very nice neighborhood. He has a single story ranch style house with three bedrooms. For a bachelor, his house is very neat and well-decorated. When I walk in the living room, he has a beautiful black painting hanging on the wall.

"I didn't know you were into art," I say, shocked.

"Yeah, I'm into a lot of things you probably don't know about. Have a seat. I'll be right back."

He goes into the kitchen and came out with a fruit tray and chocolate fondue sauce. He also brings out two champagne glasses and a bottle of Moet. Jerell lights the candles. "This is your appetizer. You can watch TV while I set up dinner."

"You cooked me dinner by yourself?"

"Yeah, I can cook. I even made dessert. Chill out for a minute. I'll be right back."

I turn on the fifty-seven inch flat screen plasma TV and lie back on the forest green Naturri Italian leather sofa. About fifteen minutes later, Jerell comes back in the living room "Dinner is ready. Come this way."

He leads me into the dining room where everything is set up. Pink, white, and purple balloons fill the room. Those are my favorite colors. There is also a bouquet of candy roses of the same colors on the table. He hands me a birthday card.

"Happy Birthday, baby."

"Thank you. Don't you want to wait until the party to give me my gift?"

"No, I can't bring your gift to the party. Well, not this one anyway. Don't worry, I bought you more than one gift. You will get another one tomorrow as well."

"Okay, sounds good."

I open my card. It's a Mahogany Hallmark card. The words and design are so beautiful.

"You told me that you never had a man cook for you. So I thought it would be special if I cooked you dinner on your birthday. We always go out to eat, and I know you've never been to my house, so here we are. I hope you aren't still mad."

"No, I'm not. Actually, I feel quite stupid. I'm sorry. Everything is beautiful. Thank you. This was a wonderful idea."

"You're welcome." Jerell plays some soothing slow music.

Dinner is great. He cooked a T-bone steak with grilled onions, sautéed mushrooms, shrimp scampi, scalloped potatoes, broccoli and cheese, and buttermilk biscuits. He even made a cheesecake with strawberry topping. I am pleasantly surprised that he can cook so well.

"Now it's time for your gift. Are you ready?"

"Yes, where is it?"

"Close your eyes, I'll be right back."

Jerell goes into one of the bedrooms and returns with a small white toy poodle wearing a pink heart-shaped dog tag that read Princess.

"This is for you. Her name is Princess. She's already house broken. She can keep you company when I'm unavailable. That way you won't need Chris."

"Very funny. She's adorable, I love her! Thank you so much."

"You're welcome, and I'm serious, but we'll discuss that another time."

I move the puppy off my lap and move close to Jerell. I begin kissing him on the lips. He winks at me and says, "Let's go into my room."

In his room are purple rose petals on the bed. Purple scented candles that smell like lavender fill the air. The room is dark, and our silhouettes cast a pretty picture on the wall. Our bodies connect as if we are one. I feel something deep down in my soul when I make love to Jerell. It feels like liquid fire running through my veins. He sets my body on fire. It's safe to say he quenched all my sexual desires. We fall asleep in each other's arms. Princess joins us at the foot of Jerell's California king bed. This is a wonderful birthday.

I wake up with my skin glowing.

"Good morning, precious. Did you sleep well?" Jerell asks, kissing me on the forehead.

"Yes, I did. Your bed is very comfortable. What are you getting into today?"

"I was hoping you. Nah, just kidding. I'm going to get a haircut, go to the gym, then stop by your party. But before I do all that, I'm going to cook you breakfast."

"Get outta here! I get breakfast too? It's going to snow tonight," I joke.

"I hope not! I want you to have a good party. Do you need any help setting up anything?"

"No baby, it is all taken care of. You better start cooking, 'cause I got a hair appointment at nine."

"Your hair already looks good, but I'll get on it. I was going to cook an omelet."

"Do you have oatmeal?"

"Yeah, baby. I can make that too. Why don't you take a shower while I cook breakfast?"

"Good idea."

I jump in the shower and wash my hair. I figure it will save Coco some time.

"Thanks, for everything. I had a great time. I'll see you tonight." I kiss Jerell goodbye.

"A'ight baby, I'll holla at you later. Your boy is going to show up fresh to death."

***

I hurry over to Coco's house. I'm thirty minutes late, but she doesn't mind.

"Girl, sorry I'm late, but I already washed my hair. I just want some kind of up do."

"A'ight, I gotcha. So how was your birthday?"

I tell Coco all about my dates with Jerell and Chris.

"Girl, you are one crazy chick. I don't know how you do it. I can't believe you let a dog in your house."

"Oh, I left her at Jerell's house. I'ma pick her up Monday. I got to get some food, a bed, and a doggy door for her."

"I want to see the dog. Bring her over here when you pick her up. Come on sit under the dryer for a minute."

"For how long? You know I hate sitting under here. I'll bring the dog over Monday, since you're off and so am I. I took a couple days off."

"Don't take too many. You know we're going to Montego Bay for Jazz's birthday. I'm in the process of organizing things with her now. You are going, right?"

"Hell yeah, I wouldn't miss it for the world."

After I get my hair done, I have to go pick up my birthday cake and decorate the club. Jazz comes by to help me out. My party starts at 9:00P.M., but me and Chris arrive a half hour early to make sure everything is in order.

"Damisha, you look absolutely gorgeous."

"Thank you, baby. You are one handsome brotha. I'm proud to have you as my date."

"I'm honored to be your escort."

By nine-thirty, people start rolling in by the packs. The dreaded moment has arrived. Omar and Dontaé are here.

"Hey sis, you look beautiful. Happy belated birthday!"

"Thank you. You didn't bring your groupies with you?" I joke.

"Nah, I thought I would find some new ones here."

"Mm hmm." I smack my lips.

"Happy birthday, Damisha. I bought you a gift. I promise not to cause any problems." Omar states.

"Am I supposed to believe that? Look Omar, this is my big night. It has nothing to do with you or Skye, so I would appreciate it if both of you leave the drama outside. If you start acting crazy, I'ma have you thrown out. Am I making myself clear?" My hand is on my hip.

"Yes. Loud and clear. I won't mess up your night. Dontaé already threatened me."

"Good. You both remember Chris, my date for this evening."

"Yeah, hey man. How has it being going?" Dontaé asks Chris, shaking his hand.

"I'm good. Can't complain."

"This is my boy, Omar."

"Nice to meet you," Chris says while shaking Omar's hand.

"Please excuse us, we have other guests to greet," I say, pulling Chris away.

"I take it you don't care for Omar too much," Chris replies.

"You're absolutely right. I just hope he doesn't start anything with Skye."

"Oh, that's Skye's ex-boyfriend."

"Yep."

"Is she coming, or does she know he's here?"

"She knows he's here, she's just late as usual. Knowing Skye, she wants to make a grand entrance."

Our conversation is interrupted by Jamyya and Keenan. "Hey, girl! You look so pretty. I love your dress," Jamyya compliments.

"Thanks, girl. You are doing the damn thing yourself. I can't believe you got Keenan to dress up. You look good too Keenan."

"I know it's going to snow tonight. Damisha is giving people compliments. What? Nah, but seriously, thank you," Keenan laughs.

"You're welcome. You both know Chris, right?"

"Yeah, you look very handsome in your black and red as well," Jamyya tells Chris.

"Thank you. You are radiant too."

"Skye is in the house, so the party can start now!!" She hugs me.

"Thanks for coming, late as usual I see. Trying to make a grand entrance. You know Omar is already here."

"I figured as much. Girl, you know it takes time to look this good! Hey Jamyya and Keenan."

"Hey, miss diva. I thought that looked like Omar."

Are you okay with him being here?"

"No, but I'm not going to let him steal my joy. I'll be fine. Just keep him away from me."

"We already had a talk. You should be okay. He's going to be cool," I reply.

At last Jazz, Shawn, Coco and Jerome show up. Everybody is complimenting each other and making small talk while drinking and eating. The DJ's crunk with the music. Everything is flowing smoothly. Omar does not go near Skye all night. He's dancing with Aisha, one of my coworkers. Skye starts to get jealous.

"Look at Omar over there all up on that girl. That shit is just disgusting."

"Don't start no shit, Skye. Omar hasn't bothered you all night, so let it go," Coco states.

"He's doing it on purpose, he's just trying to make me mad."

"Well, if you know that's what he's doing, don't feed into it. Ignore him. Have a drink, then find somebody to dance wit'," I suggest.

"Good thinking. That's exactly why I love you." Skye goes off in search of a dance partner. The time is ticking by and Jerell still hasn't gotten here. I'm talking to Coco and Jamyya.

"I wonder where he is. He said he was coming. It's almost eleven o'clock. I hope nothing happened to him."

"Maybe he changed his mind. This would be an awkward situation for both of them to be here at the same time," Jamyya replies.

"Maybe so. I'm a go check my cell phone. Excuse me, ladies."

I go to the back office and look at my caller ID. I had two missed calls. I check my voicemail, but there's no message from Jerell. When I go back out into the club, I see Jerell standing beside Shawn and Jasmine. I walk over to him, trying to remain calm.

"Hey, beautiful. I'm sorry I'm late, but I'm here now. Where is your man?"

"Somewhere around here. I'm glad you made it."

"I wouldn't have missed it for the world. Now give me a hug before your date comes over."

I give Jerell a tight, long hug.

"I love you," he whispers in my ear.

"What?" I am truly in a state of shock.

"You heard me but I'll say it again. I love you."

I smile as wide as I can. "I love you too."

"Oh, I gave your gift to Jamyya, she put it up for you. I hope you like it."

"I'm sure I'll love it."

"Here comes Chris," Jazz whispers, nudging my arm.

A slow R & B song was playing. "Damisha would you like to dance?"

"Yeah, sure but first let me introduce you to Jerell, one of my friends."

"Nice to meet you," Jerell says, shaking Chris's hand.

"Mm hmm, likewise."

It appears Chris has an attitude. I guess he knows exactly who Jerell is. Chris takes my hand and leads me to the dance floor. "Please excuse us, everybody," he says.

Once out on the dance floor, Chris speaks quietly. "So you were bold enough to bring your other man to the party too. You are one brave sista. I thought you two were through."

"I'm sorry if I hurt your feelings. I just wanted everybody to share my day with me. He's still my friend; we grew up together. Jerell knows I'm with you, and he respects that."

"Are you sure? 'Cause you two were hugging pretty tight for a long time. I saw that big Cheshire cat grin on your face when you saw him."

My face looks surprised.

"Oh, you didn't think I saw you. Why did you think I came over to ask you to dance? Mm hmm... you ain't slick at all."

"I wasn't trying to be. I don't hide anything from neither of you. That's why you know about one another. We never agreed to be exclusive. Let's not do this here. Can we pretend to have fun until we leave? Please," I beg.

"Yeah, I'm cool. I don't want to be the one to spoil your party. This can wait till later, but we will talk about it."

"Thank you, baby," I kiss his cheek. He just looks at me funny.

"What's wrong now? Do you want me to tongue you down?"

"No, it's all good."

Dontaé gets on the microphone. "May I have your attention please? It's time to sing Happy Birthday. Then Mimi is going to open her gifts and then the cake will be served. Thank you."

I go to the front table and stand in front of the cake. Coco lights the two and seven candles on the cake. "One, two, three, happy birthday to you." Everyone sings the birthday song Stevie Wonder style.

"Now make a wish and blow out the candles," Dontaé says.

I close my eyes and think long and hard about what I want. Truth is, I want Jerell to be my boyfriend and possibly one day my husband. At that moment, I actually realize I want a relationship and a family. Almost all my friends have kids and are married. I believe I want the same thing.

"Mimi, we don't have all night," Jazz teases.

"A'ight, already. I'm finished." Everyone claps.

"I think we should cut the cake first, then I'll open presents while everybody is eating," I suggest.

Jamyya serves the cake for me while Skye and Dontaé bring up the presents. I'm so proud of Omar and Skye. He does not once bother Skye. It's a miracle.

"Ladies and gentlemen, may I have everyone's attention. First, I would like to thank everyone for coming out to help celebrate my twenty-seventh birthday. I appreciate all the gifts and compliments. A special thanks goes out to Jazz for helping me decorate and Coco for hooking up my hair. Dontaé, my big brother, rented this club for me, and I thank you. He's the one who made this possible. To Chris, thank you for being a gracious date. You look very handsome, and I love you. Thanks for understanding me. Now it's time to open some gifts."

"Here, open mine first." Chris hands me a rectangle-shaped gift. I tear off the paper. Wow, it's a pink diamond tennis bracelet!

"Thank you baby, it's beautiful." I kiss him on the lips. I figure Jerell won't care. He never seemed like the jealous type. Next I open Skye's present; it's a soft leather fuchsia Baby Phat coat. It's just my style. Even though Dontaé paid for the club, he still bought me a gift. It's a black and gold Dooney & Burke bag.

The last gift I get to is Jerell's. I'm really excited. He gives me a twenty-four-karat gold necklace with a heart locket on it. Inside of the locket is a picture of me and him. I quickly close the locket and thank him. All my gifts are great, even the ones from my coworkers. I get six hundred dollars in cash and gift cards. Coco buys me a dog bag like the one on <u>White Chicks</u>. It is so cute! By now I'm tired and my feet are sore.

"Chris, baby, I'm ready to go. Dontaé is going to stay and clean up. I'm really exhausted."

"Yeah, I bet you are. Why don't you tell everybody goodnight, then we can leave."

"Okay. Can you wrap me up some cake to take home?"

"I can do that. I'll be waiting at the bar."

When I go to make my goodbye rounds, I see Skye and Omar talking. I can't help but eavesdrop.

"Skye, I'm not trying to bother you. I just wanted to say hello. I think we could at least be cordial. You look very nice tonight, as always."

"Thank you. Now why don't you go back over there with that chick you were grinding on all night."

"I know you're not jealous."

"No, I'm not. I'm just tired of dealing with you. So excuse me, I have to go." Skye walks off.

Well, that went better than I would've thought. I say my goodbyes, hug everybody, and am on my way out when I run into Jerell.

"Thanks for coming. I hope you had a good time. I really like the necklace. I guess I'll see you Monday. How is Princess?"

"She's cool. I'm kind of getting attached to her. You better hurry up and come get her. She's good company."

"You can't have her, she's mine. Maybe you can bring her over Sunday night."

"A'ight. Just holla at me. I'm out. Have a good night. Don't do nothing I wouldn't do."

"Ha, ha, very funny. I'll see ya around."

I go back over to the bar. "Are you ready?" I ask Chris.

"Nah, sit here for a minute, I'ma help your brother put the gifts in the car."

"Okay."

I sit at the bar and talk to Skye until Chris comes back.

"Skye, are you okay?"

"No, I'm jealous. I can't stand to see Omar with another woman. I guess I see how he felt when he saw me with Jeff. I still love him a lot. I never thought I would miss him so much. The funny thing is, he didn't bother me all night. But deep down inside, I wanted him to. I'm just as crazy as he is."

"No, you're not. You're just used to him hounding you, that's all. Love doesn't go away just because someone has hurt you. Omar has been your boyfriend for almost five years. Y'all have a child together. Whether you want to be with him or not, you two have a bond. Now, I admit I don't care for Omar too much, but he does have some good qualities too."

"I hate to admit it, but he does. It just seems like he's destroying himself. He has started drinking and smoking weed. Devin called me 'cause he's worried about him, and so am I. I don't know what to do. Lately, I've been tired and really emotional. This breakup has taken a toll on me. I can't hide it any longer."

"The worst thing you can do is hold it in. Let it out, it's okay to cry sometimes. Talk about it, I'm willing to listen. We all have done some dumb shit in our lives. For example what I did tonight. I'll probably be calling you crying tomorrow, 'cause Chris is really upset with me."

"He knows who Jerell is, huh? I told you this wasn't going to work. But nah, you're hard-headed just like me. One day, we are going to actually follow through with the advice we are giving."

"Hopefully, one day soon. Call me tomorrow afternoon so we can talk."

"Okay, I love you, Mimi, and I hope whatever that long wish was comes true for you. You are a wonderful friend, and you deserve it."

"Thank you, ma. Trust me when I tell you, everything is going to work out. You are a bit spoiled and you got them mood swings, but you are a smart, beautiful, fashionable, and caring woman. You will find the right one, or maybe you and Omar just need a break. Whatever the case may be, just know I got your back. And I love you too." We hug and I wipe the tear from Skye's eye.

"Goodnight. I'll holla at you."

"A'ight, birthday girl. Try not to hurt 'em too bad."

Chris comes back then we leave the club.

Dontaé is waiting at the car for me. "Nice party, li'l sis. I hope it was everything you wanted it to be. I love you, and if you need me to help you spend that money, let me know," he laughs.

"You should know I don't need any help when it comes to spending money."

"That's for sure," Chris replies.

"Anyway, I love you too, Dee. Thanks for cleaning up. I owe you one. Goodnight and stay out of trouble. Don't take nobody home with you."

"I'm cool tonight. My hormones are under control. Just make sure you got yours in check. I'll holla at y'all later. Nice seeing you again, Chris. Y'all drive safe."

"You too. Goodnight." I kiss my brother.

"Yeah man, its' been real. See ya." Chris does the little head nod to Dontaé.

The ride home is silent. I can tell Chris is very upset. I try to ease the tension.

"Baby, I'm sorry. Sometimes I can be very selfish, and I wasn't thinking about your feelings when I invited Jerell. I shouldn't have insulted your intelligence. My only concern was me. Please forgive me."

"I don't think you understand the real reason I'm mad. For one, you should have told me. He just pops up like a surprise gift. Second, you could have kept the physical contact to a minimum, but it's all good. I see how you really feel about me. You don't even look at me the same way you do him. I know it's not intentional, that's just how you feel about him. I'ma do both of us a favor and step off. It's been real."

"I really don't want you to go, but I'm not going to be selfish this time. I'm going to respect your decision whether I like it or not. I can't change how you feel, but I do really care about you. I love you, and either way I will continue to care about you."

"I don't doubt that you care about me or even love me, but you're not in love with me. You don't love me the way you love Jerell. I think you want us to be friends, and that's cool, but I can't do that right now. It's going to take awhile, cause I love you like you love him. I really want to be in a monogamous relationship with you. I guess that's why it hurts so much."

"Does this mean we're breaking up?"

"Yes, for right now. I need some time alone to think. I'ma drop you off, then I'm going home. But first, I'll help you take the gifts inside."

At that moment, I feel worse than shit. My eyes begin to tear up. I don't want to lose Chris, but I don't want to let go of Jerell either. My heart is torn between the two. I'm in love with both of them.

Damn, what should I do? My first thought is to beg him not to leave, but my pride won't let me. Damisha never begs anybody for anything. I pull myself together. I hold my head high, give Chris a goodbye hug, and shut my front door.

After I'm sure he's gone, I scream and cry like a two-year-old having a tantrum. This is not how the night was supposed to end. Life …

I cry myself to sleep and wake up with a headache. I look out the window and it's snowing. So much for going shopping to make myself feel better! I take four Advil and make a pot of coffee. I decide to call Jerell. "Hey baby. Are you busy?" I inquire.

"No. What's up?"

"I'm here by myself, and it's snowing outside. I need some company. Can you bring Princess over here?"

"Yeah, but not right now. I got to put some clothes on and I gotta make a quick stop."

"You promise? It's snowing hard. You might get stuck in the snow."

"Yes, Mimi, I promise. It won't take me long. Give me an hour and a half, okay?"

"Mm hmm, alright."

"I'll see you in a minute. Do you want me to bring anything else? I know you don't come out in the snow."

"Yeah, can you bring some hot cocoa and milk?"

"Yeah, now let me go get dressed."

"Bye."

I hang up feeling a little better. Really, I want Jerell to come over, but I don't want to ask. My eyes are puffy from crying all night, so I put cucumber slices on them and lie back in a tub of hot water. Since I'm not going anywhere, I throw on my sweat pants and T-shirt then lounge around on the couch. I watch three movies on Lifetime and cook a DiGiorno pizza, but Jerell still hasn't came yet. I am starting to miss Chris even more.

***

It's about 4:00 P.M. I call Jerell to see what's keeping him but he does not answer. I don't bother to leave a message. Next I call Chris, but he doesn't answer either. I'm not surprised. I guess I should just give him time.

My next call is Skye. If she isn't available, I'm just going to give up.

"Girl, let me tell you what happened last night. Chris broke up wit' me, and now Jerell is back to his same ole bullshit. How could I be so stupid?"

"I told you to leave Jerell alone. He don't want you, but he don't want anybody else to have you either. He's playing you, Mimi. Wake up, the dick can't be that good. Jerell knows he can do as he pleases when it comes to you. You know why? 'Cause you let him. Learn to put your foot down. I know it's going to be hard, but it's okay to be alone. I have to learn that myself. If you need a friend, you've always got me, Coco, Jazz, and Jamyya."

"Yeah, I know, but I need a man's affection. Y'all just can't give me that. I'm missing my other half."

"And I don't want to give it to you either! Find yourself first before you look for someone else. Only you can make yourself happy, not anybody else. True happiness comes from inside."

"I knew calling you was a good idea. You always manage to tell me what I need to hear, even if I don't like it. Thanks."

"You're welcome. Anytime. You know what's ironic? We always seem to help each other out, but we can never solve our own problems."

"I guess if you're on the outside looking in, it's easy to pinpoint the problem. No one ever wants to examine their own flaws."

"That's so true. So what are you up to today?"

"Girl, you know I don't come out in the snow. I'ma just chill, eat some cake and popcorn while watching movies."

"You suck. Do you want me to come over to keep you company?"

"Nah, I'm good. I'll see you later on in the week."

"Well, if you change your mind, I'll be here. You know I don't have a life."

"A'ight. Holla at me if you need to talk. The least I can do is listen to your hang-ups."

"You got it. Bye."

I resume watching TV and eating. I must be depressed, 'cause I rarely eat a lot, but today I am the junk food queen. Something is really wrong here. By eight o'clock I figure Jerell isn't coming, so I pour me a glass of E & J, and then another and another. After awhile I lose count. Finally I pass out. Around 3:00 A.M., Jerell rings the doorbell. I stagger to the door.

"Hey baby, were you asleep?" he asks, holding the cage that contains Princess in his hand.

What a dumb ass question, I think to myself. "What do you think?" I slur with attitude.

"Damisha, are you drunk?"

"Don't worry about me. You didn't care several hours ago. You said you would be here in an hour and a half; that was at 10:00 A.M. I called you. You didn't answer or have the fucking decency to call back. Then you just show up like I'm supposed to be happy. Well, I'm not. Actually, I'm thoroughly pissed. Just kiss my ass, Jerell, 'cause I'm tired of your lame ass excuses. Save it for one of your dumb ass hoes."

"I don't feel like hearing this shit. I could've just gone home. Instead, I came over here in the fucking snow to bring your damn dog so you wouldn't be lonely. Here, take the damn dog."

"You forgot my damn cocoa and milk. Just go. Get the hell out. I can't take this no more. I'm tired of being treated like a high-priced whore. You came this late on purpose 'cause all you want to do is fuck. Well, not tonight. Not with me."

"That's cool, I always got a backup. I'll go somewhere else where I can be appreciated. Don't call me next week trying to make up, 'cause someone else will be taking your place. You're going to have to work your way back up into my top five."

"Jerell, do me a favor and just shoot yourself! Now get the fuck out!!" I damn near fall trying to push him out the door. Damn, I'm heated! I have to run to the bathroom to throw up in the toilet. He literally made me sick, or maybe it's the E & J.

Oh well, the point is, I've had enough. Conceited bastard! The nerve of him! I'm so mad I can't even go back to sleep. I put my coat and shoes on and drive to Krispy Kreme in the snow. I make it to Broad Street just fine, but I get too cocky on my way back.

Now normally, I wouldn't drive in the snow, but at that moment I'm not in my right mind. I'm still drunk, 'cause I drank another two glasses of E & J straight after Jerell left. I'm eating a glazed doughnut riding down 64 going east when I slide on a patch of ice and run into the side of the highway railing. Good thing I have my seat belt on! The front of my car is smoking. A man comes and knocks on the window,

"Ma'am, are you okay? Do you need an ambulance?"

"No, I'm fine," I slur.

"Do you have a cell phone?"

"Yes. Can you call my boyfriend for me?"

"Yeah. You know you shouldn't drive drunk. You could really hurt yourself or somebody else. Get in the passenger seat so I can move your car. I'ma help you out this time. Please don't make this a habit."

"Thank you, sir. No I won't. I don't usually drink this much. Here is my phone; my boyfriend's name is Chris. His number is in my phone book."

"Okay, let me move the car first."

He cuts the car on. It sounds horrible, and the engine is smoking. He looks at me. "It might damage your engine more if I move it, but frankly, I think it's already a total loss. Do you want me to still try?"

"Yes. I got AAA. They can tow it to my house. Can you call them too?"

I dig in my purse for the card. The nice citizen moves my car to the right shoulder of the highway. It's quarter to five in the morning. He calls AAA, then he calls Chris. AAA says it will take them about an hour or more to come, so they said I can leave and they will bring the car to my house.

At first Chris, is very rude. He asks the man to put me on the phone.

"Damisha. Are you crazy?" he screams. The man told him I was drunk and in a car accident.

"No, I'm depressed. Can you please come get me?" I whine.

"I don't feel sorry for you. Where is Jerell? You couldn't call anybody else?"

"No one else would answer. Look, I'm outside in the snow, drunk with a complete stranger. I got a big knot on my head and a headache. Are you coming or not?" I'm starting to get agitated.

"Against my better judgment, I'll be there. Stay put." He slams down the phone.

"Thank you, mister. He'll be here shortly."

"You're welcome. Here's your phone. I'll sit in my car and wait. You can stay in your car. The heat should still work."

"Okay, thank you again."

I wait about thirty minutes and Chris shows up.

"Thank you for coming. I'm sorry for waking you."

"No you're not. You just got to have your way. You really need help. Getting drunk is not going to solve your problems. That man should have called the police on you. You were lucky no one else saw you. Someone else always cleans up your mess. You need to grow up and learn how to make adult decisions. The only reason I came is because I still love you, but I can't deal with this. I don't want nothing bad to happen to you, and you know that. Please make this the last time you do some stupid shit like this."

"I promise, this is the last time."

"Mm hmm... I'm glad I took today off. You are really messing up my life. I've been really down since Saturday, but I didn't resort to drinking. You need to deal with the decisions you make."

I'm already fucked up, now I got to listen to a lecture all the way home.

"You got a knot on your forehead. Do you need to go to the hospital?" he asks.

"No, I should be fine."

"Well, don't go sleep for about three hours. I wouldn't want you to have a concussion. Do you have coffee?"

"Yes," I say, exhausted. Chris helps me into the house and makes me coffee. He makes sure I stay up, but he doesn't say much of nothing else. The look of disappointment on his face breaks my heart.

"Thank you for everything, Chris. I really appreciate it."

"You're welcome. Where did the dog come from?"

"It was a present from Jerell."

"Cute gift. Well, I guess it's time for me to go. You should be good now."

"Actually, I'm hungry. Could you fix me some breakfast, please?" He looks at me strangely.

"Yeah, but then I'm leaving."

The AAA people finally knock on the door. Chris signs the form and takes the keys from the man, then serves me breakfast in bed.

"Here's your breakfast. I can let myself out. Don't drink anymore, but if you do, stay in the house. You may want to consider counseling. If you really need to talk to somebody, call Skye or one of your friends. I'll try to check on you later on in the week. I love you, Damisha, but right now I can't be with you. You've hurt me too bad. I gotta go. See ya. I'll lock the door behind me."

Chris leaves and the tears begin to fall. I eat the food, but I throw up minutes after. I have a terrible hangover to sleep off. I finally fall asleep and I have a beautiful dream. I dream that me and Chris get married then we have a cute little baby girl. Her name was Danayshia. She looks just like Chris. My dream is so lifelike; it feels so real. I wake up with tears in my eyes. I know I fucked up. Princess starts barking at me. Oh shit, I forgot all about her! She is probably hungry. I go to the kitchen to get her some food, then I see her bowls have water and food in them. Chris must have done it. How sweet!

Maybe she wants to play, but I don't feel like it. She follows me around the house. I take her outside to use the bathroom.

Oh, that's what she wanted. I take a long hot shower. The snow has started melting 'cause the sun has come out. Well, at least the day is bright. It's Monday, and Coco is the only one off besides me. I start to call her, then I change my mind. I forgot I had a big bruise on my forehead I don't want to explain. I call my doctor to see if I can come in today. She says sure.

I know I will need a doctor's note for work. I call and tell them about my accident, but I leave out the part about being drunk. I tell my manager I will be back on Monday. That reminds me, I need to call the insurance agent.

My doorbell rings. I wonder who this could be? It's a delivery man with flowers. I sign for them and go inside. I wonder who these are from. I read the card and I'm shocked. The flowers are from Chris. The card reads, "Here is a little something to lift your spirits. Right now I can't help you, but I want you to remain positive. I know how it is to be depressed. The best advice I can give you is to pray and go to church. Seek God first, and everything else will fall in place. Love, Chris."

Aw, he is the best. Why did I ever let him leave? My stupid pride. I want to call and thank him, but I know he doesn't want to speak to me. So I do the next best thing, I text message him. He texts me right back two words: You're welcome. Right then, I know I can't get him back.

My insurance company arranges for me to get a rental car until a claims adjuster can come out to assess the damages. I call Coco to take me to Enterprise Rent-a-Car.

"Coco, I got in a car accident last night. My car is totaled. Can you take me to pick up a rental car at Enterprise?"

"Sure. How did you get in an accident? Are you okay?"

"Yeah, I just have a big bruise on my forehead. I was wearing my seatbelt though. I wanted some Krispy Kreme doughnuts. On the way back, I was eating a glazed doughnut and my car slid on some ice. I hit the highway divider barricade head on. The hood is smashed, my car is a total loss."

So I lied a little. Coco is a mother, I don't feel like another lecture. Chris laid me out enough for two people.

"When do you want me to come?"

"Now, if possible. I have a doctor's appointment at three o'clock. I need a note for work 'cause I'm not going back until next Monday. Plus I need proof I was driving for the insurance company. I called AAA, but didn't call the police 'cause I was the only car involved."

"Who brought you home?"

"Chris did. I got the dog here now, so you can see her when you come."

"A'ight, I'm leaving now."

"Thanks, boo."

Coco comes to pick me up. She comes in and plays with Princess for a few minutes, then we leave. On the ride to Enterprise, I tell Coco all about the incident me and Jerell had last night. She isn't surprised. Basically, she tells me the same thing Skye said. I feel really dumb and naïve. They give me a Toyota Camry to drive. I like it a lot. I go to the doctor, then decide to comfort myself by going shopping.

I spend all my gift cards at the mall. I even buy Princess some toys from Pet Smart. Before I left the house I had put some foundation on my face to cover the bruise. It worked good. I also stop by the grocery store to stock up on junk food before I head home.

As soon as I go in the house I eat three bowls of ice cream. Then I eat two cupcakes and a whole bag of Doritos. I even drink a whole two liter Pepsi.

My phone rings. I look at the caller ID 'cause I don't want to be bothered. It's Jerell, so I don't answer. I have no words for him. Wait a minute… I take that back. I have plenty of words for him, but none of them are nice. I don't feel like dealing with him right now.

Coco told me all about the trip to Montego Bay when we were together earlier. She booked all our tickets and everything. I'm going to use my tax money to pay off my credit cards and use some as spending money for the trip. I didn't have any money when she booked the trip, so I put it on my Visa card.

January can't come fast enough for me. I need a vacation. I just hope I don't get fired from my job. I'm about to be broke 'cause I'ma have to get a new car. I think I might get a Honda Accord. Who knows?

Princess sits in my lap while I watch TV. Jazz and Jamyya call me, but I don't answer. I am tired of people. I don't feel like being social. Jerell calls again, but I don't even bother to check my voicemail. I feel myself sinking deeper and deeper into depression. For the next couple of days, I shut myself off from the world. I don't talk to nobody. I just eat and cry.

Chapter Sixteen
Coco

The time has come for me and Alana to attend the visitation hearing against André. It's Friday, December 19th. I'm glad it's not snowing today. I hate going to court, especially Juvenile and Domestic Relations. They take forever to call your case. We are on the docket for 2:00 P.M., but I arrive at 2:30P.M. 'cause I know how they do. I do not feel like sitting in the waiting area looking at Tyesha and André.

Sure enough, when I arrive, Tyesha's fat ass is there supporting André. He looks like a broke-down Snoop Dogg. Anyway, I ignore them and sit beside Alana.

"Hey girl, y'all still waiting I see."

"Mm hmm, I wish they'd hurry up! I got other stuff to do. This is a waste of time anyway. Once they give him visitation, he's going to get them for two weeks, then he ain't going to want to be bothered with it again."

"You ain't never lied! He just wants to be in control, that's all. He don't have shit of his own, so he wants to control something. Just look at his dumb ass sitting over there," I whisper.

"I know. Tyesha keep looking over here rubbing her stomach; she must be hungry. Big ass cow."

"Girl, you are so crazy."

At three-thirty, they finally call our case. I am first. After the judge hears the case, this is his ruling: "Mrs. Knight, I grant visitation to Mr. Smith every weekend from 6:00 P.M. on Friday to 6:00 P.M. on Sunday. He also gets visitation on holidays from 8:00 A.M. till 4:00 P.M. Failure to comply with this order will be contempt of this court. Order starts on today's date. So if you want to see Corey today, Mr. Smith, you may do so at six o'clock. Anyone have any questions?"

I stand up. "Yes, Your Honor, I do. What is going to keep Mr. Smith's girlfriend from mistreating my child again?"

"Very good question. Mr. Smith is, if he wants to continue to see his son. If anything happens that is child abuse, you need to report it, Mrs. Knight. Don't engage in vigilante activity. If that is all, court is adjourned."

André has a big smile on his face like he won the lottery. I knew all along he was going to get visitation, I just wanted to be difficult. Alana's case goes the same way. She calls and tells me about it, 'cause I wasn't waiting around any longer. Alana refuses to let André get Brianna for Christmas or next weekend. Oh well, that's their fight. Personally, I'm sick of trying to find somebody to keep Corey. Jerome is getting on my last nerve, so this is one last thing I need him to do. I hate asking him to do shit. I can't wait till I go to Montego Bay.

Since I had to come to court for this bullshit, I left work early. I don't have any more appointments for today, so I'll just do some Christmas shopping.

Damisha has been depressed lately. Maybe I should see if she wants to come along. I call her cell phone first.

"Hey, Mimi. I was going to go Christmas shopping, would you like to go?"

"For what? I don't have anybody to shop for. I already bought all the girls their gifts and Dontaé something. Nobody is left, I don't have a man."

"Well, just go to get out of the house. Even though you and Chris aren't together, you can still get him a gift. Maybe you can have it delivered to him."

"Yeah, I guess I could. A'ight, I'll go. Are you coming to get me?"

"Yeah, I'll be there in thirty minutes."

"A'ight. I'll be ready."

When Mimi comes out of the house, I can't believe my eyes. Her stomach is so big.

"Girl, are you pregnant?"

"No, I'm just fat and depressed. All I do is eat."

"I see. Well, you need to stop. You ain't going to be able to wear your bikini at Montego Bay if you keep going the way you going."

"Do I really look that bad?"

"Your stomach does. Put down the spoon and fork. Are you sure you're not pregnant?"

"Yes, I came on my period, plus I took a test, it was negative. It's just food, Coco," she explains, shaking her flabby stomach.

Mimi has always had a flat stomach. It's hard to believe she gained so much weight in only two weeks.

"Can you still fit your clothes?" I am curious.

"Let it go, Coco. I already feel bad enough."

"A'ight. I'm sorry."

Hmm, I know what to get her for Christmas, a membership to American Family Fitness.

We shop for a couple of hours, but I can tell Mimi still isn't herself.

"Mimi, if you need to talk, I'm here for you. You are not alone. I'm worried about you."

"I'm fine, but thanks for caring."

When I get home the kids are still up, so I leave my bags in the car. When they go to sleep, I'll sneak everything in.

"Hey Corey and Christian. What are y'all doing up?"

"Just playing, Mommy," Corey says.

"Well, it's late. You and your brother need to get ready for bed."

"Okay, Mom."

Before I can even get comfortable, Jerome starts fussing. "Where have you been? André called here wanting to get Corey, but you weren't here. I called your cell phone, but you didn't answer. Now he's pissed 'cause he said the court order says he can get him. I didn't let him go, 'cause I knew you would throw a fit."

"Well, I didn't think he would get him today. All I did was go Christmas shopping. I knew the kids were up, so I left the stuff in the car. I didn't even know you called. I must've left my cell phone in the car."

"You got an excuse for everything."

"I refuse to fight with you. I can't wait till I go to Montego Bay. You are really starting to aggravate me."

"Go where? When? You didn't ask me if you could go anywhere?"

"I don't need your permission to go anywhere. Last time I checked, I was a grown-ass woman. I paid for the trip, which means I can go."

"A'ight smart ass. Who is going to keep the kids, 'cause I'm not. Plan that shit out. I'm tired of your smart-ass comments. We are married, or have you forgotten? You are supposed to discuss shit like this with your husband."

"I was going to discuss it with you, but you act a damn fool all the time. I really don't feel like going through this with you. I don't need your permission to do a damn thing. Yeah, it would've been nice if I told you, but I didn't. I'm still going whether you like it or not, case closed."

"Fine, do what you want, but don't expect me to be happy about it. Just make sure you have proper care for Corey and Christian, 'cause I need a break too."

"A'ight, no problem."

I slam the bedroom door, then go downstairs to the family room. I refuse to be in the same room with him. I call André, 'cause I have to go to work tomorrow and I know Jerome isn't going to keep Corey.

"André, can you get Corey tomorrow from my shop around eight in the morning? I'm sorry I wasn't home earlier. I didn't think you were going to get him today. When we were at the courthouse you didn't mention it. I went Christmas shopping. My bad."

"Mm hmm, I can get him in the morning."

"Good. One more thing. I'm going on a trip January 16 through January 24th. Can you keep Corey for me while I'm gone?"

"I don't know about that. You know I gotta work, and you be acting funny about Tyesha. She is not feeling well either. I can't keep him that long. I can only do some weekends."

"That doesn't surprise me, you don't never do shit anyway. Can you pay child support since you're working? Or maybe buy Corey some shit for Christmas? Can you do anything besides be an Internet hoe?"

"I ain't going to listen to this. Grow up, Coco. I'll see what I can do about Christmas. I got bills to pay too. It don't seem like you hurting for money if you're going on a trip."

"Forget it, André. Just pick Corey up tomorrow. Bye." I slam down the phone. What an asshole!

***

When I woke up this morning, I packed Corey's bag and took him to work with me. It's Saturday and I'm booked. André comes to get Corey, but of course he's late. Skye, Jamyya and Jazz come to get their hair done. Skye comes first.

"Hey boo. How is everything going with you?" I ask.

"I'm good. Sometimes I miss Omar, but Omari keeps me happy."

"That's good. Have you talked to Mimi?"

"Not in a couple of weeks. I call her but she doesn't answer. Why? What's up?"

"We went shopping the other day, and her stomach looks terrible. She has gained so much weight, I thought she was pregnant. All she does is sit in the house and eat. She looks so sad."

"Aw, I wish she would talk to me. Maybe I'll just pop up over there when I leave here. She needs to get out the house. All she's doing is feeling sorry for herself."

"I know. I'ma buy her a gym membership for Christmas."

"Don't do that, Coco. That will be mean."

"Yeah, I guess. Make sure you comb her hair when you go over there, too."

"A'ight."

When Jazz comes, she tells me Chris called her to check up on Mimi. He said he was worried about her.

"Yeah girl, Chris said Mimi has been getting drunk and everything. I told him that she hasn't been talking to anybody. He said he was going to try to see her, but he don't know if he can do it," Jazz states.

"Aw, poor thing, he's really hurting too."

"Yep, he sure is. Make sure you make me pretty, 'cause I got a Christmas party to go to tonight. Shawn's company is having one at the Radisson Hotel."

"Sounds nice. I'ma give you a classy updo. You are going to be absolutely gorgeous. Those eyebrows need to be arched too."

"Work your magic, girl," Jazz says, snapping her fingers.

I can't wait for Jamyya to come so I can get some advice from her. She is the only one of my friends who is married.

"Hey, Jay, I need some advice. Jerome is mad about our trip to Montego Bay. He won't keep the kids. We had a big argument. What should I do?"

"Why is he mad?"

"'Cause I didn't ask him to go before I paid for the tickets."

"In that case, you were wrong. You should have discussed it with him, not ask him. I can see why he was mad. Put yourself in his shoes. How would you feel if Jerome planned something and didn't consult you?"

"I would be mad, but he does it all the time. So, I can relate, but since he does it to me he shouldn't have a problem when I do it."

"You need to stop all that tit for tat bullshit and go to counseling or something, y'all need professional help. Both of y'all have a problem communicating with each other."

"You think you know, but you're right. I'll work on it."

"You promise?"

"Yeah, I do."

I leave the shop with a different attitude. I'm ready to go home and apologize to Jerome for cussing him out. When I pull up to my house, I can't even park in my driveway. Cars are everywhere. Balloons are hanging outside the house.

"What in the world is going on?" I wonder. I park the car half way down the street. I can hear music blasting before I open the door. People are everywhere in my house. Kids are running and dancing.

I see Jerome in the kitchen. "What the hell is going on here?" I scream.

"Jermeka's birthday party. Remember, her birthday was Thursday?"

"Oh, yeah, but why is her party here? You didn't tell me nothing about it."

"Her party is here 'cause I'm her father, and this is my house. I didn't think I needed to tell you. I know you would be at work anyway."

Someone busts out laughing. I turn to look; it's Shameka.

"Oh, hell no! Not in my damn house! This bitch has got to go! Get out of my damn house!"

Shameka puts her hands on her hips. "You are making a fool of yourself. Children are in here, just calm down. I always knew you were an ignorant ghetto bitch."

Before she can utter another word I punch her dead in the mouth. "Talk shit now, you tacky bitch! Take all these damn people and their wild ass kids and get out! Get the fuck out!"

Jerome grabs me by both arms. "Coco, I can't believe you! You are ruining Jermeka's birthday party! You are a selfish, inconsiderate…you know what, I'm not even going to go there. I'm leaving. I can't put up with this shit no more."

By now everyone is gone but Shameka and Jermeka.

"You know what, Jerome, just leave. Go now before I hit you too. I'm furious right now, ain't no telling what I might do. Get this bitch out my face."

Jerome grabs Jermeka's hand and looks at Shameka. "Come on, let's go."

Shameka's lip is busted. "You must wanna go back to jail. You crazy bitch."

"Oh, if I do, you better hope I don't get out, 'cause I'll whoop your ass again."

They both leave.

That bitch slams my door so hard I think the glass is going to break. I hope this bitch don't call the police on me. Wait a minute, how do she even know about my charge?

Oh, hell naw! I know Jerome has not been telling this hoe my business! He has truly violated this time! I am fuming! All I could do is pace back and forth.

"Mommy, are you okay?" a small timid voice asks.

"Christian, oh baby! I'm sorry. Mommy didn't know you were still here."

"Yes. I eat ice cream. You want some?"

"No thank you, baby. Come here, put your coat on. We are going to go bye bye, okay?"

"Okay."

I put Christian in his car seat and we drive to Skye's house. I didn't even call first, I hope she's home. When I get to her house, I see the Lexus in the driveway. Good, she's home. I ring the doorbell.

Skye opens the door surprised. "Hey Coco, what's up? What are you doing here? Hi, Christian."

"Hi, Auntie Skye," he replies.

"Girl, me and Jerome just had a big fight. I need somebody to talk to."

"Aw, damn! I don't mean to sound insensitive, but I was on my way out. I got Mimi to agree to go out for drinks tonight. If you didn't have Christian, you could come too. Do you think you can get a babysitter?"

"I don't know. Listen Skye, I don't think it's a good idea to let Mimi drink. She has an alcohol problem. Chris told Jazz about it. He's worried about her. Maybe y'all could just have dinner, no alcohol."

"Oh, I didn't know. Well in that case, you can bring Christian."

"No. I don't want him to hear our adult conversations."

"Yeah, true. Call your mom I bet she might watch him."

"Nah, I need her to keep both the kids when we go to Montego Bay. Oh, I can ask Torey. Let me use your phone, I left mine."

"Okay."

I call my brother, and he says Christian can spend the night.

We pick Mimi up first, 'cause Skye said she was scared she might change her mind. Then we drop off Christian. It's hard finding a place that doesn't sell alcohol.

"Let's go to Friday's," Damisha suggests.

"Too many bad memories for me," Skye replies.

"Okay, let's go to Red Lobster."

"Yeah, that'll work. Good choice," I agree with Mimi.

For a Saturday night, Red Lobster is pretty empty. While we are waiting for our food, we chat. Mimi doesn't order any liquor, but she damn sure orders enough food. I have never seen her eat so much.

"What do you want to talk about, Coco?" Skye asks.

"Jerome. I talked to Jamyya at the shop, and she made me realize I was wrong. I went home all set to apologize to him, but when I got there, a party was going on. He gave Jermeka a birthday party in the house. The music was blasting, children running around, adults dancing and eating. He even had Shameka up in my house. I put everybody out."

"Did he tell you about the party?"

"No, that's the point. He's mad 'cause I didn't tell him about Montego Bay before I bought my ticket, but he can do whatever he wants without consulting me. What makes matters worse is he's been telling Shameka my business. She made me so mad I punched her in the mouth. Jerome got mad and left with her."

"Do you think Jerome and Shameka are fucking?" Mimi bluntly asks.

"I don't know what to think anymore. We have been having so many problems lately, he just might be. Even if he's not, that's how she makes it seem, and he doesn't seem to care. When it comes to Shameka, he thinks she can do no wrong."

"Well, why aren't they still together?"

"'Cause they were young and she's a hoe. She broke up with him to be with somebody else, then that dude ended up leaving her a couple months later. After that, I guess she couldn't find anybody like Jerome's dumb ass, so she's been trying to get him back."

"Seems like she wants him bad. A female Omar." We all laugh.

"Are you feeling better, Mimi? We're concerned about you," I say.

"Yeah, I'm a little better. I'll be okay. It just takes time to get over a broken heart. I had two breakups at one time that's all. I'm not contemplating suicide or anything drastic."

"If you say so. You need to stop eating so much. Go to the gym and work out. Start the new year off right," Skye tells her.

"I'll see if I can fit it into my busy schedule."

"What busy schedule? All you do is go to work and sleep then wake up and eat."

"I also walk my dog and clean up my house. I'm in the process of donating my old clothes to charities."

"That is so sweet! You keep on eating like that, by summer you will be donating everything."

"You are such a smart ass." Mimi rolls her eyes.

"Stop, Skye. Don't make her feel bad. We are supposed to encourage her, make her feel better."

"You're right. I'm sorry. I'm just not used to seeing you like this. You're depressing me."

"Thanks Skye, you really know how to cheer a girl up," Mimi sarcastically states.

"I don't know if I should go back home or not. I'm not in the mood to see Jerome right now."

"You can spend the night at my house. I don't mind. It would be nice to have some company. Oh, I got an idea. We should have a sleepover. Mimi, you can come over too. We can stay up and talk, do each other's hair, do nails, watch movies. You know, girl stuff."

"Yeah, it sounds like fun. What do you think, Mimi?"

"I guess I can come. I don't have any prior engagements. Just stop me by my house so I can get some clothes. Can I bring Princess?"

"Yeah, I want to see her anyway. Is she house broken?"

"Yeah, she got her own bed she sleeps in too, she's a good dog."

"A'ight, let's go get some movies from Blockbuster."

"Don't forget the snacks. I need ice cream. Can we go to Pizza Hut too?"

"Mimi, we just finished eating."

"Yeah, I know, but in a couple of hours I'll be hungry again. What's a sleepover without pizza?"

"We can order pizza later on tonight before they close, okay? Now let's go get this party started."

This is the first time we've had an adult slumber party. It's really fun. We don't even drink alcohol 'cause we know Mimi has a problem. We dance, sing, talk, cry, watch movies, and eat like pigs. How I wish I was young again!

***

I leave Skye's house early the next morning 'cause I have to pick up Christian. Torey's girlfriend Chantel is cooking breakfast when I walk in.

"Hey Coco, would you like to stay for breakfast? I cooked plenty," Chantel says with a smile.

"Yeah, if you really have enough. I'm really hungry."

"Yeah girl, sit down. Tell me what you did last night."

"Nothing really, just hung out with Mimi and Skye. Me and Jerome had a big fight as usual. Where is Christian?"

"He's still asleep. Takori had him up all night playing wit' toys. She was so excited he was here."

"I guess she's still asleep too."

"Yep. I'ma wake them up when I finish cooking."

Chantel is cool, but I'm not trying to tell her all my business. Plus, she's the nail tech at my shop. I don't need all my workers in my business. Christian and Takori finally wake up. We eat breakfast, then I leave. Takori wants to come home with me, but I tell her she can spend the night next weekend.

When I get home, Jerome isn't there. It looks like he never came home last night. I start to get furious. These anger management classes are not working. Six o'clock comes, and still no sign of Jerome.

André calls for me to meet him at the mall to pick up Corey. While I'm out, I go to the grocery store. I'm tired of eating out, so I cook pepper steak for dinner. Monday comes, no Jerome. Tuesday, no Jerome. This nigga hasn't called or nothing. When I look in the closet, I notice some of his clothes and shoes are missing. He even took all his personal hygiene items off the dresser.

I take a deep breath then check my messages. Maybe he left a message on the landline. I dial the voicemail number. The first one is from Shameka.

I start to skip it, but something tells me to listen to it, so I do. "Hello, Mrs. Coco, this is Shameka. If you want to know where your husband is, he's here with me. Yep, he's been sleeping in my bed every night since Saturday. Just thought you should know. Next time be careful who you cross, bitch."

Oh, no this heifer didn't! I am raging mad. I start slamming shit and just tearing up stuff. Oh, I got something for her ass! I glance at the clock, mm hmm, it's only 5:00 P.M., the kids don't have to be picked up from daycare until 6:30 P.M. That gives me plenty of time to kick Shameka's ass. I jump in my car and headed to her house. I call my brother while driving.

"Hey Torey, can you please go to Home Depot and buy me two new deadbolt locks where you need the key for both sides, and two new doorknobs? Then come straight to my house and install them."

"Look Coco, I think you are overreacting. Just calm down tell me what's going on," he says in a calm voice.

"This nigga hasn't been home in four days and you are telling me to calm down? He hasn't called or nothing, and I know he's alive 'cause I called his job yesterday and he answered the phone. I hung up when I knew he was all right."

"It's your call, but don't say I didn't try to stop you."

"Just do what I ask you. I'll pay you back when you get to my house. Are you going to see Dad for Christmas?"

"Yeah, we can go up there for a couple of hours. You want to see him?"

"Mm hmm. I haven't been in a while. I wrote him and sent some money a couple of weeks ago."

"Cool, I'll drive. I'll talk to you when I get to your house. In the meantime, please try to chill out."

"I will, I'ma go pick up the kids from daycare. If I'm not home when you come, I'll be on the way."

"A'ight. Bye." So I lied a little. I am going to make a special trip to Shameka's house first. When I get there, Jerome's truck is parked out front. No this trifling mothafucka don't have the nerve to really be here! I'm too through wit' this hoe.

Since I already have an assault charge, I decide to take my crazy ass home. Shit, she can have his lying ass! I am so mad I get a migraine headache. Tears are pouring out my eyes. I try to get myself together in the daycare parking lot. I'm in no mood to cook, so I take the boys to Pizza Hut for dinner. Actually, I get the pizza to go.

I let them play video games in the family room until they get tired. After Torey installs the locks, I give him some money and he grabs a couple of slices of pizza. I explain to him how Shameka left a message and I saw Jerome's truck at her house. Torey has an excuse for everything. You would think he's Jerome's brother.

"Coco, maybe he was visiting Jermeka. His child does live there. You know how Shameka lies. Don't let her get to you. I'll do you a favor. I'll ride over there, and I bet you $20.00 that his car is gone. He's probably staying at a friend's house or wit' his sister. Have you called Lisa?"

"No. I'm not trying to bring everybody into our business. Besides, I'll just look stupid if he's not there. Fuck him, 'cause he still didn't come home no matter where he's staying. He could have at least called or left a message. He did neither, so if he decides to sneak in again when I'm not home, he will have to break in. I changed the alarm code too."

"You are real cold. I'm leaving now. I'll call you when I get to Shameka's house. She still lives in the same place, right?"

"Yeah, that trifling bitch hasn't moved."

"Get a glass of wine or something to calm you down. Do you want some weed or Newports?"

"Yeah, I want a cigarette. You got a pack on you? You know I'm on probation for beating Tyesha's ass."

"Oh, that's right. Here, take these, I'll just buy some more. Don't leave this house, 'cause you don't need to get into no more trouble."

"I know. That's why I didn't beat Shameka's ass when I went over there earlier. She's trying to trap me. She wants me to beat her ass so I can go to jail, but I ain't falling for it. I'm smarter than that."

"That's good to hear. Get a drink, turn on some slow music and chill out or call up one of your girls and talk about Jerome like a dog. That's what y'all normally do anyway. Here are your new keys. I replaced the front and back door locks."

"Thank you. Now go, I don't need any more advice. You need to get home before Chantel starts tripping on you. I know you don't want to be in the dog house."

"Oh, so she be talking about me at work?"

"No. Well, not to me, she knows you're my brother and I don't play that shit. And don't be telling my business to her, 'cause I don't want the whole shop knowing what goes on in my house."

"Your secret is safe with me. I love you, sis. Goodnight. I'ma call you."

Torey goes to Shameka's house, and sure enough, Jerome's truck is still there. Dirty little bastard! I don't want to become like Mimi, but I need something to relax me so I get a glass of Moet and chain-smoke ten cigarettes. My throat is burning; I haven't smoked in awhile. Jerome always hated cigarette smoke, so I tried to quit for him, but he's not here anymore, so I can do what I want.

I run around the house doing all the little petty things he hated just to spite him. The funny thing is, he's not even going to know, 'cause he ain't here. I can't wait to see the look on his face when he tries to unlock the door! Hmm, he must think I'm a fool. I can excuse one night, but not coming home for four days? Now that's just plain ridiculous! He must've truly lost his mind. I can't even go to sleep, I'm so upset.

I take two Advil PM's so I can sleep. I've got to get some sleep, tomorrow is Christmas Eve and I'm swamped with clients. Jamyya offered to help me so she could make some extra money, but she said she has to leave at three o'clock 'cause the mall closes at six. Some help is better than none.

I know you aren't supposed to mix medicine and alcohol, but God willing I'll wake up in the morning. Oh, yeah, that reminds me, I need to return all of Jerome's gifts and Jermeka's too.

Fuck everybody. That's going to be my new motto. Now I know just how Mimi feels. I start to call her, but my eyes start getting heavy so I just go to sleep. Good thing my alarm clock is set for the same time every day.

Daycare closes early today, so I asked my mom to pick the kids up. She agreed to keep them until seven o'clock. She has a Christmas Eve party to attend at nine o'clock. I still need to wrap presents.

I call Jamesha to see if she's busy. I tell her I will pay her one hundred dollars to wrap presents for me, and she quickly agrees. I drop off the gifts and wrapping paper at her house on my way to work. I'm not in the mood to do hair, but I can't let my clients down. They are looking forward to looking good for Christmas.

Even though I'm not in a good mood, it doesn't show in my work. I hook up every last one of my clients' heads. I take a lot of my tools home so I can do my own hair tomorrow. Damn, I'm tired as hell! I still need to pick up some last minute gifts, but don't feel like shopping. I buy Visa gift cards from Wal-Mart and some Christmas candy, then go to my mother's house.

"Mommy, is Daddy home?" Christian asks.

"I don't think so, sweetie. We'll see when we get home, okay?"

"Okay."

Whew, that was easy! I've been avoiding that question all week. I have a habit of not telling my mother stuff, and this time is no different.

"Is everything alright, boo?" my mother asks.

"Yeah, I'm just a little tired. The shop was packed today."

"I can imagine. I know how people get during the holidays. Are you coming to Grandma's for dinner?"

"Yeah, but I might be a li'l late. Me and Torey are going to see Dad tomorrow. I sent him a Christmas card with some money about a week ago."

"That's nice. I'll send him something too when the post office opens back up. Tell him I asked about him and I hope he's a'ight."

"I will. Maybe you can go with us next time we visit."

"Yeah, I'll see. Just let me know in advance. Now y'all got to get out, 'cause I gotta get ready for my party. Take them babies home so they can go to sleep before Santa Claus passes by y'all house."

"Uh huh, Grandma, I've been a good boy. Santa Claus is coming to my house. Ain't he Mom?" Corey screams.

"Yes baby, he's coming to our house. Now let's go so you can get in the bed."

I look at my mother. "See what you started, Ma? You know how kids are. Now he's going to worry me half the night about whether or not Santa is coming. Bye Ma, see you tomorrow."

"A'ight. Bye, grandma's babies. I love you. Be good and go straight to bed. Oh, here are the chocolate chip cookies we made for Santa Claus. I hope y'all got milk."

"Yeah, Ma, I have to go to the grocery store. Bye. Love you. Don't have too much fun at that party."

"Oh, I will," she laughs.

I speed home, hoping Jerome is not at the house waiting for us. I don't see nobody when I pull up. Good. I take the kids and we run in the house. I put them to sleep then Jamesha and Devin bring the wrapped gifts to my house. I give her the money and give Devin twenty dollars for gas.

"Merry Christmas, y'all. Thanks so much," I tell them.

"You're welcome," they reply.

I feel good helping out the young kids. They are trying so hard. They make the cutest li'l couple. The kids wake me up Christmas morning, I try to act happy.

"Mommy, Mommy Santa Claus came! Can we open our gifts?" Corey asks, while Christian jumps up and down on my bed.

"Yes, let me get myself together first. I want to take some pictures."

"Hurry up, Mommy, I'm excited!"

"I see. Calm down, the gifts are not going anywhere."

"Where is Daddy?" Christian asks, looking around.

"He ain't here. He don't live here no more," Corey replies.

"Be quiet, Corey. Look honey, your daddy went bye bye for a little while, okay. He will be back soon."

Christian has tears in his eyes. "But where him at mommy? I miss him."

"I know you do. He had some business to take care of. Come on, let's go open the gifts."

"Yeah!" they both scream.

This is going to be hard to discuss with the kids. Maybe just for today, I can keep them distracted. They run to the Christmas tree and start tearing open gifts. As they smile, I snap pictures.

The phone starts ringing; it's probably just Skye or one of the girls. I check the caller ID, and it's Jerome. Oh, now you want to call after four days just 'cause it's Christmas? Well, you know what, fuck you! I don't bother to answer the phone.

"Mom, the phone is ringing!" Corey yells.

"I know, but I'm busy. I'll call them back later."

"Okay."

Jerome calls so much I turn the ringer off. I quickly get me and the kids dressed, then drive to Torey's house. I'm hoping he's ready to go see my dad. Jerome calls my cell phone while we are en route.

"I've been calling you all morning. Where are you? I went to the house; I see you've changed the locks. You're trying to be funny, I see."

"Me, trying to be funny? Ha, this is the first time you've called since you've been gone. Don't call now 'cause it's Christmas. Did you forget you have a son who's been looking for his daddy? What do you want me to tell him?"

"The truth. That his mother is a crazy bitch who can't control her anger. You are my wife, you shouldn't be jealous of Shameka. Coco, you need to grow up. You can't be ghetto all your life. I was calling 'cause I want to see Christian."

"Well, he already has plans for today. Maybe you can get him this weekend."

"Oh, now you wanna pull that shit? I'm not André. You are not going to keep my son from me."

"I'm not keeping him from you. You made the choice to leave. Now I said you can get him tomorrow or tonight when I'm finished doing what I'm doing."

"A'ight, fine, have him ready at eight o'clock tonight."

"I will, and I'll appreciate it if you pick him up from Mimi's house. I'm going to visit her, so you can just meet us there."

"Whatever."

I don't hear anything else 'cause I hang up.

Torey glances at me. "So y'all still beefing, huh?"

"Yep, he can go to hell for all I care. He gets on my damn nerves."

"You're just mad right now. You just need some time apart that's all. Maybe y'all could get some marriage counseling."

"We don't need none 'cause we don't have a marriage. That counseling shit doesn't work. I paid all this money for anger management, and look at me, I'm still fucking pissed. The only reason I go is 'cause the court ordered me to. Look Torey, it's Christmas, I'm really not in the mood for a lecture. Let's just have a good time."

"A'ight, but it's not just going to go away. You need to talk about it to somebody. You need healing."

"Enough. I will talk about it, but not today. The kids are in the back seat. Just let it go, please."

"Oh, I forgot about them. A'ight I'll drop it."

My dad is very happy to see us. We have a good visit. I tell him what my mom said. He smiles. I think they still love each other, but him being locked up so long drove them apart. After visiting my dad, we go to my grandma's house for dinner. It looks as if the whole family is there. I see people I haven't seen in years. I throw all my problems on the back burner and I put my happy face on. No one knows that anything is wrong with me. I'm good at hiding my feelings when I want to.

My mother asks, "Where is Jerome? Is he coming later?"

"No, we came straight from the prison. Jerome is at his family's house. I don't feel like being bothered with them today. I'm just in one of my moods."

"Mm hmm, you must think I'm stupid, you know kids talk."

"Yeah, I do, but not now. Can we discuss this later? I can't run to you every time me and Jerome have a fight. If that was the case, I would stay at your house or on the phone all day. I'm not a child anymore. I can handle my own problems."

"If you say so. Just know I'm here if you need to talk."

"Thanks Mom, I appreciate it. Now just drop it."

"Okay Coco, it's done with."

My mother hugs me. We all exchange gifts with each other. I only bought gifts for my mom, Torey, Takori, and Grandma. My mother gave me a gift card to Macy's and Torey gave me a charm bracelet. I'm going to use my gift card to buy an outfit for Montego Bay. I leave my grandma's house and go to visit Jamyya.

Every Christmas, we all go to one another's houses to visit and see their gifts. Skye is already there, and she has Omari with her. By this time, I only have Christian 'cause André came to get Corey while I was at my grandma's house.

"Merry Christmas, everybody." I hand out all the gifts. Jamyya's family was expensive. She has four kids, then I had to get her and Keenan a gift. I couldn't leave Jamesha out either. I was glad her mom was gone.

"Merry Christmas to you, too. Where is Corey?" Jamyya asks.

"He's with André. I was court-ordered to let him get him for at least eight hours."

"Oh, well how was your Christmas?"

"I'll just say it was good. We have to talk later when less people are around."

"Okay, I catch the hint. Little ears are listening."

"Exactly. Hey, Skye, I'm surprised you got Omari with you."

"Oh, Omar had her this morning. He just brought her back about an hour ago."

"So are y'all getting along?"

"Ask me that question another day. I'm going to be happy today if it kills me."

"Okay, then let's just open presents. Where is Mimi?"

"Oh, we are going to her house as soon as Jazz gets here."

"Just call her and tell her to meet us there. I don't want to be out all night with Christian. Jazz is probably caught up with Shawn."

"A'ight, I'll call her."

Jamyya calls, but Mimi didn't answer. I'm kind of worried.

"Maybe she's still with her family," Skye states.

About fifteen minutes later the doorbell rings; it's Damisha. She actually looks cute; the old Mimi is back. Well, almost; she's still a lot bigger. Hopefully she will start to lose some weight.

"Merry Christmas, everybody!" Mimi sounds happy.

"Same to you. Who put that big smile on your face?" I ask.

"I got a Christmas gift from Chris. He's still not talking to me, but he wrote a note that said 'I bought this before we broke up and I still want you to have it. Cheer up and have a Merry Christmas.' Look, do you like them?"

Mimi shows us her pink heart-shaped diamond earrings.

"They are beautiful! Chris has got some good taste. Did you give him your gift?"

"Well, not in person; I had it delivered to his house. He texted me a thank you so I assume he liked it. He's probably busy with his son."

"True. I'm glad to see you happy. Have you been drinking?" Skye asks.

"No, I'm on a natural high. Can't a girl just be happy?" she laughs.

"Yeah, I guess someone needs to be. We can't all be down and out at the same time. Otherwise we wouldn't have anybody to lift our spirits," I say.

"You're right about that. It seems like we take turns going through things," Skye replies.

Jazz finally comes over. Now it's time to get down to business. We have to go over all the arrangements for the trip. I still haven't asked my mom to keep the kids. Now I need her more than ever, 'cause at first I was just going to leave them with Jerome. I wasn't going to tell him I was going to Montego Bay. I would just let him pick up the kids, then I was going to go to the airport. He was going to be pissed, but I didn't care. So eventually he was going to leave me anyway. Oh, shit, I forgot I told Jerome to meet me at Mimi's house! I call and tell him there's a change of plans and to come to Jamyya's house. Christian has fun playing with the twins.

Jerome comes and gets Christian. As soon as I see him, I get mad.

"I'll bring him back Sunday around six o'clock."

"Okay, you can meet me at the same mall André drops Corey off at."

"No. I need to go to the house to get the rest of my stuff."

"We can talk about this later. Don't do this here."

"You're right. I'll call you"

"Mm hmm. Whatever."

Little did he know he didn't have any more stuff. As soon as I got home, I packed up all his stuff and took it to the landfill. It was not open, so I left it right outside the gates. I wanted no remembrance of him.

For the first time in years, I am home all alone. No husband or kids. I don't know what to do. The house is so quiet it scared me. I refuse to sit around and eat all night. I don't need to gain any weight! I'm already a size 8. I want to look good in my two piece Gucci swimsuit. I watch TV and fall asleep.

My cell phone ringing wakes me up. "Hello," I answer in a raspy voice.

"Coco, were you sleep? Girl, get up, it's still early!" Mimi yells.

"What time is it anyway?"

"It's eleven-thirty, get up and get dressed, let's go to the club. I feel like dancing."

"You must be drunk. Who else going?"

"Just me and you. Do everybody else have to go too? You can't just hang out with me? Skye wants to spend time with Omari, and you know Jamyya and Jazz with their men."

"Oh, so we are the only men-less ones out the crew?"

"No. Skye don't have a man either, but she has a child. You don't have your kids right now. Look, just get dressed so we can go. I promise you will have a good time. If not we can leave."

"A'ight, give me thirty minutes. You gotta come pick me up. I'm not driving."

"Fine. I'll leave my house in thirty minutes. Be ready to have fun."

"Yeah, right."

I get out of bed and jump in the shower. I throw on a dress and some pumps, spike my hair, and put on my makeup. Mimi's blowing the horn. I grab my purse and leave the house.

"Girl, you wasn't playing was you? You sure know how to be on time. I had to rush," I say, gasping between breaths.

We go to the VIP. It's packed. The club is hot as hell. I can barely breathe. This is not my idea of fun.

Against my better judgment, I sit at the bar and get a couple of drinks. Once I start to relax, I feel a lot better. Mimi wants to go out onto the dance floor. We dance with several different guys. I can truly say I had a good time after all. Surprisingly, Mimi doesn't give her number to any of the guys who buy us drinks. She is truly growing, I'm so proud of her.

Time flies by so fast. Sunday comes before I know it. Against my wishes, Jerome comes to the house to bring Christian home.

"Why are you here? I thought you were going to meet me at the mall?"

"I changed my mind. I live here, so I don't understand why I can't come to my own house."

"I forgot to tell you. Love don't live here anymore."

Chapter Seventeen

Yolanda

Things are going so well in my life. Me and Omar have been kicking it since Thanksgiving. We've only had sex a few times, but I love his company. We go out to eat, to the movies, and play pool. He is a really cool guy. I go out shopping on Christmas Eve with Charmese and Star.

I buy Omar all kinds of stuff for Christmas. I'm glad I got this new job so I can start saving money. After I quit the Marriott, I found a job working at Bank of America as a Customer Service Supervisor. I make about $35,000 a year. It's not much, but it's better than what I was making.

I have to spend the rest of my Christmas Eve alone, but Omar did promise to visit me on Christmas. He's going to see his daughter, but he said he would stop by after six. I wake up Christmas morning feeling nauseated.

Today is special. I'm supposed to be happy. Instead, I look like the dawn of the dead. My skin is pale and my eyes are glassy. "Please don't tell me I'm getting sick," I say to myself. I wash my face then attempt to fix me some breakfast. Before I can eat, the smell makes me throw up. I get back in my bed and lie down. I feel weak. Maybe I have the flu.

I get myself together and throw on some clothes. I drive straight to St. Mary's emergency room. After waiting for what seems like hours, I am seen.

They take my blood and urine for test. I tell the doctor my symptoms. She comes back smiling. "Congratulations, Ms. Winston, you're pregnant. I'm showing your iron is very low. This is probably the cause of your fatigue. I'm prescribing you iron pills and prenatal vitamins. You should make an appointment when the office opens. Is this your first child?"

"Yes. I'm in shock. I didn't think I was pregnant."

"Yes, you definitely are. Drink plenty of milk and eat healthy. I know it may be hard at first 'cause you have morning sickness. Here is a list of stuff that should help with that. Get some rest. How do you feel about being pregnant?"

"Oh, I'm happy! Very happy! I just had no clue it happened. I've been trying for awhile."

"Well, I'm glad it finally happened for you. What a nice Christmas gift."

"I'll say!"

"Get dressed and I'll get your discharge papers ready. Good luck."

"Thanks, doctor."

I'm elated on the inside, but my body just won't show it. On the way home, I stop by Walgreens to have my prescription filled. While waiting, I pick up some ginger ale, crackers, and parenting magazines. I call Star to tell her the good news. "Hey Star. Merry Christmas. Are you busy?"I ask.

"A little, I can talk for a minute. What's up?"

"I'm pregnant! It finally happened. I thought I had the flu, so I went to the emergency room. The doctor said my iron was low so I got a prescription for iron pills. A baby! Isn't it great?"

"Yeah, I'm happy for you. Have you told Omar yet?"

"No, but he's supposed to be coming over later. I'll tell him then. I really don't know how he's going to react. To tell you the truth, I'm kind of scared."

"Well, just come right out and tell him. Don't act too happy about it though. You don't want him to think you planned it. Look, I gotta go. I'll call you tomorrow so we can *really* talk."

"A'ight. Have fun. I got your gift under my tree. Maybe you can get it tomorrow."

"Okay. Enjoy your evening."

"Trust me, I will. Bye, girl."

I go home, climb into bed, and eat some crackers. My plan is to go to my mom's house for dinner, but it looks as though I won't make it. Every time I eat, I vomit. My head is spinning, I feel awful. I never knew being pregnant would feel like this. I hope it gets better. I manage to gather up enough strength to call my mom.

"Merry Christmas, Mom."

"Merry Christmas, baby. Are you okay? You sound horrible."

"Actually that's the reason I called. I'm sick. I've been throwing up all day. Can you have Derrick bring me a plate?"

Derrick is my younger brother. He's twenty-four and has two kids. Deja is four and D. J. or Derrick Jr., is two. Everyone thought by me being the oldest, I would have kids first. Well, it didn't exactly happen that way.

"Do you have a stomach virus or something?"

"No, just morning sickness. I'm pregnant."

"Wow, what a surprise! How far along are you?"

"I'm not sure, probably two months. I just found out today, I'm going to make a doctor's appointment Monday."

"Okay, sweetie. I hope you feel better. Call me and let me know what's going on. Are you excited about the baby?"

"I'm not mad, if that's what you're asking. Just make sure Derrick stops by to visit me."

"I will. I'll personally fix you a plate and send your presents over by Derrick. I love you, and get some rest. Oh, drink plenty of milk."

"If I can keep anything down. Thanks Mom, I appreciate your concern. Love you too." I hang up.

My mom can be so talkative at times! Today I am not in the mood. I take my vitamins with a glass of water and take a nap. I wake up to someone banging on my door. "I'm coming!" I scream. "Who is it?" I look out the peephole.

"It's Derrick."

I open the door. Of course he has my niece and nephew wit' him. "You look terrible, Yoyo! Mom told me you were pregnant."

"Yeah, I wish I had known it was going to be like this."

"It won't last long, hopefully. Here are your gifts. What you want me to do with your food?"

"Just put it in the fridge. I'll try to eat later. Come give auntie a hug and kiss," I say to Deja and D. J.

"Hi auntie, you got a baby in your stomach?" Deja asks, touching my belly.

"Yes, I do."

"Can I play with her?"

"When she gets big enough to come out."

"Okay, when is she going to come out?"

"I don't know yet. When I find out, I'll let you know."

The phone interrupts her twenty-one questions. "Hello."

"I'm on my way over, is that okay?" Omar asks.

"Yeah, that's fine. I'll see you in a minute."

"Did you go out for dinner?"

"No, I'm not feeling well. My brother came over and brought me a plate though."

"You're still sick? Maybe you got the flu. Do you want me to bring you some medicine?"

"No, medicine won't cure this. I'll talk to you when you get here. I'm not contagious though."

"Okay, whatever that means," he replies.

As I hang up I notice Derrick staring at me strangely. "Who was that?"

"My baby daddy."

"Oh, well are we ever going to meet him?"

"I hope so. Just give me time to work things out with him. I'll let you know. Now I need y'all to leave before he gets here."

"Fine, I don't want to stay where I'm not wanted."

"It's not even like that. Here, these gifts are for you and the kids."

"Thanks, Yoyo, take care of yourself."

"I will. Love y'all. I'll come get the kids when I feel better. Where's their mom?"

"She's at home sick. She has the flu for real. I need to get home to her anyway."

"Tell her I asked about her and I hope she feels better."

"Me too, cause she's a bit worrisome."

"You are so mean!"

"I'm just kidding. See ya later, sis."

"Bye, auntie," Deja says, waving

"Bye, sweetie."

I lock the door and go to the kitchen to get a glass of ginger ale. Maybe this will settle my stomach. I turn the TV to Lifetime and watch a movie. Omar arrives about fifteen minutes later.

"Oh, my goodness! You look really sick," he says.

"Thanks," I reply sarcastically.

"I'm sorry, I didn't mean to hurt your feelings. It's just that I'm used to seeing you pretty. You know, with your hair combed and nice clothes on."

I guess I do look a mess. My hair is all over my head and I have on some old sweatpants and a T-shirt.

"No need to apologize. I do look kind of rough today. I've been vomiting and sleeping most of the day."

"Maybe you got a stomach virus or something."

"No, I'm just pregnant. At first I thought I had the flu, 'cause it's going around, but I went to the emergency room earlier and that's how I found out I was pregnant."

"Wow! I didn't expect this. How far along are you?"

"I'm not sure. I haven't really missed a period. My period has come every month, but it lasts like two days and it's light. Monday I'll call to make an appointment with my gynecologist."

"Don't be mad at what I'm about to ask you. Is it mine?"

"Yes, it's yours! I haven't been with nobody else."

"Umm… well what do you want to do?"

"I want to keep it. This is my first time being pregnant. I didn't even think I could have kids. I'm kind of scared though, 'cause I'm still having periods, but I want it."

"I feel I should be honest with you. I'm still in love with Skye and I was hoping we would get back together. I like you and everything, but I don't know how this is going to work. Skye is going to kill me when she finds out."

"Well, don't tell her. Look Omar, whether you are with me or not, I'm going to keep my baby. I'm not having an abortion just to spare Skye's feelings."

"I'm not suggesting that you kill my baby. I don't believe in abortion either. What I'm trying to say is, I'll take care of my baby no matter what. I just don't know how our relationship is going to be. I really like spending time with you, but my heart is somewhere else. I'm kind of torn between you and Skye. Do you understand what I'm saying?"

"Yeah, I understand. I'll be lying if I say I don't want us to be together, but you have to do what's best for you. I love you no matter what decision you make. I know you're a good man and an even better father."

"Thank you, Yolanda. I'll be here for you if you need anything. So I guess you got morning sickness bad?"

"Yes, but I don't know why it's called morning sickness, 'cause I've had it all day."

"Yeah, Skye had it really bad too. She got better when she was about four months. Oh, I'm sorry. I'm sure you don't want to hear about Skye."

"Actually I don't, but that information was helpful. I'm going to need your help, 'cause this is a first for me."

"I'm here for you. Let me know when you go to the doctor. I would like to go with you."

"I sure will. I guess our baby and Devin's baby can grow up together."

"Yep, they sure can. He will really be surprised, and so will my mom."

"Did you want more kids?"

"Yeah, I love children. I just always thought I would be married and my kids would have the same mother, but I guess things don't always work out like we plan."

"Ain't that the truth. Well, let's lighten things up a little. Open your Christmas gift. It's under the tree right over there."

Omar goes and gets the gift and opens it.

"Thank you. You didn't have to buy me anything."

"I know, but I wanted to."

"You really know my style too. I can wear this to my brother's basketball game. Would you like to go?"

"Sure, I would love to, if I'm feeling better. Thanks for asking."

Omar pulls a small box out of his pocket. My eyes get very big, I am shocked! I didn't think he had bought me a present.

"This is for you. I didn't really know what to get you, so I figured I would buy some jewelry. All women love jewelry. I hope you like it."

He hands me the box. It's from Jared jewelry store. I open it slowly. It's a pair of diamond hoop earrings.

"Omar, these are beautiful, thank you. I absolutely love them."

"I'm glad you like it. Have you eaten anything at all today that has stayed down?"

"Not really. I drank a glass of ginger ale, that's it."

"Are you hungry? Maybe you should try to eat a little now."

"I am hungry, but I'm scared to eat. I hate throwing up."

"I know it's not fun, but you need to put something in your stomach for the baby. How many months or weeks are you?"

"I don't know. The doctor didn't tell me. Actually, I was surprised when she told me, 'cause I haven't missed a period. I hope nothing is wrong. Here's my paperwork from the hospital."

"Did you tell the doctor you were still having a period?"

"Yeah, but she said it happens sometimes. She told me to let my OB/GYN know when I go for my appointment."

"Maybe you should stay off your feet too. Do you want me to fix you something to eat?"

"No, my brother brought me a plate from my mother's house. Do you mind heating it up for me in the microwave?"

"No, I don't mind."

Omar goes into the kitchen and gets the plate. He comes back out. "Maybe you shouldn't eat this right now. I'ma go to the store and buy you some chicken noodle soup with some crackers."

"Oh, I got some in the cabinet already."

"Well, you can eat what you want, but I think it would be a good idea to start off light."

"You're right. Soup is fine. It would come up easier if I can't keep it down."

He goes in the kitchen to fix me a can of Campbell's Chunky Chicken Noodle Soup. My cell phone starts ringing.

I answer it quickly. "Hello," I whisper.

"I'm mad at you! I can't believe you're pregnant and you didn't tell me!" Diamond screams.

"I'm sorry, a lot has been going on. I just found out this morning. I don't feel very good. I got morning sickness bad."

"Mm hmm, you found time to call Star. So what are you doing now?"

"Lying on the couch. Omar is in the kitchen cooking me some soup. Well, heating up a can of soup."

"Oh, you got company? I see why you couldn't call me. Did you tell him yet?"

"Yes, and he's okay with it. He bought me a pair of diamond hoop earrings for Christmas. Now I have to go, but I promise to call you tomorrow with all the details."

"You better call me first."

"Okay, I will. Bye." I hang up just in time, 'cause Omar is coming holding a tray with a cup of ginger ale, a bowl of soup, and crackers on the side.

"It's very hot. So eat it slow," he says.

"Thank you."

He sits beside me on the couch and we watch TV. I eat the soup and crackers. About ten minutes after I'm done I'm throwing up everywhere. I couldn't even make it to the bathroom. Omar is so sweet. He cleans it up for me. I take a hot shower and get into bed.

"I'm sorry you're still sick. Maybe you should stick with just liquids."

"Yeah, I give up for today. I'll try again tomorrow."

"Well, I'ma leave so you can get some sleep. I'll call to check on you tomorrow." He kisses me on my forehead.

"No, don't leave. I've been in the house all day alone. I want some company. Can you stay and just hold me?"

He pauses for a moment. "Yeah, I guess I can do that." He takes off his shoes and clothes and climbs into bed with me. Omar wraps his arms around me and I fall straight to sleep.

I have the most beautiful dream. Me and Omar are getting married in the park underneath a white gazebo. Then we have a beautiful baby girl. Our house is very big. The dream seems so real, everyone is so happy.

***

I wake up with my stomach hurting really bad. It feels like cramps followed by sharp pains. I manage to roll out of bed and get a glass of cold water. No sooner have I gotten to the doorway of the bathroom than I'm spitting up water. I'm coughing and gagging very loud. I throw up so much that only stomach juices are left to come out.

Omar wakes up. "Yolanda, are you okay?"

I shake my head no.

"Maybe I should take you to the hospital. Something's not right. Can you get dressed by yourself?"

I nod yes. He throws on his clothes while I brush my teeth then slip into a sweatsuit. We drive to Henrico Doctor's Hospital. I sit in the emergency room for an hour before I am seen.

My skin is pale and I'm hot. The nurse takes my temperature; it's 101.5 degrees.

"Oh my goodness, you are burning up! What are your symptoms, ma'am?"

I tell her all my symptoms and that I had gone to St. Mary's Hospital yesterday. That's when I found out I was pregnant. She takes some blood and urine from me. Another nurse comes in and hooks me up to an IV. I lie in bed drifting in and out of sleep.

Omar sits in a chair right beside my bed. He brushes my hair with his hand. "Everything is going to be all right."

"Are you sure?"

"I sure hope so. I have faith that it will."

"Thanks for being here with me. It means a lot to me."

"I'm glad I'm here too. I wouldn't want you to be alone at a time like this. I don't want you to doubt that I have feelings for you, it's just that I thought things would turn out differently."

"No need to explain, I understand."

The doctor comes in with the test results. "Ms. Winston, you are pregnant, but you have the flu as well. You're also dehydrated. We are going to give you some Tamiflu and you should be good as new in a couple of days. Get plenty of rest and try to drink plenty of fluids. Good luck with your pregnancy."

"Thank you, doctor."

Omar drives me back home.

"I'ma stay here with you to make sure you're okay. I got to go to work tomorrow, so when you go to sleep, I'ma run home and get my clothes."

"Okay, thank you for being so concerned."

"No problem. Just follow the doctor's orders so you can get better."

The weekend flies by, and so does the word about me being pregnant. Diamond told Charmese, who in return calls to cuss me out for not telling her. Now everybody knows what is going on. I call and schedule my doctor's appointment for January 5th. I take Monday off, 'cause I still feel queasy. Being pregnant is hard work!

Diamond, Charmese, and Star think it will be fun to go out shopping to catch the after-Christmas sales. I have an outfit to take back that my aunt bought me. It's just not my style even if I am pregnant. I show off the earrings Omar bought me for Christmas.

"So tell me, what did Omar say about the baby?" Star pries.

"He said he will take care of it even if we aren't together. He doesn't believe in abortion, but he knows Skye is going to kill him when she finds out."

"Kill him and you!"

"I'm not worried about her. I told him not to tell her. I could care less whether she knows or not."

"Yeah, but it would be to your advantage if she does know, 'cause that would mean she wouldn't never take him back," Charmese replies.

"You've got a point. I'm sure he's going to tell her anyway."

"I'm so happy for you. Now I can have a godchild," Star says, smiling.

"Yep, I wish you could have these symptoms for me. Omar has been so sweet. He comes over, cooks and cleans for me. I hope things work out between us."

"They will. The baby will probably bring you two closer together. Just play your cards right," Diamond advises.

As soon as I walk past the food court, I start getting sick. Just the smell of food makes me vomit. I try to run to the bathroom, but I don't make it.

"Damn Yo, we can't take you nowhere!" Charmese yells.

"I told you I had morning sickness. Shit, you act like I did it on purpose. Trust me, I'm tired of throwing up."

"Yeah, Charmese. She can't help it, you got kids you should know how it is. Chill out. Yolanda, I'll take you home," Star states.

"Thanks, girl. See y'all later. Sorry to ruin your trip, Charmese." I roll my eyes.

"I didn't mean it like that."

"Mm hmm. I'm sure you didn't."

Star leaves them at the mall to shop while she drops me off at home. Damn, I can't even go shopping! This pregnancy thing is starting to get on my nerves.

Omar is spending time with his daughter today, so I don't get to see him, but he calls. Since I'm still in a bad mood 'cause I can't eat or smell food, I call in to work. My manager tells me to bring a doctor's note. No problem, I tell him.

Chapter Eighteen

Omar

Why me? I'm so damn stupid. Skye will never take me back now. I don't know what to do. What will I tell my mother? She is going to have a fit too. My life is destined to be fucked up. I have been staying at the hotel and Tyrone's apartment since Skye put me out. On the nights Tyrone's girl comes over, I stay in one of the rooms at work.

I need to talk to somebody about Yolanda's situation, but who? Nobody will understand but Tyrone. Tyrone is my best friend, but when it comes to advice, he never gives any good ones. If I call Dontaé, he'll tell Damisha and then Skye will know for sure.

Hmm… Oh, I'll call my brother.

"Yo, Damon. What's up, man? Are you busy? I need to talk to you."

"No, I'm just chilling. What's on your mind?"

"Can we keep this just between us for now?"

"Yeah, I can keep a secret. What have you gotten yourself into?"

"You won't believe it when I tell you. I'm still in shock myself. The girl Yolanda I cheated on Skye wit' is pregnant. She wants to keep the baby. I don't know what to do. I want to be there for my baby. I can't just abandon it, but I'm still in love with Skye. I always thought we would get married. My plan was to try to win her back slowly."

"Well, you can cancel that now. You know better than anybody how Skye is. She's going to lose her mind when she finds out. Do you plan on telling her?"

"Eventually, but not no time soon. I'm still trying to wrap my mind around the idea."

"Does Yolanda have any kids?"

"No, this will be her first. She thought she couldn't get pregnant, and she's having complications already. I don't know if she will have a miscarriage or not."

"Hopefully for you she will."

"That's fucked up to say. Even if I'm not in love with her, that doesn't mean I want something bad to happen to my baby. If that happens, Yolanda will probably go crazy. This baby means a lot to her."

"I don't know what to tell you. Just wait till she's about five months pregnant before you tell anybody. If she makes it that long, she might have a chance."

"Yeah, I wanted to have another baby, just not with her."

"I know the feeling."

"Oh, you do. How do you know? Are you hiding babies?"

"Noooo. I don't have any. Latrice was pregnant, but she had an abortion"

"Tell me you didn't suggest that?"

"No, she decided on her own, and I agreed with her decision."

"A'ight. 'Cause I don't want you to be trifling. I raised you better than that."

"You sure did. Anything else I can help you with?"

"No, have you talked to Kenya lately?"

"Yeah, she wants me to be in her wedding. What about you? Are you okay with her getting married now?"

"I'm dealing with it. Omari is going to be the flower girl."

"Is Skye going to let her be in the wedding?"

"Yeah, she's helping Kenya plan it. I don't have a problem seeing Omari. She's been good about letting me spend time with her."

"That's good. Well, call me whenever you need some more advice. Looks like you and Devin will have kids around the same time. More power to you, bro."

"I appreciate your input. Remember, don't tell nobody about the baby. I'll tell them when the time is right. Holla at you later."

"A'ight, bro. It'll all work out somehow."

When I tell Tyrone about it, he has a totally different outlook on the situation. He said, "What you need to do is tell her to have an abortion. Make her understand that she's just a rebound chick and you don't want her or her bastard child."

"I can't say that to her. That's mean and inconsiderate."

"So, fuck her feelings! Obviously she don't care about yours if she knows you don't want it and she has it anyway. The baby is a trap to keep you. Don't fall into it. She knows you're a good guy. That's why you need to hurry up and flip the script on her. Show her your bad side."

"I ain't got a bad side. My mother taught me how to treat women. Shakita will kick my ass if she ever found out I abandoned one of my kids. She's determined to keep the baby. This is her first. I don't think nothing I say will convince her to change her mind."

"Well, you could at least try. Do you want me to do it for you?"

"No, please don't, I'll handle it myself. Thanks for your input. I'm the one who fucked up, now I got to deal with it."

"Yep, you're right. I don't know why you want Skye back anyway. She is a spoiled, stuck-up little brat. She treats you like shit, and you just take it. Skye deserves not to be happy. Payback is a bitch. You worry about other people's feelings too much. And they don't give a shit about yours. You are better off without Skye. Move on, be with somebody who appreciates you."

"Easier said than done. I've invested almost five years into my relationship with Skye. I love her, we have a child together. It's hard just to let all of that go. Love takes time to wear off."

"I'm glad I've never been in love. I'ma keep being a playa. I don't have time to have some woman wrap me around her finger. You need to tighten up. Be a man, learn how to control the ladies, don't let the hoes control you."

"A'ight, Ty, I got it. Thanks for the pep talk. I gotta get going. I'll holla at you."

"Do that. I hope the next time I see you, you'll have your shit together."

"Before I forget, I would like it if you didn't tell Dontaé. I don't want Skye to know yet. I know as soon as he finds out, he'll slip up and tell Damisha."

"Ain't no slip up in it. He'll just straight put you out there. I think he likes Skye. Anyway, he's always stirring up shit. Have you noticed that?"

"Nah, I've never paid it any mind. I don't really think he's that sheisty."

"Never underestimate a nigga. You know I'ma keep it real wit' you. I don't give you advice unless you ask, but that nigga always got something to say about your relationship. All I'm saying is keep your eyes open."

"Well, you've definitely given me something to think about. I'll keep it in mind. You always keep a nigga on his toes."

"Fo' sho. Peace, my nigga."

I leave Tyrone's house feeling more confused than I did before I came. Me and Tyrone have been tight since eighth grade. We go way, way back. I met Dontaé through Skye 'cause he use to hang out with Damisha all the time. Somehow, we became friends, even though his sister despises me. Dontaé gets a lot of women throwing themselves at him, so I don't understand why he would want Skye. Shit, he knew her before I did, so if he wanted her, why didn't he just go for it? I'm thinking so hard my brain starts hurting. None of this shit makes sense. I need a drink. I ride around the way and cop a bag of weed from my man. I don't want to smoke in the hotel room, so I ride to Yolanda's house after I make a stop at the ABC store. I knock on the door.

"Hey, I'm sorry for popping up at your house. Do you mind if I come in?" I ask.

She smiles. "Of course not, baby, come on in. You look troubled; is everything okay?"

"Yeah, I'm just a li'l stressed. I just need to relax. Are you feeling better? I know I haven't seen you in a couple of days. Things have been a li'l hectic at work lately."

"I'm feeling better. I only threw up twice today. It seems like I can eat late at night without getting sick. So now I try to eat around eight or nine at night. My doctor's appointment is Monday at three o'clock. Will you be able to make it?"

"Yeah, I'll take that day off. Do you mind if I go in the bathroom and smoke this blunt? I need a drink too. Do you have some ice?"

"Yeah, I got ice. Is things that bad that you need to smoke and drink? Do you want to talk about it?"

"No, I just want to get drunk and smoke. Maybe we can talk about it later."

"Okay, I guess you can smoke in the bathroom, just light some scented candles while you're in there."

"Okay, thanks."

I sit in the bathroom, smoke my blunt, and drink three glasses of Hennessey and Coke. By the time I come out I'm tore down. My eyes are bloodshot red.

"Omar, are you okay?"

"Mm hmm, I'll be a'ight. Can I sleep here tonight?"

"Sure, let me help you to the room."

She takes my clothes off and helped me into the bed.

"I'ma wash your clothes, 'cause the smell is making me sick. They should be dry by the morning."

"My bad, I forgot certain smells get to you. It won't happen again. Do you want me to take a shower?"

"That would be nice, but I think you might hurt yourself and I can't pick you up."

I start laughing. "I won't fall. I'll just wash my hair real quick and take a shower."

I get up and stagger to the bathroom, wash my hair and body. When I get out I feel a little better. I think the shower sobered me up a little.

"Do you still want to talk?" I ask Yolanda.

"No. I feel bad though 'cause I think it's all my fault that you are becoming a weed-head-alcoholic. You didn't act like this before you and Skye broke up. Now I'm pregnant and things are worse."

"Baby, it's not your fault. I'm just going through something. I'll be okay. You and the baby have nothing to do with it. I made my choices, and now I got to live with them."

"Can you deal with it sober? I don't want an alcoholic baby daddy."

"I'm not an alcoholic. I don't drink all the time. I just needed one today. Let's change the subject. Do you want to spend New Year's Eve with me? That way you can make sure I don't drink. That will be my New Year's resolution."

"I would love to bring in the New Year with you! We can have our own little private party. I can try to cook dinner for you."

"That's all right. I love your cooking, but I can wait until you feel better. I can cook us something. Remember, the doctor told you to stay off your feet."

"You know what I want? I got a taste for some Krispy Kreme doughnuts and orange juice."

"Do you want me to go get you some?"

"No, you can't drink and drive. I can wait until the morning. Do you have to work tomorrow?"

"Yeah, but I get off at six o'clock. I didn't want to bring in the New Year at work. I can go get you a dozen of glazed doughnuts before I go to work."

"That will be great."

"Oh shit, I forgot I'm supposed to keep Omari tomorrow night. Skye wants to go out."

"You can bring her over here. I don't mind. I love kids. She can sleep in here with us. I got a Disney Princess blow up mattress my niece sleeps on when she spends the night."

"Okay. I'll bring her over, but she acts kind of funny about where she sleeps. I might have to leave early if she cries."

"That's fine, I'll understand. I don't want her to be uncomfortable."

"I'm glad you are so understanding. Why can't all women be like you?"

Yolanda smiles. "I don't know. It takes time. I wasn't always so understanding. I had to work on it."

"I'm glad you did. I'ma go to sleep now so I can get up in the morning. Goodnight, baby." I kiss her lightly on the lips.

"Goodnight," she replies. She climbs into bed with me and cuddles up next to me. I have to admit it feels good.

Skye barely ever wanted me to touch her after she had Omari. I still wonder how things got so bad between us. Yolanda is so sweet, loving, and caring. I don't know why I can't just love her the way she loves me. Maybe in time, my feelings for her will get stronger. No one knows what the future holds. Maybe the baby is a way to bring us closer. My mother told me that babies are a blessing. Considering the fact that Yolanda has never been pregnant before, I guess this would be considered as a miracle. From this moment on, I'm going to think positive about this relationship. My mind finally becomes blank and I fall off into a deep sleep.

Yolanda wakes me up so I can get ready for work.

"Good morning, sleepy head," she says, smiling.

"Good morning. You look much better today. How do you feel?"

"I feel good today. I think I'm getting over my morning sickness."

"That's good. Let me go get you some doughnuts. What kind of orange juice do you want?"

"It doesn't matter. You can get me two bottles from Krispy Kreme."

"Anything else you want?"

"No, that's all. Get half glazed and half chocolate iced."

"Gotcha. I'll be right back."

I go to Krispy Kreme to get Yolanda's order. Then I stop at Chick-fil-A to get me some breakfast. I just go ahead and order two number one combos. I drop off the food and rush to work. Today will be an experience. I hope Omari likes her, and if she does, she's going to tell her mom all about it. I will never hear the end of this! What the hell am I doing? I just shake my head at what I am thinking. I'm digging my own grave.

Chapter Nineteen

Yolanda

Omar is bringing his little girl over for the first time. I'm so excited! I hope she likes me. I deep-clean the house from top to bottom, then child-proof all the electrical sockets. I even go out to Wal-Mart and buy some toys for her to play with. I really want to make a good impression.

Diamond wants me to go to the club, with her but I say, "No. Omar and his daughter are coming over tonight. I think this is a big step for him to introduce me to her."

"Yeah, it is. Have you met the rest of his family?"

"No, not yet, but he tells me about them. His sister Kenya is getting married March 28th. Maybe he'll take me to the wedding."

"That would be nice. You'll be showing by then."

"I know. I can't wait to get a li'l round belly. It looks so cute."

"They all don't turn out little and round. Sometimes your whole body gets big. It just depends. I was lucky"

"Hopefully, I will be lucky too. I'm going back to work on Jan 6th. Can you do my hair at your house Monday around ten?"

"Yeah, I'll do it, 'cause last time I saw you, your hair was tore down. Are you feeling better now?"

"Yeah, I'm almost back to normal. It's still certain things I can't eat, but for the most part, everything stays down. I think the worst is over. Hopefully my period will stop too."

"Let your doctor know when you go. She or he can give you some pills to stop your period."

"Really? I didn't know that. My doctor is a woman, Dr. Hoffman at Henrico Doctor's."

"Oh, well just tell her your medical history so she can make sure everything is okay with the baby."

"I will. I'll see you Monday."

"Bye. I hope everything works out. You know kids can be very protective of their parents. If she doesn't like you, don't take it personal. You're not her mom, that's all she knows."

"I'll remember that. Bye."

I buy juice boxes and all kinds of snacks from the grocery store. I want Omari to be comfortable. I believe her reaction to me will determine Omar's relationship with me.

Omar and Omari come over around eight o'clock.

"Hello, how are you, sweetie? Aren't you a pretty little girl?"

Omari smiles. "Hi, lady."

"Her name is Yolanda. This is my friend," Omar states.

"How are you?" I ask him.

"I'm cool, and you?"

"I'm doing better. Have y'all eaten dinner yet?"

"Yeah, her mom fed her before I came. I'm hungry though."

"Well, I got some baked spaghetti in the oven. It should be ready soon. Would you like some?"

"Yeah, that'll be good."

I go to my room and pull out the toys. I bring them into the living room. "Would you like to play with my toys?"

"Yes, I like 'em. Thank you," Omari replies.

"You're welcome."

"You play wit' us, Daddy?"

"Yeah, I'll play too."

We all get on the floor and play with the toys until the food is ready. I fix me and Omar a plate.

"I want some too," Omari says, tugging at my shirt.

"Okay sweetie, I'll fix you some."

I put a little in a bowl for her and sit her at the table. She's too short. "Come on, sweetie, you can sit in my lap," I say. She climbs in my lap and eats her food. She cleans the bowl.

"It's good," she says, wiping her mouth with her hand.

"Come on Omari, get down. Let Yolanda eat her food." Omar takes her off my lap.

"Are you gon' play when you finish, Yolanda?" Omari asks, smiling.

"Yes, sweetie. I'll be there in a minute."

After I eat, we play some more, then we eat ice cream. Omari falls asleep on the couch while we watch a children's movie.

Omar looks at me. "I can't believe how she opened up to you that fast! She doesn't usually like people she don't know. I'm glad y'all get along good."

"Me too. I was so afraid she wouldn't like me. Most kids love me though, but you can never tell what will happen. I love kids. She's very cute. I see a lot of you in her. She seems like a sweet little girl."

"She is. She acts nothing like her mother, and I'm glad."

"I hope our baby is this pretty."

"It will be gorgeous. I just hope Omari is not going to be jealous. She's used to being the only one. She'll be three and a half by the time the baby comes."

"Well, we will just make sure that she feels included. She will be the big sister."

"I love the way you say we. I appreciate you going through situations with me. I admire that about you."

"Thank you. I will always be here for you, no matter what."

"I appreciate that."

Omar has no idea how touched I am by his comments. I'm so relieved that me and Omari bonded. Me and Omar sleep in my room. In the middle of the night, I see Omari standing in the doorway. I purposely left the door open just in case she woke up. I whisper, "Come on in, honey. Do you want to sleep in here?" She nods her little head yes. I pick her up and put her between me and Omar.

"Do you need to use the bathroom?"

"Yes." she replies.

I take her to the bathroom, then we get back into bed. We both go back to sleep. The next morning, Omar takes us to Shoney's for breakfast because it's Omari's favorite place, next to Chuck E. Cheese's. I have fun spending time with her.

"I noticed your eating has picked up," Omar states.

"It sure has, I can eat without getting sick. I feel much better. I'm going back to work Tuesday."

"That's good. I'm happy you're feeling better. Now I don't have to worry about you as much."

"Right. Do you remember your New Year's resolution?"

"Mm hmm, to stop getting drunk and smoking weed when I have a problem."

"No, to stop doing it period."

"Come on, I'm a grown man, I can drink socially. I'll cut out weed altogether, but I'll drink occasionally. Not get drunk, but have one or two light drinks"

"Okay, deal."

"Good, now what is your New Year's resolution?"

"To save money for you-know-what and to move into a two bedroom apartment."

"Can you afford to move?"

"Not really, but the little person needs somewhere to sleep."

"You have a point. We'll talk about it later. You know ears are listening."

"I know. It was fun having her around. Maybe we can take her to Chuck E. Cheese's when I get my niece and nephew next weekend."

"That would be cool. How old are they?"

"Deja is four and D. J. is two years old. They are my brother Derrick's kids."

"I didn't know you had a brother."

"Yeah, he's twenty-four. It's just me and him."

"Oh yeah, Devin's basketball game is Friday, January 9th at seven o'clock. Do you still want to go?"

"Yeah. I'm better now."

"Okay, I'll get him to buy us some tickets."

I go back home and Omar takes Omari to her mom's house. I spend the rest of New Year's Day with my girls. Charmese couldn't find anybody to keep her kids, so we hang out at her house, 'cause Danger was out hustling. The kids stay downstairs in the game room. Everyone is sipping on their apple martinis while I drink fruit punch.

"I'm glad to see you're feeling better, 'cause you was looking tore down. I thought you was going to scare the man off," Charmese says, laughing.

"Ha ha, very funny!"

"No, but seriously, I'm glad you're better. I got a gift for you." Charmese hands me a gift bag. In it is a book called What to Expect When You're Expecting.

"Aw, thank you. This is just what I need."

"So how are things going with Omar? Did his daughter like you?" Diamond asks.

"Yes, she did. She's such a sweet little girl. I was surprised at how well we got along. Omar's taking me to his li'l brother Devin's basketball game next Friday."

"Oh, he's taking you to meet the family in a casual sort of way?" Star says.

"I didn't think of it like that, but yeah. I guess."

"What do you want to have, a girl or boy?"

"It doesn't matter to me. Either one would be great. I just hope it's healthy."

"I know that's right! Everything should be okay."

"Guess what? Omar is thinking about moving in with me. I told him that I wanted to move to a two-bedroom apartment so the baby can have its own room. He knows I can't afford it, so he said he'll consider moving in."

"What I suggest you do is play nice. Don't push the issue of commitment or moving in. You don't want him to think you're trying to trap him. If he feels like you are smothering him, then he'll back off."

"Yeah, and don't be too needy. Do things for yourself. Since you are feeling better now, do something special for him. Make him feel loved and appreciated," Diamond adds.

"Girl, don't listen to them. All you gotta do is throw that pussy on him good, and he will do whatever you want. Shit, if you can suck it just right, he'll be begging you to move in."

"Star should know better than anybody the power of pussy," Charmese snaps.

"What is that supposed to mean, Charmese?"

"I was simply stating that you get paid every night to shake yo' ass for men, and in return, they give you money. You tease them then leave them, or do you fuck them too?"

"No, I don't fuck them. Some girls do, but I don't go that far. I dance and I get naked, that's it. Maybe a li'l touching, but no sucking or fucking on my part."

"What you mean on your part?"

"They can suck and lick me but I'm not doing them. It's strictly one-sided. Some men like to pay to eat pussy, and I like to let them."

"So how much you make a night?" Diamond asks.

"Like five hundred on a slow night and a thousand to fifteen hundred on a busy night."

"Damn! It's like that?"

"Yep, a sista is getting paid. How much do you make?"

"My slow day is about three hundred, on a good day about seven fifty."

"I'm in the wrong business," I say, laughing.

"No. You are doing exactly what you should be. You'll get a raise soon enough. If Omar moves in with you, you will have two incomes in the house. Everything will work out," Star says.

"Everybody keeps saying that, but I'm not so sure. I guess my conscience is getting the best of me."

I'm starting to feel really bad about what I did to get Omar. Now that it's done, I'm not happy like I thought I would be. What if somebody does the same to me and takes Omar away from me? I guess I would deserve it.

***

Monday comes and it's time for my doctor's appointment. When Omar comes to pick me up, I look really pretty. Diamond did my hair in twists and curls. I even got my eyebrows arched. I put on the earrings Omar bought for me.

"Wow! You look really beautiful. Welcome back. It's nice to see the old Yolanda."

"I was never gone, just hiding underneath the sickness. Let's go so we won't be late."

"A'ight. Where are we going?"

"To Henrico Doctor's Office Park."

The office is packed with women, some pregnant and others not. Finally my turn comes. I have to fill out a stack of papers and pee in a cup for the thousandth time. They also take blood, my weight, blood pressure, and temperature. I have lost five pounds. I guess it came from the days when I couldn't keep anything down. I also have to have a pap smear. The doctor lets us hear the baby's heartbeat. After the doctor finishes examining me, she gives me some disturbing news.

"Good afternoon, Ms. Winston. I'm Dr. Hoffman. I noticed during your pap smear that the lining of your uterus is very thin. Have you been bleeding heavily?"

"No. But I have had my period every month but it lasts for two to three days. The bleeding was lighter than normal though."

"Okay, well I'm going to give you a prescription to stop your menstrual cycle. Hopefully your uterus will thicken on its own. Don't lift anything heavy and avoid long periods of standing and walking. What kind of work do you do?"

"I'm a Customer Service Supervisor at Bank of America. I sit down the majority of the time at work."

"That's good. So you're over your morning sickness?"

"Yes, ma'am."

"Good, because you need to gain weight, not lose any. Make sure you take your prenatal vitamins and iron pills. I want to see you back next month. You appear to be nine weeks. Your due date is August 8th. I'm going to schedule an ultrasound for your next visit. Do either of you have any questions?"

"Yes. Can I have sex?"

"Oh yes, but just go easy for right now. I want to make sure everything is okay. Just don't do any strange positions."

"Is the baby going to be okay? What happens if her uterus doesn't thicken?" Omar asks.

"Well, it just means she could have a miscarriage or the baby might be born early. If that happens, I would have to put her on bed rest. Constant motion is not good for her if things don't get better. But I don't foresee that happening. The pregnancy is very early so the uterus still has time to develop."

"Okay. I'll make sure she follows your instructions."

"Thanks, doctor," I say.

I feel really bad. This is all my fault. My baby has complications 'cause I stole somebody else's man. Karma is a bitch. Tears stream down my face as we drive down the street.

"Don't cry baby, everything will be okay. Let's stop by Walgreens so you can get your prescription filled. You heard the baby's heartbeat. The doctor said it sounded strong. Just chill out and take your medicine. Things will get better. You got over the morning sickness, right?"

"Yeah, but that was different. I don't know what I'll do if I lose this baby. I'll just die. I've always wanted to be a mom. Now I have a chance, and things are not going good."

"You have to think positive. Look, I was thinking maybe I should move in with you now so I can keep an eye on you. The doctor said stay off your feet as much as possible. I can cook and clean for you. I don't have a steady place to stay right now anyway. I'll help you pay rent. Do you mind if I move in?"

"I don't know if it's a good idea. I love you, but I don't want you to feel obligated to take care of me. I'll be okay, trust me, I'ma follow exactly what the doctor says. I don't want to put the baby in jeopardy."

"I want to move in because I want to be here for you. I want to support you emotionally. I don't feel obligated at all. Please let me do this for us. We need to get close before the baby comes. This is the only time we will have alone, once the baby gets here it's over. It's all about him or her then."

"I guess you're right. I could use your help. I just want you to be with me 'cause you love me, not because I'm pregnant. I'm not trying to trap you. You can be part of the baby's life without being with me. I don't have a problem with that."

"That's good to know, but I love you. I care about you, it's just that I still love Skye too. I'm working on falling in love with you. You are a wonderful person. I'm just not allowing myself to feel that way about you. You are good for me. I need you in my life. Let's just see what happens. If it works out, good, if not, at least we can say we tried. Deal? Are you willing to try?"

"Deal. We can try, but not hard. I'm sure it will happen naturally if it's meant to be."

Omar is so sweet. He always knows what to say to make me feel better. I don't understand why Skye is so mean to him. I bet she misses him now.

That night, Omar packs his stuff and moves into my apartment. I am smiling so hard in the inside, but at the same time, I'm worried about the baby. We don't have sex again that night, but we cuddle, and Omar gives me a bomb-ass back massage. I go to sleep in his arms. Little does he know, he's slowly spoiling me.

The next day, I go back to work with my doctor's note. Everyone tries to act concerned, but they are really being nosy. I'm not too much of a people person. I already have friends, so no need to fake it on the job. I don't like people in my personal business. By the end of the week, everything is back to normal.

I love having someone to come home to everyday. I take my friends' advice and plan a special night for Omar. I fix all his favorite foods and I give him a back massage with hot massage oil. The night goes extremely well. For the first time in what seems like forever, we make love. He is so gentle with me. My body yearns for more when he is finished. I could really get used to this.

Finally, the time comes for me to meet some of Omar's family. His mom and sister are going to be at Devin's basketball game.

"Now, my mom is very outspoken. Please don't take offense to what she says. Her and Skye are kind of tight, so she may not be too polite. My brother Devin is easy, he pretty much likes anybody. On the other hand, Kenya is a lot like my mom. She's good friends with Skye too. They still talk, she's helping her plan her wedding. She might not like you too much at first, but she'll get over it. I don't think anybody else is coming besides Jamesha. She's Devin girlfriend. She don't really count. Just be yourself."

"That's the only thing I can do. Your little pep talk just made me more nervous."

"I didn't mean to scare you. I just want you to be prepared. We'll get through this. Let's keep the baby a secret for right now. We should start off slow."

"I agree one hundred percent."

I try to look as calm as possible. Omar told me his mom had him young, but I couldn't believe it was his mother. She looks more like an older sister.

"Hey, Mom. I would like you to meet my friend Yolanda. Yolanda, this is my mother Shakita and my sister Kenya."

"Nice to meet both of you," I say, smiling.

"Mm hmm, friend, what kind of friend? Is this your new girlfriend, Omar?" Shakita asks.

"Yes Ma, and please be nice."

"I'm always nice. Hello, how are you?"

"I'm fine."

"So how long have you and my son been creeping?"

"Don't answer that," Omar says.

"Mom, she has nothing to do with me and Skye breaking up. Just chill out."

"Alright, honey. If you say so."

Kenya just looks at me and rolls her eyes. Me and Omar just sit on the bench watching the game.

Omar starts talking to Kenya. "So what's up with you?"

"Nothing, just planning my wedding. Are you still refusing to participate?"

"I'm not refusing. I just don't want to be in it. I will come and support you though."

"Fine, have it your way. Will you be bringing her with you?"

"Yes, I planned on it. Is there a problem?"

"No, I guess not."

"Good. Where is Jamesha? I'm surprised she's not here."

"She is. She's sitting down front with her friends."

"Oh, that's nice. Look, can you do me a favor and at least be civil to Yolanda? You don't even know her not to like her. I never treated any of your boyfriends wrong unless they did something to hurt you."

"You're right. I can't be mad at her for your mistakes. Women come and go but you will always be my brother. If you like her, I like her too."

"Thank you. You know what, I changed my mind. I'ma be in the wedding. Count me in."

"Are you sure?"

"I'm sure. I need to stop being selfish, it's not your fault you're getting married before me. I'm happy for you."

"Thank you, O. I love you."

"I love you too."

After their little conversation, Kenya starts talking to me. Omar's mom doesn't say much. I can tell she doesn't like me.

Devin's team wins the game 40 to 32. We all go out to celebrate. Everyone wants to go to Applebee's. Omar was right about Devin, he is very polite, and his girlfriend is too. They make such a cute couple! Jamesha has the cutest little round stomach. It looks just like a basketball. Boy, can she eat! For her to be so little, she puts away some food. Overall, I think the evening goes well, even though Shakita hates me. Well, you can't win them all.

"Don't worry. My mom will come around eventually. She loves kids. Once she knows you're pregnant, you'll be like part of the family."

"I hope so. I'm not too good with mothers anyway. Most of my ex-boyfriends' moms didn't like me."

"That's surprising. You seem like a people person. I couldn't imagine anyone not liking you, especially seeing the way Omari took to you. She's a picky little girl. If you can win her over, I know you can get my mom too."

"I like your optimism. I'm sure she will eventually come around. If not, I'll just make the best of the situation."

Chapter Twenty
Skye

It's New Year's Eve. Thank you, Jesus, this year is almost over! The changes that have taken place this year are shocking. I would've never thought Omar would cheat on me, not to mention in our house. This is the first time in four years that I'm spending New Year's Eve without Omar. Strangely enough, he hasn't been following me or calling. In a twisted sort of way, I miss him stalking me.

I'm in the process of getting ready to hit the club with my girl Coco. Her relationship is on the rocks right now. Maybe we can comfort each other. Shit, I'm about to find Omar's replacement. I'm due for a little maintenance. The guy I've been creeping with seems to be too busy for my now. Picture that.

I ask Mimi to go out with me and Coco, but she says she had other plans. She's going to church this year. What a thought! To be honest we all should go. But being the heathen that I am, I decide to party. Tonight I'm driving, and yes, I'm actually on time. I pick up Coco at nine o'clock.

"Hey girl, is one of your New Year's resolutions is to be on time?" Coco says, laughing.

"Actually it is, and another one is to move on. It's time for me to find a new man."

"This time, just make sure he's not crazy. I can't deal with another Omar."

"Me neither. We are going to have fun tonight. I'm determined to."

"I didn't put on my hooker heels for nothing!" We slap hands.

We step into the club as if we are the two flyest bitches in the place. As usual, heads are turning and men are commenting. The chicken heads are hatin'. I never danced so hard in my life. You would think Ciara and Beyoncé have an older sister - me! Tonight is my night. I get two phone numbers and give mine to one man. All the others that asked aren't my style.

The one dude that is privileged enough to get my number is fine. His name is Donovan, and he's thirty-one years old. The brotha is 6'2, 210 pounds with a six-pack, golden-brown complexion and hazel eyes. His goatee is nicely trimmed, and he wears a low haircut. In the fashion department, he is dressed to impress. A lot of women in the club are throwing themselves at him, but I have his attention.

Don't think it's because I was the best looking one, even though it's true. No, but seriously, I know how to carry myself with class and sophistication.

Men are throwing money and digits at Coco, but she isn't feeling it. Technically, she's still married anyway. Deep down inside, I can tell she misses Jerome.

"Girl, are you ready to go?" Coco huffs.

"Yeah, it's almost one. We can call it a night." I say goodbye to Donovan and we leave.

On the ride home, Coco is very quiet.

"So what's your New Year's resolution?" I ask.

"I didn't bother to make one. I just hope this year is better for all of us than last year was."

"You and me both! Are you going to be okay?"

"Yeah I'll be fine. I'm getting used to being alone."

Coco gets out of the car and goes inside. I hope everything works out between her and Jerome.

Chapter Twenty-One
Coco

At first, I wasn't in the mood to go out. I wanted to stay at home alone and sulk. Strangely enough, I miss Jerome. I'm sure if he was here, all we would do is argue, but I'll take that right about now. The house is too quiet with him gone. The kids even miss him being here. I roll over in the middle of the night, but no one is there to cuddle with me. My feet are cold 'cause I have nobody to rub them on. Every time Jerome made me mad, I wished he was gone. Now that it has actually happened, I'm miserable. For some reason, I still love him.

Well, to get my mind off of that, I go to the club wit' Skye. She thinks she's the shit, as usual. Her attitude doesn't even bother me anymore. The men flock around her and she disses them one by one. She eventually finds potential in one, and shows off for him. I have a couple of guys approach me, but I'm not feeling them. Not that I think I'm fly, but because I am still married. A part of me hopes Jerome will come back. Then the other part says fuck him.

I have a couple of drinks and dance to a few songs. The fun lasts a hot minute, then I am ready to go. I go home to the same dark, quiet, empty house I left a few hours earlier. I get into bed and cry myself to sleep. This is the worst New Year's Eve ever!

Chapter Twenty-Two

Damisha

Skye calls me to go out with her and Coco to the club, but I decline. My heart is telling me to go to church. I know Chris is going to be there, and that's part of the reason for me to go. Another part is to start my year off right. I need to take my life into a whole new direction.

I get dressed, but I don't want to overdo it. If I see Chris, I don't know how he will react. Only one way to tell.

As I'm getting in the car, my cell phone rings. "Hello?" I answer. The number doesn't look familiar to me.

"Happy New Year's, baby. What's popping wit' you tonight?" Jerell asks.

"Nothing. I'm going to church. What do you want?"

"Oh, I take it you're still mad at me? I just wanted to check on you. I miss you, baby."

"Mm hmm, come up with a new line. I've heard all this shit before. It's about to be a new year and I'm moving on. I suggest you do the same."

Before he can utter another word, I hung up. I have to pat myself on the back for that.

Jerell must really think I'm stupid, or he's under the impression his dick is dipped in gold. Either way, he's dead wrong.

The church is packed. I cannot believe how many people celebrate New Year's Eve at church! I might not even bump into Chris with all these people here.

I sit in the middle of the room. Everyone at the church is so welcoming. I feel like I belong. The music is great and the preacher makes me feel the spirit.

After service is over, I'm checking my cell phone and I bump into somebody. Not looking up, I say, "Excuse me. I'm sorry."

"You need to pay attention to where you're going."

I stop texting. "I said I was sorry." I quickly look up.

Chris is smiling at me. "See, you are in church and you were ready to fight."

"No, I wasn't. I just thought you were mean."

"It's nice to see you. I'm surprised to see you here. How are you doing?"

"I'm fine, and now I'm even better since I've seen you."

"Did you come here to see me?"

"If you want me to be honest, yes."

"I'm flattered. Happy New Year!"

"Happy New Year to you."

"I hope you're not going to drink tonight."

"No, I'm not drinking anymore, that's my New Year's resolution."

"That's good. Well, I'm glad you're better. You look good, even though you've put on some weight."

"Oh, so you noticed? I'll probably lose it in a couple of months. I just need a vacation. I'm going to Montego Bay in about two weeks."

"Really? That sounds fun. Maybe you can call me when you get back. Are you still seeing Jerell?"

"No, I figured out he's not the one for me. I miss you so much. I love you, Chris."

"I love you too, but I need some more time to think things through. If you're not busy, maybe we can go out as just friends before you leave for your vacation."

"That would be great. Just call me. I'll make sure I'm available."

"All right, I'll do that. It was nice seeing you, but it's getting late. You have a good night."

"You too. I look forward to hearing from you."

"I'll be calling you. I miss you too." He kisses me on the forehead and leaves.

Just seeing his face makes me feel better. Out of all of the people in the church, I bump into him. It has to be fate. For the first time in years, I go home and pray. I ask God to bring Chris back into my life. I go to sleep peacefully without any alcohol.

Chapter Twenty-Three

Shawn

"Man, this psycho bitch keeps calling me. I don't know what to do. She's having a fit 'cause I won't spend New Year's Eve with her." I am stressed, and Dwayne is offering no help.

"Look, I don't know what to tell you. I've witnessed firsthand her craziness. You need to get a restraining order or something on her crazy ass. Why don't you take Jazz out of town? Don't tell her where y'all are going. Make it a surprise, that way she can't tell Joy."

"Good idea. I bought an engagement ring for Jazz. I'm going to ask her to marry me."

"You know when Joy finds out all hell is going to break loose."

"Yeah, I know, but I don't care. I'm tired of her blackmailing me. As long as she thinks she has the upper hand, she's going to act stupid. I have to put a stop to this."

"Good luck, 'cause you are going to need it."

"I've been praying that this baby is not mine. I don't care whose it is, as long as it's not mine. I can't deal with her for another eighteen years."

"To be honest, I can't deal with her for eighteen minutes. I hope you figure out something. Just keep her away from here."

"I am 'cause I'm about to move out. When the lease is up, I'm gone. We can get another place, or me and Jazz can move in together."

"Well, we can talk later about it. Let me know how the engagement went when you come back. I gotta go to work. I'll holla at you later."

"A'ight, dog."

Joy is constantly leaving insane messages on my cell phone. She texts me twenty times, and my battery starts dying. I hope she don't bring her crazy pregnant ass over here. Low and behold, not even an hour later, Joy knocks on the door. I open the door completely pissed off. "Joy what in the hell are you doing here? I thought we had come to an understanding."

"We did, but you reneged on the agreement. You can't play a playa. I know your game."

"You don't know shit! You're too damn emotional to even think straight."

"See, that's where you're wrong. I can think very well; actually, I'm one step ahead of you. I want you to break up with Jazz. The New Year is coming and we need to start it together. No more secrets or lies. Let's get things out into the open. I want us to be together. I've already met with a lawyer and I'm going to get a divorce."

"Slow down, I think you're moving too fast. No need to get a divorce. I don't want to marry you. To be real, I don't want to be with you at all. Go home Joy before you get hurt. I'm tired of you harassing me and blackmailing me. If you are going to tell Jazz, then just go ahead and do it."

"Oh, so you're trying to call my bluff. A'ight, I gotcha. I'ma go now before you get hurt. I'm getting really angry and I don't want to have my baby in jail."

"You need some medicine, 'cause you have serious mental problems. Get that shit checked out. I would hate for our child to be crazy."

"Go to hell, Shawn! Jazz will eventually find out that you ain't shit, and when she does you are going to be history."

"And at the same time, she's gonna know her sister is a psychotic hoe. I got shit to do. Get to stepping."

I push her out the apartment and shut the door. As soon as she leaves, I make plans to go to New York. At least I know me and Jazz won't be interrupted there. I hope she can get off work. This is going to be the best trip ever. I can't wait to see the look on her face.

Chapter Twenty-Four

Jasmine

I'm so excited. Me and Shawn are going to New York City to watch the ball drop in Times Square. This is the first time I've ever spent New Year's Eve with a man. I usually go to the club and hang out with my girls. I feel it is important to bring in the New Year with my man. It's Shawn's idea for us to go to New York.

We actually leave Virginia on the 30th. We go shopping and see "A Raisin in the Sun" on Broadway. The hotel we stayed in is very elegant. I notice that Shawn's cell phone keeps ringing, and he cuts it off. We are having such a good time, I don't even bother to ask him about it. We stand in the crowded streets as the balloons and fireworks go off. Shawn kisses me and tells me he loves me as the ball drops.

We go back to the hotel and I get the biggest surprise of my life. Shawn gets down on one knee and pulls out a small black box. He opens it, and a two karat diamond ring is inside.

"Jasmine, I love you. You are my world. I never had anyone in my life that made me feel the way you have. I want you to be my wife. I want to wake up with you beside me every morning. Jazz, will you marry me?"

"Baby, I love you too, but this seems kind of sudden. Can you give me time to think about it?"

"How much time do you need? We don't have to get married right now. Our engagement can last for a couple of months. Baby please, I'm pouring my heart out to you. Do you want to be with someone else?"

"No. I only want you. Okay, I'll marry you but we need to have a long talk before I go to Montego Bay."

He places the ring on my finger.

"Shawn, this is beautiful. Thank you, honey. I love you."

"I love you too, with all my heart. You have made my New Year's wonderful."

I want to call and tell everybody the big news, but I figure they are either busy or asleep so I text message them. Damisha is the only one who texts me back. I guess all the other hoes are asleep. I'm sure I'll hear something from them by morning. We make a toast with some champagne and make love all through the night. I think it's the best sex I ever had.

Chapter Twenty-Five

Jamyya

Keenan is so sweet. I don't know what's gotten into him lately but he has been so nice lately. I guess deep down inside, he feels guilty for calling the police on my mom. I was furious at first, but I eventually forgave him. Keenan's mom is keeping the kids for us tonight.

I don't know what he said to her, but whatever it was, it worked. Keenan takes me to Kabuto's for dinner. He doesn't know how to cook that well, so we eat out. It's nice, just the two of us enjoying each other's company.

"Honey, we should do this more often," I say.

"Yeah, we do need more alone time, but you know what that leads to."

"Yep, more babies."

"Exactly, and I think four is enough."

"More than enough."

When we leave the restaurant, I am surprised by our next stop. "What are we doing here?" My eyebrows are raised.

"We are spending the night here. I thought a change of scenery would be nice. Plus I wanted to get in the Jacuzzi. I told Jamesha that Devin could come over to keep her company. I know she wouldn't want to be at home all alone."

"That's cool. She's already pregnant, what more could happen?"

"Not much."

The hotel suite is beautiful. We sit in the Jacuzzi drinking red wine and eating chocolate-covered fruit. Candles are lit all around the bathroom.

We have sex in the Jacuzzi; it's so fun! I feel like a young woman being wooed by her man. "Keenan, I love you. This has been the best New Year's ever. Thank you."

"You're welcome, and I love you too. Don't ever forget that. I really do appreciate all your hard work. I'm so proud of you for getting and keeping your job."

"Yeah, I actually like working. It makes me feel useful, like I have a purpose."

"You've always had a purpose. You have filled my life with a lot of love and beautiful children."

"Aw, that's sweet."

We kiss each other as the New Year rolls in. When we get out of the Jacuzzi our bodies are wrinkled 'cause we stayed in so long. Keenan plays the Midnight Soul CD and we slow dance in the bedroom.

"Sweetheart, I have a gift for you."

"You do? What? What is it?" I ask excitedly.

"Open it and see for yourself."

"I can't believe you did this. It's so cute! You're going to let me wear this without you?"

"Yep, I trust you."

"You better. I ain't going nowhere. Besides, who would want me with four kids, a sister, and a niece or nephew on the way?"

"You got a point. No, I'm just kidding. I would want you."

Keenan bought me a hot pink Baby Phat one-piece bathing suit with matching flip-flops. For a one piece, it is very revealing. I'm surprised he picked it out.

"Try it on for me. Let me check you out."

"A'ight, big daddy." I put the bathing suit on and strut around like I'm on America's Next Top Model.

"Work it, baby!" Keenan shouts. I pose as if I'm taking pictures. We have so much fun acting silly. It's a big relief from everyday life. It feels good laughing and joking with my husband. This past year has been so crazy! I am totally stressed. My mom living with us put a big strain on my marriage. Not to mention Jamesha's pregnancy. I hope this year is better. I'm glad my vacation is coming soon. Watch out, Montego Bay!

Chapter Twenty-Six

Jasmine

Everyone must have finally checked their cell phones, cause mine's starts ringing off the hook. It's early in the morning on the 1st and I'm still in New York.

"Hey, ma. Congratulations. I'm sorry I didn't hit you back last night, but I was knocked out," Skye says.

"No problem. I figured as much. You know I'm going to need your help planning my wedding."

"I'm on the job. You know I have to be the maid of honor, 'cause I met you first."

"Of course. You know my sister ain't going to be it. I can't believe I'm going to get married before you."

"Who would've thought? I'm really happy for you. Does everybody else know?"

"I texted everybody, but Mimi is the only one who texted me back last night."

"Aw, that's sweet! I wonder how things turned out for her?"

"I don't know. All she said was congratulations and Happy New Year. My line is beeping. It might be her or somebody else. Hold on a minute."

"No, that's all right. Just call me back. Bye, Ms. Bride-to-be."

I click over. "I know you're not getting married!" Coco screams.

"Why you say that? Aren't you happy for me?"

"I just think it's a little too soon. You and Shawn just got back together not too long ago. Do you even know if he stopped cheating? Plus you haven't even been together a year."

"You make a valid point, but we love each other. I thought it was a bit soon too, but Shawn insisted. He said we could have a long engagement."

"Don't let him pressure you into something you're not ready for. You're still young, and marriage is a huge commitment. I just want you to be sure this is what you really want. If Shawn really loves you, he will wait."

"I was thinking the same thing. I'm real confused, 'cause I have a feeling he's hiding something from me."

"Does he know about your trust fund?"

"No, and I'm not going to tell him right now. I don't feel comfortable talking about that with him."

"Girl, that's a sign right there. If you don't trust him enough to tell him about your money, then don't marry him. Just think about what I said. What are you going to do with your money anyway?"

"I'm going to open a retail store. I'm still researching where and what type, but Damisha is going to help me with it."

"Really? I thought you were into the daycare thing."

"I was, but my focus is on my true passion and that's shopping. I love clothes and fashion."

"Don't we all? In that case, we all need to work with you."

"You know what? That just gave me an idea. I could open up a vintage boutique. Mimi can be the Head Buyer and order all the merchandise and I will manage the place."

"Sounds good, but what would you call it?"

"I don't know, but I'll work on it. Maybe when I get back to Richmond we can all get together and come up with a name."

"Count me in. I would love to help you."

"You don't have to leave your shop. Maybe we could have a shop connected to my store. You would still own your shop, but now you could have two locations. Think of it as an expansion. You could work in one shop but manage both."

"I think I get it. I'll just move my clients to the new shop and work there and still keep the old shop."

"Right. Now, we'll have to talk more later 'cause Shawn just came back from getting us some food."

"A'ight, Jazz. I'ma work on a proposal and meet with you later on in the week. Don't forget the rest of the conversation."

"I won't. I appreciate your honesty. Talk to you later."

I get off the phone feeling totally confused. Leave it to Coco to be honest. She tells it just like it is. Now what should I do? I don't know. Well, I'll think about it later, but right now I'm hungry.

"Hey, baby. Who was that?" Shawn asks.

"Oh, that was just Coco. She called to wish me a happy New Year and congratulate me on our engagement."

So, I lied. Shit, he does it all the time. Watch what he says when I ask him about the constant calls he got last night.

"While we are on the subject, who was blowing up your phone last night? I saw you finally turn it off. You didn't even bother to return the call."

"It was nobody. You know how Dwayne is, he and his girlfriend are having problems and he needed to talk. It was our night, so I didn't answer. I didn't want to ruin our moment. He can talk to me when I get home."

What a crock of shit! "If you didn't answer, how do you know that's what he wanted or if it was even him? You know what? Don't even answer that, 'cause all you are going to do is lie. Just forget it."

"Come on, baby, don't be like that. So now you don't trust me? That's real fucked up."

"No, what's fucked up is that you think I'm stupid. I may be young, but I'm not dumb."

"I don't think you're dumb. Let's just drop it. I don't want to fight with you. Let's just eat."

"Yeah, let's do that, then we can leave, 'cause I got some business to handle back home."

"What business?"

"I'm planning on starting my own company sometime this year. Whenever I get everything straight."

"What kind of business?"

"Look, I don't know yet. I'll tell you all about it when I figure it out. So just eat."

I eat my food then packed my clothes. I am so ready to go home. I am getting more irritated by the minute. Maybe I'm PMS'ing. We drive halfway home without words. I go to sleep the majority of the way.

"Hey baby, would you like to stop and get something to eat?" Shawn asks timidly

"Yeah, stop at wherever is closest."

"What's wrong with you? Ever since you talked to Coco you've been acting funny. Why you got so much attitude?"

"I've just been thinking about some things. Shawn, we've only known each other for about seven months. I think we are rushing into this marriage thing. Maybe we should live together first to see how we get along."

"You know what? Living together is a good idea. But I still want you to keep the ring. Let's just stay engaged for about a year. Then if things work out, we can get married or start planning the wedding."

"A'ight. I'll try it. I've already found a house. Jerome is preparing the paperwork. I should be moving in the 1st of February."

"You are buying a house?"

"Sort of. It's a lease town property. After a year of on time payments, I have the option to purchase. The house is beautiful. It's a three-bedroom ranch with a sunroom attached."

"So I assume you want me to move in with you?"

"Yeah. You live in an apartment with Dwayne. You don't honestly think I'm going to move in with y'all?"

"Nah, I didn't think that at all."

We stop at Burger King to eat and use the bathroom. Back on the road we go. I was never so happy to get back home! I miss my friends. I can't wait to share my ideas with them. My birthday is coming up. I'ma be the big two-five.

When I return home, Joy is her usual moody self.

"Where the hell have you been?" she yells with her hands on her hips.

"Hello to you too! You do realize I'm grown. For your information, I went to New York with Shawn for New Year's Eve to see the ball drop in Times Square."

"Mmm, must be nice. Did you have fun?"

"I sure did. Shawn asked me to marry him and I told him yes. I'm engaged."

I hold out my hand to show off my ring. Joy's expression turns really mean. Her mouth twists up and her eyebrows furrow.

"I don't believe this shit! Shawn can't marry you! He's a fucking liar and a cheater. You are one stupid bitch. I hate you! Just get out of my damn house! You can't live here anymore. Get out!!" she yells.

This bitch has really flipped her lid! "Fine, I'll leave, 'cause I'm tired of your shit! You need to take some medicine for your bipolar disorder. I'ma pack my shit now. I'll be back for the rest when you calm down."

"Kiss my ass, Jazz. You think your hot shit 'cause you got a boyfriend and a trust fund, but really you ain't shit. Everything you got, I done already had. Get all your shit out tonight! I'm leaving, and by the time I come back, I want you and your shit gone."

"No problem. I'll be glad to leave. I got my own house now anyway. I hope you don't ever need anything from me, 'cause your ass won't get it! I no longer have a sister."

I push past Joy and go in my room to pack.

"Crazy bitch!" I scream out loud. I pick up the phone and called Skye and Mimi to help me move my stuff.

"We need a truck and a man to move this furniture. Why don't you call Shawn to help?" Skye asks.

"Yeah, I guess I should call him." I dial Shawn's number but he doesn't answer. I call again but no answer. Finally I leave a message.

"He's not picking up the phone."

"Who else can we get? Hmm… what about Mario? Where is he?"

"He's probably at work or else he just don't want to come home. She probably pissed him off. I'll call him."

I call Mario's cell phone and explain the situation to him. He says he will be home soon to help. While we're waiting for Mario to come home, we pack up all the clothes and other small stuff. Mario finally comes home with his friend John. John has a pickup truck that he let us use.

"So what happened between you and Joy?" Mario asks, confused about the whole situation.

"Nothing. I just told her me and Shawn got engaged. I showed her my ring then she went slam off. She's just plain crazy."

"She has been a little moody lately. Maybe once she calms down we can resolve this. Where did she go?"

"I don't know and don't care. She just stormed off and told me to be gone by the time she comes back. I'm sick and tired of her shit. There is nothing to work out. I planned on moving the 1st of February anyway."

"Good luck. I'm sure she'll call to apologize eventually."

"I won't hold my breath."

"So where are we moving your stuff to?"

"I'm going to stay with Skye until my house is ready."

"A'ight. I'm ready whenever you are."

Mario and John move all the rest of my stuff. It takes about three hours to move it. I buy them some pizza and beer for helping. Plus, I give John fifty dollars. Mario doesn't get any money 'cause it was his crazy ass wife that put me out. I call Shawn again to tell him what happened, but he doesn't answer. What the hell could he possibly be doing?

This is one rough day! Jamyya calls to congratulate me on my engagement. I am exhausted, so we don't talk long. Skye makes me feel at home. She cooks me dinner, then I go upstairs to take a bath. After soaking for twenty minutes, I wash and go to bed.

I hope Shawn is okay! It's not like him not to answer his phone and not to even call me back. That's kind of strange. Hopefully he'll call in the morning. Wow, what a way to start the New Year!

Chapter Twenty-Seven

Shawn

Once Jazz got home, she must've told Joy about our engagement, 'cause she started blowing up my cell phone. She comes to my apartment and I don't open the door. The next thing I heard is screaming and glass shattering. I look out the window and this crazy bitch is busting out the windows on my car! She slashes all my tires and dents my hood.

She is yelling, "Come outside, you piece of shit! I know you're home! Oh, you thought you could get away with it, didn't you? Well, not this time! Bring your ass outside!"

I am raging mad! I slip on my Timberlands and go outside.

"Joy, get the fuck away from my car! You are a crazy bitch! You must want me to beat your pregnant ass! I'm warning you."

"How could you, Shawn? How could you do this to me? To our family? You can't marry her! You just can't!" She is crying hysterically.

"Calm down, Joy. Come on, let's go in the house before somebody calls the police. You know I got nosy neighbors. I know you don't want to go to jail." I try to reason with her.

"No I don't, but I'm hurt. I'm really hurt. I cussed Jazz out and told her to get out the house."

"You did what? How could you? You're going to attract attention to us. What's wrong with you? You need to learn to control your temper."

"You need to learn that you are my man. I'm the one having your baby, not her. I demand some attention."

"Fine, you got, it now let's go inside."

I grab her by the arm and we go inside my apartment. I am not in the mood for round two so I do the only thing I know will shut her up. I walk up on her quick and kiss her. Then I pull her body close to mine. At first, she tries to act as if she doesn't want it.

"Get off me, Shawn! I'm mad at you. Don't touch me." She tries to push me away. I swoop her up and lay her on my bed.

"Damn baby, you're getting heavy! You need to slow down on the food." I start undressing her quickly. Without any clothes on, I notice her belly starting to protrude. I kiss her hard round belly. Then I unhook her bra and slide off her panties. I place both of her legs on my shoulders and I begin to swirl my tongue around her clit. Joy begins to moan softly. I slowly work my way up to her soft, supple breasts. After I finish sucking each one, her nipples become erect. I suck and kiss her all over her neck. My hands explore every part of her body. Once her pussy is gushing wet, I slide inside her tight warm walls. Tears began to roll down her face as I thrust in and out.

"What's wrong? Am I hurting you?"

"Not physically but emotionally. You can't expect sex to fix everything. Your dick is good, but not that good."

"I'm sorry, baby. I didn't mean to hurt you. I love you. Now stop crying, everything will be all right."

"Stop playing with my emotions! That's why I'm crazy now. One minute you want to be with me, then the next you don't. Make up your damn mind!"

"Can we talk about this later? Just relax and enjoy the moment."

"All right."

We continue to make love.

My cell phone is vibrating but I can't stop to get it. The sex is too good, plus Joy would have had another episode. I don't want no more drama. When Joy finally falls asleep, I tiptoe into the bathroom to call Jazz back. This time she doesn't answer. I leave her a message.

"Hey baby, sorry it took me so long to get back to you. Somebody stole my car and vandalized it. I just got back from sitting in the police station. Dwayne took me to the police station. I left in such a hurry, I left my phone at home. I'm fine, and I got my car back, but it's damaged pretty bad. Call me when you get up in the morning. I love you. Goodnight."

Yeah, that sounds like a pretty good lie. That covers all the bases. Now I don't have to try to explain why my car is fucked up.

When I come back out of the bathroom, I wake Joy up. "Baby, it's late, you should be getting home. Now what am I supposed to do about my car? My insurance is going to go up."

"Stop your whining! I'll pay for it. Just go get an estimate and I'll cover the charges. How much is your deductible?"

"It's five hundred dollars."

"Well, just call the police once I leave and file a report. I'll write you a check for $500 to pay the deductible. Oh, here is some money for some tires and a rental car."

Joy throws the check and $250 on the bed.

"Thanks for a good time. Next time I see you I want you to have that ring back. And don't think I'm stupid, 'cause I know what it looks like. She made sure she showed it to me. This engagement needs to be called off. Tell her you changed your mind. It's too soon."

"Joy, be for real. You're still married. Let's just take this thing one step at a time. Chill out. You are going to upset the baby if you keep acting crazy. When is your next appointment?"

"I have one Feb 4th and then March 6th is my ultrasound. Are you going to come?"

"Yeah, I'll take that day off. Now goodnight. Drive safely. I love you. I'll call you sometime this week. Remember to stay calm, think about the baby."

"Okay. I love you too. Now you remember. No more games. My feelings are real and I don't want to get hurt."

"I hear ya."

Once she leaves I call the non-emergency number to the police to report vandalism. I act as if I have no clue as to who vandalized my car. At least the insurance will cover it and I don't have to come out of pocket. I'm really broke now 'cause Jazz's ring cost a fortune. I gotta pay $150 a month until it's paid off. But she's worth it. I still have no clue what to do about Joy. She gets crazier by the day. Somebody please help me! I'm in deep shit.

Chapter Twenty-Eight
Jasmine

Considering I'm away from home, I sleep well. I decide I'm going to go to work anymore because I have too much stuff to do. I had already turned in my two week notice, but my last day was supposed to be January 9th. Oh, well, I'm just leaving a week early. I call to let my boss know that I 'm not coming back anymore. I'm going to get paid next Friday, and then the next week is my birthday, so I will just use my trust fund money.

After ending my call, I notice I have a voicemail message. I check the message; it's from Shawn. Oh, he finally decided to call back! Let's hear his excuse. I listen to the message. *Mm hmm... Whatever!* I think. He has more stories than anybody else I know. I don't bother to unpack many boxes because I will be leaving in about two weeks for our vacation then moving out when I get back. I go downstairs and make a cup of coffee. Skye left me a note on the counter.

"Good morning sleepy head. Well, I guess by now you know I'm at work. Make yourself at home. If you need anything don't hesitate to call. I left a spare key on the counter in case you need to go out. See ya later. Love Skye."

Great, I do have a lot of errands to run. I have to see Jerome about the house. I feel funny dealing with him after what happened between him and Coco, but she says it's fine. I also need to stop by the library to do some research on my business idea. I don't bother to call Shawn back 'cause I knew he's at work. I take a shower and am off to start my day. I go to Jerome's office first.

"Good morning, Ms. Taylor. How are you?" Jerome asks.

"I'm fine. Now what's the deal with the house, can I move in early or not?"

"Yes, as of right now the house should be ready by Jan 26th."

"Thank you. So what do you need from me?"

"I just need you to sign these papers."

He gives me a couple of papers to sign.

"Jazz, how is Coco doing? She won't talk to me and she threw all my shit away. What's going on with her?"

"I'm not one to get all up into other people's business, but what you did was foul.   I understand Jermeka is your daughter, but you allow Shameka to overstep her bounds. Coco thinks that you and Shameka are sleeping together. Now don't tell her I told you, but that's why she changed the locks."

Jerome starts laughing. "You have got to be kidding! Why would she think that?"

"Because the night you left, Shameka called her talking shit, and she rode to her house and your truck was there. Later on that night it was still there."

"I can explain that. I was watching Jermeka 'cause Shameka went out with one of her friends. Her car was there but she was gone. She didn't come back until late. As soon as she came back, I left. I've been staying at my friend Justin's house."

"Well, why don't you call her and explain. I know she misses you."

"Nope, I'm always the one that gives in and patches things up. If she can't trust me, then we don't need to be together. Let her get herself together and figure out if she really wants this marriage."

"You know what, Jerome? It's partly your fault. If you would stop giving Shameka so much control in your life, you wouldn't have these problems. Open up your eyes. She wants you bad, and she's causing problems between you and Coco on purpose. You just refuse to believe she is capable of wrong. Are we done here?"

"Yeah, I'll mail you the rest of the paperwork along with your copies of everything."

"Okay, let me give you my new address because I have already moved out. My sister is deranged, and I can't stand it any longer."

I write down Skye's address and leave the office. Jerome has pissed me off being so stubborn.

I go to the library and check out a lot of books on owning your own business and business plans. Skye has a computer with a printer and the Internet at her house, so I can just use hers. I never knew so many people came to the library. All the computers are taken anyway. On my way out, I notice André sitting at one of the computers. I guess he's still shopping for hoes on the Internet. I don't even bother to speak.

I stop by Arby's for lunch and go to the house. It is quiet and peaceful. I eat my food and watch The Young and the Restless. After that goes off I take a nap. When I wake up, I get on the Internet and start planning my business goals. Surprisingly, I get a lot done.

Around four o'clock, Shawn calls me. "Hey baby, did you get my message?" he asks.

"Yeah, I got it this morning, but I knew you were at work so I didn't call you. By the way how did you get to work?"

"Dwayne dropped me off, but now I got a rental car. The insurance appraiser will be over Monday to give me an estimate."

"Well, who stole your car?"

"I don't know. The police found the car abandoned. It was probably some li'l young kids from around here."

"It just seems funny. All the time you have been living there nothing like this has happened before."

"I know. Maybe it's a sign telling me to move out. So what did you need last night?"

"I called to tell you that Joy was tripping about our engagement. She cussed me out, then told me to get out. So, I packed my stuff and came to Skye's house."

"Well do you want to stay with me?"

"No. I wanted you to help me move, but it's done now."

"Well, what else did Joy say?"

"I didn't pay much attention. She's crazy. All she does is rant and rave. I got pissed and she left the house. I was two seconds from whooping her ass. It's over now. I don't want to talk about it anymore."

"Do you want to go out tonight? You could come spend some time with me?"

"Not tonight baby, I got other plans. I'll see you Sunday."

"Wow! Your plans take that long?"

"Yep, I got important things to handle. Once I get it all together I'll share it with you."

"A'ight, baby. Well just call me if you change your mind."

"Are you going to be available if I do?"

"Sure will. I love you."

"I love you too. Bye."

Something is certainly strange about Shawn's behavior. Right now, I don't even have time to worry about it. When Skye comes home, she cooks dinner. I go into the kitchen to talk to her.

"How was your day?" I ask.

"It was good. I had a couple of meetings today. I need a break though. I'm counting down the days until we leave."

"You and me both! I saw Jerome today, and he asked about Coco. We got into it, then I left. The good news is, the house will be ready on Jan 26th."

"That works out perfect. You know I don't mind you staying here. Actually, I like the company. I've been kind of lonely since Omar left."

"I haven't heard you talk about him lately. What's up with him?"

"Girl, I don't even know. He hasn't been calling or following me. The only time I see him is when he gets Omari. He'll speak and that's it. It's strange, but I even miss him following me."

"Do you want him back?"

"I'm confused about that. My heart says yes, but my mind says no. I don't know which one to listen to."

"I couldn't tell you either. I always choose the wrong one."

"Me too."

We talk some more and I tell her my business idea. I call Mimi and Coco so they can hear it too. Everyone comes over but Jamyya. All of us talk and brainstorm. We have so many good creative ideas.

Later on that night, I get a phone call from Chris. We talk for a while. I see why Damisha wants him back. He is so sweet! He offers to take me out to eat dinner Sunday evening, and I accept. I guess Shawn will just have to wait.

***

It's Friday January 16th. I'm more excited today than I was on my birthday. I'm now twenty-five years old and I have $75,000 at my disposal. Yesterday I acted a pure fool. I got my hair braided for my trip. Then I got a pedicure, full set of nails, and my whole body waxed. My eyebrows are already arched. I went on a mega-shopping trip. I spent $3000 on clothes and shoes. Then I bought jewelry and picked out furniture for my new house. Me and the girls go out for breakfast, but the rest of my day is spent with Shawn.

Mario calls to wish me happy birthday, but my loony bird sister doesn't even bother. In a way, I'm glad cause I don't have time for her drama. While packing my clothes, my cell phone rings. The number is blocked out. I answer it 'cause I'm curious to know who it is.

"Hello?" I hear nothing but hard breathing.

"Hello?" I huff.

"Stupid bitch!" someone screams. I open my mouth to retaliate, but the bitch had hung up. Who the fuck was that? I shrug it off. No one is going to spoil my day.

I yell downstairs to Skye, "Are you ready?"

"Yeah, I'm about to call everybody to see what's holding them up. Coco is supposed to drive us there, and Keenan is going to drop Mimi and Jamyya off at the airport."

"Well, I'm almost ready. By the time Coco gets here, I will be."

It's killing me to keep a secret, but I have to. I can't tell anybody about the dinner me and Chris had.

Damisha has never been on a plane before, and she is freaking out. I have to give her some medicine to calm her down. The flight is long, but we have first-class seats. Mimi goes to sleep while the rest of us read books and chat. The resort shuttle bus picks us up from the airport. The scenery is beautiful. The resort is very high class.

I went all out when it came to this trip. I wanted everything to be lovely. Our condo is nice. It has three floors and a Jacuzzi. There are five of us and we only have three rooms. Since it's my birthday, I have my own room. Coco and Jamyya share a room and Skye and Damisha share a room. At the last minute, I manage to get an adjourning condo with two rooms. No one knows about it. I'm going to keep it a secret until the right moment.

We are excited about our first major vacation together. We are anxious to hit the town. Everybody changes clothes for a night out on the town. We go to a reggae club. It is jam-packed. Guys are buying us drinks left and right. Coco is winding her hips and some Jamaican dude is grinding all on her booty.

"Look at Coco out there, acting like she ain't married! That's why Keenan didn't want me to come," Jamyya says, turning her nose up.

"She ain't doing nothing but dancing. We are here to have fun. Stop hatin'," I say.

"I know, don't spoil the mood. Let's let our hair down and be free," Mimi adds.

Jamyya rolls her eyes and sits at the table. The rest of us go to the dance floor and dance. We don't leave the club until it closes. Coco gets the man's phone number. His name is Kingston.

"Whew, y'all! I haven't had fun like that in a long time. I'm actually sweating, I danced so much."

"I saw you out there doing your thing. He was cute too," Skye states.

"Yeah, he was, and I got his number. I might call him before we leave."

When we get back to our rooms, everybody is tired. Coco gets in the shower while the rest of us go to sleep.

I call Shawn to let him know I am back at the condo safe, but he doesn't answer. I have no idea what time it is in Virginia anyway. For the rest of the weekend, we take tours, shop, and go to the beach.

Jamyya can't wait to show us the bathing suit Keenan bought her. It does look really nice on her. Mimi isn't too excited about wearing her bathing suit. She has gained a lot of weight, but she's still pretty.

"Mimi, just put a sarong on. You look fine, you are still beautiful," I tell her.

"Thanks, but I feel so ugly. I got to lose some of this weight. It's just not me."

"It's not you. I'm sure this vacation will give you a new prospective on life. You will lose all that weight when you get home."

"Yeah, I will. I gotta get right for Spring Bling. I forgot to tell you that I sold Princess."

"You did what? Why?"

"Because Jerell gave her to me, and every time I look at her I think of him. I'm starting the New Year differently - without him or his dog! I can always get another one. It's time for me to move on."

"Now that's what I like to hear!"

Skye calls to check on Omari while me and Mimi chat. Jamyya lounges on a beach chair while Coco splashes in the water. Eventually, we all get in the water and splash. Some guys are looking at us. One comes over and introduces himself to Mimi. "Hello, how are you today?"

"I'm fine."

"That you are! I think I already know the answer to this question, but I'ma ask anyway. Are you taken?"

"I'm sorry, but yes, I do have a man."

"Well, tell him I said he is one lucky man."

"Thank you. I will." That puts the biggest smile on her face. I'm glad that happened for her. I can't wait to see her face this evening!

Some ladies come over and offer to braid our hair. Jamyya decides to get hers done. It looks really nice too. I'm mad as hell that I paid $250 for the Africans to braid mine, and hers only cost $50 for the same style.

For lunch, we go out to eat at a little restaurant on the strip. The food there is good. Skye orders curry chicken. About ten minutes after we leave the restaurant, she starts throwing up. We go straight back to the condo. Skye runs to the bathroom. She has diarrhea and is still vomiting. I knock on the door. "Skye, are you okay?"

"No, I feel like shit."

"Do you want to go to the hospital?"

"No, it's probably just the food. I'll be okay once it all comes out."

"Okay, let me know if you need anything."

I go outside on the patio to get some fresh air. The view of the beach is beautiful. I hope Skye feels better soon, 'cause my plans for tonight require all of us to go out. Hmm... What can I do?

"Hey, what's got you so deep in thought?" Coco asks.

"Ah, nothing, just wishing Shawn was here with me."

"Aw, ain't that sweet! So what's up for tonight?"

"It depends on how Skye is feeling. I wanted us to go to the party the resort is having on the beach."

"Sounds fun. Maybe I can get my groove back like Stella," Coco laughs.

"Girl please, you ain't nowhere near Stella's age."

"Well, you know what I mean."

Skye lies in bed while we hang out on the strip. I kind of feel bad leaving her alone. But we have fun walking around viewing the sights. When we get back, she isn't feeling any better, so we take her to the hospital. I have to make Damisha stay at the room just in case somebody calls, 'cause our cell phones are out of range. Nobody understands why whoever called couldn't leave a message.

We wait in the hospital for three hours. Finally, Skye is discharged.

"What's wrong? Was it food poisoning?" we all ask.

Skye's face looks sad and tears fall from her eyes.

"I'm pregnant. That's what's wrong. I guess the baby doesn't like curry chicken."

"You're what?" Jamyya shouts.

"I'm pregnant. Damn, I know you heard me the first time. Look, I'm in no mood for questions. I'm pissed off right now, so let's just drop it. I'm tired, so let's just go. Y'all can go out without me tonight. I'm just not in a partying mood."

"It'll be okay. You're just in shock."

Skye shoots Jamyya a look of death.

Damn, I thought our trip was going to be joyous!

Chapter Twenty-Nine

Damisha

Everybody is gone and I'm sitting here alone. Jazz has some nerve making me stay. Why did she pick me? I know … she thinks I'm too fat to go out with them. Fuck 'em all! Even if I have gained a few pounds, I still look good. Well, besides the gut.

After sitting around being bored for thirty minutes, there's a knock on the door.

"Who is it?" I yell, opening the door simultaneously. My mouth dropped wide open. I cannot believe what I am seeing! I am completely speechless.

"Can I come in, or do you want me to stand out here all night?" Chris's deep voice asks.

"I'm sorry… I guess I'm just in shock. Come on in."

"Thank you. You look beautiful. These are for you."

He hands me a bouquet of flowers.

"These are beautiful, thank you. How did you get here?"

"I flew on a plane."

"Yeah smart ass, I know that, but how did you know where I was staying?"

"I called Jasmine about a week ago and we talked. She arranged for me to meet you here."

"Oh, so that's why I couldn't go to the hospital. So, Skye is not really sick then."

"Unfortunately, she is. That wasn't part of the plan. I hope she feels better. Enough about her, I came to see you. Come give me a hug. Act like you miss me."

"Trust me, I do miss you, more than you know."

I hug Chris so tight, I don't wanna let go.

"So you missed me, huh?" I ask, smiling.

"Yes, I did. For some reason, I couldn't shake you. I thought about you every day. I couldn't stop loving you no matter how hard I tried."

"That's sweet. I realized how much I need you in my life. You see how fat I've gotten. I've been really depressed. When you left, all my joy was gone. So you coming here, what does this mean for us?"

"I want us to be together, just you and me. If you are willing to let go of Jerell, I'm willing to take another chance with you. I love you and I believe we can make this relationship work. I'm looking for a future wife, not a playmate."

"Well, me and Jerell are through. I even sold Princess, 'cause I wanted no reminders of him. It's definitely over between us. All I want is you."

"You sold the dog? Wow, that had to be hard. I know how much you loved her."

"Yeah, it was, but I can always buy another one."

"You sure can, but another one of me is hard to find."

"You're right about that."

"Enough talking. Let me show you how much I miss you. Come with me to my room." Chris leads me to the condo next door. We barely make it inside. He pulls me close and tongue-kisses me passionately. My panties instantly become wet. It has been almost a month since I had sex.

Now I know what you are thinking, a month is not long. Well, for me it is. I'm used to every-day love making sessions. I pull Chris's shirt off, mmm … mmm … mmm… even better than I remember!

This man's body is sexy, not to mention the big-ass dick he has. Oh yes, he knows just how to work it! I unbuckle his belt and unzip his shorts. Next thing you know, his boxers are around his ankles. I waste no time putting his dick into my mouth. My goal is to please my man, 'cause I have no intention on letting him leave again.

Chris undresses me then sits me on top of the breakfast bar.

"Damn baby, you are getting a li'l thick, but I like it."

"Don't worry, I'ma going to lose it all when I get home."

"I'm just joking. I love you big or small. It really doesn't matter to me."

"Mm hmm … I bet."

"Shh." He places his pointer finger over my lips. We continue kissing and his fingers begin to explore my treasure chest. He moves down to suck on my perky breasts. My heart starts beating fast. My pussy starts pulsating as his tongue goes in and out of my opening.

Damn, I missed him! The anticipation of feeling his hard long dick inside me is too much to bear. "Baby, please… put it in. I'm ready," I whisper in his ear. He complies without hesitation. As our bodies become one, I feel something that I have never felt before. I am in pure ecstasy.

The orgasms keep coming back to back. My body quivers with every stroke. The passion that ignites between us causes a tear to drop from my eye. This man has me whipped! I am so exhausted afterward, all I can do is go to sleep.

I remember Chris kissing me on my forehead and saying, "I love you" before my eyes closed.

When I wake up, it's eight o'clock at night. I call over to the room to find out what happened at the hospital.

"Skye, do you feel better? What did the doctor say is wrong with you?" I inquire.

"I'm pregnant and depressed. I can't believe this shit. I take my birth control pills every single day. I've never missed a pill, not even now and I ain't even having sex. This shit sucks."

"Well, you always have options. How far along are you?"

"I don't know. I have to make an appointment with my gynecologist. I'm not trying to have another baby right now. This is not a good time."

"I'm sorry, boo. I don't know what else to say. Are you there by yourself?"

"Yeah, everybody went to the beach party. Why don't you and Chris go? Jazz told us about her plan to bring him up here. I'm glad y'all are back together. Jamyya is really pissed about him being here, but she'll get over it. She's been acting crazy since we got here anyway."

"She sure has, but why? Do you want some company?"

"Nah, I actually want to be alone. I need time to think. As far as Jamyya goes, I don't know what's up with her attitude. Maybe she's PMS'ing, or her and Keenan got into it before we left. Who knows?"

"Well, since you're okay, I guess me and Chris will go to the party too. I'll talk to you later."

"Have fun for me too. Tell Chris I said hi."

"I will." I hang up feeling a little depressed, but one looks at Chris and my smile instantly returns.

"Is everything okay wit' Skye?"

"Yeah, she's okay now, just a little tired. Do you want to go to the beach party? Everybody else already went."

"Sure, seems like fun."

We jump in the shower and get dressed. I have to admit, my man is looking fine and so am I! Even though I went up two dress sizes, I am still fly. We wander around the party for about fifteen minutes when we bump into Coco and her new-found friend Kingston.

"Hey, Coco. What's going on? Where is everybody else?" I ask.

"Nothing. I'm just having a good time. You remember Kingston right?"

"Yeah. Hi, how are you?"

"Fine. You look lovely," he says, shaking my hand.

"Excuse my manners. This is Chris, Damisha's boyfriend," Coco says.

"Nice to meet you," Chris says, shaking Kingston's hand.

Coco pulls me to the side and whispers in my ear, "Jamyya got a real attitude problem. She's mad at you 'cause Chris is here. Then she's mad at me for having fun with Kingston. Jazz told her she was being selfish, and they got into a big argument, so Jamyya stormed off and Jazz went back to the room to check on Skye."

"Damn," is all I can say.

Me and Chris hang out with Coco and Kingston. I can tell he is a pretty cool guy. I am glad me and Chris have our own condo, 'cause it's going to be too much drama with Jamyya having an attitude. We have two rooms in our condo. Chris said that Coco can stay with us, that way everyone can have their own room. Actually, it works out perfect, 'cause Coco is barely here.

Skye spends most of her time sulking in her room while Jazz and Jamyya try to hang out. I spend the majority of my time with Chris. I never knew we could have so much fun together! This is the best vacation ever! Well, for me; I guess I can only speak for myself.

Chapter Thirty

Skye

Ain't this some shit! This was supposed to be a nice getaway; instead I get the worst news of my life. This has got to be a bad dream! Would somebody please wake me up? I should be the one with the attitude, but instead, it's Jamyya.

She's walking around here acting like everybody's mother. She's mad at me 'cause I don't want to discuss my problems with her. What's the point? She can't fix it. Before we leave, we all decide to leave our problems at home. And that's exactly what I'ma start doing. I ain't going to lie, I sit in my room for two days straight, but on the third day I wake up. Fuck this shit! I'm not going to let an unwanted pregnancy ruin my dream vacation.

"Hey, Jazz. What you got going on today?"

"I haven't decided yet. I'm sick of hanging out with Jamyya. All she does is bitch and complain about Mimi and Coco. The madness has got to stop. Mimi and Coco agreed they would leave their men at home Friday and we will spend our last night here together."

"That's good. But what are we going to do today?"

"Whatever you want to do is fine with me."

"Are you sure?"

"Absolutely positive."

"Good. First I'm going to get Jamyya straightened out. Then us three are going to go to the club and have some fun."

"Good luck with Jamyya. That girl is a piece of work."

"Yeah, I probably need it. Where is she anyway?"

"Sitting on the balcony."

I go outside to talk to her.

"Jay, what's up with the attitude?"

"You should know. Nothing is turning out how it's supposed to. I left my husband at home, but Mimi and Coco are spending all their time with men. If I would've known that, I could've brought Keenan. Then you don't want to talk about your condition. I thought we were best friends. We talk about everything."

"Look, it's a time and place for everything. Now is not the time to discuss this. Remember what we said before we left Virginia. We said we would leave the drama at home. Now, that's exactly what I'm trying to do. You should be happy for Damisha. You know how hard she took it when

Chris left her. She's happy, now don't spoil it. And as for Coco, you're not her mother. She is a grown-ass woman, her marriage is between her and Jerome. Obviously, he's not taking their vows seriously. Take time off from trying to fix everything; you just can't do it. Relax and enjoy yourself. Now, we are going out tonight, and I demand you have fun! Jazz has arranged for all of us to go out tomorrow night. Just us girls. No men allowed. Now go put your freak'em dress on, 'cause we are going to the club."

I give her a big hug.

"Thanks, Skye. You always know what to say. I do need to let loose and have fun. I just feel so guilty for leaving Keenan alone with the kids. The whole time we've been married, the only place we've been is Virginia Beach. We should be taking a vacation together. He works hard. He deserves a vacation too."

"I understand, but so do you. You have always taken care of somebody else. Now it's time to take care of you. Maybe this summer you and Keenan can take a vacation. You should have a top paying job by then. You know Jazz wants us to work at her company."

"I know. I'm really excited about it. I can't believe, I'm going to be a part of something big. Hopefully, it won't take long for her to get off the ground."

"She will do fine with all our help. Now you know how long it takes me to get ready so I better start now."

She laughed. "You're right. I'ma apologize to everybody."

"Good idea."

I go into the closet to find a cute outfit. It's strange. I haven't even gained any weight. Mimi must've done it for me. Needless to say, we go to the club and have a great time. Jazz gets drunk and dances on the tabletops. Jamyya finally lets loose and dances on the stage and I have a couple of drinks too. Yes, I know I'm pregnant, but right now I don't care. I need to have fun.

Chapter Thirty-One

Jamyya

At first, I'm pissed off, 'cause things aren't going as planned. Jazz takes it upon herself to invite Chris as a surprise for Damisha. Then Coco meets some Jamaican dude named Kingston. She's running around like a single woman with no ring on her finger. Skye found out she's pregnant, and she don't want to talk about it. Things are a mess. I'm pissed off at everybody. I call home, thinking that will calm my nerves, but all it does is make me more upset.

Keenan's fussing 'cause the kids are running wild. Jamesha's been working all week, so she's tired. Things are just plain chaotic.

Skye finally manages to get herself together and we have a long talk. She has no problem putting me in my place, and I thank her for that. After our talk, I decide to let loose, and we have so much fun. I never danced so dirty in my life. I am bumping and grinding with just about everybody on the dance floor. I have plenty of drinks too. I can honestly say our trip turned out better than I expected. I'm glad I came. This was a well-deserved gift.

Chapter Thirty-Two

Coco

Whew whee! If somebody would've told me that I would've met a fine Jamaican man, I think I would've said that they were lying. Kingston is absolutely gorgeous. He has a pretty chocolate complexion with skinny, shoulder-length dreads. His teeth are pearly white. I met him at the club the first night here. We have been kicking it ever since. He shows me all around town, and we have so much fun. I even smoke weed for the first time. I don't know what comes over me, but I feel like letting loose. The whole time I've been married, I have never slept with anyone but Jerome until now. After I have sex with Kingston, I just can't believe it's me doing these things. My sex life with Jerome is great, but I've never been the freaky one. Kingston has me swinging off the chandeliers. I wish I can say we only did it once and the alcohol made me do it, but that would be a lie. We have sex on the balcony, in the shower, on the beach, and of course the bed.

Yeah, yeah, I know, of course we used a condom. I'm not that damn crazy! Staying in the condo with Damisha and Chris is fun 'cause they are happy. The depressed angry bunch was right next door.

Chris and Damisha have sex just as much as we do. I have fun hanging out late and enjoying myself. Kingston is so cool and laid back. I'm going to miss him when I leave.

Jazz calls and wants all the girls to get together for one last night here. I agree, but Jamyya better not start no shit! Since Chris and Kingston seem to be getting along, they hang out together while me and Mimi go out with the girls. I am dressed to impress. This better be worth my time!

Chapter Thirty-Three

Jasmine

The vacation started out rocky, but is ending on a good note. I'm so happy Chris and Damisha got back together! Sometimes I feel a little lonely 'cause I', missing Shawn like crazy. Anyway, I am happy that my friends are having fun.

Coco found a man to have a fling with while Skye found out she is pregnant. I try to plan for a fun night since we are leaving the next day. I think it will be nice if we go to dinner and a reggae concert in the park. All of us meet at the room.

"Okay girls, this is our last night together. Let's have fun. No fussing or attitudes. We are going to leave here with a bang."

"I agree. I apologize for not spending more time with my girls. I was just so excited about Chris being here that I lost my cool. Please forgive me," Damisha says to all of us.

"We forgive you," Jamyya answers for the group.

"Let's go get this party started!" Skye shouts.

"Just remember not to eat the curry chicken this time," Coco replies.

"Oh, you got jokes? That shit ain't even funny."

"You can take a joke. Don't get mad."

"I ain't mad. Well yes, I am, but not at you. I'm mad about the situation, but we'll talk about this another time. Tonight we are going to have fun."

"We sure are."

At the restaurant we eat and talk. Everybody shares their story about what they did this past week. I notice Skye was drinking alcohol but I didn't say anything cause I didn't want to upset her. Everything is flowing so smoothly.

We go straight to the park from the restaurant. The weather is nice and the sky is beautiful. The concert is a stand-up affair. Three different reggae bands perform that night. Everybody dances, laughs, and has a good time. This trip is so relaxing for me. It gives me time to think about my relationship with Shawn. I realize I don't want to be alone. I love Shawn and I'm going to marry him. I enjoyed myself in Montego Bay, but I can't wait till I go home so I can see my baby. I hope he's being a good boy.

Sometimes I wonder if Shawn is still cheating on me. Maybe I should start doing some investigating before we get married. Some of the things that have been going on lately seem mighty strange. Why would somebody steal his car just to vandalize it? Nothing was missing. Shawn has a CD player with the MP3 attached, two CD books, and he leaves his bankcard in the glove compartment. Out of all that stuff, the car thief took nothing.

Usually women are the ones who slash tires. Maybe he broke it off with the girl and she got mad and fucked his car up. That sure does sound like something me and my friends have done plenty of times. It happened to Damisha's brother not too long ago. I'm asking some questions when I get home.

Chapter Thirty-Four

Skye

I make a doctor's appointment while I am in Montego Bay. My appointment is for Thursday, but I can't wait that long. I refuse to believe I'm pregnant. I was only sick that one day. They probably thought I was going to sue, so they tried to cover up my food poisoning.

As soon as I get home, I jump in my car and head for Walgreens. I immediately start having flashback of when I first found out I was pregnant with Omari. Maybe Walgreens isn't such a good idea. Instead, I go to CVS, like that will really make a difference. I get two different pregnancy tests and rush home to pee on the sticks. I sit on the toilet, impatiently waiting for the results. All the tests read the same. It would have been obvious to a sane person that I am pregnant. I, for one, refuse to believe it.

When Monday comes, I go to the walk-in clinic at Planned Parenthood. I demand a blood test, 'cause in my mind, the urine ones is faulty. After days of denial, I finally try to accept it.

I go to my regular doctor. Her name is Dr. Seagram.

"Ms. Jordan, how are you doing today?"

"To be honest, I'm bugging out. I've been taking my birth control pills everyday at the same time for two years. I just don't understand how I could be pregnant."

"Are you using any other form of birth control?"

"No, I wasn't at the time."

"Birth control pills are only 99% effective. You should also use condoms as a backup. Enough of the lecture. Let's do some blood work and find out what's going on."

I go through the whole rigorous process of a full examination. The doctor once again confirms I am pregnant. She said I'm eleven weeks pregnant and I'm due August 21st.

Somehow, I wish it all was just a bad dream. I don't feel like going to work, so I go home. The question still plagues my mind, "How could this happen?" My next question is, when did this happen? I haven't had sex in awhile, but to be honest, Omar wasn't the only one. Damn, damn, damn! I am starting to freak out again. I have to do something to calm my nerves.

I call Jazz since she is the only one I know isn't at work. "Jazz, I'm buggin' out. I really need your help. Can you meet me at the mall in thirty minutes?"

"Yeah, which one?"

"Um... Virginia Center Commons is cool."

"A'ight, I'm leaving now. You aren't going to do anything stupid, are you?"

"Not yet. That's why I need to see you."

"Just hold tight. I'm on the way. Let's meet in the food court."

"Okay. Bye." I hang up.

The only thing that will calm me down is shopping. I need a good distraction. I really shouldn't be shopping, 'cause I already spent too much money in Montego Bay. Oh well, I get paid tomorrow anyway. What's the use of having money if you can't spend it?

I hop in my Lexus and drive recklessly to the mall. Jazz is sitting at a table waiting for me.

"So what's up?" she asks.

"I went to the doctor earlier, and I'm definitely pregnant."

"I never doubted it. You are just in denial."

"Not anymore. I want to have an abortion. I can't have a baby right now. I'm just getting started with my career. Plus, Omari is only two years old."

"So, you are just making excuses. Omari will be three by the time the baby comes. You know Omar will help you. Have you told him yet?"

"No, and I don't plan to. Come on, let's talk and shop."

"Skye, honey, you are deeply disturbed. Shopping should be the last thing on your mind. Don't you think Omar has the right to know?"

"I believe he lost all his rights when he cheated on me. If I have an abortion, he really don't need to know. The situation will already be taken care of."

"You know how I feel about abortions. It's your choice, but I prefer you not do it. You are just in shock and upset. Wait a couple of days and see if your mind changes."

"Yeah, I am upset. Can you blame me? Shit is just so messed up nowadays."

"You ain't never lied!"

We walk around the mall, and I purchase a couple of items that I really don't need.

"Are you cool now?" Jazz asks.

"Yeah, I feel better. Thanks for listening."

Actually, I feel about the same. I go home broke and depressed.

Omar is supposed to get Omari this weekend, but I don't think now is the right time to tell him.

My phone rings, and it's Donovan. "Hello, lovely. How are you?" Donovan asks.

"I'm fine. I just got back from my vacation. Sorry I haven't returned your calls."

"No problem, I understand. Maybe we can go out to dinner and a movie this weekend."

"Sure, that sounds nice. My daughter is visiting her father this weekend so I have a sitter. What day is good for you?"

"Saturday around six o'clock is good for me. Shall I pick you up?"

"Yeah. I'll be ready. I promise." I give Donovan directions to my house and we chat for another fifteen minutes. He has never been married and has no kids. He works as a contractor for Verizon Telephone Company. Donovan seems to have it all together. Hopefully he's not a nut like Omar.

***

Saturday comes and Donovan picks me up. We go out to eat, then the movies as we planned. He is easy to talk to and he has a wonderful sense of humor. We have a great time. I make plans to see him again. By Monday, things are back to normal. I am back at work and Omar starts stalking me again. I catch him following me to Applebee's on my lunch break. It would have been a miracle if he would have really stopped stalking me.

On Tuesday, I get a strange call from Dr. Seagram. She asks me to stop by her office and bring my birth control pills. My test results are back. The test shows a high level of estrogen in my system. Dr. Seagram said this is not normal, so she wants to test my pills. On my lunch break, I drop the pills off at her office. She said it will take two to three days for the tests results to come back. I am scared something will be wrong with the baby. I pull out my cell phone to call my friend for comfort.

"Hello," the deep voice answers

"Hey, I got something real important to tell you. Do you have time to talk?"

"I always have time for you. You, on the other hand, are always too busy for me. So tell me what's going on."

"I'm pregnant, and I want to have an abortion."

"Why, 'cause it's my baby, or cause it's Omar's?"

"I don't know whose baby it is. But I do know I don't want it if it's Omar's baby. He'll want us to get back together. If it's yours, everyone will know our secret. I just can't do it. The baby has to go."

"If your mind is already made up, why did you tell me?"

"'Cause I thought you should know. I had to tell somebody."

"I'm sure your girls already know. I think the real reason you told me is so I can talk you out of it."

"No, Jazz already tried that days ago."

"Do Mimi know you are pregnant?"

"Yes, I found out in Montego Bay when I got real sick. All the girls know."

"I don't believe you will go through with it. It's your choice. Do what you feel. Would you like me to come over?"

"No, not tonight. I already feel guilty enough."

"You're already pregnant. What else could happen? I just want to comfort you."

"We could get caught. Have you ever thought of that?"

"We are two mature adults. I'm not worried about what other people might think. That's your problem. You are too concerned with appearances. You need to relax. Just live a little."

"You are starting to piss me off. I'll just call you back another time."

"Yeah, do that."

He hangs up. Damn, he's an arrogant bastard! I don't have time to deal with him.

Thursday, I go to the abortion clinic. I don't tell anyone I am going. I sit in my car outside the building for ten minutes. When I get out of my car to go inside, there are people holding picket signs marching in front of the door chanting "Give life. Don't kill. Babies are a blessing."

I burst into tears and run back to my car. He's right. I can't do it. I'm too weak. What am I going to do now? Everybody will automatically thinks it's Omar's baby anyway. I'm sure I can pull it off.

The week is coming to an end when Dr. Seagram calls me to have a meeting at her office. She wants to give me an ultrasound and talk to me about the test results. It must be bad if she won't tell me on the phone.

I go straight to her office. "What's wrong, Dr. Seagram?" I ask, panicking.

"The pills you gave me aren't birth control pills; they are fertility pills. Do you know who might have switched your pills?"

"Yes, I have a pretty good idea."

"Well, the reason I called you in is I want to take a look at the baby. Make sure everything is okay. You know taking fertility drugs often times causes multiple births. Lay back on the table so we can take a look."

My mind is somewhere else. I'm getting hotter and hotter by the minute. I can't believe that son of a bitch changed my pills! I'm so deep in thought I could swear I mishear the doctor when she says I'm having twins.

"What did you just say?"

"I said, you are having twins, Ms. Jordan. I told you that multiple births were a possibility. The good news is, the babies are fine. I'm surprised you aren't showing. You appear to be a little further along than I first anticipated."

"This just keeps getting worse and worse. Are there any special requirements, since it's more than one?"

"Just eat more healthy foods, drink plenty of milk, and take your vitamins. Here are your ultrasound pictures. You can get dressed now. I'll see you next month."

"Thank you, doctor."

This is the final straw, I can't take it anymore. I call up Omar and go slam off. He answers the phone unexpectedly. "Hello."

"You stupid ass bastard! I can't believe you would stoop so low! I should have your psycho ass locked up! How could you switch my birth control pills? I know it was you. You are so dumb!"

"I-I-I don't know what you're talking about," he says, stuttering.

"Don't play dumb with me! 'Cause of your crazy scheme, I'm pregnant with twins. Twins that are going to die. I'm killing your babies' jackass."

"You know what? I don't give a fuck! I'm having a baby anyway with my new girlfriend, so you can kiss my ass. At least she appreciates me. Go to hell, Skye. Straight to hell! Your selfish ass don't need to be anybody's mother anyway!"

"You got what on the way? Oh, so your trifling ass is walking around making babies! Well, I hope the trick bitch marries your crazy ass too, and she must not be that great, 'cause you still stalking me!"

"Get over yourself Skye! You ain't shit, for real! Yolanda is all the woman I need and then some. Go suck a dick! This conversation is over."

"It ain't over till I say it's over!"

Little did I know that last comment was not heard. Omar has already hung up. I immediately redial his number, but he doesn't answer. I repeatedly call him. Finally, I leave several messages. I leave so many messages, his voicemail box is full. When I'm mad, I can't calm down until I get out everything I need to say. Lucky for him I don't know where he lives. I wonder if he was at work. I drive to the Marriott in a haze. Boy, I was lucky! As I'm approaching the hotel, I see Omar's Escalade pulling out of the parking lot. I follow him to an apartment complex that isn't too far down the street. When he gets out of the car, he goes to the door. I pull up closer so I can see. I notice he uses a key to get in. Hmm... he must live here. I sit for awhile debating on whether or not I should knock on the door. I park my car a little ways down the street. As I'm walking to the door, I see a woman coming out of the same apartment. Oh, this must be his new bitch. When she turns around, my heart drops. This is the same bitch's ass I beat back at Friday's last summer. So he has been creeping with her all along.

I step right in front of her path. "Do you remember me, bitch?" I say in a harsh tone. I walk right up on her.

"Yeah. What do you want?" she replies smartly.

"If you want to keep that baby you're pregnant wit', I suggest you change your tone of voice."

"How do you know I'm pregnant?" she seem puzzled

"'Cause Omar told me. Let me tell you something. Keep your crazy-ass boyfriend away from me. You wanted him so bad, now you can have him. Tell him to stop following me. The next time I catch him, I'm calling the police. It's a violation of the restraining order. If you weren't pregnant, I would whoop your ass again."

"I'm not going to be pregnant forever. I'm due Aug 8th. Obviously, you know where I live. I look forward to seeing you then. Oh, by the way, how do you know where I live? You must've followed Omar home. Why don't you practice what you preach? You had a good man, but you lost him. Too bad. Now if you'll excuse me, I have more important things to do." She begins walking off.

My first instinct is to trip her up, but something deep down inside tells me to let it go. She gets in the car and drives off. I decide not to knock on the door after all. I take the childish way out.

I flatten all Omar's tires and scratch up the doors. Ah, I felt better. I'm exhausted, so I stop by Wendy's to get something to eat, then go home to take a nap. I don't think he will be seeing Omari for a while.

When I wake up, I call a couple of daycares to see if they have any openings. I don't want to take a chance of Omar popping up to the daycare taking Omari without my permission. I find a private daycare not far from my job. I enroll Omari there. The director says she can start Monday. Instead of letting Omar keep Omari this weekend, I take her to my parents' house. She needs to spend time with her grandparents anyway. I'm supposed to meet with Kenya this weekend to help her plan the wedding. Even though me and Omar aren't together, I'm still close to his family. I would hate to back out of an obligation, so I try to act happy and I keep my word. Helping Kenya plan her wedding kind of takes my mind off things. It's actually fun. Too bad Omar isn't like his sister. Me and Kenya are real cool, but I decide to keep my pregnancy a secret for as long as I can.

I haven't had a heart-to-heart talk with my mother in awhile, so when I go to her house to pick up Omari, I decide to tell her about the twins. I need some advice.

"Mom, I have something really important to tell you."

"What is it, dear?"

"I'm fourteen weeks pregnant with twins. I don't know what to do. I told Omar, and he's acting stupid. He has a girlfriend and she's pregnant too."

"I can't believe Omar would do something like that! He's always been such a nice young man! Well, it's your choice Skye. Your father and I will support you with whatever you decide. I know raising twins alone won't be easy, but I'm sure in time Omar will come around. If not, you know you can always count on me. I love babies, I will help you as much as I can. Don't worry, everything will be all right. Life is not supposed to be easy. We have to learn to live with the choices we make, good and bad."

"Thanks Mom, you make a lot of sense. I should have talked to you sooner. I've been so stressed out lately."

"Don't worry about things you can't change. Just pray, and God will take over the rest. It's not healthy for the babies if you worry. Skye, you are my only child and I love you with all my heart, but sometimes you can be a real bitch. You need to spend some time thinking about all the wrongs you have done to Omar. Maybe you two can get some relationship counseling. If you don't get back into a relationship with him, you will still be connected to him by your children. Just think about what I said. Everyone makes mistakes. I think it's time you forgive Omar for his."

"It's not as easy as you think, Mom. You have a valid point, but right now, I'm just not ready. Maybe in time I can. Where's Omari? I should be getting home."

"She's at the store with your dad. He went to get groceries. I'm cooking dinner; would you like to stay?"

"Yeah, that would be nice. I haven't seen dad in a while."

I stay and eat dinner with my parents. I tell dad about my situation. He agrees with my mom. I'm shocked she called me a bitch, but she is right. I feel bad about not telling her the whole truth, but I couldn't have my mom thinking I'm a hoe.

Weeks go by, and Omar harasses me about seeing Omari. Finally, I break down around the beginning of March and I allow him to get her for the weekend. By now I am four months pregnant, but I look like I'm six months. Omar is shocked when he sees me.

"I thought you were getting an abortion," he says calmly.

"I changed my mind. People are entitled to change their mind, right?"

"I guess. Why didn't you tell me you decided to keep the babies?"

"'Cause I didn't want to. You're busy with your new family anyway. I really didn't think you would care."

"Well, you are wrong. I still love you, Skye. I will always love you. Of course I care about our babies. Is there anything you need?"

"No, we are fine. I had an ultrasound; they are both girls. I found out a couple of days ago."

"That's nice. I guess I'ma have three girls now."

"Oh, so is your girlfriend having a girl too. When is she due?"

"Aug 8th. No, she's having a boy. My sister told me you were coming to the wedding, and I'm bringing Yolanda, so can you please act like somebody with some sense? I don't want my sister's big day to be ruined."

"Of course I can. I love Kenya like a sister. I would never ruin her day. I'll be on my best behavior."

"Thank you."

Chapter Thirty-Five

Coco

When I come back home from Montego Bay, Jerome's truck is parked in the driveway. I get out of my car and go up to the window. No one is inside.

I wonder where he is? I think.

I unlock the front door; only the bottom lock is on. When I left, the deadbolt was on too. I got halfway up the stairs when I hear little feet running.

"Mommy, Mommy I'm glad you're back!" Corey screams.

"Hi, Mommy!" Christian yells, hugging my leg.

"Hi sweetheart, how are my two favorite boys?" I kiss both of them.

"Where is your dad?" I ask.

"In the bedroom watching football," Corey replies.

"You and your brother go to your room and play. I need to talk to your dad."

"Okay. Mom did you bring us back a treat?"

"Yeah, I got both of you something, but it's in my suitcase. I'll give it to you after I talk to Jerome."

"A'ight, hurry up." Corey and Christian go to their rooms.

"Hey baby, how was your trip?" Jerome asks.

"Baby? I'm not your baby anymore. What are you doing here? I changed the locks for a reason."

"This is still my house, and you are still my wife. I know I left things fucked up between us, but we need to talk and work things out. I love you, Coco, and I miss you."

"You didn't love me enough to be faithful. You always take Shameka's side, even if she's dead wrong. I'm your wife. You should support me sometimes."

"Coco, what are you talking about? I've never cheated on you since we've been married."

"You've been sleeping with Shameka. I saw your truck at her house. She called and told me you've been staying at her house ever since you moved out."

"Now that's a lie! When I first left, I stayed at the Marriott. Omar hooked me up with a room, then I moved in with Justin. My truck was at Shameka's house 'cause she went out to the club, and I stayed there to keep Jermeka. Shameka wasn't even there, she rode with one of her friends."

"If that's the truth, then you see what type of conniving little bitch she is. She made it a point to call me every time you were there."

"I'll prove it to you."

Jerome pulls out his cell phone and calls Shameka. "Hey, Shameka. Where is Jermeka?"

"In her room playing with one of her li'l friends. Are you coming over tonight? I'm cooking dinner. I know you could use a home-cooked meal and some good pussy."

"No, thank you. I don't feel like your mess tonight. Can I please speak to my daughter?"

"Why you try to be stingy with the dick, Jerome? You and Coco ain't together no more. I know you staying at Justin's house. Kandice told me you are still there. Come on over here. I'll make sure you are comfortable."

"Look, I'll just call her back later. Bye." He hangs up.

"You still think I'm fucking her? I'm not a liar, nor a cheater."

"Yeah, I believe you. But I got a question for you. You see what type of person she is? That's exactly why I don't want you around her."

"Yeah, I see now. I guess I just didn't want to believe she would do something like this. I'm not going to let her interfere with our relationship anymore."

"I'm not either. I got something for her ass. Excuse me for a moment. I got something to take care of."

I grab my keys and dash out the house. I am sick and tired of this bitch ruining my marriage! It's time for me to give her the ass beating she deserves! I knock on Shameka's door like I'm the cops. I cover the peephole wit' my finger. Dumb bitch didn't even ask who it was. As soon as she opens the door, I hit her right in her mouth. No words were exchanged, just licks! I just keep punching her over and over again. She grabs my hair like the punk she is. It's hurting, but I don't care, I just keep hitting her until she lets go. Shameka hits me one time in my chest and bites the side of my face. She is down on the ground when Jerome pulls up. Jermeka must be busy playing, 'cause she never comes out her room. The neighbors don't even come outside. I guess nobody likes her either. Jerome pulls me off her.

I begin shouting, "You raggedy bitch! I bet not ever catch you trying to take my husband for granted again! He don't want you, so you can't have him. Get over it. He's mine now!"

I kick her one last time.

"You are going to jail, bitch! You are going to pay for this. I'm calling the police!" she screams.

"If you call the police, I'll never speak to you again. You bet not ask me for shit! It's over, you were wrong. You deserved a good ass-kicking. I'll still see my daughter, but the days of me trying to help you are through. I mean what I say," Jerome threatens Shameka.

We both get in our cars and leave. Jerome didn't bring the kids, he left them with our next-door neighbor. I knew he would come rescue her. When I get home, I think I'm going to hear a lecture, but instead Jerome consoles me. We talk for hours and I let him move back in. I decide to go to marriage counseling so we can work out our problems.

Shameka never did call the police on me. Maybe I should've beaten her ass a long time ago. Well, at least I got my husband back, but now I feel guilty about what I did in Montego Bay. Like the saying goes: whatever happens in Montego Bay, stays in Montego Bay. I sure won't tell.

Chapter Thirty-Six

Jamyya

Don't get me wrong, I had fun in Montego Bay, but I'm glad to be back home. When I come in, I'm greeted by all my kids. "Hello everybody. I missed all of you. How are my babies doing?"

"Fine. I been good, Ma," Tamia says, smiling.

"I'm glad, what about your brothers?"

"They was a'ight. Daddy had to beat Deontaé one time."

"Stop snitching!" Deontaé yells.

"A'ight, y'all. Let your mother get in the house good before you act a fool," Keenan says.

"You missed me?" I ask.

"Of course. I haven't had a good night's sleep since you've been gone. Your mom called a couple of times."

"From where?"

"I don't know, but it wasn't jail. She didn't leave a message. I told her you would be back today. So, how was the trip?"

"I had fun, once I got over the surprise guest."

"Who?"

"Chris came to surprise Damisha. Jazz helped plan the whole thing. I was mad 'cause she spent all her time with him. Then Coco hooked up with some Rasta, trying to get her groove back like Stella. Skye got sick. Things started off bad, but at the end, everyone got together and we had a good time."

"That's good. I'm glad you had fun. This has been an experience. I realize how much work it is to run a house. I'm sorry if I ever belittled you as a housewife. This shit is hard. I took two personal days from work 'cause I was so tired. Jamesha was a big help though. She cooked dinner for us when she wasn't working."

"Where is she?"

"She's over Devin's house. She should be back in a couple hours. I told her it was okay."

"Yeah, it's fine. I wanted to talk to her about a new job. Jazz is going to open up a boutique, and she's hiring. So, I wanted to see if Jamesha was interested."

"That's a good idea. We need something like that around here."

"I can't wait to be her first customer."

"I'm sure she knows she can count on her shopaholic friends to support her" Keenan laughs.

"She sure can! In other news, Skye is pregnant. She found out on our trip."

"Damn! I know she is mad."

"Mad ain't the word. She wants to have an abortion. We tried to talk her out of it. I hope she changes her mind. I just wish she would talk to me about it. Ever since she found, out she's been withdrawn."

"Just give her time. She'll come to you when she's ready to talk. Meanwhile, I need some attention. I haven't seen you in a week. We have some reconnecting to do."

"We sure do, but I need to spend time with the kids first. I'll take care of you tonight."

I am so happy to be back home with my family! I play Twister with Tamia and Ke'Asia then play Lego with the twins.

When Jamesha comes home, we talk about the job at the boutique and her prom. Even though she's pregnant, she still wants to go. I told her I will buy her a prom dress or get one made, depending upon how big her stomach is. The baby is due May 10th, so she might have it before the prom. Her prom is May 16th; hopefully, she will have recovered by then.

After the kids are asleep, I give my husband the special attention he wants. It feels good being back in his arms. I wish Coco and Skye could work their relationships out! We could all be happy.

Chapter Thirty-Seven

Jasmine

I miss Shawn so much that I drive straight to his house. I can't wait to see him! When I pull up in the parking lot, I notice a car that looks just like Joy's. But why would Joy be over here? So I shrug it off. I skip up to his apartment. I hear yelling and screaming. My heart begins to beat fast. I can't make out what is being said, but it's a man's and a woman's voice. I knock on the door very hard. As I stand outside, I hear a mumble and some scuffling.

Joy snatches open the door. "Surprise!" she yells.

Dumbfounded, I asked, "What kind of surprise is this? I thought you weren't speaking to me?"

"I'm not, and I'm about to tell you why. You are messing up my family. Shawn is my man now. We're having a baby."

Joy lifts up her shirt to expose her hard round belly. My mouth drops open. I can't believe my ears.

"Stop playing! This shit ain't funny! A'ight Shawn, joke's over."

"This ain't a joke, boo. Tell her, Shawn. Tell her how we've been fucking for five months. How my pussy is so much better than hers."

Shawn steps in front of Joy. "Just shut the fuck up!" he screams, shaking Joy.

He turns towards me. "Look baby, I'm sorry. I never wanted you to find out this way. Please forgive me, it was a mistake."

Tears run down my face. Words can't express how hurt I am.

"Yeah baby, I forgive you," I say calmly. Shawn goes to hug me and I punch him in the eye, stomp on his foot, then knee him in the dick. I push past him and tackle Joy. I don't care if she is pregnant; I beat her ass too. I try to avoid her stomach, so I tear her face up. Shawn makes several attempts to pull me off of her.

"You dirty bitch! I'll kill yo' trifling ass! You are so lucky you're pregnant, 'cause it would have been a lot worse! You bitch, I'll never forgive you! And Shawn, fuck you too!" I scream.

Shawn tries to hold my arms, but I struggle hard to break free. The neighbors must have called the police, 'cause they show up and arrest me. At that point, I really didn't care. They take me to Henrico County Jail on Parham Road. I'm charged with two counts of assault and battery, trespassing, and destruction of property. When I was beating Joy's ass, I broke the coffee table and a vase.

On the way to the police car, I kick a dent in the side of Joy's car with my Timberlands. Since this is my first time being in trouble, the magistrate releases me on my own recognizance. I call Skye to come pick me up. She said she will be here in fifteen minutes. She asks me what happened. I run the whole story down to her.

"That's fucked up," is all she can say. She says she's going to bring Coco so she can drive my car back to her house before somebody vandalizes it. I am tired and pissed. I had just had the best vacation ever, now my sister is pregnant by my fiancé. This is some Jerry Springer bullshit! My arraignment is tomorrow at 8:00 A.M.

When I get back to Skye's house, I'm still pissed. I look down at my hand and notice I am still wearing my engagement ring. In a fit of rage, I snatch it off, peeling a piece of skin off with it. I throw the ring to the floor.

"I hate him, that son of a bitch! How could he play me like that? Ahh, I'm so fucking stupid!" I scream, pulling my hair.

"You are not stupid. You were in love, that's all. Love makes you do some crazy things. We all are guilty of that. Don't beat yourself up. You did nothing wrong. Just try to calm down. Trust me, I understand. Your situation is a bit worse than mine, 'cause Joy is your sister, but I know how it feels to be lied to and cheated on. In time, your wounds will heal."

"I don't know about that. I don't think I can ever forgive either one of them. I don't want to talk about it anymore, it's just making me upset. I'ma go upstairs, I'll see you later. Thanks for picking me up."

"You're welcome. If you need anything, just let me know. I can take tomorrow off if you want me to go to court with you."

"Yeah, you can go if you want. Nothing is going to happen though it's just an arraignment."

"Well, I just want to comfort you. I'll be downstairs if you need me."

"Cool."

I go upstairs and take a hot bath. I took a couple of Advil PMs so I can sleep. I just wish this day could be over. I appreciate Skye being so unselfish and standing by me when she has her own drama going on.

Months go by and it's now March. Today I'm going to court for sentencing. I am found guilty for the two counts of assault and battery and destruction of property. The trespassing charge is dropped. The judge gives me a year for each assault charge, but suspended all but three months. Then I get thirty days for destruction of property but he suspends all of it. Altogether, I have to serve ninety days in jail and enroll in an anger management program. I'm pissed, but I have no choice but to do my time. My release date was June 15th. This is my first time being locked up, but I make it through. Everything happens for a reason, and I think I found my purpose.

Jamyya's mom Rhonda is in the same pod I am. It's nice to see somebody I know. Rhonda has been locked up before, so she takes me under her wing. My goal is to reunite Jamyya and her mother. Jamyya can be stubborn at times.

"So why are you here, baby girl?" Rhonda asks.

"I beat my sister's ass 'cause she slept with my fiancé and is pregnant by him. I tried to beat his ass too."

"Oh, well I'm sorry you are here, but she deserved it. How are Jamyya and Jamesha doing?"

"They are both fine. Jamesha is doing good, she's having a little boy. She got an 1100 on her SATs. She also registered for college at VCU. I'm going to open a boutique when I get out. Jamesha and Jamyya are going to work there with me."

"That's nice. How much time you got to do?"

"Only ninety days. My release date is June 15th. When do you get out?"

"I get out July 20th. I'm here on a violation. I'm still clean though. I haven't used drugs since I got out of prison. I even stopped drinking. I go to AA meetings and everything. I got violated when Keenan called the police on me back in November."

"Oh yeah, I remember that. Do you still have a job?"

"Sort of, I was working up until I got locked up. I explained the situation to Omar. He said he would see what he could do. But I've be gone for four months and I got four more to do, so I don't know."

"Well, you can come work for me. I would love for you to be a drug counselor. Just think about it. I'll leave my info wit you so you can call me when you get out."

"Thanks."

"No problem."

We talk off and on about a lot of different things. I am surprised at how much work I get done in jail. I read a lot of books on retail store and owning my own business. Skye and Damisha also sent me information off the Internet. I cannot believe how dedicated Damisha is in helping me get my business started.

I finally convince Jamyya to visit her mom. Even though I am locked up, I manage to accomplish a lot.

As the days go by, my anger starts going away. I am so lucky to have friends who care! I get a visit twice a week and tons of mail. Mario comes to visit me as well. He found out about everything and moved out. I let him stay in my house until he found something. His apartment was going to be ready June 1st. I'm glad Shawn never moved in with me. Mario didn't divorce Joy but they are separated. He told me that her and the baby are fine. Shawn doesn't have anything to do with her.

Coco comes to see me too. I'm glad her and Jerome are back together and doing good. Skye is not due until August, so at least I won't miss the twins being born. Something good can come from something bad.

My life… who would have thought it would be like this? When I get out of jail, I'm going to Philly for a week to visit my brother and sister. I need to get out of Richmond for a while.

The world didn't stop while I was locked up. When I get out, everything seems different. I have definitely changed for the better.

Skye is big as a house. She is now seven months pregnant. The doctor moved her due date up to Aug 2nd. Jamesha had her baby on May 4th. She named him Javon Kevin Rhodes. He has Devin's last name. The baby weighed 6 pounds 2 ounces.

Rhonda was surprised when Jamesha wrote her a letter and sent her pictures of the baby. I'm glad Rhonda got her kids back.

Chapter Thirty-Eight

Damisha

I love Jazz. She's the best friend a girl could ever have. Since Chris came back into my life, I've been so happy. When I get back home, I decide to make a change. I decide to use my gym membership. I'm determined to get this weight off of me. I want to be a size six again. My self-confidence is back up. Don't get me wrong. I don't need a man to validate me, but it's nice to have one to share my life with. Lately, I've been thinking about getting married. Coco and Jamyya are already married. Jazz is engaged to Shawn. Now it's just me and Skye who are single. I'm twenty-seven years old with no kids. I think it's about time I grow up and take on some responsibility. I've always wanted kids, but then I wouldn't be the center of attention anymore. I'm getting older and my biological clock is ticking.

I can't believe Skye is pregnant again. Strange things are definitely happening. My brother left me a message talking about how I'm going to be an aunt. I can't begin to picture Dontaé being a dad. But hey, if he's happy, so am I.

Chris comes over Monday night with a dog. He felt bad about me selling Princess, so he bought me a male Yorkshire terrier name Jodeci. Jodeci is my favorite R & B group. I'm glad I finally came to my senses and chose Chris. Jerell is never going to change, and it's time I realize that.

Coco calls to tell me the good news about Jerome coming back home and how she beat Shameka's ass for once. Her ass whooping was long overdue. I am more than shocked when she tells me about Jasmine's arrest and what led to it. I can't believe Joy would do something like that to her own sister!

Shawn was wrong too, but men are dogs, so I expect nothing less than bad behavior. I want to go to Joy's house and stomp the shit out of her myself. But what would that solve? As the months pass by, me and Chris become closer. I start going to church every Sunday and Bible study on Wednesday. My life has gotten so much better. Jazz, on the other hand, has been going through hell. She got sentenced to ninety days in jail, and her sister is pregnant by her ex fiancé.

Since Jazz has done so much for me, I feel compelled to help her out. I do all kinds of research for her. I even contact Jerome to help find a building for the boutique. We find a great space on the Northside of town.

I'm really excited about the boutiquer. I can't wait for Jazz to come home so we can open it! I'm going to be the Buyer. Finally, it's June 15th and Jazz is out of jail. I am kind of disappointed when she decides to go straight to Philly. I pick her up from Henrico County Jail and drop her off at Amtrak Train Station. She says she will be back in a week.

"Mimi, thanks for having my back. I couldn't have done none of this without you. You are my best friend. I promise I will spend time with you when I get back. I love you. Tell everybody I miss them."

"A'ight, have fun with your family."

"I sure will! I trust you to take care of things while I'm gone."

"You know I'm on it! I got your back. I'm really excited about this boutique. You know I love to shop."

"It sure is! Don't forget to save a position for Rhonda. She'll be out soon."

"I got it covered."

While Jazz is in Philly. I decide to plan a coming-home cookout for her. I call Jamyya and Coco to help me out. Skye is too tired to do anything but eat. I'm surprised her and Omar didn't get back together yet. Of course she's invited.

Jamesha graduates high school with a 4.0 GPA and she got accepted at VCU. She is majoring in Nursing. Devon graduates too. He decides to go to ECPI for Graphic Design. Both of them are doing so well! Just looking at babies makes me want to have one.

I look at Chris. "I want to have a baby."

"You what? I don't think I heard you correctly."

"Yes, you did! I want a baby. Let's have one. I'm ready."

"Don't you think we should get married first?"

"Okay, let's get married then. Chris will you marry me?"

"That's not how it's supposed to happen. I'm supposed to ask you with a ring down on one knee. Like this... let me show you how it's done."

Chris gets down on one knee in Coco's backyard. We decided to have Jazz's cookout here. Jamyya went to pick Jazz up from the train station so she isn't here yet. Chris pulls a small black box from his pocket and opens it. A pink diamond engagement ring is shining bright.

"Damisha Monaé Miles, will you marry me?"

"Are you serious?"

"Yes, I am. I've been wanting to ask you for a long time. Now, will you marry me?"

"Yes, yes, yes!" He slides the ring on my finger. It's a perfect fit.

"You've made me the happiest man in the world. I love you."

"I love you too."

I have no idea that Jazz has come in and is watching us.

"I'm so sorry, Jazz. This cookout was meant for you." I didn't know how she would react. I know how sad she was about her relationship with Shawn. The last thing I want to do is flaunt mine in front of her face.

"No need to be sorry. I'm happy for you guys. Thanks for throwing me a cookout. When my girls are happy so am I. Now where is big mama?"

"I assume you're talking about Skye."

"Yep."

"She's in the house sitting in the living room. You know how she hates bugs. Plus it's too hot out here for her."

"I'ma go inside and get her."

Jazz and I go in to get Skye. "Damn girl, you sure look like you're having twins! You are big as a house! No more cute outfits for you," Jazz teases.

"Shut up. I'm still cute. You don't like my outfit?" Skye gets up and twirls around.

"Yeah, it's cute. When did Baby Phat start making maternity clothes?"

"It's plus size, girl. I only wear a size 14. I'm doing good. It's all baby weight, I'll lose it after I have them."

"Yeah, I guess. If Mimi can get back down to a size four, so can you."

"Yep, and I'll help her," I respond.

I am so proud of myself! I stayed determined and I lost all the weight I had gained. Now I'm engaged; I feel so lucky. I'm really loving life again. I invited my brother Dontaé and his girlfriend to the cookout, but she didn't come. He said she isn't feeling good, that the baby is wearing her out. I really want to meet the woman that was having my niece or nephew! Maybe another time.

"Isn't it funny, Skye, that Dontaé's girlfriend is due around the same time as you?" I say to Skye.

"Mm hmm… it sure is. I guess everybody got pregnant around the same time. Omar's girlfriend's baby is due in August too."

"Wow, I guess Omar was on a roll!" Jazz states.

"Is he going to help you take care of these twins?"

"Yeah, he said he would. He wants us to get back together, but I don't want to."

"Why?"

"'Cause he's happy with somebody else. Let her keep him. I don't want him anymore. My parents will help me. I'll be fine."

"Okay. You know you got us too. Come on, let's go outside and mingle." Jazz grabs Skye by the arm and pulls her up.

We go outside and join the party. Jerome plays some music while Chris and Mario cook on the grill.

"Oh shit, Skye! You missed my engagement. Chris proposed to me."

"Congratulations! I'm sorry I missed it. Why didn't somebody come get me?"

"'Cause then we would have missed it too!"

"Good point!"

Everything is finally starting to fall into place. Jazz opens the boutique called Jazzy's Place on July 1st. She even got Power 92 to come out for the grand opening. We have balloons everywhere and a clown to paint faces. There's pizza and sodas for the guests as well. The boutique sells a variety of vintage shoes, handbags, and accessories. I resign from Virginia Power and became the Head Buyer of the boutique.

Chapter Thirty-Nine

Joy

Finally, the day has come for me to have this baby! My ultrasound says it's a girl, so I buy pink, yellow, and purple outfits. The baby is born exactly on my due date, June 30th. It's a five pound, seven ounce baby girl. She is so beautiful!

Since the day I told Jazz about the baby, Shawn hasn't spoken to me. I called him but he changed his number. I went by his house then he got a restraining order. He calls me from a blocked number occasionally. I hope he calls so I can tell him I had the baby. I decide to name the baby Jashauna Alicia Jackson. I give her Shawn's last name.

I don't have many visitors at the hospital. A couple of my friends and coworkers come by. My family is still pissed off at me because of what I did to Jazz. I really don't care. I got my baby, and that is all that matters. I stay in the hospital for three days 'cause I had a C-section. On the third day before I am discharged, Shawn calls my cell phone.

"Hello," I answer cheerfully.

"Did you have the baby?"

"Yes I did, and you missed it. I had her three days ago. Her name is Jashauna Alicia Jackson. She is so beautiful, you should come see her."

"Why did you give her my last name? I want a blood test. What hospital are you in?"

"I'm at Henrico Doctors, but I'm about to be home by then."

"A'ight. We need to talk about the baby."

Later on that evening, Shawn comes by. He insists on a blood test before he signs any papers. I schedule a blood test for the following week. When I get the results in the mail, I am shocked: 99.98% Shawn Jamal Jackson is not the father of Jashauna Alicia Jackson. I'll be damn. How could this be? Now I know what you're thinking but I'm not a hoe. The only other person I slept with is Mario, but the doctor said he is infertile. Hmm. I call Mario.

"Hello," he says, with an attitude.

"Look, I have something very important to tell you. I had the baby, it's a girl. Shawn took a blood test, and the baby is not his, so it has to be yours. Can you take a blood test for me, please?"

"How many people have you been sleeping with?"

"Only you and Shawn."

"You expect for me to believe that?" Mario starts laughing.

"Believe what you want. This child is yours, either you want to be a part of this child's life or not. It's your choice."

"All right, I'll take a blood test, but you bet not be playing with my emotions."

"I'm serious, Mario. Shawn is the only other person I slept with. I just wanted to have a baby. Now I got one; it's yours."

"We'll find out soon enough."

I guess Shawn must have got the paternity papers, 'cause he calls and calls, but I don't have the heart to answer the phone. He leaves a message though. It said "You lying bitch! I knew that baby wasn't mine. You ruined my relationship for nothing! You are a deranged, psycho bitch! I hope you get what's coming to you. I'm glad it's not my baby; now I can get rid of you. Stop stalking me, bitch! You need to go on Maury to find your baby daddy, trifling-ass skank!"

Seems like Shawn took the news rather well. I'm glad I don't have to deal with him anymore. Now that I know the baby is Mario's, we can get back together. I know he still loves me 'cause he hasn't filed for divorce yet.

At the end of the week, Mario shows up to take the blood test. When the results come back, he's shocked that the baby is 99.99% his. It's a miracle. I talk Mario into moving back in with me so we can raise our baby together. He said on one condition - I have to change the baby's name, and I do. I'm glad she's only two months old. I change her name to Jaslyn Alicia Allen.

Mario is such a good father. He helps me with everything. Don't get me wrong, he is still pissed at me. For right now, he's sleeping in the guest bedroom. We talk every now and then, but he's mostly consumed with work and the baby. Sometimes I want to call and apologize to Jazz, but then I get scared and chicken out. Mario stays in contact with her.

He tells me about the boutique she opened. It appears she is doing good. I give Mario some pictures of Jaslyn to give to Jazz. Mario tells me that even though Jazz still hates, me she loves her niece. I don't have a problem with her seeing Jaslyn.

While I'm on maternity leave for work, I go to Philly so my family can see the baby. Once everybody finds out the baby is Mario's, they aren't so mad with me anymore. Only time will tell what will happen next. I hope Mario can learn to trust me again. Even though no one believes me, this was the first time cheating on my husband and the last.

Chapter Forty

Jasmine

Everything in my life starts getting better. The boutique is a complete success. Rhonda got out of jail and started working as a salesperson. I'm so proud of her! She's doing so well! Jamesha and Jamyya forgave her, and they are becoming a close-knit family. Jamesha is my cashier part-time. She's going to VCU in August. Damisha buys all of the merchandise for the boutique and hires the staff. I handle the payroll and oversee the daily operations.

One day, I get a call from Mario telling me that Shawn is not the baby's father, he is. I almost drop the phone. Mario is nice enough to bring the baby to the boutique so I can see her. She is absolutely gorgeous. I can't believe Joy named her Jaslyn, cause it's too close to my name. I will never understand why she hates me so much.

Mario says she's jealous of me, but I have no idea why. She's beautiful and she has a wonderful job. Joy gets the same amount of money I got when she was my age. I don't know, I think she's just crazy. Even though I despise Joy, I love my niece with all my heart. I'm so glad she turned out to be Mario's! I guess Shawn must have really thought I was stupid.

Once he found out the baby wasn't his, he called me trying to get back. Nigga, please! He is too full of himself. Life goes on and I'm doing fine without him.

Chapter Forty-One

Skye

The doctor moved my due date up, which confuses me even more. I still don't know if Omar is my baby's daddy or not. Me and you-know-who have been kicking it off and on. He wants the twins to be his, and honestly I have a weird feeling they are. It seems like everybody is having a baby this month.

Mimi calls me; she wants to plan a baby shower for Dontaé's girlfriend.

"Have you even met her?" I ask.

"No, but I want to. Every time I set up something, she always gets sick or they have to cancel. Even if she doesn't want to meet me, I want to get some stuff for the baby."

"Yeah, that's a good idea. Maybe you can give it to Dontaé and he can take it to her. Some people are really shy. She could just be a private person."

"Could be, I don't know, but I'm tired of trying to figure out. Now let's plan your baby shower."

"It's already set. My mom is giving me one. You should be receiving your invitation shortly."

"Well, I guess I'll have to wait till I have my own baby to plan a shower."

"Sorry. You can have a bridal shower once you set a date for the wedding."

"True, but that won't be until next year. We decided on May 5th."

"Good, I should be back in shape by then."

"Yep, now I just hope nobody else gets pregnant before then."

"It won't be me, for damn sure! I'm getting my tubes tied."

"I don't blame you. Well, I gotta go, Chris should be home soon."

"Bye, girl."

I'm glad I had my baby shower early, 'cause the twins can't wait to come out. At ten o'clock on Aug 3rd, I start having contractions. For some reason, the first person I called is Omar.

"Omar, I'm in labor. I need you to come over. Omari is here and I'm by myself. Hurry, I need you to take me to the hospital."

"A'ight. Calm down, I'll be there in a minute."

"Okay, but you are coming, right?"

"Yes, Skye, I'm putting on my clothes now."

"Thank you, see you soon."

I hang up and call Jazz to keep Omari. I was not in the mood to deal with my mom. She would've came to the hospital too. I'm not for that right now. Jazz pulls up about five minutes before Omar comes. I can't believe Yolanda let him leave the house by himself.

"Thanks for coming. Where is Yolanda?"

"In the house asleep. I hope you didn't call me just to piss her off?"

"No, I'm not that petty. I'm really in labor, but if she's pissed that's just an added bonus." I start laughing until a contraction hits.

"This shit ain't funny!"

We pull up to the hospital and Omar helps me inside. Since I'm having twins, Dr. Seagram decides to do a C-section. Omar's cell phone starts ringing while we are in the delivery room.

"Excuse me, I have to answer this." He answers the phone.

"What? Not now! Tell me you're lying! Okay. Yeah I'm already here. I know, I know… Okay I won't miss it." He hangs up.

Me being the nosy person I am, I ask, "Who was that?"

"It was Yolanda; her water broke. Her friend Star is going to bring her to the hospital."

"You've got to be kidding! She's lying, she just wants some attention."

"I don't think so, she's nothing like you. Just concentrate on having these babies."

"What if she really is in labor? Are you going to leave me to be with her?"

Omar pauses for a minute. "Yes. You decided you didn't want me anymore. Now you have to deal with it. I'll call your mom if you want me to."

"Fuck you, Omar, just go! Go now, I don't care!"

"Skye, shut up and calm down."

It's now 11:30, and I am being prepped for surgery. Finally, at 11:50, the first baby comes out. It's a girl. Then the second comes at 11:54.

"Aw. Omar, look, aren't they beautiful?"

"Yeah, they are."

Yolanda is in a labor room next door to mine. She is still having contractions. Lucky for Omar, he got to see all of his kids being born. Yolanda has a little boy at 1:05 A.M. on Aug 4th. All the kids almost had the same birthday. Who would have thought?

I name the twins Horizon and Rain. Rain looks like me; her eyes are green and her hair is sandy brown. Right now, both of the twins are really light. I checked both of their ears, but it isn't much darker. The twins look just alike except Horizon has hazel eyes. Neither one has dimples. The more I look at them the more it becomes clear that Omar is not their father.

After I take a nap, I call the man who is possibly the father.

"Look, I'm at the hospital and I just had the babies. I need you to come take a blood test. I really think you are the father, but I need to be sure."

"A'ight, I'll be there in an hour. Do you need anything?"

"Yeah, some food. Bring me something from McDonald's. Oh, and be careful, 'cause Omar is here with Yolanda. She just had her baby too."

"Damn, that's crazy! I'll call him so he can tell me what's going on, so if he sees me he'll think I came to visit with him."

"You are so devious! Good thinking."

"What did you name the babies? Are they okay?"

"Yeah, they are fine, the two cutest babies in the nursery. I named them Rain Storm and Horizon Sunshine."

"Were you still drugged up when you named them?"

"No, I think it's cute."

"Mm hmm. Well, what is their last name?"

"I don't know yet. That's why I need you to take a blood test."

"I'm about to leave now. Give me a couple minutes, I got a stop to make."

"A'ight, but you know my girls and family will be up here in the morning"

"Who knows you had the baby?"

Nobody but Jazz. I told her not to tell the others yet. Plus, it's in the middle of the night; everyone is probably still sleep."

"Okay, I'll be there soon. Just sit tight," he responds.

While waiting for this jackass to show up, I fall asleep. I awaken to someone coming in my room. "Good morning, Ms. Jordan, how are you feeling?" the nurse asks.

"I'm fine, just a little sore," I say as I try to sit up.

"Well, that's normal. I'll give you something for the pain, but first I need to check to make sure everything is okay."

She checks me out then gives me two Percocet and a cup of water.

"The orderly should be in shortly with your breakfast. If you need anything, just call the nurse's station," the nurse says as she walks out the door.

"Thank you."

I noticed that the sun is shining bright, so I decide to check the clock to see what time it is. The clock reads 8:00 A.M.

"What the fuck?"

Why is it taking him so long to get here? I call him about five hours ago; he should have been here by now. He's probably doing this shit on purpose. I grab the phone and angrily dial his number.

"Yo, what's up?" he asks as if nothing is wrong.

"What the fuck you mean, what's up? I just gave birth to two kids or did you forget? You need to stop smoking that shit. I thought you were coming to the hospital to see me and the babies!" I yell in frustration.

"Keep your panties on, I'll be there in a minute," he says, laughing.

"This shit ain't funny. You know what, fuck it don't come at all. I don't want you here anyway. I regret that I ever met you. Just stay your trifling ass home."

"Calm down, I'm on my way."

He hangs up before I can get out another word. Damn fool, gets on my nerves. What an asshole! Why did I ever get involved with him? Before I can finish my thoughts, Omar came in. "Are you and the twins okay? he asks.

"Yeah, I'm fine and so are the twins. They are in the nursery right now, but the nurse should be bringing them any minute now. How is your other new baby?"

"He's fine, a little small, but healthy. He was born two weeks early, but the doctor said he should be all right."

"That's good to hear. Is there anything else you want?"

"Well, I just kind of wanted to talk to you about visitation as far as the kids are concerned. Even though we are not together, I want to be a part of the twin's lives too. By the way, what did you name them?"

"I named them Horizon and Rain. What did you decide to name your son?"

"We decided to name him after me, so he's a junior," Omar says, blushing.

"Oh, that's nice."

I give him a fake smile. Even though me and Omar are not together anymore, I am still jealous that he has a baby with someone else. He still is attractive to me, and I miss all his attention so much. Damn, I fucked up!

Omar sits down in the chair beside my bed and we continue to talk. We try to come up with a solution that will work for both of us. As we are talking, my man on the side comes in carrying a light pink gift bag and a ton of balloons. Omar has a shocked look on his face.

"What are you doing here?" Omar questions.

"I just came to see my twins and check on my girl," he says nonchalant-ly.

I can't believe he just said that! He is one cocky nigga, and must be even crazier than Omar! There is no doubt about it, all hell is going to break loose.

Omar stands up. "Man, you play too much, stop joking."

"This is no joke. I guess Skye didn't tell you that I was coming to see my twins. Oh, my bad. I guess you thought they were yours, huh?" A sly grin creeps across Tyrone's face.

"You sneaky bastard!" Omar yells, standing up and walking over to Tyrone.

"Well, what can I say? I guess I can say that I've been fucking your girl for about a year and a half. Oh, my bad, your ex-girl. I guess if you was taking care of home then this would not have never happened. Better me than some scrub-ass nigga," Tyrone gloats.

Before he can utter another word, Omar punches Tyrone in his mouth so hard that blood flies out of his mouth. They are fighting like two niggas in the street. They're knocking over everything in the room. I start screaming at them both to stop, then I push the button for the nurse. Needless to say, they are both escorted out of the hospital.

Damn, why did he have to do this now? All I can do is cry. How the hell did I end up in this situation? I have truly fucked up my life. After things calm down, Jazz comes by and I tell her all my secrets.

She reaches over and gives me a big hug and says, "I guess everybody has a little drama."

I'm glad that Jazz doesn't give me an hour -long lecture or judge me in any way. She is really a good friend. I don't know what I would do without her.

"A li'l drama, yeah right! Little is an understatement."

After Jazz leaves, I close my eyes and try to go to sleep. Boy, today was a total wreck! Hopefully things will get better. Oh boy, am I wrong! Tyrone's girlfriend Star busts in my hospital room with rage in her eyes. I can't even scream, because her hands are so tight around my neck. Damn, so much for a happy ending! The drama continues.......................

About the Author

Latisha Patterson was born and raised in Richmond, VA. She is currently working on her Bachelor's degree in Business Management. After spending years searching for the "right" career, she discovered writing was her passion. She started taking writing seriously in 2006. Shortly after, she began writing her first novel *Airing Out Dirty Laundry*. Latisha is the mother of two beautiful daughters. In her spare time, she enjoys reading, writing, shopping, and being involved in several book clubs and organizations. She is currently working on her second novel *Three Way Love*. For more information about her upcoming projects, visit www.latishapatterson.com.

The End

www.ingramcontent.com/pod-product-compliance
Lightning Source LLC
Chambersburg PA
CBHW071204250626

47159CB00001B/194